"*Saint X* is hypnotic. Schaitkin's characters . . . are so intelligent and distinctive it feels not just easy, but necessary, to follow them. I devoured [it] in a day." —Oyinkan Braithwaite, *The New York Times Book Review*

"Richly atmospheric, by turns coolly satiric and warmly romantic, Alexis Schaitkin's brilliant debut novel, *Saint X,* imagines a chorus of voices in the aftermath of the alleged murder of a privileged American girl vacationing in an exotic Caribbean country. Part 'true crime' thriller and part coming-of-age novel narrated by the deceased girl's younger sister, *Saint X* is irresistibly suspenseful and canny." —Joyce Carol Oates

"*Saint X* is slightly miraculous. Funny, chilling, moving, and deeply intelligent throughout. We follow Emily into the depths of her obsessive quest with fascination and, in the end, rise with her as she moves on. This is an utterly original and engrossing novel written with the surest possible hand." —Christopher Tilghman, author of *Thomas and Beal in the Midi*

"Here is a marvel of a book, a kaleidoscopic examination of race and privilege, family and self, told with the propulsive, kinetic focus of a crime novel. Brilliant and unflinching, *Saint X* marks the debut of a stunningly gifted writer. I simply couldn't stop reading." —Chang-rae Lee, author of *On Such a Full Sea*

"*Saint X,* Alexis Schaitkin's atmospheric new novel, is ostensibly about a young American girl who goes missing while on a family vacation in the Caribbean. But it is more than that. The book also unpacks timely social and cultural issues—about grief, truth, white privilege, and our murder-as-entertainment culture." —*The Washington Post*

"A smart, socially conscious thriller that will take you away." —*People* (Book of the Week)

"This debut novel is hypnotic, delivering acute social commentary on everything from class and race to familial bonds and community, and yet its weblike nature never confuses or fails to captivate." —*The New York Times* (Editors' Choice)

"This writer is fearless, and her gamble pays off. This killer debut is both a thriller with a vivid setting and an insightful study of race, class, and obsession."
—*Kirkus Reviews* (starred review)

"There's one moment in every person's life, posits *Saint X,* that will define the rest of it. For many in this novel, it's the death of Alison Thomas, a teenage girl who perishes while vacationing with her family on a Caribbean island. The mystery remains unsolved until years later, when her sister, Claire, runs into one of the original suspects in New York and befriends him, hoping to piece together what happened to Alison." —*Entertainment Weekly*

"One of the year's buzziest debuts."
—*Bustle* (22 Most Anticipated Books of February 2020)

"Alexis Schaitkin's stunning debut novel is an examination of race, privilege, family, and self as a teenage girl vanishes during her family's luxury Caribbean vacation on the island of Saint X. Though the lives of the privileged tourists and the island locals are seemingly unrelated, in the aftermath of this single dramatic event, they're inextricably bound to each other forever."
—*Good Morning America* (20 Books We're Excited for in 2020)

"A deft, absorbing study of how death changes everything and obsession can take hold."
—*Library Journal* (Fall/Winter Bests)

"This is a smart page-turner, both thought-provoking and effortlessly entertaining."
—*Publishers Weekly*

"On a family vacation to the Caribbean island of Saint X ('a lovely nowhere'), an eighteen-year-old American is found murdered, sparking a media frenzy. Schaitkin's pulse-pounder of a novel picks up two decades later, when the victim's younger sister crosses paths with a lead suspect."
—*O, The Oprah Magazine* (14 of the Best Books to Read This February)

"A gripping page-turner about two sisters . . . Set among the atmospheric backdrop of the Caribbean, get ready for an emotional ending."
—*Parade*

"Alexis Schaitkin's debut novel, *Saint X,* delves into what it means when beautiful, promising young women go missing in foreign lands—and the

ripples that emanate out from their disappearances. . . . If you're looking for something that will stay with you long after the sun goes down on your holiday, *Saint X* marks the spot." —*Rolling Stone*

"Taking place between a Caribbean holiday and a particularly brutal New York winter, *Saint X* is an exhilarating thriller about race, loss, and America's obsession with dead girls."
—*Harper's BAZAAR* (Best Summer Books to Read in 2020)

"Eerie and complex, the shifting perspectives will certainly keep you intrigued until the very end." —*Mashable*

"Readers will gladly fall headlong into this brilliantly conceived novel."
—*New York Journal of Books*

"One of *the* thrillers of 2020." —*Business Insider*

"Mystery fans will appreciate this engrossing read about two sisters."
—*Vogue*

SAINT X

Alexis Schaitkin

CELADON
BOOKS
— NEW YORK —

SAINT X. Copyright © 2020 by Alexis Schaitkin. All rights reserved. Printed in the United States of America. For information, address Celadon Books, a Division of Macmillan Publishers, 120 Broadway, New York, NY 10271.

www.celadonbooks.com

For seal on cover:
From *The New York Times*. © 2020 The New York Times Company.
All rights reserved. Used under license.

The Library of Congress has cataloged the hardcover edition as follows:

Names: Schaitkin, Alexis, 1985– author.
Title: Saint X / Alexis Schaitkin.
Description: First edition. | New York : Celadon Books, 2020.
Identifiers: LCCN 2019036360 | ISBN 9781250219596 (hardcover) |
    ISBN 9781250219589 (ebook)
Classification: LCC PS3619.C32534 S25 2020 | DDC 813/.6—dc23
LC record available at https://lccn.loc.gov/2019036360

ISBN 978-1-250-21957-2 (trade paperback)

Our books may be purchased in bulk for promotional, educational, or business use. Please contact your local bookseller or the Macmillan Corporate and Premium Sales Department at 1-800-221-7945, extension 5442, or by email at MacmillanSpecialMarkets@macmillan.com.

First Celadon Books Paperback Edition: 2021

10 9 8 7 6 5 4 3 2

For M & E

CONTENTS

Contents

INDIGO BAY

BEGIN WITH AN AERIAL VIEW. Slip beneath the clouds and there it is, that first glimpse of the archipelago—a moment, a vista, a spectacle of color so sudden and intense it delivers a feeling like plunging a cube of ice in warm water and watching it shatter: the azure sea, the emerald islands ringed with snow-white sand; perhaps, on this day, a crimson tanker at the edge of the tableau.

Come down a bit lower and the islands reveal their topographies, valleys and flatlands and the conic peaks of volcanoes, some of them still active. There is Mount Scenery on Saba, Mount Liamugia on Saint Kitts, Mount Pelée on Martinique, the Quill on Saint Eustatius, La Soufrière on Saint Lucia and also on Saint Vincent, La Grande Soufrière on Guadeloupe's Basse-Terre, Soufrière Hills on Montserrat, and Grande Soufrière Hills on tiny Dominica, which is beset by no fewer than nine volcanoes. The volcanoes yield an uneasy sense of juxtaposition—the dailiness of island life abutting the looming threat of eruption. (On some islands, on some days, flakes of ash fall softly through the air, pale and fine, before settling on grassy hillsides and the eaves of rooftops.)

Roughly in the middle of the archipelago lies an island some forty kilometers long by twelve wide. It is a flat, buff, dusty place, its soil thin and arid, the terrain dotted with shallow salt ponds and the native vegetation consisting primarily of tropical scrub: sea grape, cacti, wild frangipani. (There is a volcano here, too, Devil Hill, though it is so small, and the magma rises to its surface so infrequently, that it is useless as both a threat and an attraction.) The island is home to eighteen thousand residents and receives some ninety thousand tourists annually. From above, it resembles a fist with a single long finger pointing west.

The north side of the island faces the Atlantic. Here, the coast is narrow and rocky, the water seasonally variable and sometimes rough. Nearly all of the residents live on this side, most of them in the tiny capital town, the Basin, where cinder-block schools, food marts, and churches mingle with faded colonial buildings in pastel hues: the governor-general's petal-pink Georgian mansion; the mint-green national bank; Her Majesty's Prison, eggshell-blue. (A prison next to a bank—a favorite local joke.) On this coast, the beaches' names bespeak their shortcomings: Salty Cove. Rocky Shoal. Manchineel Bay. Little Beach.

On the south side of the island, the gentle waves of the Caribbean Sea lap against sand fine as powder. Here, resorts punctuate the coast. The Oasis, Salvation Point, the Grand Caribbee, and the island's crown jewel, Indigo Bay, all of them festooned with bougainvillea, hibiscus, and flamboyant, beautiful deceptions meant to suggest that this island is a lush, fertile place.

Scattered in the sea around the island are a dozen or so uninhabited cays, the most notable of which are Carnival Cay, Tamarind Island, and Fitzjohn (famous, at least locally, as the home of the Fitzjohn lizard). The cays are popular spots for excursions—snorkeling, romantic picnics, guided expeditions through their limestone caverns. The closest of the cays to the main island is the ironically named Faraway Cay, which sits not five hundred meters off the coast at Indigo Bay and which, owing to its nacreous beach, its wild landscapes, and the pristine waterfall at its center, would be a popular destination like the other cays, were it not overrun by feral goats, which survive on sea purslane and prickly pear.

The island's visitors have little sense of its geography. If asked, most would be unable to sketch its basic shape. They cannot locate it on a map, cannot distinguish it from the other small landmasses that dot the sea between Florida and Venezuela. When a taxi brings them from the airport to their hotel, or from their hotel to a Caribbean fusion restaurant on Mayfair Road, or when they take a sunset cruise aboard the catamaran *Faustina,* or disembark their cruise ship at Hibiscus Harbour, or when a speedboat whisks them to Britannia Bay to tour the old sugar estate, they do not know if they are traveling north or south, east or west. The island is a lovely nowhere suspended in gin-clear water.

When they return home, they quickly forget the names of things. They do not remember the name of the beach on which their resort was situated, or of the cay where they went for their snorkeling excursion. (The beach there was littered with sand dollars, as if they were entirely unprecious.) They forget the name of the restaurant they liked best, remembering only that it was some exotic flower. They even forget the name of the island itself.

ZOOM IN closer on Indigo Bay and the resort's features come into view. There is the long drive lined with perfectly vertical palm trees, the marble lobby with its soaring domed roof, the open-air pavilion where breakfast is served until ten each morning, the spa, the swimming pool in the shape of a lima bean, the fitness and business centers ("CENTRE," on the engraved placard outside of each; the American guests are charmed by this Briticism, which strikes them as quaint and earnest on this island so distant from England). There is the beach where lounge chairs are arranged in a parabola that follows the curve of the bay, the local woman set up on a milk crate beneath a sun-bleached blue umbrella at the beach's edge, braiding young girls' hair. The fragrance is tropic classic, frangipani and coconut sunscreen and the mild saline of equatorial ocean.

On the beach are families, the sand around their chairs littered with plastic shovels, swimmies, impossibly small aqua socks; honeymooners pressed closely together beneath cabanas; retirees reading fat thrillers in the shade. They have no notion of the events about to unfold here, on Saint X, in 1995.

The time is late morning. Look. A girl is walking down the sand. Her gait is idle, as if it is of no consequence to her when she arrives where she is going. As she walks, heads turn—young men, openly; older men, more subtly; older women, longingly. (They were eighteen once.) She wears a long, billowy tunic over her bikini, but she has a teenage knack for carrying it with a whiff of provocation. A raffia beach bag is slung casually over her shoulder. Apricot freckles crowd the milky skin of her face and arms. She wears a silver anklet with a charm in the shape of a star, and rubber thongs on her long, archless feet. Her russet hair, thick and sleek as a horse's, is tossed into a bun of precise messiness with a yellow elastic band. This is Alison, never Ali.

"Good morning, sleepyhead," her father says when she reaches her family's lounge chairs.

"Morning," she yawns.

"You missed a cruise ship go by right out there. You wouldn't believe how big that thing was," her mother says.

(Though the guests at Indigo Bay are apt to complain when these hulking ships lumber into the vista, they also derive a certain satisfaction from these moments, when the bad taste of others reaffirms their own quality—*they* have not chosen to spend their vacations in the vulgar opulence of a ship with all the beauty of an office park.)

"Sounds riveting." Alison drags a chair out of the shade of an umbrella and into the sun. From her beach bag she removes a yellow Walkman. She lies down, puts on her headphones, and pulls her sunglasses over her eyes.

"How about a family swim?" her father says.

Alison does not respond. Not pretending she doesn't hear him over whatever she's listening to, her father decides, just ignoring him.

"Maybe in a little while everyone will be more in the mood," her mother says with prodding cheerfulness.

"Hey, Clairey," Alison says. "I'm going on a treasure hunt and I'm bringing a starfish."

She is speaking to the little girl sitting in the sand between her mother's and father's chairs, who until this moment had been piling sand into small mounds with intense focus.

"I'm going on a treasure hunt and I'm bringing a starfish and a dog," the little girl says.

She is as peculiar in appearance as her older sister is appealing. Her hair is nearly white, her skin extremely pale. Eyes gray, lips blanched. These features combine to create an impression that manages to be at once arresting and plain. This is Claire, age seven. Clairey, to her family.

"I'm going on a treasure hunt and I'm bringing a starfish, a dog, and a piccolo."

"A piccolo," Claire whispers. Her eyes widen with wonder.

The father flags down one of the men who work on the beach. There are two of them, both dark-skinned, in white slacks and white polos with the resort insignia embroidered on the breast pocket in gold thread. The skinny one and the fat one, in most of the guests' mental shorthand. The man who approaches the family now is the skinny one, Edwin.

When he reaches them, Alison sits up and smooths her hair.

"How are you all doing this morning?" he asks.

"Excellent," the mother says with a bright display of enthusiasm.

"First time to our island?"

"Yes," the father confirms. "Just flew in last night."

The family vacations at a different resort on a different island every winter, weeklong respites from their snowbound suburb that steel them for the remaining months of darkness and cold. They have seen palm trees bent to kiss the sand. They have seen water as pale as glaciers and walked on sand as soft as cream. They have watched the sun transform, at the end of the day, into a giant orange yolk that breaks and spills itself across the sea. They have seen the night sky overcome with fine blue stars.

"Look at our island pulling out she most beautiful day for you." He gestures generally with his skinny arm at the sky, the sea. "What can I be getting you this morning?"

"Two rum punches and two fruit punches," the father says.

Alison emits a small sigh.

The skinny one returns some time later. (Too long, the father thinks, as fathers all along this stretch of sand think; the skinny one is a chatterbox, and a dawdler.) He bears a tray of drinks garnished with maraschino cherries and hibiscus blossoms.

"We have a volleyball match this afternoon," he says. "We hope you will join us."

"Oh, honey, you would love that!" the mother says to Alison.

The girl turns to face her. Though she wears sunglasses, the mother has no doubt that behind them her daughter's gaze is withering.

The skinny one claps his hands together. "Excellent! May we count you in, miss?"

The girl adjusts her sunglasses. "Maybe." (She has developed a talent lately for delivering even the most innocuous words as thinly veiled innuendo. The mother has noticed this.)

"More of a sunbather, are we?" the man says.

Alison's face turns crimson.

The father reaches into his wallet and pulls a few singles from the thick stack he took out yesterday at the bank. (Was that really just yesterday? Already he can feel the island beginning to work its rejuvenating magic on him.)

"Thank you, sir." The skinny one tucks the money in his pocket and continues down the beach.

"Nice guy," the father says.

"Friendly," the mother agrees.

"Well?" the father says, and raises his glass.

The mother smiles. Clairey stares intently at her cherry. Alison swirls her fruit punch with practiced boredom.

"To paradise," the father says.

IN THE hot afternoon sun, the fat one makes his way down the beach, pausing at each cluster of chairs. "The volleyball match will begin in five minutes," he says softly. He nods uncomfortably, tugs at the collar of his shirt, and walks on. The guests watch as he passes. He is big, the kind of big that draws attention. This is Clive. Gogo, to those who know him.

"You best sell my game hard, man! We still four players short!" the skinny one shouts from the volleyball court, hands cupped around his mouth. "Volleyball of champions! Last call!"

People who were sleeping or reading shake their heads at his shouting and smile indulgently. They understand that the skinny one is an essential element of this place, granting the beach its energy, its sense of fun, its luscious, gummy vowels.

Alison takes off her headphones and stands. "Want to come watch me play, Clairey?" She reaches her hand out to her sister.

As the sisters cross the sand to the volleyball court, young men rise from their chairs and stroll casually in their wake. They are in the mood for some volleyball after all.

THE SKINNY one counts off the players, one, two, one, two. Claire takes a seat on the sideline.

"You're my extra pair of eyes, little miss," he says to her with a grin. He tousles her hair and she stiffens at his touch.

Just before the game begins, Alison slips her tunic up over her head and drops it in the sand beside her sister. The eyes of the other players land on her, noticing while trying to appear as if they have not noticed the large conch-pink scar on her stomach. For a moment she stands perfectly still as they take in her secret spectacle. Then she snatches the ball from the sand and tosses it into the air.

IT IS not much of a game. A few high schoolers and college kids, a couple of young dads with some lingering fitness, a woman who ducks whenever the ball comes near her, a husband and wife in their mid-thirties—a slight paunch spilling over the waistband of the husband's pink dolphin-print swim trunks, the wife's immaculate body casting off the aura of frantic hours at the gym—and one genuinely skilled guy whose overinvestment in the game (unnecessarily aggressive spikes, the frequent utterance of the phrase "a little advice" as he attempts to whip his team into shape) quickly begins to grate on everyone.

As the game progresses, the players converse about the usual things. It is established that two couples are from New York, one is from Boston, and another from Miami. The woman who ducks is from Minneapolis. A Chicagoan on his honeymoon has left his brand-new wife, whose langoustine last night must have been off, holed up in their room.

"She made me leave," he adds quickly. "She said there was no point in both of us missing the day if I couldn't be useful anyway." Having repeated his wife's words, he furrows his brow; it occurs to him that he may have misunderstood her and failed one of the first tests of his marriage.

"Welcome to the next forty years of your life," says the overinvested man. He and his wife have been at Indigo Bay for two days. Don't get him wrong, it's fine, but they prefer Malliouhana on Antigua, or was it Anguilla?, where they stayed last year. The couple from Miami has friends who swear by Malliouhana.

"Are we the only ones who find the food here pretty subpar?" the overinvested man asks.

The woman from Minneapolis finds the food delicious but outrageously overpriced.

"It's because they have to bring everything in on boats," says the man in the dolphin swim trunks.

"That's just what they say. It's because we're a captive audience," corrects his wife.

"And the service charge is killer."

"When the bill comes, I don't look. I just sign."

"Smart man."

"Almost, honey!" the wife of the man in the dolphin swim trunks says when he serves the ball into the net. The trunks embarrass him, but they were a gift from his wife, and she was so excited about them he didn't want to offend her by returning them, though he suspects she was excited not because she thought these trunks would make him happy, but because they made her happy, because on some level she wants a husband she doesn't have to take seriously. He noted this but said nothing, figuring it would be cruel and pointless to call her attention to the ugliness in intentions she believed to be pure. When they separate three years from now, he will become aware of how many things he noted silently, of how much time he spent smiling at her while rebuking her in his mind.

A discussion is had about the pros and cons of the various excursions offered by the resort. Somebody wonders whether the snorkeling trip to Carnival Cay is decent.

"We went yesterday. You'll see so many fish you'll be sick of them," says a husband from New York.

Someone has heard that the scuba excursion, to the site where a ship called the *Lady Ann* was wrecked in a hurricane fifty years ago, is not to be missed. Somebody else spent the morning golfing and can report that the course is top-notch. The wife of the man in the dolphin swim trunks has decided against the tour of the old sugar estate and rum distillery. Another husband from New York highly recommends the romantic picnic on Tamarind Island. The beach is exquisite. He and his wife had it all to themselves. He does not mention the fake rose petals he kept finding on the beach, half buried in the sand, remnants of other people's romantic picnic excursions on Tamarind Island, and how they have burrowed into his mind, souring his memory of an experience he knows was very nice.

The boys who followed Alison down the beach include a short, muscle-bound kid with a frayed braid of hemp around his neck; a boy who wears a T-shirt emblazoned with the Greek letters of his fraternity; and a tall blond boy who, when pressed, admits to attending Yale. There's a girl, too, a communications major. For a few minutes they run through the people they know at each other's schools, looking for connections. The ex-girlfriend of the boy with the hemp necklace is in Developmental Psych with the fraternity brother. The sleepaway camp bunkmate of the communications major is in orchestra with the blond boy from Yale. The blond boy plays the cello. He is going to Saint Petersburg on tour in March.

"Small world," the blond boy says when he puts together that a teammate from his high school soccer team is in Alison's dorm at Princeton.

"In the sense that our worlds are small," she retorts.

He laughs. "Good point, Ali."

"Alison."

"Good point, *Alison*."

The players serve and spike against a dichromatic backdrop of sand and sky. They clutch their knees and say, "Whew," after a particularly aerobic play. They watch Alison. She leaps and dives, flinging herself after the ball with abandon. Her body is lithe and athletic. Even when she's still, an energy simmers about her. When the wife of the man in the dolphin swim trunks catches him staring, he pretends to be extremely absorbed in the view of the ocean.

From her spot in the sand, Claire watches and wonders whether the sluicing beauty of her sister's movements will be hers, too, someday, when she grows up. She doubts it, but this doesn't really make her sad. It is enough to bask in the warmth of her sister's light.

When the game ends (defeat for the team of the overinvested man, who now declares the game to have been "all in good fun"), the blond boy approaches Alison. They talk a bit. The other boys eye him with annoyance and self-recrimination, then turn their attention to the communications major, reassessing. The blond boy touches Alison's shoulder, then trots off down the sand. When he's gone, she brings her hand to the spot he touched and brushes her fingertips against her own soft skin.

AS AFTERNOON slips into evening, the guests drift away from the beach. They spend the hours before dinner recovering from the day—the sun, the heat, the booze, beauty so vivid their eyes crave a rest from it. They shower. They check in with the office. (Their expertise is needed to resolve some particularly thorny issue, and they provide the solution with relief; or they are told to enjoy their vacation, things are chugging along just fine without them, and for the rest of the evening they are cranky and short-tempered.) They have sex in the fluffy white hotel beds. Afterward, they eat the mangoes from the welcome baskets, letting the creamy juice run down their hands. They investigate the small bottles in the minibars. They flip on televisions by force of habit, watch a few minutes of a news program from Saint Kitts, a *Miami Vice* rerun, a documentary about a reggae singer who is neither Bob Marley nor Jimmy Cliff. They sit on the balconies, smoke loose joints rolled with the mediocre grass they've managed to procure on the island, and watch the night begin: the sun go down, moths bloom from the darkness, the palms turn to shadowy windmills, the first faint stars pierce the sky.

The sisters lay side by side on Claire's bed and let the air conditioner blitz their bodies. One day on the beach and already Alison has turned nut-brown. Her freckles, faint apricot this morning, are auburn sparks. Claire's skin, meanwhile, is angry pink.

"You poor thing," Alison says.

She fetches the bottle of aloe vera from the kit in the bathroom and squeezes some into her palm. She soothes her sister inch by inch. Claire closes her eyes and slips into the blind dream of her sister's touch.

Alison has been away at college for four months. Sometimes at home Claire goes into her sister's room and sits on her bed. The room looks as if Alison went out just a minute ago. On the desk there are messy piles of snapshots and, mixed in with the pens and pencils in a blue ceramic mug, a tube of sparkly strawberry lip gloss. (Once, she opened the tube, slicked some on, and inhaled her sister's smell on her own lips. She has not dared to do this again.) There are band posters on the walls. The clothes her sister didn't take to college are sloppily folded in the dresser. But the room no longer feels inhabited. Sometimes, when she closes her eyes, she cannot picture her sister's face. She cannot hear her voice, and when this happens a wave of panic washes over her.

Now the hotel room they share is humid with Alison's presence, and everything Claire has missed comes rushing back. Her sister's savage nail biting. Her habit of stroking her scar through her clothes when she's thinking. The way she dances a little, small private movements, when she moves around a room. Her sister is a secret whispered in her ear.

WHAT DOES a father think about when he wakes at dawn on the second morning of vacation? The damned birds. The roosters crowing away, from somewhere behind the resort. Some incessant yellow-breasted bird making a high-pitched racket on the balcony. (This is the bananaquit, an infamous island nuisance.) He throws on a robe, goes out to the balcony, shoos the bird away, and returns to bed. But it is back a minute later. He does this three times, thinking with increasing agitation of some prior guest in this suite who must have offered the bird scraps from his room service *pain au chocolat*. He tells himself to relax. He's awake anyway now, might as well get his day started. He kisses his wife, who is still sleeping soundly, and steps onto the balcony to appraise the morning. It is a clear day. A few squat clouds move slow as cruise ships across a pure blue sky. Faraway Cay appears so near he half believes he could reach out and touch it. He can make out individual palm trees on the shore. He can see the cay's black rock faces, mossed with growth, and the shadows of its ravines. The cay's intense greens simply do not exist at home. A father reflects momentarily that most people will live their whole lives without getting to see a place this beautiful. He reiterates to himself, as he tries to do often, that he is fortunate. He paused to allow a similar reflection on the shuttle ride from the airport to the resort, a journey whose features—children playing in dusty yards; women sitting somnolently behind dented tin pots at roadside stands; concrete houses that must once have been turquoise, yellow, pink, but whose paint had nearly all peeled away; strays—summoned the equivalent features of his own life: his beautiful daughters, wife, house (the eaves tufted now with shimmering snow), Fluffernutter the dog.

His thoughts are interrupted by a mechanical noise. A tractor is making its way along the beach. He notices now that the sand, which was immaculate yesterday, is strewn with mats of brown seaweed. Two men in overalls are raking the seaweed into piles. The tractor follows after them, scooping up the piles. Behind the tractor, a fourth man uses a push broom to smooth away the tread marks.

A father stands on the balcony and watches this procedure for some time. He understands now that the beach is not naturally pristine, which, he admits, should have been obvious, and this knowledge taints his enjoyment of it. His reaction bothers him. Why should these men's labor make him appreciate the beach less instead of more?

As his second day at Indigo Bay unfolds and he grows accustomed to the resort's beauty, to the bushes everywhere weeping pink blooms and the brazen teal water, he begins to perceive a new set of information. He notices, for instance, that the milk at the breakfast buffet in the open-air pavilion is ever so slightly sour, leaving an unpleasant aftertaste on his tongue. He does not say anything about this. He does not ask the woman who greeted his family so warmly at the pavilion's entrance to rectify the situation. He simply registers it. He also registers that in a few places at the resort he routinely catches the whiff of certain unmistakable odors. At the far side of the swimming pool, warm garbage. At the turn in the gravel path that leads from their room to the beach, sewage. He would never dream of complaining about such things, as other guests might. He likes to think he wears his affluence tastefully. He does not move through the world expecting things to be perfect. He tries to like everything and everybody as much as he can. Even this orientation toward the world he recognizes as a benefit of the position he occupies. It is easy to make allowances when you live a fortunate life.

Only now it is all a bit spoiled, isn't it? This same disappointment every year; childish, he concedes, but there it is: he still hasn't found paradise, not quite. Because, like everywhere else, when you get down to it, it is all just bodies and their manifold wastes and where to put it all, it is all just disorder two days from taking over. The week before he flew down here, a blizzard had prevented trash pickup in Manhattan for a few days. On his walk from Grand Central to the office, the sidewalks were piled five feet high with black trash bags. At street corners, the garbage pails were overflowing, the pavement around them littered with chicken bones, half-eaten hot dogs, diapers, frozen rivers of old coffee. He saw a little terrier in a red sweater urinate at the base of a pile of trash bags; he saw a thick beige puddle beside another pile, and stared at it curiously for a moment before the smell hit him and he realized it was vomit. As he walked past all of this he had fixed an image of a tropical beach in his mind and thought, *Thank god I'm getting out of here.* But now that he is out, now that he is here, he cannot help but wonder whether the only damned difference is the bougainvillea, whether this place is nothing but the same old ugliness, spackled with an unconvincing veneer of beauty.

A YELLOW rubber ball rises high in the air. A dozen children dash across the sand to catch it. It is ten in the morning, the start of the resort's daily hour of children's games and relays. While the children play, their parents use the free time. At the moment the yellow ball reaches its apex, a mother shudders with the force of her first orgasm in a month. Another mother is getting close and hoping ferociously that her husband lasts. A husband and wife who fully intended on sex snore in bed. Couples drink tequila sunrises in the hot tub, read on the beach, pound away side by side on treadmills in the fitness center. A wife poses for her husband in front of the ocean, trying her best to hide her soft thighs. For a moment their children slip from view. Briefly, they seem not to exist at all.

CLAIRE IS no good at games. She falls during the crab walk. "Come *onnn,*" her partner urges during the three-legged race. Two strides into the egg-and-spoon relay the egg rolls off her spoon and cracks on her foot. But most of all she is no good at the mysterious process by which children sift out into pairs and clusters, securing their buddies for the week. Even Axel from Belgium, who doesn't speak English, slips right in with another rowdy boy. They kindle friendship so quickly it leaves her dizzy, as if she's been spinning; when she stops, the world tilts back into place and the business of making friends is done, settled, without her.

THE FAT one brings the family's lunch. They watch him come up the beach, the heavy tray balanced on his shoulder. He stumbles. French fries rain onto the sand.

"I apologize," he says when he reaches them. "I'll bring you more chips."

"Oh, don't bother. There's still plenty," the mother says encouragingly. "Clairey, sweetheart, no writing."

The little girl freezes, caught with her index finger in midair. The word she had been writing was *chips*. She was up to *p*. She shoves her hand down at her side. She can feel her finger itching with the half-finished *p* and the *s*. She will have to finish later.

"Leave her alone," Alison snaps at her mother. She takes Claire's hand, raises it to her lips, and gives it a peck.

The mother sighs. This habit of her younger daughter's emerged a few months ago, her index finger wiggling and looping through the air. "I'm writing," Claire had mumbled when the mother asked what was going on. They'd met with the school psychologist, a mistake—after that Claire got furtive about it, sneaky, only doing it when she thought no one was paying attention. It is a constant struggle for the mothers: How do you know what is merely odd and what is worrisome? How much damage can you inflict upon your child if you treat something like it is one when it is really the other?

After Clive sets out their food on the low tables between their chairs, he takes a small towel from his pocket and wipes the sweat from his brow.

"Must be hot out here in long pants," the father says.

Alison shoots him a disapproving look, which he ignores. If fathers only said things their teenage daughters approved of, they would never speak at all. The mother and father exchange glances. A change has come over their daughter. Lately, her teenage moodiness carries a whiff of moral judgment. Newer still is this sighing dismissiveness, as if they are hardly even worth the effort of her judgment. Make no mistake, she's a college girl now.

"It's not so bad," the fat one mumbles. "Are you having a cold winter at home?"

"Brutal," the father says. "It's been snowing nonstop. I envy you, waking up to this every day."

"We do have our hurricanes," the fat one says.

"You had a bad one this season, right? José?"

"Luis."

The father claps his hands together. "Luis! That's the one."

"We had six hundred homes and many of our schools destroyed."

"How awful," the mother says.

The father cannot comprehend how people can be willing to live in a place where something like this can happen. He decides that a sense of the perpetual potential for destruction, for incurring a total loss, must be baked into people's temperaments here from birth, so that living like this is easier for them than it would be for him. Which is not a deficit in his character, for presumably if he had been born here he, too, would be such a person, able to bear unpredictability with stoic equanimity. He pauses to imagine himself as such a person—a pleasurable leaving-behind of himself as he enters a self more connected to and at peace with the planetary vicissitudes.

"Tell me something," the father says. "Where do you recommend for some local food? You know, something authentic."

The fat one gives him the name of a restaurant in town. His friend works there; his friend gives tours of the island and the cays, too, "At a good price." The mother and father smile and thank him, but something silent is exchanged between them: they enjoy receiving local knowledge, but they are also on guard for local slipperiness.

Up and down the beach, fathers sign bills for lunches and drinks. They try not to think about the numbers. Five bucks for their kid's Orangina, eighteen for their wife's goat cheese salad. They do not want to linger on the ways they are being nickel-and-dimed in paradise. Besides, what price can one put on such moments? Here is the sea, the blue water and the milky froth. Here is the soft, sun-warmed sand. The grains of sand on earth, a father read somewhere, are fewer than the stars in the universe. How unlikely, then, what an unbelievable stroke of luck, his family on this beach.

SOME TIME later, the skinny one comes to clear the family's plates.

"What are the sisters planning the rest of the day?" he asks.

"We're going to build a castle, right, Clairey?" Alison says.

"Did you know I was this year's Carnival Sandcastle Competition champion?"

"Is that so?" Alison sweeps her hair off her neck and gathers it into a ponytail.

"For true. Well, honorable mention." He grins. "If you girls need any consultation on your design, just let me know."

"We like to build our sandcastles solo, thank you very much," Alison says with a fetching smirk.

Edwin squats in front of Claire. "And you, little miss? Do you, too, prefer to build your sandcastle *solo*?" He smiles at her.

Claire nods rigidly.

He laughs. "Okay, little miss." He tousles her hair. "See you later, sisters."

As he heads off down the beach, the mother notices that her daughter has her eyes on him, watching him go.

THE SKINNY one is the prince of the sand. The social hierarchy of the guests flows through him. Those he anoints with his gregarious approval seem to possess an invisible status. It is true he takes a lot of breaks and his tendency to stop and chat slows down service on the beach, but this is forgiven, even embraced. What's the rush? They're on island time. He is adored, too, by the young children, who follow him around like a fan club.

Then there is the fat one, Gogo, clumsy in the sand, clumsy with a tray of cocktails on his shoulder, clumsy adjusting the umbrellas to keep up with the movement of the sun, his voice rarely rising above a mumble. But he is Edwin's friend. The closeness between the skinny one and the fat one is clear. When they pass each other on the sand they exchange high fives and chummy insults. Often, Edwin returns from his break with a grease-spotted paper bag in hand—lunch for Gogo.

When a guest asks Clive about their friendship, he says simply, "We're best mates."

"Me and the Goges?" Edwin says, asked the same question. "We come up together from small. Me and he go back to primary. Who you think it was named he Gogo? I'd tell you why but he'd kill me."

One sundown, the man with the dolphin swim trunks is jogging down the beach when he sees Edwin struggling to drag a stack of chairs across the sand. Clive hurries over and, without a word, lifts the load from him. The man feels something crack in him. He loves his wife, don't get him wrong, but somehow he had forgotten until this moment—maybe he has forced himself to forget—the sweetness of friendship.

THE SISTERS do many things together. They collect seashells. They trade underwater messages in the pool: "Mayonnaise is gross." "Fluffernutter is the world's best dog." In the ocean, Alison scoops Claire into her arms and Claire wraps her arms around her sister's neck.

"Our ship sank and Mom and Dad and everybody else is dead," Claire says. "We're in the middle of the ocean."

"See that island out there?" Alison says, pointing to Faraway Cay. "We're going to have to swim for it. It's our only chance. Can you make it?"

Claire nods, sober and brave.

They build castles, Claire happily submitting to her sister's vision and management. She fetches buckets of water and collects twigs and pebbles, while Alison carves bridges and archways and spiral staircases to the sky.

Edwin comes by and appraises their progress. "Look at your bridge there caved in. Guess you girls aren't having much luck building *solo* after all." He grins.

"It's a ruin," Alison replies. "We're building something ancient."

A ruin, Claire whispers to herself as she fetches more water. *A ruin. A ruin.*

A CELEBRITY has arrived at Indigo Bay. He is an actor, a man in late middle age known for playing offbeat characters, mostly sidekicks, with a signature misanthropy. He has brought with him a supple young girlfriend, black-haired and splayfooted.

News of his arrival spreads quickly among the guests, who go intensively about the business of pretending not to recognize him. The chairs to either side of the actor and his girlfriend at the pool remain unoccupied. When the newlyweds (the wife by now recovered from her bad langoustine) find themselves in the hot tub with the actor, the husband goes so far as to ask him what he does for a living.

In the actor's vicinity, the guests laugh more loudly. The men stand straighter and touch their wives more. The women sway their hips. (They tell themselves, though, a bit smugly, that they would not go to bed with him. He was handsome once, but he has let himself go and turned flabby and dissipated. They've heard rumors for years that he is in and out of various rehab facilities in the California desert.)

Though he has been a public figure for more than three decades, the actor has never grown accustomed to the way people adjust themselves in his presence. He can feel it, a shrill solicitousness like a current in the air. While his girlfriend gets a massage, he takes a seat at the poolside bar and orders a vodka with a twist. The couple at the barstools next to him hush. Then the man says loudly to the woman that he wishes there were bigger waves here; he would love to go surfing. He begins to recount a story from long ago. Hawaii, a big wave seized at the perfect moment and how he rode the white curl of it to shore. The actor understands that this is one of the man's moments of personal greatness. One of the unusual features of his life is how often such stories are offered up for him to overhear.

This man could not know that the actor himself possesses a paralyzing fear of the ocean. This trip is his girlfriend's idea. (Whose idea his girlfriend is, is anyone's guess. He has a way of finding problems and holding tight to them. Always has.) If it were up to him, he would vacation in the comfort of his own house, just take a week away from people. After all, it is people, not work, from which he craves respite.

When they arrived here, his girlfriend flung open the curtains in their room and urged him out onto the balcony. Beyond the sand, the ocean arranged itself in bands of deepening blue. The sun blinked on the water like infinite strobe lights.

"See? Not so scary, right?" She patted his arm as if comforting a twitchy dog.

Then it happened as it always did. The sea rose into a wall, higher and higher, until there was no end to it. He opened his mouth and the water flooded him.

EVERY FAMILY has its documentarian. Say it is the father. He squats in the sand, a position his sorry knees can barely handle these days, and captures his girls at work on their castle. At dinner, he nabs an action shot of Alison cracking a lobster claw with her hands. He snaps Clairey marveling at the whorls of a seashell. This task falls to him because his wife never takes pictures; she says she will but she forgets, or doesn't bother, he's not sure which. Anyway, it has worked out. He has found an avocation and become, if he says so himself, a pretty decent amateur photographer. What a relief to find, in middle age, that there are still interests waiting inside you to be discovered, that you just might have more artistic heft than you long ago made your peace with having.

At home a family's walls are decorated with photographs from their travels. The father and mother went on an African safari last year to celebrate their twentieth anniversary. A black chain of elephants against an orange sunset. A flock of birds like a vast swath of silk in the sky. A gathering of local children craning their faces up at the camera. Their guide, Buyu, kicking at the embers of their campfire with his black rubber boots.

And what a disappointment it is to see, on the walls of their friends' homes, *their* fauna silhouetted against the sunset, *their* gathering of enthralled local children, *their* diminutive guide in black rubber boots. (All over the world, it seems, in Tanzania and Vietnam and Peru, short, wiry men lead tourists across savannas and through jungles and up mountains in these same black rubber boots.) For fleeting moments, he bore witness to something beautiful; to see these moments of personal sanctity duplicated— a father knows it shouldn't matter so much.

It's a relief to be on a straightforward beach vacation. No endangered species or ancient city walls to capture. Clairey at play. His wife, modest and lovely in the whisper of early evening. After many days of disinterest and outright refusal, he prevails upon Alison to let him take some pictures of her. She takes her hair out of its ponytail and lets it fall around her shoulders; she leans against a palm and looks at the camera with a pensive expression, her lips slightly parted. He is so touched by her effort to style herself that for a moment he pulls the camera away from his face and simply looks at her.

In the distance he sees the fat one and the skinny one coming up the beach. He catches the skinny one's eyes on his daughter. If the father is honest, if all the fathers of teenage daughters here are honest, they do not like the way this man looks at their daughters. He is so informal. There is an unconcerned quality in his gaze, as if the father's daughter, while appealing, is not special.

They can acknowledge that their concern has at least partly to do with the color of this man's skin. But they aren't even *concerned*, really; they are merely entertaining the possibility of concern. It is nothing. The people here are simply very friendly. It is their culture, the warm and open way of people on a small island. You know you've gone too long without a vacation when you start seeing friendliness as some kind of problem.

ONE AFTERNOON, the blond boy from the volleyball game stops by the family's chairs on the beach. The mother watches Alison wave at him as he approaches, a gesture she executes with delicious casualness.

"What happened to your leg?" he asks when he is standing beside Alison's chair.

The mother looks over and sees that her daughter's calf is scraped and bloody.

"Tripped," Alison says, and shrugs.

The mother wants to tell her daughter to get bacitracin and a Band-Aid at the front desk and clean out the cut; she wants to get the bacitracin herself and patch up her daughter's scrape, but she holds her tongue.

"I'm going to hit some golf balls into the lagoon. Thought you might want to come," the boy says.

The mother watches him. His hair falls shaggily around his face—he wears it long and a bit disheveled. His skin is golden, like the outside of a perfectly baked vanilla cake. He wears his swim trunks slung low on his waist. On his chest, she sees a few strawberry blond hairs.

"Sure," Alison says. "Why not?"

The mother watches her stand. She walks beside the boy down the beach with an aloof strut, just right. This age, this moment. A woman flares in ultraviolet bursts on the hot surface of her child.

BY THEIR fourth day at Indigo Bay, the mother and father doze on the beach with ease. Sometimes they nod off with their books still in their hands. The longer they are on the island, the more easily and frequently they slip into sleep. All around them, other guests experience this same psychic loosening. In their regular lives, they make choices with high stakes every day: forty million dollars, the life of a patient, a thousand manufacturing jobs in the Midwest. If you catch her in a vulnerable moment at the bar, the wife of the man in the dolphin swim trunks will confess that by the time she leaves the office at night, sometimes the choice of where to order takeout is enough to crumple her. At Indigo Bay, they unwind into a world of choice without consequence. Beach or pool? Beer or margarita? They submit to the tonic regiment of such days gratefully. They begin to fantasize about saying goodbye to their lives back home. They could quit their jobs, buy a little villa down here, and never look back. They could spend every day on the beach and never tire of it. They could remain here forever.

"DON'T LET them get into any trouble while I'm gone," Alison tells Claire, nodding at their dozing parents. Claire watches her sister until she disappears down the beach, then she turns her attention to the bucket of seashells she and Alison collected earlier in the day. She spreads them out in the sand and sorts them into rows according to size, then piles them together and sorts them according to shape, color, favorite to least favorite. She goes down to the shore and spells her sister's name in the sand. She watches a wave wash the letters away. She returns to her seashells. She holds her favorite tightly in her fist and closes her eyes.

The mother opens her eyes and yawns.

"Where's your sister?"

"Bathroom?" Claire says, though her sister has by now been gone a long time. When she finally returns, their mother asks her where she has been.

"Just went for a walk. It's really beautiful down at that end." She points to where Indigo Bay ends at a barrier of black rocks. "Hey, Clairey, I'm going on a treasure hunt and I'm bringing a lime."

Her sister has told a lie. On her breath, as she says *lime*, Claire smells smoke. It's her turn, but she can't think of a word.

"I'LL BE back," Alison says the next day. It's the in-between time after the beach and before dinner, and Claire is coloring at the coffee table in their room. After her sister leaves, Claire counts to ten, then follows.

She keeps her distance. Her sister walks back to the beach. She moves along the water's edge, skimming her toes in the froth. Claire takes big steps, planting her feet in her sister's melted footprints. Alison does not go to the pool, or to the bar. She walks past the water-sports cabana, the kayaks and Sunfish lined up tidily on the sand. She walks to the end of the beach and continues onto a narrow path, then disappears into the sea grape.

When Claire reaches the path, she hesitates. It is getting dark. What if their parents open the door that connects their rooms and find that they are gone? She takes a deep breath and steps onto the path. After a minute or so, it ends abruptly at an asphalt parking lot full of small shabby cars, their windshields covered with accordions of silver foil.

She hears laughter, a man's, and follows the sound. The asphalt burns her feet, but she stays quiet. There, next to an eggplant-colored car, her sister stands between the fat one and the skinny one. The skinny one digs into his pocket. He pulls out a small box and, from it, a cigarette. Her sister leans toward him and he slides it between her lips.

HUSBANDS AND wives have lost track of time. It is Tuesday or Wednesday, but perhaps it is only Monday. They have been on the island four days, no—five, possibly six. Within these lost days are lost moments, hours, mornings. Minutes diffuse like perfume into the air. The passage of time is of consequence only for the spectacles it reveals: The sea transforms to liquid silver as the day draws to a close. Sunset yields to the lavender fleece of twilight. Stars blink awake.

NIGHT. AT the hotel bar, couples drink elaborate cocktails as the lilting cadences of reggae float through the speakers. An elderly widow steps into the pool for her nightly swim. (She doesn't swim during the day. The pool is too busy then with the splashes and laughter of people together with their people.) A security guard with a corona of white hair plucks an empty chip bag from a bed of portulaca and deposits it in the trash.

In their room, the sisters lie together on Claire's bed. Alison weaves her sister's hair into a loose braid, unspools it with her fingertips, then braids it again.

"I'm going on a treasure hunt and I'm bringing a pearl," Alison says.

"I'm going on a treasure hunt and I'm bringing a pearl and a pizza."

"I'm going on a treasure hunt and I'm bringing a pearl, a pizza, and the stars."

"You can't bring the stars."

"Why not?"

"You can't carry them."

"I'll bring whatever I want."

A RAINY day. Guests flip fruitlessly through the television channels. They sit on balconies and watch the rain. They order room service. They doze and make love, make love and doze. Some perceive the rain as a personal slight from the universe, a tax on their happiness. Others are secretly grateful. The rain absolves them from the burden of spending the day well; they hole up in their rooms with peculiar relief.

In the afternoon, Alison finds a cartoon for Clairey on TV.

"I'm going to the gift shop to poke around. Back soon," she says, not asking if her sister would like to come along.

Though she does not like cartoons, Claire watches dutifully. When the show ends, Alison is still not back. Claire walks out to the balcony. The rain falls in silver curtains. Palms toss in the wind. She looks out at the ocean. There is a person out there, swimming—she can see the head bobbing in the waves; it glints in and out of visibility in the surf, there and not there, back then gone again. Far out, the swimmer stops. The head bobs in place, facing away from shore, in the direction of the little island that is shrouded in mist, like a place in a fairy tale. As Claire looks at it, her heart flutters, and she remembers again the disappointment of mist—how you can never be *in* it; how as soon as you walk into it, it vanishes through your fingers, so that the little island as it appears from here is a place you can never, ever reach, no matter how you try.

The swimmer begins to stroke again. Claire watches as the figure moves around the black rocks that jut out from shore at the edge of Indigo Bay and disappears.

"Got you something," Alison says when she returns to the room later.

From a shopping bag she removes a puka shell necklace. Claire bends her head and her sister slips it over, twisting it into a double strand.

"Look at you, pretty," Alison says.

Her hair is wet.

THAT NIGHT, Claire is awakened by the sound of a key rattling in the lock. As she surfaces from dreams, she watches the door to the hotel room open. Her sister tiptoes across the room and slides into bed. In the morning Claire wakes at dawn to find her sister's bed empty. She is on the balcony, her eyes fixed on something in the distance. It seems her sister is hardly sleeping at all.

THE ACTOR cannot set himself at ease. The ocean is too near. His girlfriend tests him. She frolics in the waves, dives into the crests. Each time she disappears, fear grips him. She knows this and enjoys it, and the pleasure she derives from his fear makes him want to wring her.

She keeps pestering him about chartering a boat to Faraway Cay. The concierge has advised against this, on account of the goats, and recommended Tamarind Island instead, but she has decided this makes Faraway Cay off the beaten path and, therefore, more desirable. She says the beach is supposed to be even more beautiful than at Indigo Bay. (Is Indigo Bay not beautiful enough? Is there no such thing as enough beauty, as all of it you could possibly need?) In Faraway Cay's interior there is a waterfall. They must see it. He must overcome this silly fear once and for all. She will help him. (How nice for her.)

At night he dreams of death by water. A whirlpool sucks him into its maw. The deep seas swell and swallow him. Dead, underwater, he feels his body bloat and stiffen. He hears the roving cries of gulls.

ON NEW Year's Eve, Indigo Bay holds a dinner barbecue on the beach. There is a live calypso band—three men in matching tan fedoras and short-sleeved floral button-downs, the cheerful reverberations of a steel-pan. Tiki torches. A buffet of local specialties—roasted sea crayfish, conch creole, mashed dasheen; chicken nuggets and spaghetti for the children. The guests drink piña coladas. They pick and suck the crayfish clean and lick the sweet ocean juice from their fingers. Small children toddle, woozy with happiness, before the torch-lit faces of the band.

When the band begins to play "Day-O," Alison sings along.

"Come on, Clairey. You know the words," she prods.

Claire is tentative at first, her voice barely a whisper, but as the song continues, it grows louder.

Six foot, seven foot, eight foot bunch.

The mother and father smile. Their shy little Clairey letting her voice be heard. Alison seeming finally to have unclenched. The mother and father join in. For a moment they are a family, singing.

Daylight come and me wan' go home.

A father knows it already: this is a memory.

As the night deepens, people kick off their sandals. Husbands reach for wives. They dance and drink and feast beneath the star-crammed sky. All the while, though they don't feel it, sand flies devour their flesh. The next morning at breakfast the guests scratch furiously at their limbs.

"I didn't feel a thing."

"Sneaky little suckers."

Claire is bitten terribly. Her legs and feet are covered. A bite on her eyelid causes it to swell so that she can hardly open her eye. The mother purchases Benadryl at the resort shop and Claire spends the day in a groggy haze, scratching.

Alison takes her sister's hand and pulls it away. "Don't." She presses her palm to her sister's skin. For a brief moment Claire is soothed. "Poor Clairey. You're just too sweet."

DURING THE last days of vacation, adults begin to speak of their return.

"When we get home, remind me to take the car in."

"Let's be sure to call the Vitales about dinner."

"Don't let me forget to sign the boys up for Little League."

The sisters' parents are no different. Two days before their departure, as they lie on the beach, the mother remembers that she has unread library books, by now overdue, on her bedside table. When they get home she will return them and take out new ones, and this time she will actually read them. This vacation has reminded her how much she loves to read. The father announces that when they get back he will start going to the gym in the morning before work like he used to, no excuses. They are energized. Excited, even, to be off this island and back home, where their plans can be implemented, this energy put to use. The vacation has served its purpose—it has made them eager to be home.

A few days ago, they imagined leaving their jobs, their houses, their lives behind and moving down here. Some of them even spent an afternoon viewing properties with a Realtor. Now they see that they were simply indulging a fantasy that, like most fantasies, is not something they actually want. They would grow bored here. The bright colors would grate on their eyes. The sound of the ocean would torment them.

GUESTS DEPART daily. The resort shuttle takes them in reverse, up the palm-lined drive, onto the rutted public road, past concrete houses, roosters and goats, clothes on clotheslines fluttering over sandy yards. At Sir Randall Corwin International Airport, they walk back across the tarmac, up the stairs onto a plane, speed back down the runway, and lift into the sky. They touch down in Boston or New York or Chicago amid a papery snowfall and drive the dark roads home.

Inevitably, they leave things behind—in their rooms, by the pool, buried in the sand. The staff gathers these objects at the lost and found, but they are rarely claimed. Once a month, Gwendolyn from the spa drives the items to Bendy Harbour Baptist Church. A gold necklace with an amethyst pendant. A denim jacket. A red shawl. Infinite sunglasses. A camera (the roll of film inside never to be developed). A legal thriller. A wristwatch with a green face.

ON THE day before they return home, Alison, Clairey, and their father walk down the beach to where the local woman who braids hair sits beneath a faded blue umbrella. Their father hands the woman sixty dollars, takes a picture of the girls (the woman looking up briefly—humorlessly, the father thinks—from combing Claire's fine white hair), and returns to his lounge chair.

As the woman braids Claire's hair, the sisters sift through the basket of beads, picking out purple and white.

"I'll come back to check on you," Alison says. She pecks her sister on the forehead and is off.

The braiding takes nearly two hours. The woman does not try to get her to talk, which is a relief to Claire. She likes sitting here, the silence and the feeling of the woman's hands working quickly yet gently through her hair. The sun is hot, the bites on her legs beg to be scratched, but she stays still, fortified by an image of herself returning to school with these braids, the beads tinkling as she walks, and how, for a rare, brief time, the other girls will envy her.

When the woman is finished, she hands Claire a clouded plastic mirror. It is better than she dared hope.

The woman looks at her. "My, you a patient child."

THAT NIGHT, Claire claws through her sleep. No matter how she scratches at the bites, she can't make the itching stop. All night she tosses in and out of dreams. When she wakes up it is dawn, barely light. The bites on her legs are crusted with dried, rust-colored blood. The blood has stained the crisp white sheets, too, blots so perfectly red it makes her dizzy. She looks around the room. Alison is gone.

WHAT DO a mother and father do when they are awakened by one child to the news that the other is missing? First, they tell themselves not to panic. Their daughter must have simply gone off somewhere on the resort grounds. It is a large property and there are any number of places she could be. Perhaps she has gone for a jog, or to smack tennis balls against the backboard at the courts. The small red blip of a kayak far out on the water might be her—maybe she decided to squeeze in one last water sport before their departure. Perhaps she got too drunk at the hotel bar last night and is sleeping off a hangover in the room of one of the other girls her age. (The parents are not naïve; they know that a teenager is apt to have one daiquiri too many after her parents have gone to bed on the last night of a Caribbean vacation.) Surely she will come groggily across the sand anytime now, and how furious they will be! And how pleasurable it will be to be furious with a daughter who is perfectly fine, and who will be snotty and dismissive when they tell her how worried they have been.

But she is in none of these places doing none of these things. By late morning, a mother and father's faith that their child will turn up any moment has given way to terror. Everything but Alison is forgotten. Breakfast, lunch . . . Claire is starving but says nothing.

Word spreads quickly among the guests.

"Did you hear? That pretty girl with the auburn hair is missing."

"The one with the scar?"

"They're saying she never came home last night."

The police are summoned. The chief of police asks the mother and father a series of questions, and they tell him about their vacation in precise, dutiful detail. As guests sun themselves by the pool and climb the StairMaster to oblivion in the fitness center, the Royal Police Force of Saint X combs the property. The time for the family's flight home comes and goes.

ON THE first night after Alison's disappearance the sunset is the most beautiful yet, a flashy display of scarlet and violet that deepens, as the sun slips below the horizon, until it is the shade of a bruise. On the balcony, a mother watches the sun go down, then sinks to the floor. She crouches on hands and knees and dry-heaves over the cool terra-cotta tiles. A father goes to her, holds her. He tells her that everything could still be okay. She repeats this. Everything could still be okay. Hearing these words echoed back to him from his wife, a father breaks down. They remain on the balcony, intertwined, for some time. A sense of distance from the day's events comes over the mother and she wonders, with detached curiosity, whether she is becoming—whether she is already—the one thing none of the mothers ever want to be. A father is seized by the most unaccountable memory: Alison, one year old and bald as could be, blowing raspberries against his cheek.

From inside, where she has been set up in front of the television, Claire watches her parents. Later that night, they put her between them in their bed. In the middle of the night she wakes to the feeling of a hand on her back; for a moment, she thinks it is Alison. Then she remembers. It is her father's hand, checking for the rise and fall of her breath. Claire lies awake, eyes wide open in the dark.

ON THE second day, the chief of police asks the mother and father to take him through their time on the island once more. The father tells him again about their arrival, ten days ago, on a TWA flight out of Kennedy. Alison slept late the next morning. She drank a fruit punch.

"He was after her all week," the mother interrupts. Her body trembles. "That blond boy. He couldn't leave her alone." As she speaks, a film reel of horrible possibilities flickers through her mind. She'd liked this boy, found it sweet the way he lingered, at once cocky and unsure, around her daughter. What if she'd misjudged him? What a fool she'd been, thinking herself a good mom, a fun mom, for letting her daughter go off with him. How had she allowed herself to forget that in the end a mother has only one job? Suddenly she cannot breathe. The warm tropical air clogs in her throat. When she begins to hyperventilate, the chief of police calls for the hotel doctor, who arrives promptly, examines the mother swiftly, and writes a prescription for a sedative. A porter is sent to the local chemist's to collect it. The doctor pulls the father aside. "I might suggest that you have a babysitter called for the little one," he tells him quietly, gesturing at Claire, who is sitting in a wicker chair, eyes on her mother. "Give yourselves some time and space."

"If you think we're going to let our daughter out of our sight, if you think we're going to leave her with some person who could be anyone, you're out of your mind."

"Of course. I apologize."

"Everyone here could be anyone. *You* could be anyone."

"I'll go now, sir."

THE COUPLE in the room next to the family's asks Indigo Bay's manager, very tactfully, if they can be relocated.

"It's so awful, what's happened. The thing is, we can hear them," the husband says.

"Going through . . . what they're going through," the wife adds. She places a hand protectively over her stomach; she is four months pregnant, this trip a last hurrah before their lives change. She laces her other hand through her husband's and squeezes, a gesture that means, *Something like this could happen to us.* Her husband squeezes her hand back, an assurance that it won't and, more generally, that this thing that has occurred is not a bad omen, not some harbinger of terrible things on the horizon. (He will turn out to be right. Often, in the decades to come, as their son grows up and their family's own small troubles reveal themselves, the wife will think that this ruined vacation was the darkest of blessings, because however her child struggles, however he tests her, hurts her, what does it matter when she carries within her the indelible sounds of another mother's undoing?)

The manager upgrades them to a private villa.

The rest of the guests do their best to balance concern with the pleasure of their days. They do not know the girl, after all. Their worry is tinged with excitement. There are rumors.

"They say the police are questioning that blond boy."

"Did you hear they're talking to the skinny one and the fat one?"

"I heard the police picked them up for something the night she went missing. People are saying they spent the night in jail."

"It's always the pretty ones, isn't it?"

THE ISLAND is turned upside down with searching. Members of the civil service are given days off to join the search. Prop planes loaned from a larger island nearby scan the shallow seas. The lagoon into which, mere days ago, Alison watched the blond boy hit golf balls is trawled to no avail.

The search turns up answers to other, older mysteries. The body of a beloved family dog, who disappeared during a storm last season, surfaces in the thickets beside a salt pond. A wedding band is found in the dusty lot behind Paradise Karaoke. In a limestone cavern on Carnival Cay, a customs worker uncovers a small black notebook in which are recorded the debts of a local man who left the island in an unexplained hurry last year. But no sign is found of Alison.

When the chief of police arrives at the family's hotel room on the third day after her disappearance and delivers this update, the father looks around—at the marble floor, the scarlet orchid in the white vase, the canopy bed—his gaze darting and unfocused, as if the coherence of these things is beginning to come apart before his eyes. "I don't understand. What's taking so long? Where is she?"

"I assure you we are deploying every available resource. Our officers are working in fifteen-hour shifts. We are coordinating with the Federal Bureau of Investigation. We have search-and-rescue units from three islands and a patrol ship from the British navy devoted to finding your daughter."

"But this island is tiny." The father squints at the chief of police. "Why the hell can't you find her?"

THE ACTOR'S girlfriend finally persuades him, grudgingly, to charter a boat to Faraway Cay. As they slice through the water, he keeps his eyes shut tight and listens as his girlfriend chats up the two men who comprise the boat's crew. ("I *love* reggae. That whole rasta spirituality, you know? I've always found that so interesting." "I'm an L.A. girl. But he"—gesturing, he knows, at him—"grew up in a really small town in Kentucky." He knew she'd tell these men this; she mentions Kentucky to anyone who will listen. It hurts him. His childhood was not a happy one. If he asked her to stop mentioning it he knows she would, but she wouldn't understand why, so he doesn't ask.) Each time the boat lofts over a swell, time becomes a glass cube he's trapped in.

The cay is only a few hundred yards off the coast, so the ride must take only five minutes, though to him it feels much longer. They anchor off-shore, so he has to climb the metal ladder down from the boat and wade through the shallows; he keeps his back to the open water, his eyes fixed on the land. She's right—it is beautiful. The cliffs are covered in green growth, a color so vivid it seems to cast out vibrations. The beach is a crescent of sand so brilliant he has to shield his eyes. Palms curve outward in invitation.

While the men prepare a picnic for them on the beach, the actor and his girlfriend hike a path inland to the waterfall. When the ocean slips from view he feels like himself again. At first, they climb steeply uphill through humid green growth, the birdsong so thick you couldn't sort through it if you tried. The understory is a sprawl of ferns and vines and the buttressed roots of trees that rise to form a nearly solid canopy high overhead. (The trees are silk-cotton, and have stood for centuries.) After half a mile or so, they summit abruptly onto an arid plateau, silver scrub and cacti and dust, a transition like leaving one dream and entering another. A few stark, knotty trees jut from the cracked earth, leafless and stunted. Lizards that seem made of nothing but dry air scuttle in and out of the scrub. A small white butterfly floats over the hot earth.

Not far from the path, a cluster of goats snort and chomp at the scrub.

"Gross," the actor says.

"I think they're cute."

"I think *you're* cute."

Whether he says it because he means it or because he doesn't but wishes he did or simply because it's the sort of thing he knows she wants him to say, he couldn't tell you.

The path descends back into dense and steamy thickets. He smells growth, soil, sweet wet rock. He hears falling water. They are close.

Around a bend, and there it is. The water sluicing down the rocks is glitter and mist. The pool into which it tumbles is utterly circular and glassy. At the pool's edge, mosses fur the stones in newborn green, and white flowers bloom, their perfume carried lightly on the vapor cast off by the waterfall. He has the feeling then that he is seeing something he shouldn't be seeing, that maybe there really is such a thing as too much beauty, as so much you can never move on from it.

"You like it?" his girlfriend says. He notes the curl of triumph in her voice and a familiar urge rises in him to fuck her till she hurts for days. But then he looks at her and sees that there are tears in her eyes. She laughs at herself, wipes them away. "I know, I'm a sap."

He has been unkind. All she wants is his happiness. Is that so terrible? He takes her in his arms, feeling the blunt realness of her. What the hell is wrong with him? Where is the problem here? He leads her to the water's edge, holding her hand in case she should slip on the slick rocks, and they wade in. He surrenders to it. They swim together to the very center of the pool. The water is so crisp and clean you could understand how a baptism could change everything. He squeezes his hands together and squirts her.

"Hey," she splashes back.

He wraps his arms around her. "You're mine."

She shrieks and kicks and protests with delight. "Let me go! Let me go!"

"Never." He makes a silent vow. From now on when she asks for things he will do them, give them, say them.

They swim to the waterfall. They dunk their heads beneath the rushing water and let it pummel them. They slip behind the curtain of water. They kiss. She reaches for him but he shakes his head.

"Lie back," he says. He cradles her head as she lies against the wet rocks. When she comes, her cries are lost in the roar of water.

After, they float, spent and open on the surface of the pool.

"They'll be waiting for us," he says finally.

"Do we have to?" she pouts.

Together, they stroke toward the edge.

Years from this moment, the girlfriend, who by then will have been the girlfriend of quite a few Hollywood men, will publish a memoir (the back cover promising to reveal "the juicy private details of the lives of some of America's favorite leading men"). In the chapter about the actor, these details will include his thalassophobia and his various chemical dependencies, which the girlfriend will theorize stem from a loveless childhood. It goes without saying that the memoir will recount this day: the boat ride across the topaz shallows to the cay, the birdsong and the goats, the waterfall and how, just before leaving it, the girlfriend looked down and saw an arm, puffed and white, reaching up from the bottom, as if frozen in the act of beckoning.

"Why did the chicken cross the road?"

"To give Officer Roy the busiest day of his life."

This is a popular joke here and I don't mind it. The things the police handle on this island are mostly small. Mr. So-and-So cut down Miss So-and-So's sugar-apple tree. A scuffle at Papa Mango's. Floyd Vanterpool operating an unlicensed taxi again. We do see a few cases of domestic trouble each year.

Much of my job involves helping our children here grow up safely and become upstanding citizens, and I like this work. Every year I visit the island primaries and teach a lesson on bicycle safety. For my demonstration I ride a small pink bike with streamers on the handlebars, and this always receives a good laugh. When children see me around they shout, "Officer Roy!" "Officer Roy!" just to say hello.

When the young folk have a late-night bacchanal on Little Beach I have no choice but to bust it up, but I try not to be too cross with them when I do so. I try to remember that I limed on Little Beach myself in my time. While they clean up their rubbish I make jokes. If I see a boy and girl coming out of the bushes together I say, "She out of your league, man!" If I see a boy who's small for his age I say, "Who invited this nursery child to the party?"

If I see some youths clustering outside Perry's in the Basin I pull up beside them and say, "This is loitering. I'm going to have to write you up." You should see how some of the toughest ones look like they might soil themselves until I start laughing.

"Aw, man, don't do that shit to we!" they say, but they're not really mad.

"Do it up, Officer Roy!" they beg when I prepare to drive away. *"Please, Officer Roy?"* I turn on my lights and my siren and drive off to their cheers. I have a rapport with them, you could say. I watch these kids grow and I play my part.

Edwin and Gogo—I used to shoo them away from the radio tower when they were snot-nosed little boys. I came up with Gogo's daddy, God rest his sweet soul. I pulled those two and their hooligan mates over for drunk driving all the time and took them in to sleep it off. I never saw it as punishment. I never wrote them up. I was protecting them from their young stupid selves, like pulling a baby back from the water's edge. My wife and I couldn't have children. The island children are my children.

I must have picked Edwin and Gogo up a hundred times before that night. That's how I know something happened and they were part of it. Because the ninety-nine other times I pulled them over, on the drive to the station they joked with me and made chitchat. But that time, the night Alison Thomas died, neither one of them said a word.

EMILY OF PASADENA

ON MY FIRST DAY OF KINDERGARTEN, after my father took a picture of me on our front steps in my purple overalls and before I climbed onto the yellow bus, my mother prepared me for Cody Lundgren. She squatted so her eyes were level with mine and told me that there would be a boy in my class who was different from other children, and that I must not be afraid of him, but, on the contrary, must treat him with special kindness. With a child's logic, I assumed this was simply one more part of going to school. In kindergarten, one rode the bus and learned to read (though I already knew how, and was rather smug about it), one had recess and homework, and one was especially kind to the boy who was different. I was a shy child, at once excited and tentative about taking these steps.

As soon as I stepped into the classroom that morning and saw him, I knew I could not do what my mother had asked. Cody Lundgren terrified me. His limbs jerked. His mouth hung open. Saliva pooled on his lower lip and dripped in glistening cobwebs, darkening his shirt. Worst of all were the sounds he made, viscous gurgles punctuated by high-pitched keening. Every day, while the rest of us learned our numbers or studied butterflies— larva, pupa, fly away—Cody sat with his personal aide, making his sounds and collapsing on occasion into horrible tantrums.

Then, one Monday in February, Cody Lundgren was not in school. Our teacher, Ms. D'Elia, gathered us in a circle and told us that Cody had died over the weekend. We were each made to say one thing we would remember about Cody. This struck me even then as a poorly conceived exercise, dependent as it was upon five-year-olds possessing the subtlety to craft a pleasant fiction about who Cody had been to us. (Ms. D'Elia was new that year, and more than once I'd overheard my mother on the phone with other mothers describing her as "out of her depth," which led me to imagine Ms. D'Elia in a yellow bathing cap, performing a synchronized swimming routine, her legs treading furiously beneath the water's surface.) All of the other children shared the same memory, of the cupcakes Cody's mother had brought on his birthday. They were not the homemade ones the rest of our mothers packed in Tupperware for our birthdays, but fancy ones from a bakery, with sugar flowers and perfect whorls of buttercream. It was a memory that had nothing to do with Cody, really, and everything to do with his mother's love for him. When my turn came, I said I would remember how much Cody liked to sing. Every morning during music time, Cody would squawk and moan along to "Funga Alafia" or the Erie Canal song, terrifying sounds of unmistakable pleasure. I would not actually remember this fondly, but I understood that it was the sort of thing Ms. D'Elia had in mind. Next, she read us a picture book, a parable in which a family of mice grieve and heal after one of them is eaten by a cat, and that was that.

The truth is I was relieved Cody Lundgren was dead. Death meant never seeing someone again, and I was glad I would never again see Cody or hear the yelps and gurgles that so disturbed me.

A few months later, my mother and I ran into Cody's mother at the supermarket. Mrs. Lundgren was tall, with silky black hair, far prettier than any other mother I knew, prettier than I'd previously understood a mother could be.

"Look how big you've gotten!" she exclaimed to me. Her smile was so hard and desperate that I reached for my mother's hand like a younger child than I was. I left the grocery store with a pit in my stomach, rocked by an emotion so new to me I could not identify it, though looking back I know it was shame.

THIS WAS the extent of my experience with death when my sister's body was found on an uninhabited cay in the Caribbean, many years ago now. Looking back, the things I remember most clearly from the days after Alison went missing and before she was found are strangely inconsequential. For example, I remember the hunger I experienced on that first day when my parents forgot about breakfast and lunch, and how I felt sorry for myself about it in the banal way any child feels sorry for herself when she finds herself overlooked in a flurry of attention devoted to her sibling. I remember hiding out in the bathroom to devour a Toblerone bar and a tin of mixed nuts I'd scavenged from the minibar. I was hiding because I wanted to see how long it would take my parents to realize they'd forgotten to feed me, so that I could take the full measure of their neglect. Once they *did* realize, I have vivid memories of the room service food with which I was plied, or soothed, or distracted (I'm not sure what to call it) in the days that followed—cheeseburgers and fries and sundaes and a personal pan pizza with delightful miniature pepperonis. I cleaned my plate at every meal; if my parents noticed this, I'm sure they thought my appetite was unaffected by what was happening because I was too young to grasp the seriousness of the situation, but that wasn't exactly right. I was terrified during those days, but not because of what might have happened to Alison. Even as the people around me grew increasingly frantic, I was not worried for her. I literally did not understand that what had happened to Cody Lundgren could happen to my big sister. I thought—I *knew*—that she was playing an elaborate game with us. She was watching it all, the dapper policemen with their braided gold epaulets, the resort staff in a tizzy, the entire spectacle she'd created, from some hidden perch with a smile. No, it was not Alison's disappearance but my parents' terror that terrified me. Their distraction and anguish shook the foundations of a world that had, until then, seemed to me absolutely stable.

Other memories from those days are less distinct. They have the quality of a fever dream—hazy and inconsistent, the swirling world resolving for brief instants into crystalline clarity. I remember lying between my parents at night, my father's hand on my back measuring every inhale and exhale. His words to the doctor. *If you think we're going to let our daughter out of our sight.* I remember the chief of police questioning my parents, and my mother telling him about the blond boy who'd taken such an interest in my sister. As she speaks, my mother's eyes have a wild, darting quality. The tone of her voice shifts from word to word, turning raw, then affectless, then raw again. I don't really understand what she is saying, what she is accusing the boy from the volleyball game of having done. I know only that before my eyes my mother is becoming someone I never understood she could be.

In short, a terrifying knowledge came over me in those days. It was the knowledge that I would never be safe again, because I never had been, not once in my whole life, only until then I hadn't known it, because I had believed so absolutely in the power of my parents.

. . .

THE CHIEF of police questioned me, too. My father sat me on his lap and my mother explained to me that one of the nice men who was helping to find Alison wanted to talk to me. This was the first moment I remember feeling truly afraid for my sister. I think I understood that if the police were looking to a child for help, something must be very wrong. I felt a familiar prickling in my fingertips, and as I sat in my father's lap I began to trace letters in the air. A-L-I-S—.

My mother reached out her hand and placed it over mine, stilling it. "No writing, Clairey. Please. This is important."

At the time of our family's vacation, this compulsion had been with me for several months. I'm not sure how or why it started. I would hear a word, and it would feel absolutely necessary to write it in the air. When my mother lifted her hand away, I tensed my fingers against the need—my sister's name vibrating in my bones, desperate to get out. Alison. Alison. Alison.

The chief of police smiled at me. I drew away from him. I did not like being smiled at by strangers. He asked me if I knew anything about what my sister had been doing, if I had seen anything out of the ordinary.

What did I know? I knew my sister came and went, was there and not there. I knew that eyes followed her wherever she went. I said nothing and hid my face in my father's chest. He smiled weakly at me and told me what a good job I had done, how brave I had been, which even at that age I didn't believe. A dish of vanilla ice cream with a maraschino cherry was brought for me. I hated how the bright red bled onto the ice cream, but I ate.

ON THE third morning after Alison's disappearance, my father announced with unconvincing cheerfulness that he was taking me swimming. I'd been holed up in my parents' hotel room all that time, and I understood that he'd decided this would be good for me. I changed into my swimsuit, buckled my jellies, and out we went. When we stepped onto the marble pool deck, a hush fell over the other guests. I looked at them looking at us and gagged. I had the distinct sense that they knew something about us we didn't, and that if they looked at us long enough we would have to know it, too.

"It's okay," my father said, nudging me forward.

We were not in the water long, twenty minutes at most. My father gathered me in his arms and tossed me into the air. We raced the length of the pool. We did underwater flips and handstands—my father pushed him-self into an elegant plank, toes pointed. I see now that we were trying to respool time. If only we could forget what we were beginning to know, maybe we could play ourselves back to when this vacation was just a vaca-tion. When we got out of the water, my mother would wrap me in a fluffy white towel. *Look at you, sea monkey*, Alison might say.

A few hours later, there was a knock on the door of my parents' hotel room. When my father opened it, I saw the chief of police standing very still in his uniform with the braided epaulets. A cartoon was put on the television for me, and my parents went out into the hall with him. Some-time after that, they must have told me what he told them: that Alison had been found, that she was gone. But I don't remember that part. I remem-ber those epaulets, how they seemed like something from a beautiful story.

WHAT IS known about the night Alison disappeared: At approximately 8 P.M. she was seen walking from the swimming pool to the hotel bar by an elderly security guard named Harold Moses. At the bar, she met the blond boy, a fact confirmed by the boy and three other witnesses. Alison and the boy went to the staff parking lot and smoked a joint together. At 8:45 P.M., he returned to the bar without Alison. At approximately 10:15 P.M., Alison returned to the parking lot, where Edwin Hastie and Clive Richardson picked her up in Edwin's car, a 1980 Vauxhall Astra, eggplant in color, and the three of them drove across the island to the Basin. They spent two hours at a local watering hole called Paulette's Place, where my sister was seen with the two men, smoking pot and drinking rum and dancing. Sev-eral patrons at Paulette's Place confirm that she departed with the men at approximately 12:45 A.M.

At 1:30 A.M., a police officer named Roy Cannadine pulled the Vaux-hall Astra over on Mayfair Road for erratic driving. Only Clive and Ed-win were inside. Officer Cannadine did what he always did with the young men who could frequently be found weaving down the island's roads late at night. He drove them to the eggshell-blue prison to sober up for the night. In the morning they were released, the car keys returned, and they set off on the two-mile walk to fetch the car from the side of Mayfair Road. They arrived at work on time.

• • •

CAN YOU see it? A bar, PAULETTE'S PLACE painted in white on a driftwood sign out front. Dancing and drinking and a haze of cigarette and pot smoke and, in the middle of it all, a russet-haired girl. She dances with the men. She drinks the drinks they hand her.

When she leaves with them, they tell her they are taking her someplace special.

"It's a surprise," they say.

"You'll love it."

Drunk and high but most of all naïve, she lets the twisting in her stomach push her forward when it should hold her back. They drive to the beach beyond the black rocks at the edge of Indigo Bay, where a boat is waiting. They bring the boat into Faraway Cay slowly, and she hops out into the knee-deep water and smiles, for the sea is warm and lovely and she knows that she—her thighs exposed to the starlight, the hem of her skirt soaked by the gentle waves—is lovely in it. They tell her there is a waterfall at the island's center, and they set off for it on foot. She still thinks they are having a good time.

"Not far now."

"Keep walking."

Their voices, though still friendly on the surface, have a coldness to them. No, she tells herself. She is just imagining it. Everything shifts so quickly that by the time she understands what is happening, it is too late to think about what to do. (Anyway, what could she do, way out there?)

They pull her into the scrub. She struggles at first, but one of them slaps her across the mouth. After that she is too afraid to fight. More than this, she knows there is no point. They have wanted what they wanted since the first time they saw her on the beach at Indigo Bay in the white tunic she thought made her look so very fetching. They untie her halter top, shove her denim skirt up, yank her panties down. Maybe this was their plan all along. Or maybe the night has gotten away from them. Maybe as they thrust against her, pressing her body against the hard roots of a manchineel tree, the ground littered with its sour, rotting fruit, they experience no pleasure, only terror, because it dawns on them that, having done this, they cannot allow her to live. When it is over, they dump her naked body in the waterfall. On the boat ride back to the mainland, they toss her clothes into the water, never to be seen again.

Or perhaps it was a terrible accident. They are carousing at Rocky Shoal when she trips and hits her head against one of the sharp volcanic rocks for which the beach is named. Or she stumbles into the sea and they realize too late that she is in no condition to swim. They panic. They do the first thing they can think of; they heft her lifeless body from beach to car to boat to cay.

One might imagine it differently. One might imagine it any number of ways, really, the details shifting, the outcome the same. Clive Richardson and Edwin Hastie were taken into custody.

THE NIGHT after Alison's body was found, I took off my clothes to change into my nightgown and saw that my shoulders had begun to peel. Mere days ago, my sister had rubbed aloe on my sunburned skin. If I concentrated on the memory, I could still feel her fingertips. Now I was shedding that skin. Soon there would be nothing left of me that she had touched.

For the first time since she disappeared, I cried. I was an only child now, hopelessly insufficient. I picked at the skin, wanting the new sadness I would feel when all of it had flaked away. I wanted all the sorrow I could gather.

A FEW days later, as my parents went busily about arranging the funeral and the transportation of my sister's body back to New York, the chief of police arrived with the shocking news that Edwin Hastie had been released and that Clive Richardson, while still in custody, was being held not as a suspect in my sister's death, but on charges related to drugs and paraphernalia that had been uncovered during the investigation. Despite the circumstances surrounding Alison's death, the chief of police explained, they did not have sufficient evidence to charge the two men, and they could not hold them if they could not charge them. Apparently it had been determined that the window of time between when witnesses saw Clive and Edwin leave Paulette's Place with Alison and when Officer Cannadine pulled them over on the side of Mayfair Road was not adequate for them to have traveled to Faraway Cay and back.

As you would expect, my parents were incredulous. I remember sitting with my mother on their bed, her patting my back with increasing vigor and turning up the volume on the television as, out on the balcony, my father argued more and more loudly with the chief of police.

"Explain to me, if you can, how you can be so sure the window of time was inadequate," my father said. He paced back and forth, hands jammed in his pockets.

"In the course of our investigation we have conducted numerous simulations, with boats leaving from every feasible location. The window of time during which the men in question were unaccounted for simply is not sufficient."

My father snorted. "How can you be so sure about that window? How can you be so confident it wasn't half an hour longer, or even more?"

"We have three witnesses corroborating the time of their departure from Paulette's Place. The witness who next saw them is one of our own officers."

"How convenient for you."

"I can assure you his testimony is his own."

"Well, your assurance certainly makes me feel a whole lot better. Now I have complete faith in the—what was it you called it? The course of your investigation?"

"That's correct."

My father stopped pacing. He took a step closer to the chief of police and held him in his gaze. "Those men are part of this. Maybe they weren't working alone. Maybe someone else took her out to that island, I don't know. It's not my job to know—it's your job. But I know one way or another they're involved, and you know it, too."

"I understand you are very upset."

"Oh, yes, *upset*. That's just what I am."

"I have some questions for you, sir, but perhaps we should continue this conversation at a later time."

"By all means, let's proceed." My father spread his hand in withering invitation.

The chief of police hesitated a moment, then continued. "Had you noticed any changes in your daughter recently?"

"What kind of changes?"

"For example, had she been agitated? Had she engaged in any reckless behavior? Had she been not herself or had she perhaps exhibited any signs of depression?"

My father laughed then, cold, hollow laughter. "So that's the story you want! Can't have a murder, can we? Bad for business, I'm sure."

"The only story we want is the truth."

"The truth is Alison is the very definition of a kid you don't have to worry about." He paused. "Was."

"I understand."

"Really? Because I'm not sure you do, so you listen very carefully. My daughter was killed here, on your island, and if I get the impression that you aren't really looking for the truth, I promise you I will get on every news network in America and call for a total boycott of your pretty little island, and I will not rest until every last dive shop and rum bar shuts down."

"I understand, sir. Thank you for your time."

A WEEK after Alison was found, we flew home. My father pulled two suitcases through the airport on Saint X, his and Alison's. How small we were, the three of us, barely a family at all.

"Time to go back to reality," the man seated beside my mother on the plane said sociably as we pulled away from the gate.

My mother smiled and nodded politely. She closed her eyes and did not open them again until we touched down in New York.

I had a window seat. As the plane lofted into the sky, I pressed my nose to the pane. At first the island filled the window. But quickly it reduced to a thin slash in the pale sea. Within seconds it was gone and we were moving through a vast heath of cloud.

MY BRAIDS turned limp and scraggly. Frizz haloed my scalp. There would be no grand moment of showing the braids off at school, and this disappointment still stung even in light of what had happened. Most of the time, my parents seemed not to notice how wild my hair had become. But at odd moments, one or the other of them seemed to see me vividly; they would look at the braids, then reach out to touch them as if they were some sort of curious relic.

Finally, the night before Alison's funeral, my father had me stand in front of the bathroom mirror. He unwound the rubber bands, dropped the beads into a plastic bowl, and uncoiled the braids one by one. He worked with exquisite gentleness. I think this was a necessary ritual for him, one he'd put off until he was ready for it. My hair tangled around his fingers. Loose strands floated to the floor.

"All done," he said hoarsely when the braids were out. Then he wandered off down the hall.

HUNDREDS OF people came to the funeral. High school and college classmates of Alison's, women who'd served on PTA committees with my mother, colleagues and clients of my father's. Even, in an uncomfortable gesture, the ambassador from Saint X to the United States.

The funeral is mostly a blur. Too many people. Too much perfume in the air. An itchy gray dress, purchased hurriedly for me by one of my mother's friends. What I remember most is the beautiful teenagers crying. After the service, they gathered in tight clusters on the sidewalk outside the church. The girls wore black dresses that exposed their legs and cleavage. They must not have owned clothing appropriate for a funeral, or maybe they did but chose these skimpy outfits instead because they relished this rare opportunity to explore a sad, tragic sensuality. They cried in the arms of solemn boys who, cast into this moment, appeared spontaneously to have been made into men. Among them, most beautiful of all, was Drew McNamara. Drew was my sister's high school sweetheart. They began dating in the spring of their freshman year and remained inseparable until my sister broke up with Drew the week before leaving for college. I had been heartbroken when she did it—I had believed I would scatter rose petals down the aisle at their wedding. Now here he stood, one among them. I looked around at them, these alive girls and boys, so attractive in their grief while I felt so wrong, a freak, in my own.

IN THOSE early months after Alison's death, the investigation consumed both of my parents, though it consumed them differently. My father took a leave from work; Alison became his full-time occupation. He was in frequent communication with the FBI, and he called the police on Saint X constantly to monitor the progress of their investigation, which he became increasingly convinced was not inept, but rather a dexterous charade intended to preserve the island's reputation as a place you could take your family, your kiddos and wives and pretty daughters. His desk in the basement was covered with papers and files. At one point, he even hired a private investigator to dig into Clive Richardson and Edwin Hastie, though I don't believe anything ever came of this.

My mother retreated into herself. Though she did not speak of it, it was clear to me that her thoughts never wavered from what had happened. I could see questions and theories spinning behind her distant gaze. Sometimes I overheard her speaking to herself: "I know it. I know it." In books and movies, the bedrooms of dead children become temples—untouched, everything preserved just as they left it. But my mother lived in Alison's room. I would return from school to a silent house and know she was in there, curled up in Alison's sheets. One day I opened the bedroom door to find her sitting at Alison's desk, cupping something in her hands. It was a nest of Alison's hair, pulled from her yellow brush.

For my part, if before Alison's death I had been prone to some mildly compulsive behavior, in the aftermath this spiraled into a genuine affliction. I felt the prickling in my fingertips, the need to write in the air, constantly. Alison. Alison. Alison. I also developed a second, intertwined compulsion of thinking up scenarios in which those I loved might die. It was a ritual of protection: If I imagined a specific death, it seemed nearly impossible that it would actually happen in exactly that way, so the more scenarios I imagined, the safer the people I loved became. After my mother tucked me in at night I lay awake for hours, tracing Alison's name while conjuring visions of my parents lying in parallel hospital beds succumbing to a rare infection, of our dog Fluffernutter crushed by a falling tree limb, and crying because I was exhausted and desperate for sleep and my powerlessness in the face of these rituals terrified me. I wanted to wake my parents but knew I mustn't add to their worries. I faced the long night hours alone, until the sky began to lighten and, my watch completed, my mind finally released me to sleep.

DEPENDING ON where you lived then, maybe you remember how brutal the winters were in the mid-nineties, how the Eastern Seaboard bore nor'easter after nor'easter from December straight through April. During those winters, a good number of Americans found themselves stuck inside for months on end, huddled around televisions and desperate to be entertained. If you were one of them, you will remember how Alison was all over the news the winter she was killed, as Nancy and Tonya and JonBenét were during other winters around that time. It seemed the national appetite craved—demanded, even—a dramatic story about an American beauty.

(Nancy in all those crystals, glittering across the Lillehammer ice. JonBenét the way I loved her best, *sans makeup,* as my mother would say, her natural brown hair waving out of a cowboy hat, a red bandana around her slender neck.) News vans loitered on our suburban cul-de-sac for weeks. I was forbidden from playing in the front yard. But one day I disobeyed this rule. It had snowed the night before. While my parents were still asleep, I put on my snow pants and my puffy purple jacket and slipped out the front door. I clomped through the knee-deep snow, lay down on my back, and fanned my arms and legs back and forth. I looked up at the sky. It was white, but the color didn't seem to reside anywhere. It was like the turquoise in the water at Indigo Bay, colors that were everywhere and nowhere. Had my sister slid into the infinity between color and object? Was she out there, in some incomprehensible elsewhere, watching me? Inside my mittens, my hands worked furiously. Alison. Alison. Alison.

A few minutes later my father opened the door and shooed me inside. That night, my mother was draining pasta for dinner with the small white television in the kitchen tuned to the local station, when there I was, swishing my arms and legs through the snow. "The search for answers in the death of local teen Alison Thomas continues," a woman in a magenta blazer said. "Meanwhile, on this snowy day, her sister could be seen making angels."

IN APRIL, the chief of police on Saint X called our house. We had just sat down to dinner. My father answered the call on the phone that hung on the wall beside the stove, and I watched as he listened, twisting and untwisting the cord. The chief of police had called to inform him in advance that he would be holding a press conference the next day, at which he would announce that all suspects in my sister's case had been cleared, and the department had concluded there was not sufficient evidence that Alison had died as the result of a violent crime to continue the investigation.

My father flew into a rage. I don't remember what he said, but I do remember his shouting, and how I looked down at the drumstick and green beans on my plate like maybe if only I stared hard enough it would all go away—this moment and all the others since I had awoken to find my sister gone. When my father's shouts became choked with sobs I thought I would be sick. I began to trace Alison's name furiously on the kitchen table.

"Stop that, Clairey," my mother said.

I wanted so badly to stop for her, but I couldn't. My eyes filled with tears. She put her hand over mine, but I shook it off. I cried harder, pressed my fingertip against the tabletop so hard it hurt.

"Clairey, please," she begged.

My body began to tremble.

Then my mother knelt next to my chair and looked straight at me. For the first time in months her eyes seemed animated not by some scene playing out in her mind, but by the present we shared. Though I was much too old to be carried, she lifted my tensed body out of the chair. I let myself go slack in her arms, and she carried me upstairs and tucked me into bed. She stayed there with me, stroking my hair, until I was asleep.

A FEW weeks later, my parents surprised me with the news that my Aunt Caroline would be taking me to Paris. A present for my eighth birthday, they said. Aunt Caroline was my mother's older sister. She had never married and had no children. She lived in the East Village and was the only adult I knew who smoked. For a week she and I shared a little *chambre* in the Marais. Every morning we had bread with butter and raspberry jam and espresso at a café in the Place des Vosges. ("See how butter *tastes* like butter here," Aunt Caroline said.) I forced the espresso down, trying to convince myself I liked its sophisticated intensity. We did not go to the Eiffel Tower or Versailles, nor to any of the kid-friendly attractions my parents would have sought out: wax museums, puppet shows. We did what Aunt Caroline called "being *flâneuses*." We wandered. If we passed a *fromagerie* with logs of goat cheese pressed with lavender in the window, we bought some. We ate long leisurely dinners during which Aunt Caroline drained carafes of plum-dark wine. We lazed in parks all afternoon.

Alison had never been to Paris. I had nibbled a *brioche aux pralines* in the Luxembourg Gardens and she never would. I would have this on her forever. I would have every day on her for the rest of my life. In Paris with Aunt Caroline, I finally began to understand that my sister was not gone the way she'd been gone when she was off at college—vanished from my days but still out there, living her life. She was gone not just from me and my parents and Drew McNamara, but also and above all from herself. My parents' grief might lessen, I might heal, Drew might move on, but Alison's loss—of a future, a life—would never change.

On the plane back over the Atlantic, Aunt Caroline slept with her mouth snapped open like a crocodile's for seven straight hours. I remained awake. I was anxious about returning home. I was wary of my father and even more so of my mother—how when I got home she would squeeze me in her arms so tightly I would be able to feel her thinly veiled terror that I, too, might vanish.

But when my parents met us at the airport, my mother's smile was light and clean. She'd gotten a haircut. My whole life her hair had come down past her shoulders; now it barely skimmed her chin. She was wearing a blue chambray dress and sandals.

"Did you have the very best time?" she asked.

Things were different after that. My father went back to work. If he continued to be in contact with the police on Saint X, he kept it to himself. When I got home from school in the afternoons, my mother was no longer in Alison's room; she was waiting for me in the kitchen with a glass of milk and a plate of Oreos. Always a voracious reader, she began to check out books from the library again. My father rejoined his Sunday squash game. At night from my bedroom I sometimes caught the faint sound of a laugh track—they were watching *Murphy Brown* in bed.

Every so often in the years that followed, my parents received a briefing from the police. A former maid at Indigo Bay had remembered something that might turn out to be consequential. A man from Chicago had called with a tip that seemed bogus, but which the police would of course pursue with diligence and expediency. My parents did not fixate on these developments, and in the end none of them ever amounted to anything.

When someone asked my mother how many children she had, her response was always the same. "We had two daughters but our eldest was killed."

This, in our house, was the final word on Alison. She *was killed*. Passive voice. As if Alison were the recipient of a fate inflicted by nobody.

THAT SUMMER, my parents sold our house and we moved across the country to Pasadena. I was angry at my parents about our move. I thought they wanted to forget Alison. I see now that we didn't have much of a choice. The victims of tragedies almost always depart, sooner or later. Everybody in our small suburb knew what had happened to us. Cody Lundgren's mother had made me sad and uncomfortable when I saw her at the grocery store, and now we did this to other people wherever we went. To stay would have been, frankly, *inconsiderate*. (The Lundgrens had decamped for Philadelphia not long after Cody's death.)

In New York, we had lived in a large white center-hall Colonial. There had been five bedrooms, a swimming pool out back; Alison and I each had our own bathroom. Everyone I knew lived this way, and I was young enough not to understand that most people didn't. But we lived differently in Pasadena. We moved into a small sage-colored bungalow in the hills. My mother hung wind chimes along the eaves. In New York we'd had a sprawling acre of lawn; here there was a tiny jewel-box garden. Our home in Pasadena was not inexpensive by any means, and we still lived in the sort of neighborhood that would be described as "prestigious" in a real estate listing. But the little bungalow was decidedly, *intentionally*, modest. If I found myself in the car with my mother, driving past some newfangled McMansion or an ersatz Spanish revival estate in Oak Knoll, she would scoff and say, "So tacky," and I understood she meant much more—that the people who lived there were drawing the universe's eye, leaving their good fortune out in the open, when they ought to be secreting it away.

The night before the first day of third grade, I told my parents that at my new school I wanted to go by my middle name. I could feel them exchanging meaningful looks over my head.

"Try it out," my father said. "You can always go back to Claire if you change your mind."

I never did. From that day on, I was Emily.

EVERYTHING CHANGED for me in Pasadena. I'd always been a reticent, prickly child, more comfortable in the company of my family than with my peers. I had struggled to make friends and accustomed myself to spending time alone. But in Pasadena I was new and therefore presumed interesting. Soon I was playing school and orphans in the purple enclaves of other girls' bedrooms. To my surprise, I found myself sharing with these girls the intimacy of friendship. We confessed our secrets; stuck out our tongues and touched the tips together, giggling at the contact of wriggling, tasteless muscle; carved sacred spaces in the putty of our suburban world— forts and clubhouses, hideaways in the rhododendrons. The compulsions that had plagued me for so long faded away, evaporating in the dry air of my new life. For a very long time, until the winter of my twenty-fifth year, which would find me in New York City, where events would transpire that would change everything for me again, and irrevocably, I didn't think of them at all.

AT SOME point, my father must have taken the rolls of film from our vacation to be developed, because a few months after our move to Pasadena I found the photographs in his home office, in the back of his desk drawer. Every so often I would sneak into his office and take the photos out. My father had them printed in triplicate. I did not skip through the copies. I looked at each one with the same disbelief. How could it have been real? In one picture, Alison and I were building our sandcastle. In another, the two of us smiled for my father as the woman under the faded blue umbrella braided my hair. There was a series of pictures of Alison posing beside a palm tree. On the back of one of these pictures, in my father's tidy all-caps penmanship: *MY ALI.* There were pictures of Alison and my mother walking on the beach, and of me examining a seashell with a look of wonder . . . swims and games and boat rides and half a dozen incomparably gorgeous sunsets. At first, I went to the photographs when I missed my sister. As time passed, I went to them when I had not missed her in a while and wanted to.

THE ELEVEN-YEAR gap between Alison and me is notable, and requires some explanation. I was not an accident, nor had my parents been trying for years to conceive again. I know because when I was in fifth grade I asked my mother why my sister and I had been so far apart in age, unlike my friends and their siblings. She told me that at first she and my father thought they only wanted one child. But then they realized how much they loved being parents and decided to have me. Those were her exact words: "We decided to have you." As if they had known, when they chose to have another child, that the child would be me.

When she told me this I felt sick to my stomach. I remembered something my father had said to the chief of police, when he was asked if my sister had appeared troubled in the days leading up to her death: "Alison is the very definition of a kid you don't have to worry about." His words had stayed with me, surfacing from time to time like a nagging ache. Because to say such a thing, you had to know what it was like to have a kid you *did* have to worry about. In my mother's words, I sensed her betraying insistence that it was exactly me they'd wanted. I don't mean they didn't love me; they did, everyone loves their children. But they loved me differently than they loved Alison. I don't think my parents understood their own desires when they decided to have another child. They thought they wanted to raise another kid. Really, they wanted to raise Alison again.

AS THE years passed, my mother and father continued to fulfill their parental duties. They signed me up for AYSO and pottery and displayed my endless output of pinch pots on the living room shelves. We went on trips to Yellowstone, London, Washington, D.C. They helped me with long division and took away my television privileges when I sassed. In summary, they behaved. Always fair, always reasonable. Wonderful parents, in a way. We lived on the surface, skated figure eights over a frozen sea.

WHEN I was ten, a women's television network of the feuding pageant queens and psychopathic stepmothers variety premiered *Dying for Fun*, an eight-part true crime series about young women whose hedonistic pursuits—wild parties, gap years, vacations—had gone horribly awry. Each episode was a dramatic reenactment of one woman's story. At the time, I knew only that something was being made about my sister and that my parents were upset about it, though their lawyer had told them there was nothing they could do.

The night *Dying for Fun: Alison Thomas* premiered, my parents took me to a Dodgers game. We ate hot dogs slathered in ketchup and mustard. We stood and cheered when Mike Piazza hit a home run. We sang "Take Me Out to the Ball Game" too loudly, laughed for too long, and generally tried not to think about the fact that in millions of homes across America, people were sitting on couches and tossing cheese puffs into their mouths as they watched a person who was not my sister die some version of my sister's death.

IT'S HARD for me to remember exactly what I was told about the details of Alison's death when it happened, and what facts I acquired later on. I'm fairly certain I didn't know it was the actor who'd found my sister, or who he was to begin with. But at some point I must have learned this, because there were two periods during my adolescence when I became oddly fixated on the actor. The first such period was in fifth grade. I often had sleepovers on the weekends then, which typically involved renting a movie. If the sleepover was happening at my house and it was my parents taking us to Blockbuster, I would do everything as usual, and we would come home with *Free Willy* or *Homeward Bound* or something like that. But if I was sleeping out and it was someone else's parents taking us, I'd try to make it happen that we would rent one of the actor's movies. The actor was not in children's movies, so this involved convincing my friends that a film about a bank heist or prohibition-era Chicago was something we would like. "This is supposed to be hilarious," I'd say, or, "I heard this is Sean Sawyer's favorite movie," Sean Sawyer being the boy we were all in love with. "Are you sure?" the mom or dad would ask when we handed them our selection, and if I'd done a good job, my friend would nod just as enthusiastically as me. Because the movies were actually not at all the kind of thing that interested us, often my friends would doze off after not too long, and then it would just be me, on a beanbag cushion in their playroom in the dark, watching the actor and looking for something I couldn't explain.

The second period came a few years later, when I was thirteen or fourteen and my friends and I were obsessed with *YM* and *Bop* and at night I dreamed steamy soft-core dreams about the shy, sensitive members of various boy bands. For a while during this time, I played out these extended scenarios in my mind where the actor reached out to my family seeking resolution, which he found in talking with me. Our unlikely friendship led to invitations to be his guest at awards shows, where I wore gowns and was photographed on the red carpet, stoic beauty radiating from me like an aura, and I won the attention and sympathy of all the stars I adored. I was ashamed of these fantasies, but I was helpless to stop them, unable to resist the maudlin potential of my own story. I thought I was awful, but now I think I was no more awful than any teenage girl—I simply had more potent material to spin.

I LOST my virginity in tenth grade. My boyfriend was a bassist in a band called Skar Tissue and a budding cartoonist who drew pictures of me with big anime eyes and hair made of flowers. His own hair was black streaked with violet. I helped him dye it every other week in his bathroom. My hands were perpetually stained purple, as if I'd gorged myself on berries. For as long as we were together, I was a skater girl, which didn't mean I skated, but rather that I stood around with a few other girls while the boys skated. I wore thick black eyeliner and dog cuffs on my wrists and slouched proprietarily against the gym wall when Skar Tissue played at school dances. At homecoming, they debuted a song called "Emily." I was a girl whose boyfriend wrote songs for her and played them in front of the whole school. I marveled at this, held it proudly in hand.

Four months after we started dating, on a night when my parents were at a dinner party in Toluca Lake, I told him I was ready. He treated me like I was made of glass, and I liked this. He treated sex with the seriousness of death, and I liked that, too. Afterward, it occurred to me that if Alison were alive, I would have told her every detail. Then something else occurred to me: If Alison were alive, it would not have happened at all. There was another life I might have been living, a life in which I was not Emily of Pasadena, but Claire. This other life ran alongside mine like the scenery falling away at the side of a speeding train. While Emily had sex in Southern California, Claire wrote up the mealworm lab in New York. Emily was pink-skinned from the California sun, her white-blond hair cut in a stylish crop. Claire was pale as flour, her haircut the same since she was five. What was I supposed to do with the fact that I was thrilled, I was so very relieved, to be Emily and not Claire?

I KNEW the exact day I outlived Alison. Eighteen years, three months, twelve days. I had calculated the date when I was fifteen, working it out in the back of my notebook as Magistra Kouchner chirped Latin conjugations. *Io credo, tu credi, lui crede.* For years, I dreaded the day. When it finally arrived, I marked it in secret. I considered telling my friends, who were at that time packing up one by one and saying tearful farewells as we scattered to the well-regarded colleges we would attend. (I would be the last to leave, bound for a highly ranked liberal arts college in the Midwest.) In the end I told no one. I was suspicious of my own impulse to calculate and mark the date. It seemed a theatrical and self-absorbed thing to do. Maybe part of what it means to be eighteen is to feel perpetually caught between the intensity of one's desires and the dawning self that judges them.

On the morning of the day I outlived Alison, I awoke to find my world suffused by a peculiar falsity. The sunlight streaming through my bedroom window seemed *incorrect* somehow, a shade too lemony. When I walked into the kitchen, where my mother was eating a bowl of cereal, and she said good morning, her voice, too, seemed to have shifted, like a piano gone almost imperceptibly out of tune. All day I couldn't shake the feeling that I had been transferred in my sleep to a vast simulacrum. I drifted from room to room, picking up and setting down books, beginning and abandoning the tidying of my bedroom, sitting in the garden, and then, shaken by a sense that I'd remained there too long, moving to the living room. Even my own face seemed to me a not-quite-right facsimile—I studied myself in the mirror and saw Alison's features skewed just enough to look distorted and unharmonious, my pale skin and hair like some ghostly afterimage. I'd been awaiting this day for years, but I don't think I ever really expected it to arrive. Now that the critical juncture was behind me, the tension went out of everything. My world hung slack as a sail on a windless day.

WHEN I arrived at college, for the first time since I moved to Pasadena as a girl, I found myself regularly around people who didn't know me or my story. The usual challenges and possibilities of freshman year—making new friends, conveying one's identity to others (with some fresh tweaks and adjustments from one's high school iteration)—were complicated for me by the knowledge that at some point I would have to tell these people who I was, which is to say, who my sister was. I can't express how much I disliked doing this. Though I'd come out of my shell in Pasadena, I was still relatively shy, and there was simply no way to tell people that I was Alison Thomas's little sister without drawing attention to myself.

The worst part was seeing people's surprised reactions. I don't mean the inevitable surprise of realizing that someone you know is connected to such an infamous incident. I mean the surprise, plainly visible on their faces, that this had happened to *me,* that this story was *my* story. How confused they seemed, how disappointed: something had happened to me, something huge, and yet, somehow, I had managed not to be made interesting by it.

I DATED a few boys in college. There was Nick, a pre-med soccer player who loved nothing so much as the sight of me topless in his uniform shorts.

Avi was a stoner from Toronto. Scattered between these longer relationships were brief interludes with Dave and Jordan and Zeb (whose first name was really Richard), all of them so different from one another it was like trying on funny hats in a store. With each of them I changed, shapeshifting until I fit into their world. I prided myself on my chameleonic transformations, and on not having a "type," which I thought indicated that I was open to the world, and that my essential self was so solid it could inhabit any number of forms.

They had different approaches to getting me to talk about her. But one way or another, they all tried.

"I just want you to know you can be completely open with me. Like, if there's ever anything you want to talk about."

"My uncle died when I was seven. He was basically my second dad. It really fucked up my world, you know?"

"You don't have to talk about it if you don't want to."

I could never shake the humiliating sense that, whether they realized it or not, these boys were in love with some idea of me as a tragic, wounded girl, that when they looked at me they saw a sort of double exposure—me and the sister I had lost, a second self whose presence they could sense whenever they were with me, and that it was she, not me, they were really after, that as they kissed and licked and squeezed me they were trying to draw themselves closer to her, to touch the infinite, exquisite void of a beautiful, lost girl.

(BUT WHEN I refused to open up to these boys about Alison, was it really because I couldn't bring myself to, because it hurt too much, or did I withhold to gain their admiration at my stoicism? Did I, actually, enjoy being their tragic, wounded girlfriend? Deep down, did I revel in the way Alison's death made me more than myself to these boys? To what extent was my pain a thing I cultivated, a thing I *used*? Is it possible that these relationships, these boys, were ultimately little more to me than a platform for displaying my suffering and, in doing so, for shoring up my claim to this tragedy, to the death of a sister I was barely old enough to know?)

DESPITE THESE difficulties, I would describe my "college experience" as pretty normal, which is to say that everything I did, whether a winter day spent dug in at the library or a night of dancing capped off by three A.M. pizza, felt equally, salubriously formative. I majored in English and minored in environmental studies. I made plenty of friends. The one worth mentioning, because of how she figures into my time in New York, is Jackie. Jackie was a friend I acquired at the beginning of college more due to proximity than anything—she lived across the hall. Despite our having little in common, our friendship turned out to have staying power. Jackie was an actor (*"not* musicals"). She saw nothing pretentious about referring to herself as a "thespian," and though I found this ridiculous, I was also impressed by her sheer gumption. Our relationship consisted mostly of her baring her soul and me listening and proffering advice.

Sometimes I wondered whether, when she wasn't with me, Jackie brought up her connection to the Alison Thomas murder to people as a kind of currency. I could imagine her, back home in Bethesda for Christmas break, sitting around in someone's basement with her girlfriends, drinking Yellow Tail:

"You know my good friend Emily I've told you about? Her older sister was Alison Thomas. Remember that story from when we were, like, seven?" (I would be referred to as a "good" friend not because Jackie and I were, in fact, especially close, but to emphasize Jackie's own proximity to Alison.)

"Whoa, seriously?"

Jackie would nod solemnly as if, while her friends might simply consider this to be some novel information, to her it was personal, heavy.

Oh, I didn't *wonder* if this happened. Surely it did. There was no doubt in my mind that Jackie trotted out my story for her own benefit. I didn't even feel mad about it, really, because it was so obvious she couldn't help herself, and how could you be mad at someone for being the person they were? At least at the time I thought that was why I didn't feel mad. Thinking about it now, though, the reason seems different. I never let myself get mad about anything back then.

AFTER COLLEGE, I found a job as an assistant to an editor at a publishing house in Manhattan. When I told my parents I would be moving to New York, they were supportive in the polite, aloof way I had come to expect. With Jackie and two Craigslist strangers, also recent college grads, I found an apartment in Prospect Heights. The kitchen was the size of a closet and my bedroom had no closet at all. The apartment was on the ground floor, and out back a cracked concrete patio was littered with things tenants on higher floors tossed out their windows—beer cans, cigarette butts, losing scratch tickets. We figured with some twinkle lights strung up it would be heaven.

Before I moved in and began work, I flew west to spend one last summer with my parents. Two months at home with mom and dad while my friends worked fun, sunburned jobs in resort towns in New England or retraced Che Guevara's motorcycle journey as far as Valparaíso. My parents had not asked me to do this, nor did I want to do it. It wasn't just that without Alison I felt I had to fulfill the role of two children. I did things that, were Alison alive, neither one of us would have done. I pitied my parents in a way I did not pity myself. It is easy to discern the contours of other people's pain, much harder to recognize one's own.

My parents were in their mid-fifties. My father's hair had thinned and grayed. My mother had recently had her first knee replacement. Over and over they told me how happy they were that I was there, how wonderful it was to spend "quality time" together. My mother cooked my favorite foods. My father bought tickets for the things we used to do when I was a kid—Dodgers games, sci-fi movies. Their insistence gave them away. I don't mean they weren't happy I was there. I could see it in their eyes—a love so strong it hurt. That's what I mean. They would be relieved when I left. The house would turn quiet again, and they would feel better.

One day when I came back from the gym, I entered the house quietly, and before I let them know I was back, I watched them. Through the kitchen window, I could see my father out in the yard, tending his jewel box garden. My mother sat in the sunny window seat in the living room, a chenille blanket over her feet, reading. I was seeing them without me: two people living out their separate lonelinesses side by side.

A few days before I flew to New York, I went into my father's home office. There, in his desk drawer, I found the photographs of our vacation at Indigo Bay. They were faded and splotched with fingerprints, and I wondered if looking at them had turned into a kind of compulsion for my father. Perhaps he had looked at the photographs so many times he no longer really saw Alison, had drained the power out of the images years ago. Maybe, subconsciously, that had been the point of the triplicate images to begin with: to stare at my sister until she lost coherence, like reading a word over and over until it starts to crack up. I removed one copy of each picture and brought them with me to Brooklyn. I put them in a shoe box under my bed along with a few other mementos—graduation tassel, prom corsage. The box gathered dust while, above it, I watched Netflix on my laptop while eating salt-and-vinegar chips; cuddled with Jackie after her boyfriend dumped her; had sex, often inebriated, with friends of friends. I rarely took out the photographs. It was enough just to know they were there.

LOOKING BACK, what strikes me is how ordinarily my life developed for years after Alison's death. I had friends and boyfriends. I excelled academically. Experimented in typical quantities with the kinds of drugs a fundamentally risk-averse girl could feel more or less comfortable with: I smoked pot on weekends, nibbled once on shrooms in Prospect Park, imbibed a few sips of absinthe at a party. I fretted about my weight, hamster-wheeled on an elliptical machine after work, caved and ate two egg rolls for dinner. At work, I decorated my cubicle with a framed photograph of myself on the rim of the Grand Canyon and a mediocre sketch I'd done of a cathedral during a semester abroad in Grenoble. My job paid a pittance and was glamour-adjacent, and therefore fit perfectly with a certain vision of what a girl's early years in New York ought to look like: fetching coffee for a MacArthur genius; ferrying a portfolio of illustrations through the sleet to the West Village brownstone of a writer I adored; referring to best-selling authors in the informal parlance of the office, according to which Astrid Teague was just "Astrid," and Ian Mann's forthcoming book was simply "the new Mann." On first dates, there was a nifty trick I liked to perform, where I would pull the boy into a bookstore, pick up a novel off the display table, flip to the back, and show him, in the acknowledgments, my name. Every Sunday afternoon I posted up at a café, pen in hand and the pages of a manuscript stacked before me, and when I caught the glances of people at nearby tables I quickly looked back down in a way that conveyed that I was busy making an important contribution to the creative economy.

As it happened, the editor I worked for mostly acquired mysteries. Ian Mann published a book a year about a psychologically damaged private investigator. Astrid Teague wrote atmospheric whodunits set in Cornwall, where she'd grown up (and where she was now rehabbing a dilapidated manor house, which had recently been captured in all its shabby-chic glory in a *Martha Stewart Living* profile, "Astrid Teague Comes Home"). Many of the books I worked on turned on the mystery of a girl's death. A beautiful young body turns up in small-town Maine or in an eightieth-floor hotel room in Shanghai. Sometimes the girls didn't turn up at all—they vanished without a trace, evaporated into their surroundings. In my favorite of Astrid's novels, *The Girl in the Picture*, a woman's body was discovered by a boy and his English setter in a cave on the Cornish coast. The woman had no wallet on her, no identification of any kind. Nobody came forward to claim her, nor did she match any missing person reports. But she did have a camera, and the photographs she had taken before her death became the clues a local detective used to uncover the identity of a hauntingly beautiful woman nobody seemed to miss.

It was pure coincidence, me working on these books. I had applied for over a dozen jobs, after all. I hadn't sought this genre out intentionally, any more than the girl in the next cubicle who worked on popular science, or the girl down the hall whose domain was military history and the occasional sports memoir. My boss didn't know my personal history, and I was proud of the professionalism I brought to this work. For instance, one of my responsibilities was to write discussion questions about these novels for book clubs.

What do you think would have happened if Leah had survived the fire? Would she and Colin have reconciled? Why or why not?

While Rose Van Kleef believes that Emmaline might still be alive, Orrin knows that she is dead. Which do you think is the more difficult circumstance, knowing that a loved one is dead, or not knowing?

How did you react to the comic moments in this otherwise dark novel?

I would write these questions, and my boss would tell me I had done a good job, and her praise would make me happy. If for fleeting moments the whole arrangement began to rankle, I would remind myself that people had every right to enjoy these stories, just as I enjoyed books about all kinds of terrible things that had happened to other people but not to me. What else, in the end, were stories *for*? This sentiment instantly made me feel better—not, it seems to me now, because I believed it, exactly, but because it seemed a very adult stance to take.

In any event, my living situations, too, affirmed a certain vision of what twenty-something urban life ought to be. For two years I stayed in the shitty Prospect Heights apartment. (On cool summer evenings, when the sky was the brushed-velvet way it gets after a nine P.M. sunset, the twinkle lights really did grant a celestial loveliness to that cracked patio.) From there, I moved to a brownstone in Bed-Stuy where a dozen creative types had set up a communal living system—a rotation of cooking and cleaning duties, weekly "family meetings." When the novelty of this arrangement gave way to weariness at its perpetual high drama, I left for an illegal sublet in the basement of a formerly grand, now-dilapidated old mansion on the far eastern edge of what might, with some fudging, be considered Ditmas Park, just a few blocks from the heart of Caribbean Flatbush. My studio had two half windows at the top of one wall, with a ground-level view of the sidewalk, so that from my desk I could watch the disembodied feet of passersby: black stiletto boots, duct-tape-patched Adidas sneakers, green galoshes. The room was lit by the harsh yellow light of two bare bulbs hung from the ceiling.

I didn't have to live like this. A tidy allowance from my parents flowed directly into my checking account every month. I suppose I chose this arrangement because I was a privileged kid eager to prove to myself that I didn't need the comforts I'd never been without (and eager, too, I might add, to do this before I got too old to enjoy it). It was the sort of thing, in other words, that you do not because you want to do it, but because you want to *have done* it, to have a story you'll share, you imagine, years later at a cocktail party or on the sideline at a soccer game (your child pure magic clomping through the grass in tiny cleats).

I admit I was rather impressed with myself for living in a building where I was one of the only white tenants. What a sharp little pride I felt, riding the 2 home from work and watching the other white passengers empty out, and what a sweet triumph it was on those nights when I outlasted them all. When, six months after I moved in, construction began on a luxury condo three blocks from my studio, I felt genuinely aggrieved. I suppose I must also have thought myself pretty high-minded to live where I did, among the people I lived among, despite what had happened to my sister. This must have been part of why I chose to live there, on the fringe of the largest Caribbean neighborhood in the city, right? To get to think these things about myself.

I took it as my working assumption that for my neighbors my presence was not entirely welcome, and so I smiled very warmly at everyone but spoke to no one, what I thought of as "not bothering people." All in all, I thought I was doing a pretty good job of charting a course through my life in New York that was as palatable as possible. I had not chosen to live in the lily-white postgrad brovana of Murray Hill. I was a gentrifier but, I imagined, an unobtrusive one. I see now that it was not so simple, that in keeping myself apart from my neighbors I was trying to collect a moral credit for living there without really *living* there, and that this was bound up with a set of more general misapprehensions: that unobtrusiveness was some sort of high virtue; that it was even possible at all; that I could inhabit this building, borough, world, life, without casting out ripples. But I was twenty-five—not so young I couldn't have known better, but young enough that I didn't.

Because of this stance, I came to know my neighbors only by their quirks. A stooped woman who must have been at least eighty fetched her mail each evening in a nightgown and a pair of bright white Reeboks. An old man who spoke Spanish wore a NASCAR cap and was never without his terrier, Jefe, a yappy, trembling creature with cloudy cataracted eyes. I assumed my neighbors identified me in a similar way. I was the white girl who came home from work every night toting a premade chopped salad. The only other white tenant was a man with a scruffy beard and an affinity for scarves who lived on the first floor and played guitar from two to three-thirty A.M. nightly, a habit which would have been merely aggravating someplace else, but which I found genuinely distressing here, convinced that it reflected poorly not only on him but also on me, on *us*.

During those first few years in New York I was, in short, living in that period of playacting, of whimsical elective poverty—improvisational dinner parties with mismatched plates, Saturdays scavenging secondhand shops for the perfect two-dollar blouse—that is so common among the children of affluence. The word I would use to describe myself then would not be *happy*—not that I wasn't; I was, or at least, I thought I was—but *unencumbered*. I believed I was enjoying my present life while anticipating, with a minimum of anxiety, the arrival of the next life stage, and the one after that. My illegal underground sublet in "Ditmas Park" would become a one-bedroom rental in Boerum Hill would become purchasing a brownstone in Park Slope, or a condo on the Upper West Side. Pithy remarks at editorial meetings would become acquiring my own books would become launching a best seller. That's what really strikes me, I guess, about that time. It's not that my life was ordinary, but that I fell for it so completely, that I failed so utterly to detect within myself the darker currents that must have been there all along.

SOMETIMES I thought I saw Alison. She picked up a box of cereal in the Flatbush Co-op and scanned the nutrition information. She jogged past me in Prospect Park, a beagle on a red leash tugging her forward. She slipped into a taxi in the rain. The Alisons darted. They slipped around corners. They were there and not there. They were always teenagers.

ONE DAY, I ducked out of the office at eleven A.M. for my annual dermatology checkup. It was early October, one of those blue-skied, ludicrously crisp days when the bustling midtown sidewalks seem to hum. At the dermatologist's I sat for over an hour in the waiting room, occupying myself with whatever inexplicable magazines the office subscribed to. In the examining room, I changed into a paper gown. "Sorry for the wait. I was held up by a gangrenous toe," Dr. Schwartz said when he finally came into the room. He made small talk as he inspected my skin with a small magnifying glass. *Did you have a good summer? How are things at work?* He had a strategy of pretending he remembered who you were. "You wear sunscreen," he said in that doctorly way—not a question, but an entreaty for me to reply in the affirmative, whatever the truth, so that we might move this thing along.

"See you in a year," he told me when he'd completed his examination. I crunched out of the paper gown and changed back into my work clothes. I had been away from the office for nearly two hours, much longer than I'd intended, and I was in a hurry to get back. I walked quickly to Lexington, weaving around a girl with her nose in her phone, a towheaded family pointing up at the Chrysler Building. At Fifty-fourth Street, I held out my arm just as a taxi turned the corner into view—a small, delicious victory.

I spent the short ride to the office checking work e-mail on my phone—a nervous missive from Kris in publicity about an author's botched radio interview, a note from the marketing director inviting the assistants to help ourselves to the tray of leftover wraps in the kitchen. When the taxi pulled up to the curb in front of my office building a few minutes later, I entered a tip on the touch screen and swiped my credit card.

"Thank you," the driver said softly from the other side of the Plexiglas partition.

My eyes landed on the taxi license affixed to the glass: a photograph, poor in quality, of a dark-skinned man against a white background. Beneath the photo, the driver's name. Clive Richardson.

Could it be? I wanted to do something, say something, but my mind was blank. The taxi idled at the curb. My door was already open, propped ajar by my foot.

What I did next was more instinct than intention. As I climbed out of the taxi, I found myself slipping my phone beneath the driver's seat and out of view. Then I slammed the door behind me. Within seconds, the taxi rejoined the yellow sea speeding uptown.

We know what to do with death when it's close to us. Your mom dies, or an old friend, and you grieve. Maybe you're not good at it, maybe the death fucks you up, but it's supposed to be hard, it's supposed to fuck you up. We know what to do with death when it's far-removed from us, too. A sports star or a celebrity chef dies and you read the obit. You start off your lunch meeting by saying, "Did you hear about . . . ?" You read the hot-take remembrances on social media for a day or two. You move on. But we don't know what to do with the deaths of people we knew just a little.

I didn't even know Alison Thomas's name *was* Alison Thomas until she went missing. Before then, can I say this? She was the girl my wife kept catching me checking out all week. She was the reason I wanted to dish out a killer serve in the volleyball game, to impress her and to make up for the embarrassment of the stupid fucking pink swim trunks I was wearing with the dolphins on them. She was the reason my wife said this supremely condescending "Almost, honey!" when the ball landed in the net instead. In the mornings, while my wife chipped away at herself in the fitness center, I took these long, ridiculously hot showers and undressed that blithe teenage body in my mind.

I am not some pervert. We see nice bodies, young bodies, we enjoy them. We all do this, okay? It is *allowed*. But what the hell do you do when the girl you've been jacking off to every morning for a week turns up dead?

The night my wife told me she was filing for divorce, she said, "You know when I knew you were a block of ice right down to your soul? When that girl was killed and you never said a word about it. Every time I tried to get you to talk about it, every time I brought her up, because I was *reeling*, I was just *devastated*, you shut me down."

I wonder sometimes if we'd still be married if Alison Thomas hadn't been murdered. Don't get me wrong, our love was hardening into a battle of wills long before then. But that trip drove a wedge between us that never went away. I couldn't give my wife the satisfaction of knowing the number that girl's death did on me. I couldn't stand to hear her crying her self-serving dramatic tears over a girl who, let's be real, she'd viewed as nothing but competition. I would listen to my wife crying, and know that she was waiting for me to wrap my arms around her from behind and deliver some sort of Emotionally Appropriate Response, and when I tried to recall what I'd loved about her and why, in our early years together, I'd felt like the luckiest fucker on earth, I couldn't come up with anything at all.

ISLANDS

PEOPLE ARE ALWAYS LEAVING things behind. Umbrellas. Wallets. Coats. Shopping bags filled with souvenirs: I LOVE NEW YORK T-shirts, snow globes in which replicas of the Statue of Liberty or the Freedom Tower stand suspended in perpetual winter. Sometimes the objects are more uncommon, hinting at the lives of the strangers who have forgotten them. A bouquet of sunflowers, a note attached with twine: *Evelyn, forgive me.* A Senegalese driver at the garage once had a customer jump out at a red light, abandoning a tank that held a lime-green snake. Years ago, when he was new to this job and the job itself was so much more dangerous than it is now, he found a switchblade wedged between the seats at the end of his shift. He still has it, in the plastic bureau where he keeps his belongings, along with a jumble of other objects acquired over the years. A child's pink plastic watch. A ring with a translucent white gemstone, which flickers with rainbow flecks when held up to the light. A camera with a finished roll of film inside.

You were supposed to turn these things in at the garage, but it was no secret that Larry and his numbskull son with the gold chains around his pimply neck just kept the items for themselves or sold them. What he's doing is stealing, too, he supposes, but it doesn't feel wrong. Just the opposite—he is rescuing these things from the careless people who have forgotten them. Though on some nights, after a few beers or a blunt ashed into a Coke can, he wonders if this notion of the righteousness of his thefts is just a bullshit justification. Lately, it seems to him that he keeps these objects as compensation, pitifully insufficient, for his own lost things.

Today he returns home from his shift with an iPhone, the latest model, in a light-gray case, not something he can keep. Anytime now the phone will ring and he will speak to the person to whom it belongs. Maybe it will be the banker he picked up in midtown, who shouted into his phone the whole drive to La Guardia. Or perhaps it will be the Park Avenue mother in those tight black leggings with SOUL in big letters down the thigh, with the little boy in the blazer and the little girl in the blue jumper; he'd dropped the girl at Brearley, the boy at St. Bernard's, the mother in front of a cycling studio on Eighty-third. Or it will be a Russian tourist he drove to Chanel, or a sixteen-year-old girl he picked up in Dumbo who probably has no clue how much her phone costs, or a chef bound for Williamsburg, a tattoo of a pig's butchery cuts on his own fleshy hock. And when he confirms that, yes, they left their phone in the taxi and he has it, has held on to it for safekeeping, they will tell him how grateful they are, and that old feeling will come over him, a feeling that is not so much annoyance or anger as dispassion: You are invisible to them, you are the back of a head, and then suddenly you are indispensable. Suddenly they are, *like, super-appreciative*. Suddenly you are *a lifesaver, boss*. When he meets whoever it is this time to return the phone, and they try to hand him five bucks, or fifty (how variable, their sense of the value of what he has done for them), he will shake his head and politely refuse, as if it is pleasure enough just to be of service to them. His refusal will trigger a shift in the way they look at him, and he will know that they are thinking that he is a deeply good person. Probably they will tell this story: the taxi driver who returned their phone and wouldn't even accept a reward, though surely he could use the money. When they look at him in this approving way, he will simultaneously feel so good and so disgusted with himself for feeling good, for wanting that look, for chasing it, for giving one shit what they think, that he'll regret not taking the money in the first place. Because they're not wrong—he could use it.

It is early autumn, the days still mild, the trees just beginning to turn. But already he can detect faint signs of what is to come. Soon dead leaves will cover the sidewalks, revived for brief moments by swells of wind. At night the sky will turn blue-black as the open ocean, with that same tumbling depth and pitiless beauty. Then the cold will come, and with it the snow, and he will spend his shifts grinding through ice and slush, getting slammed by wakes of snow cast off by passing plows, maneuvering through the city in search of some sorry bastard in ruined wing tips trying to make it to Grand Central before the tracks ice over and the trains north shut down.

From the kitchen comes the click, click, click of a burner failing to ignite—his roommate Les reheating takeout on the stove. Through the thin wall that separates his bedroom from the next one, he hears Leon making his nightly call to his wife. Cecil has taken up residence in their small common area, the television blaring one of the reality shows the rest of them can't stand but Cecil loves, or at least seems to require, for he never exactly appears to be enjoying himself as he watches; rather, the shows seem to be a way of making time pass without feeling the granularity of each moment.

He has lived here for two years, replacing a man from Trinidad who returned home to live out his retirement in the house he'd built for his family. Les and Cecil were already living here when he moved in. Leon arrived four months ago, from Carriacou by way of Canarsie. Of these men he knows only what can be gleaned through proximity: who has a family to phone and who does not, who works the day shift and who the night. Their eating habits. The sounds of their sleep.

It is his ninth apartment in nearly two decades, all of them more or less alike—nondescript buildings in Flatbush, grease-encrusted kitchenettes, radiators that clang and keen and hiss. In his early years in New York, he had bothered to befriend his roommates. When he moved in here, Les and Cecil had tried to make conversation with him. Where was he from? How long had he been in New York? Did he have a wife? Children? To these questions he gave gruff answers or dodges, and they quickly learned to leave him alone. Now he comes and goes like a ghost. His roommates step aside when he wants to use the stove, the bathroom. They are a bit afraid of him, a big man with a look of warning in his eyes. Let them be.

At work it is the same. When he first started driving, there were many others at the garage from the West Indies, but the population has turned over several times since then, and now it's almost all Gujaratis, Sikhs from Punjab and Chandigarh, Bangladeshis, and West Africans. Their foreign tongues draw a curtain around them, leaving him to himself.

At night in bed he feels waves, mild and gentle, against his skin.

Sometimes he misses the water so much his bones ache with longing. Yet it is, ironically, all around him. In New York, he has never lived more than five miles from Manhattan Beach, hardly farther from the water than his grandmother's house had been. During his shifts, he shuttles passengers over the East River on the coral steelwork of the Williamsburg Bridge, under the Hudson through the Lincoln Tunnel, crosses the Harlem River on any number of quaint bridges. New York is a city of islands. When he was freshly arrived, he'd purchased an old guidebook from a dollar cart outside of a used bookshop. In the back of the book, along with sections on tipping and local slang ("flying rat," "bridge-and-tunnel," "yooz"), there was a map. Manhattan and Long Island and the glassy-sounding Staten Island—these he knew. But there were other islands he'd never heard of: Randall's, Roosevelt, Ellis, Wards, Hart, Governors. Over his years here he has learned many more: North and South Brother, South and East Nonations. Goose and Hog and Rat. Hunter and Shooters and Swinburne. Mill Rock and Heel Tap Rock. The Blauzes, the Chimney Sweep Islands, Canarsie Pol. Ruffle Bar and Rulers Bar Hassock and Hoffman. U Thant and Mau Mau and Isle of Meadows.

But though in New York he lives on an island surrounded by islands, sometimes—as he walks from the fleet garage to the N after his shift, or wrestles a bunch of grapes into a plastic bag at the Korean grocery on Beverley, or scrubs the toilet on a Tuesday—it will occur to him that he is, at this moment, on an island, and he will find this impossible to believe. He cannot feel the *islandness* of New York.

One day when he had been in the city two months, he took the subway out to Coney Island. He'd never seen a roller coaster before and he watched as load after load of people careened shrieking over the wooden tracks. He strolled the boardwalk, got fried clam strips and a hot dog with onions at Nathan's. It was September, and warm. After lunch, he walked down the boardwalk steps to the sand and slipped off his loafers. He walked to the water's edge, cuffed his pants, and waded in a few steps. But even then, with the water lapping against his ankles and the seabirds circling overhead and the vegetal scent of shallow water in his nostrils, he did not quite believe it was the ocean he was feeling and seeing and smelling.

Back home, whether you could see the sea or not, you sensed it. He'd sensed it in the schoolyard, tasted it in the blood from his split lip after a boxing match with his friends. When he bicycled down the road to work at dawn, the ocean was a magnet, pulling his feet through their slow revolutions until he crested the rise by the radio tower and there it was, the sea, tossed before him like a net. He'd felt it in the island's interior spaces, too, in his grandmother's kitchen with the white curtains and the refrigerator rusted by the salted wind, at Paulette's Place where he and his friends drained bottles of Cruzan and Bounty, and especially within the walls of the eggshell-blue prison on Commerce Street, where he sometimes put his cheek to the moist concrete floor and thought of wet sand warping silkily beneath the weight of his steps.

He found it impossible to separate his life there from the sensation of being surrounded by water, a sensation he hadn't realized he'd felt all day, every day, until he touched down in New York and felt its absence for the first time. It wasn't just that at home he could smell salt everywhere, or feel the humid breezes tossed off by the sea, or gauge his nearness to the water by the way the light shifted, while in New York, so remarkably, arrogantly immune to its environs, he could not. At home, the sea was consciousness itself. Always, you knew it was there, and that within it was everything else: answers and mysteries, that which could be seen and that which could not, those things that were remembered and those that had been forgotten. In New York the ocean was an irrelevancy, a vestigial thing beyond and apart from the thing itself, the city: the buildings packed in tight as tissue stanching a nosebleed, a glass-and-steel rising that pierced the sky.

THERE IS another life he lives. It flows beneath this one. He feels it like being far out in the water and sensing all that depth beneath you. In this other life, he has never driven a taxi through the snow-hushed streets of New York. He has never spent a birthday eating stale samosas in the holding lot at JFK. He has never lain awake at night listening to his roommate's snores. He has never been to New York at all. He never took a plane away from his home, never watched the island disappear into the sea as the plane lifted into the sky. Never the eggshell-blue prison. Never the shocked faces of everyone he'd ever known. Never that night and never that girl. Never and never and never.

On the table, the iPhone in the gray case rings. The ringtone is that maddening banana song. *Six foot, seven foot, eight foot bunch.* Go fucking figure. He picks it up and says hello.

THE LITTLE SWEET

COULD IT BE? Surely it wasn't him, I told myself as I sat in my cubicle that afternoon. There could easily be five men named Clive Richardson— ten, two dozen—in the five boroughs, never mind that I had no reason to believe that the man who had been a suspect in my sister's death was in New York in the first place. I stared at the manuscript for "the new Mann" on my computer, unable to think, let alone work, for the rest of the day. At five-thirty on the dot, I fled.

Back in my studio I sat on my bed beneath the harsh light of the bare bulbs. It wouldn't be accurate to say I was thinking about what to do. I had not been thinking when I left my phone in the taxi and I was not thinking now. It was more like I was waiting for my body to writhe into instinctive action and carry me along with it. I ate a few bites of my salad. I sat and felt the time drip. Then I dug a handful of quarters from the change jar on my desk, ran out of my studio and up the stairs, and went out into the evening in search of a working pay phone.

I hadn't used a pay phone since I was a middle schooler calling my parents for a ride home in Pasadena. I couldn't recall the last time I'd noticed a pay phone in New York, but it turned out there was one not a five-minute walk from my apartment. Apparently I had been walking past it for over a year without noticing it, and though rationally I knew it had been there all along, that in the city one's mind renders much of the detail in the landscape invisible out of necessity, still, in that moment, I had the uncanny impression that this sorry-looking kiosk spackled with bird droppings and gum and Sharpie graffiti tags faded as the names on an ancient gravestone, had been planted here just now, for me, to make possible whatever was going to happen. I picked up the phone and heard, to my disbelief, a dial tone. I deposited my quarters and dialed my own number.

The phone rang and rang. I was about to lose my nerve and hang up when a soft voice said hello.

"Hello?" I replied.

"Yes?" the voice said.

"Yes," I echoed. "Are you the taxi driver? I'm the one who accidentally left this phone in your cab."

I regretted the word *accidentally* as soon as I said it. Nobody who had actually left something by accident would bother to say so. It was a tell, a slip. But I was being paranoid. He would take no notice of the word. Why would he?

"My shift begins at five A.M. I could meet you in midtown tomorrow morning to return it."

"Can I come to you? I'd like to get it tonight if possible. I need it for work."

I did not need it for work. But the lie flowed seamlessly. I had to see him tonight. I had to—what? I had no plan. I felt only a need to lock eyes with this man, to speak to him, to make something happen and see what it would be.

"That would be possible. But I live in Flatbush."

"No way!" I said cheerily. "I'm practically your neighbor."

"Small world," he said with a (genuine? perturbed?) chuckle. "In that case, there's a place called the Little Sweet on Church. I can meet you out front if that would be convenient."

I knew the place; it was one of several popular Caribbean restaurants clustered near the Church Avenue subway stop on Nostrand. I had passed them many times with interest, but I had never gone inside, figuring the people there probably didn't want people like me encroaching. (Or was this a justification for staying away from places that made me nervous?)

I told him I could be there in fifteen minutes. "I seriously can't thank you enough," I said before hanging up. "I'm wearing a blue blouse. I'm Emily."

AS I made my way to the Little Sweet, I told myself it wasn't him. Though I could not deny that the voice on the phone had a familiar softness, it simply could not belong to the same Clive Richardson who'd spilled my french fries in the sand all those years ago (chips, he'd called them, and how I'd loved that), the one everybody had called Gogo, the man with whom, along with Edwin Hastie, my sister was last seen alive. I would meet him on the sidewalk and see immediately that his face was all wrong, or that he was too short, or too light- or dark-skinned. I would give him twenty bucks, thank him, and be on my way, and though I might be shaken for a couple of days, my life would quickly snap back to its usual dimensions. Whether I hoped for or dreaded this outcome, I'm no longer sure.

The landscape changed as I walked north and east. Though the building I lived in was run-down and situated on an unlovely block of vacant lots and midrise apartment buildings, it was also not far from the Edison-bulb eateries along Cortelyou Road, from cafés whose menus featured an entire section of "alternative milk" options (soy, almond, cashew) and boutiques where one could purchase a vintage Berber rug or an olive-wood cheese platter for exorbitant sums. I was just a few minutes' walk from an especially picturesque stretch of Argyle Road, where in the summertime the Victorian mansions with their wide front porches and twilight-hued hydrangeas seemed to have been lifted from some seaside idyll and set down gently on this street in central Brooklyn. Though I prided myself on living beyond such places, it was also true that I found comfort in my proximity to them. As I neared the Little Sweet, I left all of this behind. The signs on the commercial thoroughfares became more urgent: CHECKS CASHED! PLAY NOW! WIRE CASH LOW FEE!

By the time I reached my destination, the sky was dingy pink, darkness touched by neon storefronts. The Little Sweet was a take-out spot with half a dozen tables, a long steam table behind the counter, and an illuminated menu with stock photos of combination platters hanging above it. It was located between a MoneyGram and a Chinese takeout called Hunan Star, across the street from a West Indian grocery and a discount shop with a hodgepodge of merchandise on the sidewalk: coolers and pushcarts and mop heads, reflective vests and nursing scrubs. Farther down the block, a Creole and English bookstore transmitted ESL recordings into the night: *I run to the house. She bakes a cake. He goes to sleep.*

I stood in front of the narrow storefront and tried to appear occupied. I put a twenty-dollar bill in my pocket to give to the man as a reward. I cleaned out my handbag, disposing of fistfuls of receipts and a cough drop that had been floating loose in my bag, stuck with grit and lint. It had not been necessary to specify what I was wearing. I was the only white person here, with the exception of a man about my age, bearded and man-bunned, who sat at a table in the center of the Little Sweet and alternated between eating and drawing in a sketch pad.

When I saw Clive Richardson coming up the sidewalk I knew at once it was him. It was his walk. The hunched shoulders, the bowed head. He moved like he thought he took up too much space and was sorry. I clenched my jaw to quell the chattering of my teeth and willed myself to be still.

In a flash I saw my parents. They would be sitting down now to one of their abstemious locavore dinners in their kitchen in Pasadena. I imagined them seeing me seeing Clive Richardson on this sidewalk in Brooklyn. I felt them reaching out, pulling me back into the safe, blind world our family had inhabited all these years, our aftermath of SoCal sunshine and ceramics and racket sports. Forget my phone. Turn around. Run straight home and don't look back. That's what they would want me to do.

"Emily?"

I nodded. I couldn't raise my eyes to look at him.

"I hope you didn't wait long."

"Not long at all."

He pulled my phone from his pocket.

"Thank you so, so much. You just have no idea how much I appreciate this." I held out the twenty-dollar bill to him.

"I can't accept this." He spoke softly, as if worried his refusal would offend me.

"Please take it," I implored.

"I would prefer not to."

"You're sure?"

"Yes, miss."

Miss.

I looked up and for the first time our eyes met. Clive Richardson must have been at least forty now, and he looked it—his hair had already started to go white and his forehead was deeply lined. My body trembled. My jaw was clenched so tightly it would ache later. At the same time, my mind spasmed as it tried uselessly to understand that this ordinary man standing before me in a windbreaker and black loafers was *him*.

I tucked the money back in my pocket. "Well."

We stared at one another awkwardly. The moment was lifting away from me. Could it be that I would do nothing? That I would simply let him leave? But what else could I do? Even as I wondered this I was saying, "Thanks again. I really appreciate it," and Clive Richardson was telling me it was nothing, and I was wishing him a good night. The bells on the door of the Little Sweet jingled as he opened it and stepped inside. I turned and hurried down the sidewalk. My eyes filled with hot, stinging tears. It had happened too fast. I hadn't been ready, had missed my chance. My chance for what, exactly, I wasn't sure, but I was filled with the sense that I'd failed to capitalize on this extraordinary convergence and, more than this, with a sense that this failure was at the center of who I was—a person who let things slip through her hands.

THAT NIGHT I dreamed I walked out of my apartment to find that a stone staircase had opened up in the middle of the sidewalk, leading down. Only the first few steps were visible. After that, the staircase disappeared into the darkness below the city. The stairs went on and on, and I walked for what felt like an eternity in the pitch-black, *step, step, step*, down and down and down, until I found myself standing on a beach. White sand, curving palms, mint waters. It had been here all along—this place, this past, waiting only for me to return. (In the dream I knew without having to know that I was Clairey again, a child.) Some distance from me, standing at the water's edge, her ankles lapped by the gentle waves, was Alison. She was turned away from me, staring out. When I reached her, she looked down at me and smiled, and I smiled back. She raised a finger to her lips. *Shh. Don't tell.* She tossed back her head and laughed.

I awoke drenched in sweat and full of self-recrimination—I hardly ever dreamed of Alison and I'd ruined it, expulsed myself from the dream prematurely. For the first time in months, I took out the photographs from the shoe box under my bed. I needed to tell her what had happened to me and how helpless I'd felt as I thanked Clive Richardson and walked away. All this time, he had been right here. How was it possible that I hadn't known it, sensed it?

There she was, nut-brown from the sun and grinning at dinner with a giant red lobster on her plate. Singing at the beach barbecue. Smiling beside me beneath that faded blue umbrella. *My, you a patient child.* The photos felt volatile, as if they might burst into flame in my hands. There she was on a paddleboard, clinking glasses with my mother, listening to her Walkman in the shade. There she was leaning against a palm tree in her bikini, hands on hips, salt in her hair, looking off down the beach. My father had taken this picture. I remembered watching Alison pose for him. Now, looking at the photograph for the thousandth time, I saw something I'd never noticed before. Down the beach, so far in the background their bodies were nothing but tiny, blurred silhouettes, were Edwin Hastie and Clive Richardson.

I perceived something else, too. A distance in Alison's eyes. It was as if she saw Faraway Cay in her mind's eye and knew that, in the subtext of each moment, as we swam and giggled and tried to tie knots in the stems of maraschino cherries with our tongues, she was moving through the becalmed cerulean water toward it. It occurred to me that maybe I hadn't known my sister very well at all.

AT WORK the next day I was distracted and unsettled. I reread the same sentence over and over without grasping its meaning. The photograph my father took of Alison gnawed at the edges of my mind. For whom had she really been posing?

Eventually I gave up on work. Instead, I opened Facebook and searched for Clive Richardson. There were dozens of profiles, but eventually I found the one I was looking for. His profile picture was a selfie blurred by a burst of light from a lamp behind him. He was not active on the site—he had posted no other photos and had only two friends. The first was a man named Ousseini. This man did have an active social media presence; his timeline was filled with family photos and inspirational quotations set against backdrops of sunsets and mountains. Clive's only post was a birthday message to his one other friend, a man named Bryan Richardson. The post was several years old and was written the way people who do not understand Facebook write messages: *Dear Bryan, Wishing you a very happy birthday. Sincerely, Clive.* Presumably, Bryan Richardson was a relative, though he looked nothing like Clive—he was tall and slender; in his profile picture he wore a trim-cut suit and sat at a keyboard, his hands touched down lightly over the keys.

Edwin Hastie had no profile. A Google search for his name turned up nothing but old articles about Alison's case.

Next, I typed "Alison Thomas" into Google and the autocomplete options popped up:

Alison Thomas murder
Alison Thomas Dying for Fun
Alison Thomas obituary

I had never read my sister's obituary. I was too young to have read it when it came out, and in more recent years, when I might easily have found it online, I hadn't looked for it. Not that it hadn't occurred to me. But I had absorbed a lesson from my parents not to permit myself to plunge into the depths. I clicked on the link and found the brief notice that had been published by our local suburban paper.

> **Alison Brianne Thomas**, 18, died January 3rd, on a family vacation to the island of Saint X. She was born September 8, 1977, to Richard (Rick) and Ellen (Wolfe) Thomas.
>
> Alison was a talented performer and athlete who loved modern dance, swimming, tennis, and the great outdoors. A budding scientist, she had aspirations toward a career in medicine and had just completed her first semester at Princeton. While her life was cut far too short, she lived every moment to its very fullest and gave so much joy to her family and friends.
>
> She is survived by her parents and younger sister, Claire, as well as grandparents Sylvia, Edward, Jean, and Fred, and great-grandmother Helen.

A life, pared down to what were at once its most essential and meaningless facts. I was surprised to read that Alison had "aspirations toward a career in medicine." I had no memory of my sister expressing any desire to become a doctor. Come to think of it, I didn't remember her expressing an inclination toward any particular professional path at all. Maybe I'd simply been too young to attend to those aspects of her life, but I didn't think so. Something about this line rang false. Who had written the obituary? My father, presumably. Maybe he wished to suggest to the world that my sister was more directed, more fully formed, than she really was. *Here was a girl with plans!* But I think something deeper was at play: with this brief mention of Alison's "aspirations," she became not just an eighteen-year-old girl but also a medical student, a resident, a fellow, chair of Pediatric Cardiology at Brigham and Women's. *Aspirations toward a career in medicine.* A false claim, and a necessary one. To mourn a budding physician was a terrible task, but it was a thing you could do. To mourn a girl with infinite futures was to mourn infinitely.

WHAT IS the neurological experience of a person? When you think of someone, what sound, image, scent is summoned? For instance, in my mind, my father is forever bent over his African violets in our garden in Pasadena, inspecting them for aphids. My childhood friend Kelsey Johnston is the hyper-particular hammy odor of her farts. Aunt Caroline is gray roots at the nape of a long, graceful neck.

Alison is flowers and white teeth. I know where this image comes from. The high school dance recital, Alison's senior year. She wore a dove-gray leotard and a flowing chiffon skirt and leapt across the stage. I don't know the name of the song she danced to, but I remember its melancholy sound. Watching her was like watching the music itself spin and bend through the air. How deeply I felt her feeling it, infusing the auditorium with a snowy perfume of longing. I remember sitting there, watching the other people in the audience watching her. My sister. Mine.

Afterward, in the auditorium lobby, my parents and Drew McNamara and her friends piled bouquets into her arms. She wore glitter on her cheeks. She grinned. Flowers and white teeth.

This was a child's version of a person. My parents' version of Alison was different but, it occurred to me now, no more accurate. When they spoke of her, it was not to reminisce about the past, but to imagine her into the present.

Of the mandarin tree that grew in our tiny yard in Pasadena:

"Alison would have loved this."

"She would have eaten the fruit right here under the tree."

At times, their invocations struck me as almost willfully inaccurate.

At Yellowstone, beholding Old Faithful:

"Alison would have thought this was so neat."

Would she really? Alison had never been one to be especially *impressed*. In my parents' version, Alison was buffed like a piece of sea glass, her edges and points worn away over time and yielding to a pleasing smoothness.

THAT EVENING I once again traveled to the Little Sweet, drawn there as if by a spell. As I neared my destination, the racing of my heart became almost unbearable, but I did not turn back. I had to find him. I could not let him disappear. Still, I didn't expect to actually come upon him, and when I arrived and looked through the plate-glass and saw him, seated at a table in the corner beside a potted palm, a plate of crimson stew and a blue can of beer on his tray, I had the sense that this image was not, could not be, real. He sat with his shoulders hunched, his legs squeezed awkwardly beneath the small table, casting off an aura of both physical and metaphysical discomfort.

I lingered only a moment outside, terrified that he would lift his head and see me. Then I crossed the street. Hidden by the shadow beneath the awning of the West Indian grocery, I watched him. From the speakers of the bookstore down the street, a lesson on daily tasks reverberated. *They drive to work. I go to the store. He comes home.* Clive ate his meal in slow, distracted bites while he watched what I assumed must be a television on the wall, out of my view. He finished his beer and purchased another. He nodded a wordless hello to a fellow customer. With a paper napkin he kept crumpled in his fist, he wiped the crimson stew from his lips. Ordinary actions, objectively of no interest. I couldn't look away.

BACK AT my apartment later that night, I found *Dying for Fun: Alison Thomas* on YouTube. In it, my sister is played by Selena Richter, an actress who, a decade later, would rise to superstardom when she played the heroine in a trilogy of dystopian films based on a popular book series. Someone had posted each episode in the series: Kristin Broekner, Maggie Donohue, Flora Salter, Alicia Madigan. I changed into my pajamas and got in bed with my laptop to submit myself to *Dying for Fun: Alison Thomas (Selena Richter in Early Role!!!)*.

The episode had been viewed some 47,000 times and received approximately 2,400 thumbs-up and 650 thumbs-down. (Whether these "dislikes" were meant to indicate disapproval of the quality of the film, or of Selena Richter, or of the dated anti-feminism and clunky moral suasion of the entire *Dying for Fun* enterprise, I don't know.) The comments section was no more illuminating:

OMG I loved this when it aired and watching it now is a blast from the freaking past.

This is '90s AF.

Selena Richter = overrated.

I can't even with those platform shoes.

Selena Richter looked nothing like my sister. She was voluptuous and busty, while Alison's body was straight and athletic. Her portrayal of Alison featured an entire register of all-wrong sounds: squeals of delight, giggling fits, the occasional deployment of a pouty-lipped baby voice. She had none of Alison's bristle, no flash of intelligence in her swimming-pool-blue eyes. I appeared in a few scenes, though for some reason I was called Katie. I was played by an angelic child with golden ringlets and rosebud lips. When Alison's body was found, Katie cried harrowing, captivating tears, and I felt like some failed version of what Alison's sister should have been.

According to *Dying for Fun*, my sister was a sheltered girl lured to her death by tactics only a total naïf would fall for. For simplicity's sake, I assume, Clive Richardson and Edwin Hastie had been streamlined into a single character named Apollo, with dreadlocks and a gold hoop earring.

"I've never done a body shot before. Won't you show me how?" Alison implores Apollo in an early scene.

"First ya must be lickin' da salt wit ya tongue," Apollo says.

Alison gets down on her knees and licks a line of salt from his muscled abdomen. She looks up at him with guileless eyes and giggles.

In this version, my sister lies bathed in moonlight on a beach that appears made of stardust and allows Apollo to unzip her dress.

"Relax," he says with blatantly evil eyes. (The acting is uniformly one-note and overblown.)

"I want you to be my first," she whispers into his ear. She flushes and pants as if shocked by her own arousal; she is a pale pink peony, poised on the edge of blooming. "Don't you dare be gentle with me."

He presses his hands over my sister's nose and mouth. She struggles. He thrusts. The whole thing slouches to its terrible conclusion as a thousand housewives squeeze their pillows.

"I gon' be ya last."

I COULDN'T sleep that night. I kept replaying the final moments from the movie in my head. Only instead of Apollo, I imagined Clive Richardson, as I had seen him earlier that evening, transposed into each scene—laying her in the sand, unzipping her dress, smothering her with the same hands he'd used to wipe the stew from his lips. Could he have done it? Could he have played a part? Apollo was an obvious cliché, not a person but simply a murderer. But the man I had observed earlier that night evinced no coldness or cruelty at all, and this chilled me to the bone. Yes, of course he could have done it. You see a mug shot on TV and think, *Him? But he has such a kind face. But his eyes are so gentle.* Nannies drown children they cared for lovingly for years. Perfect couples become a husband who shot a wife. We see so little of people. We forget how much submerged darkness there is around us at every moment. We forget until we are forced to remember.

OVER THE week that followed, I watched the remaining episodes of the *Dying for Fun* series. I had felt guilty for ignoring the other girls. But I admit I also watched at least partly for the same reason anybody else would, for the trashy, low-fi, comically dated pleasure of it. I'd been aware of their stories to varying degrees when they happened. Perhaps you remember them, too. Maggie Donohue (Thailand, Ecstasy, a dalliance with an Aussie on his gap year). Kristin Broekner (Mykonos, an entanglement with the scion of a Russian oil baron). Flora Salter's story captured the American imagination for a few weeks' time, owing to its tragic outcomes—the apartment set ablaze in Montmartre, the suicide of that handsome young tennis phenom. Maggie. Kristin. Flora. Alicia (whose name was pronounced like satin ribbon—*A-lee-see-a*). What is the appeal of such stories? You know the kind I'm talking about. All the pretty dead white girls. The one backpacking in Eastern Europe and the one at the full moon festival in Bali and the blossom-cheeked blonde in Aruba. You see their photographs on the evening news. They wear graduation caps or prom dresses or a peasant blouse and a wreath of white flowers—it's Halloween and they're the darnedest little hippie you ever did see. You hear the eyewitness interviews. "I saw her get on the back of his motorbike." "I think she was on something." "She always had to be the life of the party." You think how stupid it was of them, whatever they did to end up as they did. You feel a bit indignant, actually. You see their honey-blond hair, their red ringlets, their auburn ponytail frozen mid-swish in the photographs, their blue, green, caramel eyes, and always, a smile so blunt it's like they don't have even the faintest notion that anything bad could ever happen to them. You find them naïve and smug. Maybe they are. Maybe Alison was.

DURING THIS same period, I walked to the Little Sweet every evening. Now that I had found Clive, it was simply not possible to stay away. He was always there, and he always sat at the same table, in the corner beside the potted palm. I would watch him from the shadow beneath the awning of the grocery across the street for as long as I felt I could without becoming conspicuous. Then I would loop the block a few times, slowing my pace as I passed the Little Sweet. I would duck into one of the nearby stores. Browse the GED prep guides at the bookstore as if they held genuine relevance for me. Peruse the unfamiliar produce in the grocery store—cassava, turmeric root, dasheen—and smile periodically at the elderly Korean couple behind the counter, purchasing a pack of gum on my way out to justify my presence.

Over these nights of observation, my inchoate need to keep tabs on Clive Richardson, to bear witness to his presence, coalesced and sharpened into a sort of plan. I would uncover everything I could about Alison, searching for clues with which to build a portrait of my sister—her emotions and relationships, the dramas and preoccupations of her life, anything that might help me to understand the kinds of dangers to which she might have been vulnerable at the time of our vacation. And I would continue to surveil Clive, watching and waiting for even the smallest detail, the tiniest slip of evidence that might point me toward the truth about the kind of man he was and the role he might have played in my sister's death. What this evidence might look like I didn't know, but I had to believe that a person couldn't take a life and simply melt back into the human crowd—such an act must leave traces, scars, and if I was vigilant, if I could attune myself to this man, I would find them.

I shared none of this with my parents. I told myself I was protecting them. But looking back, I think the real reason I didn't tell them is because I knew that if I did, they would make me promise not to seek Clive out anymore, for my own safety, and I would do as they asked because I always did as they asked, and because it still would have been possible for me to loosen my grip on him then, in the fall, in a way it no longer would be by the time winter came. I would be relieved, their concern just the permission I needed to leave it alone, to go back and continue living my life as if Clive Richardson were not living his just a few blocks east. I could no longer abide such cowardice in myself. I saw clearly now that cowardice is what it was, what it always had been—our nice family life, so remarkably functional, so totally cut off from the depths of our own pain. It fell to me. If my parents could not, would not, then I must inhabit the depths alone to uncover the truth, no matter what.

What a mindfuck. In high school I get treated like shit because I'm Shelly the theater kid, Shelly the freak. Then I show up in Hollywood, change my name to Selena, and I get treated like shit all over again, but now it's because I'm just a pretty face. I'm a weird girl, then I'm an "it" girl, and five seconds later I'm "overexposed."

I leave the house in some shit my stylist put together for me, I'm fake. I leave the house in sweatpants with greasy hair, I'm trying too hard to look like I'm not trying.

I just love how Selena Richter doesn't conform to what Hollywood wants her to be.

Ugh, Selena Richter, I just hate how self-righteously nonconformist she is.

I'm obsessed with how minimalist her acting is.

Why do people keep casting that fucking block of wood and expecting her to carry a film?

I slouch and bite my nails during an interview, where's my poise? I focus on my posture, where's my personality? I point fucking any of this out and, *Boo hoo poor Selena Richter, it must be so hard being rich and famous.* I am not saying it is harder than being a bricklayer, fucking straw-man idiots. I am saying our society is sick with a poison of its own making.

If you need proof, here is a list of just some of the shit that happened to me with my first actual role bigger than a Gushers commercial:

1. When I'm offered the part of Alison Thomas, I tell my agent I'm not sure I want to take it because it creeps me out to play a

real-life dead girl. He says to me, "This is not your last dead girl, Selena."

2. The crew is the same for all the *Dying for Fun* episodes. Sometimes in costume or hair and makeup, they do me up a certain way and then consult with each other like, "Is the braid too Alicia?" "Is this skirt too Kristin?" "Whoa, you're giving me Maggie Donohue flashbacks with that nail polish."

3. In the last scene I'm supposed to say, "Don't you dare be gentle with me," and I very politely ask if we can maybe consider cutting that line, because who says that? Like, why does she need to be such a bimbo? The director gets pissy and goes, "Say your lines, sweetheart." To put me in my place, he has us do dozens of takes. He makes me say it over and over again. The first few takes, I'm standing next to Mike, who plays Apollo. Then the director has me press myself against Mike. Then he has Mike pin my wrists against a tree. Then he has me take off my shirt so I'm just in a string bikini top.

"Please," I say. "Can we be done?"

"Are you tired, Selena? Are you parched? Somebody get this bitch a Perrier." Fucking asshat.

Poor Mike is so uncomfortable.

I lose count of how many times I've said it. Finally, Mike says, "Come on, man, she gets it."

The director puts down his stupid clipboard and walks over to me. He pulls the string on the bikini top and then I'm standing there with my breasts out in front of the whole crew. He whispers in my ear, "Do you *get it*, Selena?"

But I'm not Selena. I'm not Shelly, either. They think they've got me. They think they've pinned me down. They're not even fucking close.

OUR BEAUTIFUL DAUGHTER

From "Remembering Alison Thomas" by Jessica Nazarian,
January 10, 1996, *The Daily Princetonian:*

On Sunday, students trickling back from Christmas break returned to a campus that had been transformed into a winter wonderland of glittering quads and frosted trees. But one member of the freshman class was not among them. Alison Thomas died over break during a family vacation to the Caribbean. As the investigation into her death continues, students here paused to remember a beloved friend and classmate.

"She was really smart," said Mike Chernin, her lab partner in Molecular Biology 100. "I definitely had to step up my game with her."

Larissa Venable, captain of MoDE (Modern Dance Ensemble), shared that Alison was one of only three freshmen admitted to the selective squad this fall. "Usually the frosh hang back in rehearsals, but she was throwing out choreography ideas right off the bat. Her ideas were totally integral to our 'Like a Prayer' routine."

Alison's roommate, Nika Ivanova, reflected, "I still can't believe she won't be here when I wake up in our room tomorrow. I just want to say we will always remember her." . . .

From "For Vacationers, Grief and Questions After a Daughter's
Mysterious Death" by Vince Cerusi, January 17, 1996, *The New York
Times:*

. . . "Alison was an absolute sweetheart," her aunt, Colleen Thomas, said. "Just the sweetest, gentlest soul you could hope to meet. My dog is a rescue and he really struggles with trust, and she was just wonderful with him." When asked about reports that her niece was seen drinking and smoking marijuana at a popular local bar on the night of her disappearance, Colleen Thomas replied, "I don't care what the police down there say. It's a tourist island; they have an incentive to make her look a certain way. That is not the Ali we know and love." . . .

From "Our Town Says Goodbye" by Kate Cafferty, January 23, 1996, *The Patent Trader*:

. . . Becca Frankel, eighteen and a high school classmate, remembers Alison Brianne Thomas as being a girl who had it all. "She was totally that girl. Smart. Pretty. Great athlete. Awesome dancer. I could probably name ten guys who had huge crushes on her. She got a lot of attention, and you could tell she loved it, you know?" When it was asked whether Thomas was promiscuous, Becca replied, "She was all about Drew." Alison dated classmate Drew McNamara, who is a freshman at Rensselaer Polytechnic Institute, for three years. According to Becca, "They were *the* couple." We could not reach McNamara for comment. . . .

IT HAD been two weeks since I stepped into Clive Richardson's taxi, and at work my productivity had dwindled to almost nothing. Every morning on the subway, I scribbled a to-do list: mail off cover-art proofs, draft the back-cover copy for a movie tie-in edition, write rejection e-mails for half a dozen recent novel submissions. Arriving at the office, I hung my coat in the locker at my cubicle and settled in at my desk with every intention of getting things done. But soon, almost without realizing it, the work at hand was abandoned and I was lost in the digital sea of stories about Alison. None of the mysteries in the books I worked on could compare to my own sister's.

It seemed everyone who had known her, however distantly, had given testimony on the question of who Alison Thomas had been. The articles were filled with tidbits about my sister's last months that were new to me. She had been to an R.E.M. concert at the Meadowlands the fall before she died. She loved the mocha frozen yogurt in the dining hall. She had been a ballerina for Halloween. Each piece of information was like a wound, a reminder of how little I knew about my own sister.

From "An Enigma Abroad" by Sean Winokur, *Esquire,* June 1996:

. . . I meet Richard Conti, Thomas's high school English teacher, at the Station, a diner in the mock-Tudor downtown of the affluent suburb where she grew up. In a town whose quaint main street is crowded with dry cleaners, nail salons, and gourmet take-away shops, the Station stands unmistakably apart. The interior is beyond unfancy—it's downright dingy. Flickering panels of fluorescents overhead, a skein of mysterious stickiness underfoot, a deli case of mayonaissy potato, macaroni, and chicken salads. A jar of magenta pickled eggs occupies pride of place by the ancient cash register on the counter. My western omelet is emphatically mediocre. From the get-go, I wonder at Conti's choice of meeting place. You can sniff out someone trying to control the narrative, hoping to convince the world that Alison Thomas was not a silly little rich girl.

Conti is thirty-three, tall and handsome, with the broad and limber build of the Division I soccer goalkeeper he once was. Despite having agreed to this interview, he is hesitant, at first, to discuss his former student. As he bites into his egg and cheese sandwich, he confides that he almost canceled on me this morning. "I teach English, so I know the same story can be spun a thousand different ways."

But as we speak, Conti grows increasingly comfortable sharing his impressions and memories of Thomas. "She was a very bright girl. Not necessarily the most diligent student, but very bright. There's a type of student, and I think it was hard for me to recognize in Alison at first because it's a type that skews male. These kids do the work that interests them and say screw the rest. They turn in papers late but their work is so good you don't want to penalize them for it, even if you know they don't really give a shit what grade you give them, and also that they're kind of banking on that, kind of playing you." Asked if he'd describe Thomas as arrogant,

Conti grows flustered. "No, no, no. She was a good kid. She was just a really intelligent, nice, good kid. That's what I'm trying to say. She was a star." . . .

ALISON WAS a drama queen. She was a gentle soul. She was *that* girl. The one everybody envied. The one all the boys wanted. A star. She was what all the dead are: whatever the living make them.

AS I pored over the articles, I encountered the same two photographs of Alison over and over. The first was taken after her performance in the school dance recital her senior year. Her cheeks and eyelids are brushed with glittery makeup, so that she seems to shimmer—celestial, angelic. Her smile is soft and dreamy, an unusual facial expression for my sister. Put simply, she does not look like herself. Maybe you've experienced this: you see a photo of someone you know well, and they look like an altogether different person. What makes this phenomenon possible? Is it some trick of the light, distorting the planes and angles of the face? Something about the transference of a three-dimensional form to two dimensions? Is it that we're accustomed to seeing people in motion and the total stillness of an image throws us off? A final possibility seems most convincing to me: We don't know what people look like. We know only what they look like to us. We have an idea of them, shaped by our affections, our memories, and this is the real distortion. In this photograph my sister looks like some romantic ideal of a girl too lovely for this world. A girl fated for death.

The second picture is different. It was taken at a dorm party a month before Alison was killed. The room is dark, lit only by the harsh flash of the camera. The party must have been pajama-themed. Some boys wear boxers. Others are dressed ironically in fuzzy onesies. There is a keg visible in the corner, plastic cups in every hand and cluttering every surface. My sister wears a tiny blue slip—*negligee* would be the proper term, I think. Her nipples press visibly against the silk. She is dancing with her arms raised over her head, a cup in her hand. Her hair is sweaty, her eyes rimmed with smudged eyeliner. She smiles seductively at whoever is behind the camera.

Don't you understand? My sister was an innocent, blameless in her horrific fate. And it was all her fault.

• • •

MY OBSERVATION of Clive continued. What I saw was always the same, his habits repetitive and fastidious: that crimson stew and a beer, then a second when he'd drained the first. Silent nods hello to the other regulars. A napkin crumpled in a fist. I watched until he rose to scrape his plate into the trash. Then I hurried down the sidewalk, not slowing until I reached my apartment.

Of course, sometimes I had evening plans, or something came up. For instance, one afternoon Jackie texted that she needed to see me for "emergency girl talk," and that night we met for drinks at her favorite bar near our old apartment. Jackie ran late as a rule. I arrived on time, then sat there twiddling my thumbs and excoriating myself. Why did I always set myself up to wait for her? What was it that rendered me incapable of deviating from this pattern? (I think I know the answer to these questions now. I think I liked this pattern, this banal and benign predicament in which to seethe.) This time, my annoyance was compounded by the fact that Jackie was keeping me from Clive—what if tonight was the night something happened, and I missed it? I worked myself up into quite a state before she arrived, and as usual I shelved this feeling when Jackie whirled through the door, half an hour late and full of apologies.

The reason for the emergency girl talk was that Jackie was "just so overwhelmed." I listened for a long time as she described the sources of her trouble with mounting distress. She wasn't a priority to her boyfriend. She hated her job. She never had time to practice her "craft." (Though she seemed to have plenty of time, I thought, to attend her boyfriend's dodgeball league games and to transform bushels of produce into six ounces of juice twice a day. I didn't say this.)

"Of *course* you're overwhelmed," I said instead. "It's too much."

Jackie nodded. "Right? It would be too much for *anyone*."

There were tears in her eyes. I hugged her. I stroked her hair. I offered what seemed to me rather boilerplate advice: She should deal with one thing at a time. Step by step. Et cetera.

Jackie blew her nose into a cocktail napkin. "How are you so fucking wise?"

We stayed at the bar for another hour.

"So, what's new with you?" she asked as she tossed her credit card down on the check.

I thought of Clive Richardson, of the Little Sweet, of Alison's obituary and the golden-haired, rose-lipped child from *Dying for Fun* who was and was not me.

"Nothing much."

AT WORK one day I went on Facebook to track down Nika Ivanova, Alison's roommate at Princeton. I found her easily. She was Nika (Ivanova) Cunningham now; she lived in Philadelphia and worked for a pharmaceutical company. Her profile picture was a selfie in which she sat sandwiched between two freckle-faced boys on a chairlift. I sent her a message:

> You probably don't remember me, but I'm Alison Thomas's younger sister. I'm working on a project to compile remembrances about Alison. It would mean so much to have a contribution from you. I know you didn't know Alison long, but she loved being your roommate. Maybe we could arrange a phone call and I can tell you more about what I have in mind?

I felt weird for lying, but pinning my request to a formal project seemed to normalize it. Amazing, the power of a premise.

Nika replied that evening. She would be very happy to help me in whatever way she could. We scheduled a phone call for a night later that week, but a few minutes after we were supposed to talk, Nika texted to cancel. She had forgotten it was her turn to pick up her son's tae kwon do carpool. Twenty minutes later, I was standing outside of the Little Sweet. Stew, beer, nod hello. For over an hour, I wandered the neighborhood, circling back to watch Clive as often as I dared. The streets were busy with people. A mom herding three kids in school uniforms. An elderly man leaning against a storefront and sipping a pineapple soda. The periodic upward rush of bodies from the subway at Nostrand. A stray white kid hefting a mesh laundry basket down the sidewalk. When I circled back once more and found that Clive had departed while I was walking, I was left with the unsettling feeling of a necessary process cut short.

Nika canceled again the next time we were supposed to speak—her other son's basketball game had gone into overtime. Again I left my apartment at once and headed to Church Avenue. Stew, beer, nod hello. Clive maintained this ritual with such consistency that I half wondered if he knew he was being watched and was determined to reveal nothing of himself. At times it seemed to me as if we were engaged in a battle of wills. I had not yet found my way past the mesmeric repetition of his routines. But I was not concerned. I would wait as long as it took. I was patient.

NIKA AND I finally spoke that Sunday.

"Sorry I was so hard to get on the phone. This week was completely insane," she said, in a rote tone that suggested that for Nika, every week was completely insane. In the background I could hear the crinkle of what sounded like grocery bags being unpacked.

I had a single memory of Nika. When my family arrived at Alison's dorm room to move her in, Nika and her parents were already there, arguing with each other in urgent, whispered Bulgarian as they looked down at her bed. They hadn't known to buy extra-long sheets and now they couldn't make her bed. When they realized we were standing in the doorway, they looked stricken. Nika was dressed in a pleated skirt, a blouse, and loafers with a low, square heel. My sister wore mesh shorts and flip-flops. I understood implicitly that Alison was wearing the right thing and Nika was wearing the wrong thing. In my head she was still the painfully overdressed girl pressed close to her parents.

I told Nika I wanted to create a book of memories about my sister. "I was so young when she was killed. I've been finding it really therapeutic lately to hear stories from people who knew her."

I heard the refrigerator door opening and closing, the garbage disposal churning. Nika's inattention wasn't hurtful, exactly. It was callous in a bland, quotidian way I didn't really hold against her. My tragedy wasn't hers, and that wasn't her fault.

"Your sister was a big deal for me," Nika began. "I could not have been more clueless when I showed up at Princeton. We immigrated when I was ten, but my parents still barely spoke English. I had this horrible bushy hair. I used to go to the dining hall, fill a mug with soup, and go back and eat it in our room because I was so intimidated by the other kids at the tables. I got a sixty-three on my first calculus test. I went to this awful high school in Chicago. I had no preparation whatsoever. I just cried and cried about it. There were tutors you could go to, but I was afraid. I literally thought if I went to them, they'd realize Princeton had made a mistake accepting me and kick me out. I had no idea what to—excuse me a minute." I could hear her hand press against the receiver. *Not now, Logan, Mommy's on the phone.* "Sorry about that. Anyway, right, I had no idea what to do."

"That must have been hard." I straightened a paper clip and used the tip to clean under my fingernails. Her tragedy was not my tragedy, either.

"Your sister made such a difference for me. I'm not just saying that. She included me. The first month of school I made zero friends. I was basically a recluse. Your sister obviously knew everyone on campus within five minutes, and everyone wanted to be her friend. She just had that personal power, you know?"

"She was special," I said vaguely. Charisma, you might call it, though this word doesn't explain the mystery, because charismatic people are all different. It's the feeling they evoke in others, that tipsy glow, that tidal pull, that they share. It's Edwin Hastie with a passel of children scrabbling over him in the sand. It's a dozen men falling in love with Aunt Caroline as she peels a tangerine in the Luxembourg Gardens. Who was Nika to tell *me* about Alison's power? I thought with irritation. But I composed myself.

"Every time she was going to a party or an event or anything, she invited me," Nika continued. "I must have said no to her a hundred times. I was just scared. Finally one night she grabbed my arm and said, 'You're coming, Nika Nika'—she used to call me that, like the Singing Nun song?—and she dragged me out of our room. We went to this dorm party. I was so freaked out. I'd never had a sip of alcohol. Your sister didn't leave my side the whole night. She introduced me to everyone like I was this extremely cool person who had finally deigned to grace them with my—sorry." Her hand pressed against the receiver again. *Jackson, why do I hear video games? . . . Don't "I don't know" me . . . Five minutes . . . Fine, eight.* She sighed. "Sorry. Where were we?"

"My sister took you out with her."

"Right. Anyway, after that she basically adopted me into her friend group." Nika was speaking more hurriedly now. The video game business had pulled her out of the sea of memory and back onto the shore of her busy life. I could sense she was eager to be off the phone, to check this task off of what was surely a long list.

"And when she died?"

"We were shocked. Devastated. The way it happened. I still feel bad I couldn't go to the funeral. It was the middle of exams and I just couldn't leave. Our group stayed together, though. We're all still friends. We go to Steamboat every winter with our kids. My husband, Alex. Alison was always teasing me that he had a thing for me and I never believed her."

"That's so great."

Nika's hand went over the receiver again. *We don't interrupt people on the phone, sweetheart.* "Sorry. What was that?"

"I said it's nice to know all of this."

"Listen, I'm really sorry, but I have to go. But I have a few pictures and notes and things. I can send you color copies for your memory book." I told her I would like that very much and gave her my address. "I really am sorry to dash off. I need to help my son with this project. We're working on a Prezi about the chaparral," she said sardonically.

"I miss the days of the shoe-box diorama," I replied, as if I, too, were a harried mother befuddled by my child's Information Age assignments.

Only after I hung up did I realize that my entire body was clenched. This wasn't a nice story about the good my sister had done in her short life. It was a story about Nika's life. Alison was merely the device by which the universe had conspired to ensure Nika's destiny as Nika (Ivanova) Cunningham, mommy to Jackson and Logan. The dead's stories are lifted away from them; they are sentenced to an eternity as deus ex machina in the stories of others.

"Alison Thomas Autopsy Report, Abridged Text," Special to the *New York Post,* March 25, 1996:

Decedent: THOMAS, Alison Brianne

Authorized by: Cardigan Ralston, Coroner

Assisted by: Diandra Young, M.D.

Alexis Schaitkin

Identified by: Thomas, Ellen, and Thomas, Richard, parents of decedent.

Date of Birth: September 8, 1977

Race: Caucasian

Sex: Female

Length: 165 cm

Weight: 52.6 kg

Eyes: Brown

Hair: Reddish brown

EXTERNAL EXAMINATION

The body is presented in a black body bag. The victim wears no clothing. Jewelry includes three pierced earrings in the left ear: one gold hoop, one gold stud, and one small blue gemstone, and two pierced earrings in the right ear: one gold hoop and one gold stud. Fingernails and toenails are painted sky blue. The body is that of a normally developed, normally nourished Caucasian female. The appearance of age is approximately as stated. The eyes are closed. The irises are light brown. The teeth are native and in good condition. The tongue is smooth, bloated, and white-gray. The hair is reddish brown, straight, and fixed in a ponytail on the top of the head, secured with a yellow elastic band. It measures 35.5 centimetres at its longest length. The genitalia are that of a normally developed adult female. There is a scar measuring 12 centimetres in length on the lower left abdomen, which the parents of the decedent confirm is the result of an accidental injury sustained in 1981. There is significant bloating and draining of the skin, consistent with the body being submerged in non-saline water.

Injuries

The neck is fractured. There is a laceration to the skull measuring 3 centimetres in length, located on the left parietal. There are abrasions to the vulva which suggest recent sexual activity, but the superficial nature of these abrasions is inconclusive as to whether such activity was forcible. No semen is found within the vaginal cavity, though it is not possible to determine whether this is due to the body's submersion.

INTERNAL EXAMINATION

Lungs: Non-saline water is found in both lungs. Sand granules, beige in color, are found in both lungs.

Gastrointestinal, Cardiovascular, and Urinary systems are normal.

X-Rays

Total body X-rays reveal fracture of the neck located at the C4 vertebrae.

Toxicology

Blood and vitreous fluids positive for ethanols.
Blood and vitreous fluids positive for cannabinoids.

EVIDENCE

Items submitted to the Royal Police Force of Saint X as evidence include: vaginal swabs; oral swabs; samples of hair, eyelashes, and eyebrows; earrings; hair elastic; fingernail clippings; 3 tubes of blood.

OPINION

Time of Death

Body rigor, livor mortis, and stomach contents approximate the time of death between 72 and 96 hours prior to autopsy.

Immediate Cause of Death

Undetermined

Manner of Death

Undetermined

Remarks

Due to the condition of the body at time of autopsy, it is not possible to determine the immediate cause of death. Possible causes include blunt trauma and asphyxiation as a result of submersion. It is not possible to determine whether manner of death was accidental, intentional, or forcible.

Statement to the Press, Prentice Carter, Chief of Police, April 10, 1996:
The Royal Police Force is aware of the intense global interest in our investigation of the January 3rd death of American teenager Alison Thomas on our island. Our investigation into this matter has been conducted with the utmost seriousness and meticulousness, with the full resources of our department and in close cooperation with the Federal Bureau of Investigation. Our department has conducted interviews with over one hundred witnesses. I can share with you at this time that on the night of her death, multiple witnesses confirm that Alison Thomas was present at Paulette's Place, located at 24 Underhill Road, where, again, multiple witnesses attest that she appeared heavily intoxicated, a fact toxicology reports confirm. Witnesses describe her as wearing a revealing shirt and dancing provocatively with several patrons. A bartender has confirmed serving Thomas at least four drinks, including a shot of vodka infused with cannabis. Over a dozen witnesses provided testimony that Ms. Thomas was engaged in wild partying during the several nights preceding her death. Every effort has been made by our department to follow every possible lead in this case. Edwin Hastie and Clive Richardson are no longer considered to be suspects in this case; at present, Mr. Richardson is serving a ninety-day sentence for an unrelated charge of drug possession. At this time, there are no other suspects in this case, and we do not find sufficient evidence that Alison Thomas died as the result of a violent crime to continue our investigation.

Statement to the Press, Rick and Ellen Thomas, April 11, 1996:
We, the parents of Alison Thomas, reject absolutely the conclusions of Chief of Police Carter and the Royal Police Force of Saint X. At this time, we plead with anyone who may have knowledge of the circumstances surrounding our daughter's death to please come forward so that this case can be reopened as it should be. We will not rest until those

responsible for our daughter's death are found and punished to the full extent of the law.

We want to end with a message to other parents. Please, hug your children a little tighter tonight. We pray that what happened to our beautiful daughter will never happen to another girl.

THE BEAUTIFUL daughter had died. What daughter, meanwhile, had lived?

A COLD drizzle was falling the next evening when I made my way to the Little Sweet. I stood beneath the awning of the grocery as usual and watched Clive Richardson sit at the table he always sat at, doing the things he always did.

A few minutes later, I watched him push back his chair, carry his tray to the trash, and scrape the remains of his dinner from his plate. But this time I didn't hurry away. Instead, when he approached the door, I lowered my umbrella, concealing myself behind it. I stayed still until Clive exited the Little Sweet, walked to the end of the block, and turned the corner. Then I followed after him.

I kept my distance, clinging to the shadows cast by shop awnings, clutching the umbrella, white-knuckled, ready to hide my face should he turn around. He walked north on Nostrand, passing storefronts that would, in the months to come, become intimately familiar to me: Health-wise Pharmacy. US Fried Chicken & Pizza. Immaculee Bakery. Red Apple Nails. Winthrop Hardware. I slowed my pace, letting the distance between us lengthen. KBB Shipping. Beulah United Church of God. I followed Clive for over an hour as he turned right, left, right again, heading in no particular direction, at least as far as I could discern, down the rain-sweetened streets. Finally, he made his way to a residential area not far from where we'd begun, block after block of midrise buildings, their exteriors sand-colored brick zigzagged with fire escapes. In the middle of a block, Clive turned and walked up the steps of a building that looked like all the others. He reached into the pocket of his windbreaker and took out his keys. He fumbled a bit with the lock.

I hadn't planned what I did next. I didn't even realize I was doing it until it was done, until the shout—"Gogo!"—had left my lips and was coming back to me as an echo off the wet bricks and the soft night air.

I tucked into the shadow of a plane tree as Clive Richardson whipped around.

"Who's there?" he called out. The street was empty, silent. "Who said that?" He stood frozen halfway through the door. "Leave me alone! Do you hear me? Leave me alone!"

He let the door slam shut behind him and was gone.

GOGO

IT WAS THE WIND. It was someone on the next block yelling, "No, no, no!" It was a dog barking. There are any number of explanations for what he heard: a voice, which surely wasn't a voice at all, calling that name. In the days that follow, he is vigilant with himself. If he catches his mind spinning during his shift, he turns the radio to a Christian station and brings his focus to the words of the sermon. On his nightly walks, when he notices his pace growing frantic, he forces himself to slow down. In the apartment, he busies himself: he wipes down the stove, gives his teeth a long brushing rather than his usual cursory going-over. He even strikes up a conversation with Cecil, listening attentively as his roommate recounts the surprising turn of events from the variety show he watched the night before—a magician was beaten out by a unicyclist for a spot in the grand finale. He nods as Cecil delivers a speech that he has clearly been working out in his head for some time about what makes the show so entertaining; it has to do with the apples-and-oranges comparisons the show requires. How ought one to measure the talent of a contortionist against that of a stand-up comedian? Who is more impressive, a one-in-a-million ventriloquist or an excellent opera singer? Anything to crowd out the voice. *Gogo.* It is not the first time he has heard his name on the wind, there and then gone. He knows where it can lead, and he does not want to go back there.

The voice is mostly dormant in the daylight, so that each day he thinks he has conquered it. But at night it resurfaces, the darkness so thick with it he could choke. *Gogo.* Again and again he tells himself he did not hear what he thinks he heard. After all, how could it be? He hasn't been Gogo to anyone in a long, long time.

IT WAS the first day of second grade and Clive Richardson's grandmother had buttoned his pink uniform polo all the way to the top. They sat together at the kitchen table, where his grandmother had prepared a breakfast of fried jackfish and bakes and bush tea in blue enamel cups. As he ate, Clive tugged at the collar. His grandmother, who ate her fish in big quick bites, grabbed his hand and held it.

"None of this fidgeting."

He nodded. Things were like this with her, prickly and wonderfully firm. She removed her hand and they continued eating.

"You will make some nice friends today. Good boys."

It was a habit of hers, this way of speaking, as if the future were not in doubt; as if she were merely waiting for it to come along and cooperate. It had been less than a month since he had come to live with her, and as he sat in her kitchen, with its lacy white curtain fluttering against the open window and its smell of allspice and everything in its place—the yellow jug of oil beside the stove, pink beans soaking on the counter, margarine in the dish with the rosebud border on the table—it was still a new, miraculous comfort to be in the care of an adult who was so firmly in command and in possession of such a clear-eyed vision of what ought to happen. He would go to school and make nice friends. He wanted this very much. But he was unsettled, too, because he worried that even his grandmother's oracular proclamation would not be powerful enough to bring about something so unlikely, for he was seven years old and had never had a friend. Not really. Only if you counted Vaughn, who called him "Big Man," but Vaughn was his mother's special friend, so he knew he didn't really count. There was also Jeremiah, who lived down the street from his mother's house, but Jeremiah was simpleminded and it humiliated Clive that one of the only people he might count as a friend was simpleminded, so he did not want to count him.

"Y-y-yes, Gran," he said.

She cupped his cheek with her palm. "You a good boy, Clive." With these words, too, he sensed her trying to speak something into being, to wrangle the loose threads of the past into a neat and orderly present.

Clive had come to live with his father's mother when his mother departed for Saint Thomas to find work. His father was dead, a fact that did not make him sad because he did not remember him. This troubled him, because he was four when his father died, and he did have memories of being four. He remembered getting nipped by a black and white goat, and how his mother spanked the goat on its backside like a naughty child. He remembered Claude Félix, the old fisherman with clouds in his eyes who walked the streets of the village at sundown, stopping at his customers' houses to deliver parcels of fish wrapped in brown paper; he remembered the evening his mother told him that Claude Félix had gone to his eternal rest. But he had no memories of his own father or his death, and so these other memories filled him with shame.

On the day of his mother's departure, she packed his things into half a dozen Goody Mart bags and one of her friends drove them across the island from Bendy Harbour to his grandmother's house in the Basin. She opened the front door when they were still coming up the road. She crossed her arms and stood in the doorway.

"This how you bring my grandchild to me? With he possession all in disarray?" she said when they were standing on the porch in front of her.

"I need the suitcase, Nella."

"How silly I be! *You* need the suitcase."

"How I'm supposed to get on the plane without one?" his mum snapped.

For what felt like forever, his grandmother stood there, her arms crossed, and looked at his mum with eyes as blunt as wood.

"Convenient you not taking he with you, then, or what would you use for he luggage?"

For weeks his mother had spoken heavily of her impending departure, as if their separation were a thing over which she had no control. Now he understood this wasn't the case. She could take him. She wasn't. What a fool he was, no better than Jeremiah.

His mother knelt beside him and squeezed him tightly. "Mama will miss you so, my love."

His body went rigid. He couldn't let go. Finally, his grandmother pulled him away, uncurling his clenched fingers from around his mother's neck. She held him fast against her as his mother got into her friend's car and drove away. When the car disappeared from view, he began to sob. His grandmother patted his back. "Come, now," she whispered, and led him inside. When he had exhausted himself from crying, she changed him into an old nightshirt that had belonged to his grandfather and tucked him into bed. When he awoke in the middle of the night, aching and confused, she brought him into the kitchen and fixed him a warm bowl of the most delicious pepper pot he'd ever tasted.

It was hard to explain what he felt for his grandmother and his new life in her home. He knew that things were better here. Her house was spotless. For breakfast there was fish and corn porridge or flour pap instead of Frosties with Nido. They went to St. George's Anglican Church on Sundays. She filled a bath for him every evening, and with a rough cloth and a bar of Ivory soap she scrubbed him, a task she completed with an unceremonious physicality bereft of gentleness and harshness alike. He was required to make his bed each morning and read a psalm each evening, and even though he did not enjoy doing these things, he could feel the goodness of them.

At his mother's house he did not have a proper bedtime. Often, she went out at night, and he stayed up, snacking on crisps and pitching marbles on the floor until the house grew dark and he dropped off to sleep. Sometimes he woke in the night to voices and unfamiliar laughter. He would stumble into the kitchen to find his mother and a few others sitting around the kitchen table with the kerosene lamp with the blue base at its center, smoking hand-rolled cigarettes whose smoke tickled his nostrils with its strange funk. "Come here, Big Man," Vaughn would say if he was there. Clive would climb into his lap. "Thirsty?" Vaughn asked him once. Clive nodded. Vaughn handed him his glass. "Just a little sip, Big Man," he said. Clive sputtered as the brown liquid burned down his throat. Vaughn clapped and laughed and patted him on the head. "Look at you, life of the party."

Yet sometimes he ached for his mother's house. He missed the way she kissed his fingers, one by one. Even when she'd been gone weeks, months, years, his fingertips still prickled with her love and her leaving. He missed the flowers from their yard that she picked and tucked into her hair; sometimes at night when she wasn't around he went out into the yard in the moonlight and touched the flowers and imagined he was touching her. He missed going to the harbor with her at Christmastime, when the boat from Saint Croix brought ice to the island; on the pier, she would hold him up high above the crowd and he would watch as a man threw salt crystals into a machine, turned a crank, and churned out ice cream.

On Sunday evenings, nearly everyone in Bendy Harbour gathered at the home of the only family in the village with a generator and a television. They turned the television so that it faced the yard, and everyone sat outside together to watch. Usually he and his mother did not join their neighbors, so on Sunday nights Clive sat at home knowing everyone else was together without him. But once in a while they went, and he sat on his mother's lap among all the people he had ever known and had never not known as the sun went down. They watched *Rawhide* and *The Wild Wild West,* cheered as Andre the Giant took on Killer Khan or Kamala. When the generator wound down for the night, someone would light a lamp, and the stories would begin. This was what Clive missed most: drifting to sleep in his mother's arms as voices that were as familiar to him as his own skin conjured faraway, long-ago worlds.

There were stories about the men who had left the island at the beginning of the century and sailed to the Dominican Republic aboard the schooner *Lady Ann* to cut cane, or to Trinidad to work in the oil refineries, about fishermen and sailors and their trips to Aruba and Cuba and Curaçao and the things they had seen—the port of Santo Domingo, the club Sans Souci and the Malecón in Havana. There was the story of a cane cutter who came upon a beautiful woman one night along a desolate stretch of road. The next thing he knew, he was waking up beneath a silk-cotton tree in the forest in broad daylight. His shoes were gone—his feet were caked in dirt and blood. When he finally found his way to a road, he discovered he had traveled some twenty kilometers from where he had been walking the night before—he had crossed mountains and rivers but remembered nothing.

There were stories about the *Lady Ann*—how when Jonathan Bell's great-grandfather sailed the schooner back from Santo Domingo to see his dying father, it made the journey a day faster than ever before and he arrived just in time to kiss his father goodbye; of the salt she transported to Trinidad, and how, after the barrels had been unloaded, the deck glittered with fine white crystals like stars. There were stories about salt, how during the reaping months it was not uncommon to pull a cake heavier than a small child from the Thomasvale Pond. There was the story of Harlan Ghaut, who was walking the Old Vale Road past the salt pond when he saw a finned woman sunning herself on the rocks, or so he claimed. Harlan returned to the spot every day, but he never saw her again, until he returned late one night and found her perched on the rock, opening her fin and unfurling two human feet. Twenty years later, Harlan was sitting in his apartment in London watching television when this very same mermaid flashed across the screen.

There were stories about Janet and Alice and Carla and Camille, the great storms that had leveled the island before Clive was born—how roofs lifted off houses and people looked up from their beds into the skies of heaven, how cars spun like bottles in the streets, how the wind stripped houses clean of their paint, and how the paint, carried on gale winds, could cut you up like glass. The sinking of the *Lady Ann* in Britannia Bay.

Then there was the story Clive loved best, the one he begged his mother to tell as she tucked him in, about a long-haired woman with hooves for feet who lived on Faraway Cay.

"Is she real?" Clive would ask.

"For true. Your Great-Aunt Ruth got lured away by she. Poof. Vanish like so."

("Ha!" his grandmother snorted when he asked if she believed Ruth had been taken by the woman on Faraway Cay. "I believe your auntie had she reasons to get lost; that's what I believe.") His grandmother did not tell stories. With her, the world was just itself.

His mother had been gone less than a year when the island's first ice plant opened. You could buy a twenty-kilo block of it; men churned ice cream and shaved ice on the pier year-round. You no longer had to wait for the boat from Saint Croix at Christmastime, and you quickly forgot what a wonder it had once been to sit on the pier, your feet dangling over the flickering sea, and taste the coldness of ice cream while the sun beat hot on your shoulders. Not long after that, electricity came to the island's villages. Soon, lots of people had televisions and the gatherings and the stories ceased. Next the telephone wires went up. In no time, Mayfair Road was paved, and then Investiture Boulevard, and soon all the streets in the Basin. Then the resorts came, and with them the tourists, and everything changed.

And so, for Clive, the sleepy, magical feeling of childhood was inextricably bound up with the island as it was before—with the smell of kerosene and the sounds of stories in the dark—which were, in turn, bound up with his mother. And as the years passed without her she became, like his father, a disquieting emptiness right at the center of him where he thought there should have been sadness.

HORATIO BYRD Primary was three times the size of Bendy Harbour Primary, where Clive had attended first grade. It was a low, horseshoe-shaped concrete building painted white with blue trim. On the inside of the horseshoe, children ran and shrieked across the packed-dirt schoolyard. Clive tugged at the collar of his polo.

"Stop that," his grandmother said.

He didn't know how she saw—she wasn't even looking at him. He stopped.

"Go on," she said.

He took a few shuffling steps forward. When he turned to look back at her, she was already halfway across the yard. He watched as she strode in her black shoes through the gate and out of sight.

The classroom was not so different from the first-grade room at Bendy Harbour. The long wooden tables were the same. The girls wore the same jumpers and blouses, only here they were maroon and pink instead of green and white. The boys all wore pink polos and maroon trousers like him, though the other boys did not have their shirts buttoned to the top. He wanted to loosen his but didn't dare. Somehow, his grandmother would know. On the wall above the blackboard there was even the same illustrated alphabet: a balloon for *B*, a goat for *G*, an igloo for *I*, and, his favorite, a mermaid for *M*. He looked at the familiar picture, the pink and green scales of the mermaid's tail, her hair swirling around her head in curlicues, and felt calm.

The teacher, a tall, kind-faced woman named Miss Forsyth, took attendance.

"Annmarie Bell."

"Present."

"Don Claxton."

"Present."

"Damien Fleming."

"Present."

As she made her way steadily and inexorably through the alphabet, his mouth grew dry until it stuck together, teeth to tongue to roof.

"Edwin Hastie."

Silence.

"Edwin Hastie?"

A boy in the last row shot up as if he'd just jolted awake. "Yes!"

Everybody tittered.

"Yes what, Mr. Hastie?"

"Yes, I be present."

"I *am* present."

"I hope so, Miss Forsyth. You is our teacher."

The class broke into laughter. Clive laughed, too, though his was a nervous laughter; his turn was still coming.

"Sara Lycott," Miss Forsyth said, cutting off the ruckus like thwacking a weed with a scythe.

"Present, Miss Forsyth."

"Daphne Nelsen."

"Present."

"Desmond Phillips."

"Present."

"Ron Rawlins."

"Present."

"Clive Richardson."

He opened his mouth, but his throat wrung itself up. His ears went hot, as if pricked by bees.

"P-p-p-"

Thirty pairs of eyes converged on him.

"P-p-p-"

He searched the ceiling desperately.

"P-p-p-*present*." The word came out much too loud, like an angry shout. They were all laughing again, harder than they had when Edwin Hastie pulled his stunt.

"Enough," Miss Forsyth said. "Thank you, Clive." She smiled very sweetly at him, which made it worse.

They spent the morning on maths. Miss Forsyth wrote equations on the board. She had beautiful handwriting. Each numeral was like a flower. She called students up one at a time to work the problems out. *If Michael has seven nails and John has twelve, how many more nails does John have than Michael? Marie has seventeen yards of fabric. If she needs four yards to make a skirt, how many skirts can she make?*

Each time Miss Forsyth read a question, Clive's mind flailed. The words tumbled together, twisting into strange shapes in his head. He tried to sort it out while praying he would not be called upon, because in addition to not understanding the questions, he also had to urinate very badly. He had drunk all of his tea at breakfast. But he could not bring himself to ask to use the toilet because he knew he would not be able to get the words out.

"Johnny has a dozen eggs. If he eats four for breakfast, what does he have left? Edwin?"

The skinny boy swaggered up to the blackboard. His trousers were too big for him—they were cinched to his waist with a belt, bunched and sagging. He took the chalk from Miss Forsyth and wrote: *g-a-s*.

The class doubled over with laughter. Miss Forsyth allowed herself a very brief smile.

"The corner," she said. Edwin swaggered there, too. "You see, class, Edwin might be the smartest boy here but he treats everything as a joke so we will never know."

In the corner, Edwin Hastie played with the collar of his polo, flipping it up and down as if he hadn't heard Miss Forsyth. His eyes flashed as if lit by a brewing storm.

After maths, Miss Forsyth distributed copies of the *Higham Brothers Reader* and they went down the rows from the front of the room to the back, each student reading aloud in turn from a story about an American man who planted apple seeds wherever he went. Clive barely heard the words. He was now focused entirely on squeezing his legs together against the unbearable pressure of his bladder. He turned the page of his reader. The American, barefoot and with a tin pot on his head, lay next to a river—blue and white and foamy, full of rushing water. He could hold it no longer. As Daphne Nelsen read in the pinched, nasal voice he would hate forever after, he tentatively pressed his fingers into the air.

"Yes, Clive?" Miss Forsyth said, cutting off Daphne midsentence. The eyes were on him again.

"May I g-g-g-"

It would happen. He would wet himself right here, in front of the entire class, on his first day at his new school.

"May I go—go—go—"

Miss Forsyth saw his anguish and understood. "Yes! Hurry!"

Bent at the waist, fumbling over his feet, he dashed from the classroom. In the hall, he put both hands on his crotch and ran, and when he reached the latrine and released a torrent of urine he felt simultaneously so grateful and so humiliated that his eyes filled with tears.

WHEN PLAYTIME came, he made for a deserted corner of the yard. As the girls played marbles and the boys engaged in a rough game of tag, he sat, pulling clumps of dry grass from the dirt. He was himself all over again. In his mortification, he found a certain peace. He had his spot in the yard, and every day at playtime he would come to it and keep his own company. He thought of his mother. Where was she now? Did she know it was his first day of school? He pictured her tapping at a typewriter in a white room.

Boys were coming toward him. The troublemaker, Edwin, was leading a pack of them; he cupped his hands around his mouth and shouted: "Hey, Go-Go!"

The other boys clapped.

Don hooted. "Yes! That's right! G-g-g-go-go!"

Clive kept his eyes on his lap.

"Gogo, man, me speaking with you," Edwin said.

Clive forced himself to look up. To his surprise, Edwin was grinning down at him, his expression teasing but—could it be?—warmly so.

"We having a cricket match, we against they." He gestured across the yard, where a few other boys milled about. Clive sat, uncomprehending, until Edwin exclaimed, "What you waiting for? Get up, man! We need you!"

Clive stood, wiped the dust from the seat of his trousers, and followed.

They won the game, though no thanks to Clive, who, for the most part, stood in one place and hoped not to make a mistake. From then on, he and Edwin were always together. You never saw one without the other, and if you did, it likely meant some mischief was afoot of which you would turn out to be the unfortunate recipient. They did many things, Edwin and Clive and the rest of Edwin's band of brothers, Don and Des and Damien. They caught bait and went to Little Beach, where they fished from the pier, diving and backflipping into the sea when they were hot. They played wind-ball cricket in the sand and had swimming races—first one to the end of the pier, or to the *Atalanta* moored in the shallows. ("I get you back!" Don shouted when Edwin grabbed his leg to slow him down. "I drown you! I gonna drown you!") They built traps and caught turtledoves. They shook tamarind pods from the tree in Damien's yard and mixed the sticky brown pulp with sugar and water. Begged a dollar off Edwin's mother for sugar cakes. When Clive's grandmother baked buns, they stole them right out of the oven, slathered them quickly with red butter, then ran out of the house and down the street, tossing the hot buns in the air.

In fifth grade, they rode their bikes often to the beach that would, a few years later, become Indigo Bay. It was still wild then. The land was covered by pomme-serette trees, and they would pick the fruit, though only one in ten was sweet. The beach stank from seaweed and the seaweed was full of bad things—needles and condoms, which they would lift with sticks and fling at each other. Sometimes they would find two antimen together on the sand. They would sneak and watch them and then Edwin would shout, *Go!* and they would stampede and chase them off.

They scaled the chain-link fence and climbed the island's radio tower, a rickety structure flaking red paint. Clive was a quarter of the way up, far below his friends, when Edwin shouted down to him, "Look *out*, Goges. Why bother climbing if you don't see anything?" He gripped the metal rung as tightly as he could and raised his head. He never forgot it. He could follow the ribbon of Mayfair Road from Horatio Byrd past the governor-general's pink house and the eggshell-blue prison; he could see how the water fanned out around the island in bands of deepening hues—from a pale, milky green like Claude Félix's cataracts to a bright turquoise and finally a deep, sparkling blue. If he squinted, he could make out Bendy Harbour—hardly more than the idea of it, a loose sketch of houses, one of which had been his. He could see his whole life spread before him—past, present, future—and the solidity of this image made him want to collect it like a coin and keep it in his pocket forever.

The island's first movie hall opened when they were thirteen, and Edwin and Clive made a habit of sneaking out of Everett Lyle Secondary to catch the matinee. They waited until five minutes after the showing time so the theater was dark, then snuck in through the side door, vigilant in case Wilmot, the old man who managed the ticket booth, should come down the aisle with his flashlight. The movie hall showed a mix of old movies—westerns and kung fu, mostly—and new releases. They'd sneak into the same movie many times, timing it to catch their favorite scenes. Clive knew *Pale Rider* and *Way of the Dragon* and *Ghostbusters* by heart. Occasionally he discovered that Edwin had left school without him, and he knew that

Edwin was in the warm theater, which smelled of stale popcorn and sweat, watching *E.T.* cycle across the face of the moon for the fourth, fifth, twelfth time.

Often the movies had been out in the States a year or longer by the time they reached the island. To Clive this was unremarkable. Everything took time to reach the island. Newspapers came a week late, by way of Saint Kitts by way of Jamaica. The TV stations showed *Bonanza* and *I Dream of Jeannie* and *The Beverly Hillbillies*.

For Edwin, this was a source of immense frustration.

"When you getting *Rocky IV*?" he asked Wilmot one day on the way out.

"What are you boys doing here with no ticket?"

"I ask you first. *Rocky IV* out a year already. When you getting it?"

"When the poster go up. When you think?"

"Come on, man! Bad enough we live nowhere. Why we also have to live yesterday?"

In the beginning, Clive was wary of Edwin's friendship. Why *him*? There were other boys Edwin could have chosen. There was Arthur, for example, not a cool boy by any means and a definite brown-nose, but still miles cooler than him, and besides, Arthur came with the advantages of his father's convenience store with the satellite television in the back room. Yet Edwin had not chosen Arthur. (Nobody had chosen Arthur, who, for some mysterious reason, had been left entirely outside the world of friendship.) Had Edwin selected him merely because of his size—had he been seeking a protector, an enforcer? Or perhaps Clive had been chosen because he was quiet and went along with Edwin's schemes. But despite his wariness, Clive knew the true reason went deeper than this. In the end, friendship was not a thing that could be explained. It was a kind of magic. Either it existed or it didn't. Edwin said they were mates and so they were, and Clive was grateful for it.

Many years later, he would sit in a small restaurant in an unfamiliar city, as snow—a thing he always assumed he'd die without touching—fell from the sky, and he would trace back through his life and conclude that the moment Edwin approached him in the schoolyard was *the* moment. The one after which everything that happened was always going to happen.

The one you could wonder and wonder about but never touch: What if he'd simply stayed in the grass?

Ever after that day, Clive was Gogo. First to his classmates, then to his neighbors, then even, at times, to his grandmother. Because it was Edwin who gave him this name, and because it was also Edwin who brought him from the darkness of solitude into the light of friendship, he quickly forgot that the name had begun with his own mortification.

I wasn't trying to "control the narrative" by taking that douche journalist from *Esquire* to the Station. Sure, the kids in this town love the deli because it's a dive; they show up after lacrosse practice, or late night, six-to-a-Beemer, and chat up the counter guys like they're just regular kids. The thing is, I like these kids. For all their privilege, they're mostly unspoiled. It's a town of Nice Kids, really, just a couple of sniveling "My dad is a lawyer and blah blah blah" pains in the ass here and there. But none of that has anything to do with why I suggested we meet at the Station for the interview. It's just my usual place. I'm a teacher. Where else in this town am I supposed to go for a two-buck egg sandwich?

So, no, I wasn't trying to "control the narrative." But there are things I didn't tell him. Things I didn't trust some sleek journalist with. (Horn-rimmed glasses and a tweed blazer, and I'm the one trying to manipulate the optics? Please.) Things it wouldn't have done anybody any good to see in print.

I didn't tell him about her essays. Alison always developed these wildly contrarian thesis statements. Macbeth *can best be understood as a feminist work in which Lady Macbeth is the true hero.* Catch-22 *glamorizes war.* Or my favorite: *While it might seem to depict human nature as savage and anarchic,* Lord of the Flies *ultimately works against the author's own intentions and conveys the endurance of civilization and order.* She was one hell of a writer, and she did crazy acrobatics in the essays to defend what were, basically, incorrect readings of the texts. Intentionally incorrect. She seemed to be under the impression that the best essay is the one that gets people to believe whatever it wants them to believe, even if that thing can't possibly be true. I always wanted to tell her in my comments that just because you win an argument doesn't make you right.

But I always felt a bit nervous critiquing her, to be honest. She was smarter than me, I have no qualms about admitting it. She knew it and I knew it. I wanted to tell her that just because you're smarter than someone doesn't mean they don't have things to teach you, but I didn't tell her that, either. I gave her her A's and figured somewhere down the line of her education she'd figure out how to apply her talents in a way that went beyond hot-dogging.

I didn't tell the journalist about the time I closed the classroom door on that poor chubby kid when he was late on test day, and Alison got in a confrontation with me about it, which was entirely inappropriate. The longer the argument went on, the clearer it became that she had the whole class on her side and I was at real risk of losing their good faith in an all-out mutiny that would screw up the classroom dynamic for the rest of the school year. I've always been a really popular teacher, too. Everybody wants to be in Conti's class. That's the sway she had with her classmates.

I didn't tell him about the way she rolled her eyes at these same classmates when they made a comment in class that she found obvious or dumb.

I didn't tell him about the time I went to the Station for a late-night grading session and she was there, alone at a table in the back, eating cheese fries. She must have come from dance rehearsal—she wore leggings and a sweatshirt unzipped over a black leotard.

"Care to join me, Mr. Conti?"

Fool that I am, I sat.

"Fry?"

I ate.

I asked her how college applications were going.

"Fine," she sighed, as if she hardly cared, which I knew couldn't be true, not a smart, ambitious kid like her. "Can I ask you something, Mr. Conti?" she said.

I told her she could.

"Doesn't it bother you, spending your existence with a bunch of high schoolers?"

I said if it did, would I have become a high school teacher? I felt pretty smart about that response.

"It would make me crazy." She stared right at me as she said that. Under the table, she brushed her foot against my leg.

I told her I had to get going. She smirked, like she thought I was a wuss or something. I was totally freaked out to see her in my class the next day, but she acted completely normal, as if nothing had happened. After a few days, it started to feel that way.

After she died, the last thing she said to me that night kept coming back to me. *It would make me crazy.* What was her game with that, exactly? She was not admiring my capacity for working with young people, that's for sure. No, she was telling me she could never do what I did because she was different from me. Better.

The thing is, from then on teaching did start to drive me crazy. Before, I'd spend hours writing comments on my students' essays, and then I'd see the kids flip straight to the back, look at the grade, and chuck the papers in the trash, and I'd shrug it off. After, stuff like that enraged me. I started to see very clearly the way my life's work was just "second period" to the kids. I started seeing it the way she saw it, I started seeing *me* the way she saw me, and the foundational satisfaction of my life was chipped away at. Not completely, but some.

This is a town of Nice Kids, but Alison Thomas was not one of them. She had talent to burn. She could be very passionate. She had a personal power that she often used as a force for good. But she was not Nice.

EVIDENCE

HOW FRIGHTENED CLIVE RICHARDSON had been when he heard me call that name! The secrets of his past were there, submerged but still hot to the touch. If I played things out right, I was certain I could bring them to the surface. But what then? Was my end game public punishment? Private vengeance? Did I imagine Clive Richardson in handcuffs? Brought to his own watery end in the Gowanus? These possibilities and many others floated in my mind, but I dared not envision any of them too fully. The truth. First I must have the truth.

Autumn continued: the sidewalks grew cluttered with fallen leaves and the pink fruits of ginkgo trees, which released their bilious stink as they rotted on the pavement. I spent an evening battling with Time Warner over my spotty Wi-Fi. Jefe the dog had an accident on the faded green carpet in the hallway. It was determined that Astrid's latest novel would be titled *The Girl from Pendeen*; the fact that the titles of two of her previous novels contained the word *Girl* was decided, after much discussion, to be a non-issue, even a boon. I continued to call my parents every Sunday, conversations that increasingly became exercises in dissembling. I told them I'd begun attending yoga classes in the evenings.

"That's wonderful, sweetheart," my mother said.

"Yoga is supposed to be great for your alignment," my father said.

(I'd intended to convince them, but was still irritated by how easily they'd been fooled.)

The reality was that my evenings were now almost wholly devoted to Clive. I would linger around the Little Sweet until he departed, then follow him. Clive Richardson, I learned quickly, was a walker. He might stroll for an hour, even two, before heading home. When he reached his brick apartment building, I waited until a light on the fourth floor turned on and then, some twenty or thirty minutes later, turned off again; only then did I make my own way home. On my walk back, I would realize that I was soaked in sweat. I was terrified as I followed Clive—of being seen, of what I might see—but it was a terror that held itself at bay until I was away from him, when it came over me all at once.

On these walks, I experienced what might be described as a state of hypervigilance. I attended to every detail, every movement, searching for any scrap that might provide insight into the man Clive Richardson was and the secrets he was guarding. What ought I to make of the routes he chose? Or of the way he scuffed his black loafers against the pavement? Back at my apartment late at night, I would try to get myself to read through the mounting backlog of manuscripts in my work in-box, but I quickly found myself lost in imaginative labor: What did he think about before he fell asleep? What was in his refrigerator? What did his bedroom look like? (I pictured a stark, simple room—a rough-hewn wood floor, a simple twin bed, a small wicker chair. This mental picture had arrived fully formed, which I took as a testament to my imaginative powers; a few years later, on a visit to the Orsay, I would realize that the image was not even mine—it was *Bedroom in Arles,* Vincent Van Gogh.)

It wasn't only Clive's actions I attended to. Everything I passed seemed anointed by his presence. Graffiti on a brick wall: *Rochelle, marry me??* A man in a dastaar selling incense on a street corner. A fruit stand with a handwritten cardboard sign: BANANAS 4 FOR 1$! The sweet and sour rivulets of liquid eroding the sidewalk in front of a halal butcher. Did he notice these things? If he did, what did they make him think, want, remember? Clive's world became my evidence—a rush of details, almost unbearably vivid, the landscape infused by a sense of the significance of all things.

From "Secrets on Faraway Cay," *Dateline*, July 12, 1996:

JANE PAULEY: You worked in security at Indigo Bay.

HAROLD MOSES: [nods] For seven years. During which time I was employee of the month on four occasions.

JANE PAULEY: You saw Alison Thomas on the night of her death?

HAROLD MOSES: I certainly did, Ms. Pauley.

JANE PAULEY: Tell me about that.

HAROLD MOSES: [sips coffee] It was eight p.m. I know so because I just return from my toilet break, which I take nightly at seven-forty p.m. precisely. I was doing my rounds. By the swimming pool I see the girl dipping she toe in the water.

JANE PAULEY: Did you say anything to her?

HAROLD MOSES: [shakes head] I didn't want to disturb she. She appeared quite peaceful, like she was having some special time to she self. I saw clearly she had a sweet soul.

JANE PAULEY: What happened next?

HAROLD MOSES: [shakes head sadly] She walked away, over to the bar. This is the last time I see she. But everybody know later that night she went out with those two good-for-nothings. I have a theory about what happened to she, Ms. Pauley. Would you like to hear it?

JANE PAULEY: Please.

HAROLD MOSES: I believe it is a crime of passion. That girl was pretty. Oh, she was pretty pretty. I have one more thing I wish to say, Ms. Pauley. I want your viewers to know that I carry it heavy in my heart that for this girl I may be the last kind face of this world.

Statement to the Press, for Immediate Release, January 12, 1996:

While on a recent vacation in the Caribbean, I participated in a day trip to an uninhabited island. On this island, as has been widely reported, myself and a companion discovered the body of a young woman who had been missing for several days. Contrary to several grossly misleading recent reports, I had no involvement in the disappearance of Alison Thomas. I have participated in the local investigation to the full extent of my ability. I am not a suspect in this case. Reports suggesting otherwise are an assault on my character. I would like to extend my deepest sympathies to the Thomas family. I ask that my privacy be respected during this time.

From *Tragedy in Paradise: The Untold Story of the Alison Thomas Murder* by Craig Sheppard:

. . . The frantic hunt for the beautiful teenager continued, transforming the sleepy island with an all-out search that left no stone unturned. Unbeknownst to the police, at this same time, a Haitian man by the name of Siméon Payen was flying from Saint X to Miami, where he owned a palatial beachfront property and was well-known to law enforcement as a key player in La Petite Haïti, a small but notorious Miami cartel. By the time you turn the final page of this book, dear reader, I think you will agree that these two events were anything but a coincidence, and that on a small island, corruption can run deep. . . .

From the "Unsolved Mysteries" subreddit, Reddit.com:

I'm totally new to this sub, so bear with me, but this case is one of my first memories of being totally obsessed with an unsolved mystery and it remains one of my favorites to this day. I've read a LOT about it over the years, and I have to say I've always questioned the Haitian cartel angle, which first came out in the Sheppard book (his book on Thomas is in my personal opinion one of his weaker efforts, and I'm usually a big fan of his). I mean, doesn't it seem like a huge stretch that Payen would involve this girl in a run, with the risks that would entail for *him*? I know a lot of you here subscribe to the Payen theory, but I've always believed that the simplest and most elegant solution is usually the right one.

Stick with me here. Imagine the police know pretty much beyond a doubt it's Richardson and Hastie. Or it doesn't even have to be them—maybe it's some other local, maybe it's a police officer's kid. A PR disaster for the island, in other words. So what do they do? They fabricate evidence that these two dudes were actually locked up in jail by 1 a.m. or whenever, and once that's done, it's, "Sorry, the timeline doesn't work and there are no other suspects. Case closed, island open for business." This theory works on So. Many. Levels. Think about it. I mean, doesn't it seem just the tiniest bit convenient that the thing that gets those guys off is coming from the *police*?

That message board alone had over nine hundred posts. As I continued to search, I found countless other boards on other websites dedicated to Alison. Across the digital underworld, people were still trying their hands at solving her murder. Scrolling through these posts, reading theory after theory, I felt physically sick. There were thousands of them—these dudes (they were almost all men) using Alison's murder to distract them from their basement-and-weed lives, crafting some loser fantasy that they might be the one to solve it.

It's difficult to separate things out. To determine how much of my disgust at these men was genuine, and how much I was drumming it up, seizing upon an easy opportunity to feel disgusted, indignant, violated by anonymous people I would never know or have to confront. These online forums. Craig Sheppard lining his pockets. The memoir that actor's ex-girlfriend published where she described Alison's body. *Dying for Fun*'s absurd version of her death (Apollo! My god . . .). The whole razzle-dazzle enterprise of the Alison Thomas Economy—did these things actually pain me, did they really touch the heart of my own personal trauma? Yes and no, they did and they didn't, and this is what made it so hard to parse my own feelings, to separate what I did feel from all the things I *could* feel. At times, it could be very difficult to distinguish where my authentic pain over my sister's death ended and where a performative emotionality, a giving over to the drama opened up by *Alison,* began.

AS MY surveillance spread so, too, did Clive Richardson's power over my life. Before I began to follow him on his walks, he had been contained by the Little Sweet. It had been possible for me to leave him behind not just physically, but also mentally and emotionally—to go to the gym, for instance, and spend forty minutes on the elliptical feeling inferior to the cellulite-free woman on the machine beside me, and wonder what it must be like to have thighs like that, and remind myself that everybody has problems and surely this woman was no exception, and ponder what they might be, and imagine her cowering on a staircase as a girl, listening to her parents yell and throw things, and then, when she wiped down her machine and our eyes met briefly, to smile at her with great sympathy, and only afterward, as I engaged in some perfunctory stretching on a mat strewn with unnerving hairs, realize that I had not thought of Clive in over an hour. But once I began to follow him, he broke free. His routines became my routines, his patterns my patterns.

One night, he stopped at a church and went inside. I sat on a bench at a nearby bus stop to wait. He was not inside long, maybe ten minutes, and when he emerged, his face was composed. Whatever he had been praying over, I could discern no trace of it. Another evening, he walked by a bodega with buckets of rot-edged roses and blue daisies out front. As he passed them, he reached out his hand and skimmed his fingertips ever so lightly against the flowers.

ALISON HAD kept a diary. It wasn't the usual thing, no lock-and-key notebook with *KEEP OUT!!!* on the cover. It was an audio diary, recorded on one of those cassette players for children with a pink plastic microphone. The player had been mine originally, a birthday gift loaded with parental intentions for the shy child—*Look how much fun you'll have singing, Clairey!* I never used it and at some point Alison appropriated it for her own purposes. Many nights she retreated to her bedroom and recorded. I think she enjoyed hearing herself talk. I don't mean she was vain, nothing like that. I used to sit on the floor outside her room, letting her muffled voice wash over me with the distinct sense that on the other side of the closed door something sacred was transpiring—my sister's soul, bared to the night.

I knew my parents had the cassettes because when I was eighteen I had asked my mother what happened to them. She told me they were in the box on the top shelf of the hall closet, along with Alison's dance trophies and yearbooks and jazz shoes. When I asked if my parents had listened to them, my mother's face tightened. She was going to cry, and I felt at once guilty and angry. Guilty because I had known my question would upset her and had asked it anyway, angry because I was the child and she was the mother and shouldn't she be making things easier for me, not the other way around? "I started to once," she said. "But I only listened for a minute or two. It wasn't right."

On an evening in late October, I called my mother; it was just after six P.M. in New York, dark and cold.

"It's so good to hear from you, sweetie." This was what she always said, as if I were doing some extraordinary kindness by calling her. I winced. I pictured her in their sunny kitchen, living a falsely warm, bright existence—didn't she know it was really night? Didn't she know it was almost winter?

"You caught me in the middle of making white gazpacho. I rediscovered the recipe in this ancient cookbook I bought after college. Very *woo-woo*." She laughed self-deprecatingly. "You marinate cucumbers, green grapes, bread, and almonds in salt and let it sit a few hours. Then you puree it and whisk in some yogurt. Isn't that a neat technique?"

My mother could always be counted on to prattle about something we both knew neither of us cared about—the plot of a movie she'd seen with my father, a charity auction she had attended and the offerings donated by various local businesses, a nifty trick she'd learned for chopping onions without crying. (She would send me the YouTube.) My mother was not a superficial woman. She was, in fact, in possession of a piercing intelligence, but for some maddening reason she seemed determined to keep this a secret. She'd been a literature major in college. According to family lore, she was solely responsible for getting our father through his own college coursework. ("Your mother's so smart she tricked me into being the breadwinner," he was fond of saying.) On our bookshelves at home, dispersed among our father's legal procedurals and thick biographies of great American leaders, were my mother's volumes of poetry and the slender, peculiar novels of a female Brazilian writer with whom she was enamored. On Saturday mornings when I was a child, as our family life went on noisily around her, my mother would sit on the couch in the living room with her feet curled beneath her and read as if she were alone in a quiet room, which, in her mind, I think she was. But she never spoke to us about the things she read, and when she set down the book she became our mother again, concerned with locating shin guards and checking worksheets, a woman so ordinary and unglamorous that I remember Alison once theorizing to me that she and Aunt Caroline couldn't possibly be blood sisters—one of them must have been switched at birth, or the product of an illicit affair. I think Alison and I both grew up feeling that our mother kept the best of herself *to* herself, that she was guarding something, protecting something, from *us*. So, no, my mother was not a naturally superficial woman; superficiality was a thing she had chosen, and after Alison's death she chose it more and more. I think she was terribly lonely in Pasadena, despite the busy social life she maintained there; it was an existential loneliness that had everything to do with Alison and that therefore could not be cured. With her bland chatter, I think she was trying to talk her way out of the loneliness, to paper over all the unspoken things, but it never worked, it was all still there, and so she went on talking, and hoping, and talking.

"Very neat," I said.

"I made it once years ago but I forgot all about it. I was cleaning out— I've been trying to clean out the bookcases, and—"

"Mom."

"Hmm?"

"I was wondering. You know Alison's diaries?"

"Yes."

"Would you mind sending them to me?"

She was quiet a moment. "Sure, sweetheart," she said finally. "I'll make copies and pop them in the mail as soon as I can."

I knew she would not ask my reasons for making this request, what had happened or what I was thinking and feeling that made me want them. I didn't even bother proffering a made-up explanation. It was a little unkind of me, and I knew that; my request surely made her worry, and I could easily have told her something to assuage her concern, but I didn't. But you have to understand how much it hurt. No, *Honey, are you sure?* No, *Do you think that's really the best thing?* My mother hid away in her fragile sweetness, and I hated her for the ironic way her fragility protected her.

A COLD, clear night. Clive left the Little Sweet and headed east for some time before coming to a stop; beneath the glare of a single post light, teenage boys, T-shirts billowing from their bodies, were playing basketball on a chain-link court. Off to the side, a few young boys of about five or six played their own small game. Clive stood with his hands resting against the fence and watched. What was it about this scene that so held his attention? I stood some distance away and watched him watching the boys. They seemed to strobe with toughness and sensitivity, the two forces held in an uneasy tension. A boy dribbled the ball gracefully between his legs one moment, barreled into a defender the next. One of the young boys imitated his movements, then forgot the game and stooped to examine the clover growing up through cracks in the blacktop. A man in a tracksuit swaggered down the street in front of me, a tuckered-out girl in a tutu asleep in his arms. On the sidelines of the basketball game, a boy, still in his school uniform, punched a square of gum out of a foil packet and placed it boldly, tentatively, on a girl's waiting tongue.

There were girls and women, too, of course. Heading home from work in suits and pumps, in scrubs. Mothers with children. Clusters of adolescent girls with rhinestones on the back pockets of their jeans. But it was the men and boys I watched. I admit I had not done very much thinking about the inner lives of men. I was a girl with a sister. With my boyfriends, I saw now, I had never dug beneath the surface to find them where they hid. Perhaps I didn't want their pain to compete with my own. Perhaps my story, my tragedy, had a forbidding power over men, and I enjoyed that. Or perhaps, knowing that a man, or men, had killed my sister, I was afraid of what I might find if I looked too closely—gentleness that turned over to shame that turned over to rage; ugly, unshakable desires—qualities that might suggest a universal masculine poison I did not want to know about because it would doom me to be alone forever.

Clive continued down the sidewalk. He stopped at a newsstand and purchased a cup of coffee, which he drank as he headed north. A few minutes later, without breaking his stride, he tossed the dregs of the coffee into the street with a quick, dispassionate flick of his wrist.

THE MATERIAL on Alison was endless, so much it seemed I would never get through it. Information on Clive Richardson and Edwin Hastie, by comparison, was thin at best. One day, I told my boss I needed to consult the archives at the New York Public Library to research some details about the Cornish coast in *The Girl from Pendeen* which she had asked me to confirm, and I spent the afternoon at the main branch, searching the catalog for anything I could find that mentioned Clive and Edwin. My first discovery was an academic text, *Dark Travels: Thanatourism, Theory and Practice.*

CONTENTS

PART 1: ASPECTS OF THANATOURISM

Mediations: The Living and the Dead in Public Space
Milking the Macabre: Ethical Considerations
Kitschification and Mass-Consumption
Hospitality in Hostile Spaces: Towards a New Model

PART 2: FORMS AND FUNCTIONS

Genocide Tourism
Homicide Tourism
Disaster Tourism

PART 3: FUTURE RESEARCH DIRECTIONS

To my disappointment, the book contained only the briefest relevant passage, from the chapter on "Homicide Tourism":

. . . While Genocide Tourism is generally structured by government and nonprofit institutions, Homicide Tourism is often ad hoc, and thus represents an economic opportunity for independent local operators. Examples include Kristján Jóhannsson, who leads tours of Keflavik in southwest Iceland, a site of interest in the Guðmundur and Geirfinnur case; and Desmond Phillips, whose guided tours of the island of Saint X include visits to the houses of Edwin Hastie and Clive Richardson, suspects in the Alison Thomas murder, and a boat ride to the nearby cay where her body was recovered for a fish fry lunch. This essay will focus on the case of the Tyrolean village of Zinn am Alberg, which has rebuilt its local economy, previously dominated by dairy farming and the production of Tyrolean speck, around tourism related to the gruesome 1975 murders of the members of the Krenn family. . . .

The next few books were no more informative. An encyclopedia of unsolved mysteries. A media studies dissertation on the differing portrayals of black and white female victims of violent crime from 1970 to 2000. I had high hopes for *A Handbook History of Saint X,* the only book I'd been able to find that focused exclusively on the island. It turned out to be a self-published monograph by a retired customs worker named David Webster, a hundred spiral-bound pages, peripatetic and ambitious in its scope, with five-page chapters on such topics as the history of the salt trade and the entirety of Amerindian civilization on the island.

From Chapter 8, "1950 to the Present Time":

. . . The death of Alison Thomas on Faraway Cay (see Chapter 11: Folklore), had effects upon our island as deleterious as any hurricane. It has been speculated that the closing of the Grand Caribbee and three restaurants on Mayfair Road in a single season may be entirely attributable to the aforementioned scandal. This scandal had the additional effect of dividing the island over the question of whether its primary suspects, Misters Hastie and Richardson, were the innocent victims of a scapegoating mission by the American press, or, alternately and, this author believes, accurately, the parties responsible for single-handedly causing an economic downturn that endured for years and bringing international notoriety to our island and its people. . . .

From Chapter 11, "Folklore":

. . . Tales about the woman on Faraway Cay are prevalent. In the most widespread account of her origin, she washed up on Faraway many centuries ago in a hurricane. Nobody knows from where she came, but she can never return because as is well known, dark spirits cannot cross salt water, as a result of which she is trapped on the cay for eternity. She has white skin and long black hair and hooves for feet. Mention must be made of her odd gait, which appears in many versions of the tale, and is widely believed to be what draws people to her, as humans cannot resist that dash of salt in their sweet.

As the stories go, she lures people to cure her loneliness. She leads them across the cay and they give chase, desperate to touch some of her wildness. At last, she escorts them to the waterfall at the island's center. She allows them to draw near, but when they reach out to grasp her, she slips away into the mist. They try to follow after her and are drowned. A popular version has it that a new goat appears on Faraway Cay for every person who vanishes there. It is said that you can see the humanness in their eyes. . . .

I shut the book in disgust. A woman with hooves for feet. Humans turned to goats. Had my sister's body been dumped in that waterfall as some kind of sick joke? *Look, the woman on Faraway Cay did it! Hahaha.*

It wasn't until that moment that I realized that, from the time I was a small child, I'd found some solace in the fact that Alison had been found somewhere so beautiful. How many small, unconscious coping mechanisms, how many pretty notions, would be taken from me before I uncovered the truth?

I opened Google Maps on my laptop, a self-punishing impulse—to lay eyes on it, to force myself to picture her there, her body beneath all that water for days. But Faraway Cay did not even appear on Google Maps. Where I knew the cay must be, there was only blue.

I FOLLOWED Clive for many nights and many miles. In all that time, excepting the evening when I called his name and he responded with such terror, I never heard his voice. His nights were composed of enormous stretches of silence, and this silence was now mine, too. I would return home near midnight and realize I hadn't uttered a word since leaving work at five-thirty. Sometimes I would speak—"Hello, hello, hello," "My name is Emily," "Today is Tuesday"—just to prove to myself that I was still real. I did not hear him speak, nor did I observe any other evidence to suggest that his life connected meaningfully with anyone else's. Clive Richardson was a man hiding in plain sight, drawing no attention and leaving no trace upon the minds of others. He was an island, isolated and impenetrable.

IT WENT on like this. And something began to happen. At the beginning of each walk, I would be filled with the fear I described earlier, with a sense of the danger posed by Clive and the risk that I was taking in following him. But after thirty minutes, an hour, the experience shifted. It happened without my noticing, like slipping from waking to dreaming. It no longer felt like I was following him, but like we were on this walk together, linked. Eventually, even this *we* faded away; it was no longer the two of us traveling these dark streets, but a single mind, a memory, endeavoring through the *step, step, step* of these constitutionals to travel beyond some perimeter it could never seem to reach. If we kept walking long enough, I would be seized by the certainty that we were not alone; we were being watched, trailed by figures who flickered on the periphery, shrouded in darkness. A hand reaching out, beckoning. The pounding of hooves. A flare of laughter, rising from the streets like steam, then gone. *Shh. Don't tell.*

ON HALLOWEEN, the old woman in my building sat on the front stoop in her white sneakers distributing Good & Plenty to crestfallen fairies and firefighters. I had been invited to a party at the apartment of a college friend on Pineapple Street and decided that I would go. I'd fallen into arrears with my friends, ignoring messages and invitations; attending seemed an efficient means of digging myself out. The party was an annual thing, and in prior years I'd spent quite a bit of time and effort thinking up and executing my costume—the year before, if memory serves, I'd gone as Frida Kahlo. But this year I had neither the time nor the inclination, and so I put on brown pants and a brown sweater, picked up a few twigs from the tree outside my apartment, and declared myself a tree. My non-costume turned out to be a hit, and at first I was having a pretty good time, sliding into the social rhythm I hadn't realized I'd missed. Gin and tonic in a Solo cup. Jackie squealing, "Where have you *been,* girl?" as she petted my shoulder. Laden chitchat with a guy I'd hooked up with a few months earlier. A group of us climbing the ladder to the peach-soft roof to pass around a joint—smoke and cold air and the stark sounds of our laughter against the glitter of Manhattan across the water.

But when I climbed back down into the hot, raucous party everything was wrong. I looked around—there was a girl dressed as a Warhol painting, her face covered in red dots; Jackie was a "sexy farmer," a canny critique of the Sexy Halloween Costume that nevertheless allowed her to show off her midriff. My gaze pinged from face to face in the semidarkness. What was I doing here? Clive was out there, and I was not with him. I tried to get myself to stay, to enjoy myself, but I was startled to find that I could no longer tolerate a night away from him. I slipped out early without saying goodbye.

Looking back, I can see that my pursuit of Clive Richardson was beginning to be about something more than gathering clues, that I was falling under the grip of something I could not control. But I did not allow myself to see this then. Maybe if I had, it all could have ended differently.

I got a lot of flak for publishing my memoir. People said it was a shameless cash grab. I got called a hanger-on, a fame whore, a starfucker. I don't think any of those people actually bothered to read my book, because if they had they would have seen that I wrote every word of it straight from my heart.

After I found the girl, I went to therapy. I worked with a life coach. I embraced a vegan diet. I tried Xanax and Zoloft. I got into reiki and did a four-day silent meditation retreat. I even followed this guru for a while. Her hugs were supposed to cure you, it didn't matter what was wrong with you. During her North American tour, I went to see her at the Sheraton near LAX. I waited in line for three hours. When it was my turn, I approached the dais and the guru wrapped me in an embrace so powerful it felt like it originated at the center of my soul. I swear I could feel it wiping everything away. A new beginning. Or so I thought. But on my drive back to Santa Monica, I was stopped in traffic on the 405 and it happened again—the girl appeared in my mind. That bloated white arm, reaching out to me.

My therapist said that intrusive thoughts and images are an extremely common neurological phenomenon. To stop them, I simply needed to retrain my mind; he told me that it is not only possible to rewire the brain's neural pathways, it is easy. Plasticity is exactly what our brains are designed for. Whenever the image of the girl intruded, I was supposed to imagine that I was in the checkout at the grocery store. On the belt were different grocery items and each item was a thought, and the girl was just one of these thoughts, and I knew which items were healthy and which were not, and I could choose which ones I picked up and which ones I put down, and I could watch the unhealthy thoughts travel away down the checkout belt of my mind. I just had to put her down and pick up something else. I spent hours putting down the girl and picking up yogurt, avocados, blueberries. But the longer I spent there, the more I tried not to see her, the more I saw her. The light blue polish on her nails. Her hair swirling upward in the water.

Eventually, I decided my only choice was to accept her into my life. I still see her, but when I do, I just . . . say hi to her. I call her by her name. *Hey there, Ali.* I tell her I like her nail polish. It is not okay, and I don't think it ever will be. But I have found that this way, I can turn her from a body into a girl. And I feel damned proud that I was able to find my own solution when all these supposed experts couldn't help me.

I've been thinking about going back to school to become a licensed mental health counselor. Wouldn't that be a second act nobody expected from me? But actually, I've always wanted to help people. You want to know the real thing the men I dated had in common? It wasn't that they were celebrities. It was that they were broken, broken dudes. He was the most broken of them all. Ironic, isn't it? I made him go to that waterfall because I thought it would heal him, but instead I think it's the thing that broke him for good.

GHOSTS

IT HAS HAPPENED BEFORE. Clive has experienced several periods like this since he arrived in New York nearly two decades ago, seasons of paranoia when the girl is in the wind, when even the hiss of the radiator is full of her fury. It lasts a few days, sometimes as long as several weeks, but eventually things go back to normal. Each time it passes he thinks it will be the last time. It is over, dealt with. But it never is, is it? The old fears, the old voices—*we have found you, we know, everybody knows*—stay dormant for months, years, and then, sure as the tides, they come back.

The littlest thing can set it off. A girl rolling her eyes at her mother in the backseat of his taxi. A whiff of artificial strawberry. During that terrible episode with Sachin, all those years ago, the trigger was nothing more than the hostility with which Sachin looked at him, which made Clive certain that, somehow, Sachin *knew*. This time, it is even smaller than that, a silly mistake. He thought he heard the name that is no longer his, and now she is everywhere. She haunts him, a ghost skulking at the edges of his vision. She shape-shifts, appearing in the forms of other people. She is a girl in an NYU sweatshirt on a delayed subway train, beautifully bored. She is on his block in a pleated charter-school skirt, bathing in the adoration of the boys around her, thrusting out her chin just so. She flashes out from their eyes and catches him in her gaze.

During these intervals, nothing can quell her presence, not his walks, not prayer, for she is inside of him, too, a second self; she feels the freezing floors of his apartment beneath his socked feet, hears a customer berate him over the traffic on the FDR, sees him urinating into a Dasani bottle midshift. She reaps pleasure from each small indignity. It seems to him that this life is her doing. She has strung it together, just so. And he feels an anger at her that will never, ever be spent. Then he wonders what it says about him that he has made her into such a vindictive, punishing ghost.

At night she peers into his dreams. He is with Edwin, surrounded by everyone they know; the people shout and leer and hiss. *We have found you, we know, everybody knows.* Alison looks on from the edge of the crowd, strokes her scar, and smiles.

Old memories come unburied: Dancing with her, kissing her. The twisted string of blue fabric with which her shirt was tied around her neck. The first day he saw her walking down the beach, her stride so nonchalant he knew straightaway she'd be trouble.

Like any ghost, she radiates. She is not content to remain within her own moment. She inhabits them all—not only her aftermath, but also the time before he even knew she existed, until every memory, no matter how sweet, turns bitter on his tongue.

IT WAS no secret that Clive only had eyes for Sara Lycott. She was not one of the girls most of the boys were stuck on—Daphne Nelsen with her long sprinter's legs, or Saffy Lester with her silky hair and cashew skin, or Joy Vernon who had breasts by the time they were eleven. Sara Lycott's eyes were small and black, and they seemed to cast off bright flares of hostility. She had remained adamantly flat-chested, as if purposefully to deny any boy who looked. She and her mother had come to the island from Saint Kitts when she was a baby. Sara's mother, Miss Agatha, claimed to be the widow of a government minister who was killed in an automobile accident just before Sara was born. Clive's grandmother had declared this a "likely story." Sara didn't talk like the rest of them. She spoke properly, like a teacher, even when she was with her friends, and though she was teased for this, she didn't stop.

His devotion to her had been sealed at the Horatio Byrd Primary Christmas Pageant when they were ten. The pageant was the culmination of a week of festivities that included calypso shows and street jams and the lighting of the mahogany trees along Investiture Boulevard. Clive was an ox. His grandmother had dyed cotton batting with tea and sewn it to an old nightshirt of his grandfather's. (Though his grandfather had been dead for years, she still kept his clothes in a wooden bureau in the corner of her bedroom. It was the one soft thing about her, and it would be many years before he understood that this one thing was really an uncountable number of things, that it was merely the material evidence of an entire unseen world that resided within the grandmother he thought he knew completely.) Sara Lycott was Mary. She wore a flowing blue silk gown and a crown of white flowers. Her performance left him spellbound. Not because it was beautiful or heartfelt or pure, for it was none of these things. Rather, she commanded his attention with her magnificent vacancy. She spoke as if she cared not a whit that she was onstage in front of the entire town, playing the role of the Virgin Mary. How could she dare to give so little, to be so utterly elsewhere? When a fourth-grade boy dropped the porcelain dish that was supposed to be myrrh and the pageant fell for a moment into disarray as the wise men stooped to gather the shards, Sara Lycott reached into her dressing gown and pulled forth a square of coconut candy. There, in the middle of the stage, she bit. He could hear the candy crack against her teeth. Then she released the faintest of smiles, a secret smile at a secret pleasure. Was he the only one who had seen it? The other boys barely gave Sara a thought; if they did, it was only to joke and tease—where did such a funny-looking girl get off being so haughty? But in that moment, her prickly exterior had parted to reveal the truth of her. From then on, all he wanted was to be let back in.

He could not speak to her. By the time he moved from Horatio Byrd to Everett Lyle Secondary, his stutter had mostly faded, but in Sara's presence it came rushing back and took hold of him utterly, so that not only his tongue but his limbs, his organs, the very air inside him, were twisted and bound. His friends reaped endless amusement from this.

"Gogo, ask Sara if she wants to come to Rocky Shoal with we."

"Gogo, ask Sara if we can copy she maths."

"Gogo, Sara left she notebook. Here. Give it back to she," Don said one day in the schoolyard, shoving a yellow notebook against Clive's chest.

Sara was across the yard, giggling with her friends in a bunch tight and lovely as a flower bud. When they saw him approaching they glared at him, a wall of feminine scrutiny that withered his dick to nothing.

"Why, thank you," Sara said when he wordlessly handed her the notebook. The girls were varnishing one another's nails. In the heat, the fumes made him woozy. "How are you doing today, Clive?"

She was the only one apart from his teachers and his grandmother who ever called him Clive. He was at once proud and terrified to be called his proper name by her, to have her attention on him in this way, though he also suspected that it had nothing to do with him; probably, she called him Clive simply because she would not deign to let so foolish a name as Gogo cross her lips.

She smiled. She was tiny as a spider. The way she looked up at him, craning her neck, emphasized his bigness until he felt as if the edges of himself may as well have been miles away, for all he could do to control them.

"I'm well, and y-y-y-you?"

"Quite well, thank you."

She had the power to bind his tongue and she enjoyed it. She turned away from him and thrust out her hand so Saffy Lester could continue varnishing her nails.

He stumbled back across the yard to where his friends were doubled over with laughter.

"Check you out, ladies' man," Des said.

"Wise up, bred. Why you try to love a thing that will never love you back?" Don said.

"'Sides, I hear she mama crazy crazy," Damien said.

Edwin patted him on the back. "Don't listen to these fools, Goges. Someday that girl will be yours for true. And when she is, you remember it was me who knew it would be so all along."

GOGO AND Edwin got drunk for the first time when they were fourteen. They were walking home from school one day when Edwin stopped on Underhill Road and struck up a conversation with Jan, a Dutchman who had been on the island as long as they could remember. He wore linen tunics and leather sandals, and he could almost always be found sipping from a paper bag in the shade of one building or another in the Basin. When Jan asked if they cared for a drink, Edwin said, "Sure," as if this were something they did all the time. Jan led them to a bar called Paulette's Place, where he bought a bottle of Olde English. The three of them drank it together at the bar. When the liquid burned down Clive's throat he was back in his mother's kitchen, sitting on Vaughn's lap, the glinting faces of strangers laughing around him. He tilted his glass back again.

"An old pro, are we?" Jan said, and patted his back.

Edwin raised his glass in the air, then took a quick sip. "Sweet like a woman," he said.

"Truth," Clive replied, though neither of them had yet known a woman's taste.

THAT SAME year, for a few weeks, Edwin and Clive and their friends were seized by boxing fever. As soon as the last bell rang, they traveled in a pack down the center of Gould Road—cars honking at them to move to the side, which they didn't—to Don's house, because his father was in Tortola and his mother didn't get off work until seven. Don's family was worse off than most of theirs. The galvanized roof of his house was badly rusted. Scrawny chickens stalked the yard, pecking at the dirt. There was a rubbish heap nearly hidden in scrub. Against the house, a few desiccated pepper plants grew out of old Nido canisters. The boys liked the roughness of this. In Don's yard their jaws clenched. Their gaits simmered with an itchy energy.

They would stand in a circle and send two from among their ranks into the center. They placed bets. They jeered and clapped and egged each other on. When the sun began to set they squared up with one another, trading coins that were sour and warm from their pockets. Then they dispersed, each sore, bruised boy making his own way down the familiar roads to the lights of home.

When Clive thinks of his youth, it's this brief span of afternoons that pulses most insistently in his memory. They were after something. They ought to have been men, or so they feared, and they were trying to teach themselves the things men should know. None of them expected him to be any good, and he wasn't. Big, clumsy Gogo. He punched the air, dodged too slow, got his lip split over and over.

There was a girl from their form who liked to come around. Her name was Berline, Bery for short, and she was a solid, heavy-shouldered girl who wore her uniform loose, the maroon plaid skirt coming down to her shins. Bery had her heart set on boxing. She showed up every afternoon, lingering and begging to be included. "I been practicing with my brother," she told them one afternoon. "He says I'm better than he."

"We don't want you to get hurt, Bery," Don told her in a voice syrupy with false concern.

"What's it to any of you if I get hurt? You all does hate me."

"Go away, Bery," Des said in a bored voice. "Can't you see where you're not wanted?"

Bery marched right up to Des. "I'm just asking for one go."

"Sure, Bery," Edwin chimed in. "We'll let you have a go."

"You will?"

"Why not? You is waiting a long time now. Gogo!"

"Me?" he whispered.

"No, my other mate Gogo. Yes, you! Get in there and give Bery she turn."

"I don't want to go with no Gogo! He the worst of all you."

Don got up in her face. "You want your turn or not, Bery?"

She grabbed the gloves angrily from him and stepped into the center. Gogo followed. The worst one, good enough only for the girl. He could hear his friends sniggering as they placed their bets:

"My money's on Bery; her face all wreck like a boxer already."

"Put me on Gogo. Even he can beat a girl. If she even *be* a girl."

They met in the center, glove to glove. He could feel the humiliation in his eyes connecting with the rage in hers, sending off heat.

Don counted down from three and stepped aside.

Gogo swung.

He felt the impact of his punch like biting into a mango and letting the flesh fill your mouth. Then he heard her scream, saw her hands fly to her face. The circle fell apart as the boys rushed in.

"Bery, you okay?"

"Let we see your face."

When she took her hands away, Clive swooned. Blood spilled from her nose over her lips.

"Shit, Gogo. She all cut!"

Bery scrambled to her feet and ran off, hands over her face. When she was gone, the boys began to laugh.

"What's wrong with you, man? Breaking she nose!"

"Figure he finally throw a good punch *now*."

Gogo looked from face to face to face. When he saw Edwin, laughing with the rest of them, he was seized by an urge to run at his friend and tackle him to the ground. It was Edwin's fault. He had made this happen, matching him up with her. The blood had been thick and gummy, like the strawberry syrup at Milk Queen.

But when the sun went down and the boys dispersed for the evening, Edwin walked over to Clive.

"What you want?" Clive muttered, and kept walking.

"Come on, Goges, don't be like that!"

"Get dead, Edwin," Clive shouted behind him.

"Slow up, man!" Edwin sprinted after him. "I'm sorry, okay? For true." He put his skinny arm around Clive's shoulders, and though Clive wanted to shove his friend off, he didn't. "You know, I think you finally rid we of she for good," Edwin said. He grinned mischievously, like this had been their secret plan all along, the two of them. And Clive felt better. He smiled back at his friend. Together, they walked the darkening roads home.

WHEN THEY were fifteen, the island's first big resort, the Oasis, opened on the south coast. A year later came the Grand Caribbee, and then, in quick succession, Salvation Point, the Villas at Sugar Cove, the Oleander, and Indigo Bay. The arrival of the resorts brought other changes. Sir Randall Corwin Airport underwent a massive expansion and began offering direct flights from New York and Miami. It became unremarkable to see a white family gnawing on jerk chicken legs at Spicy's. The sleepy streets near the island's only deepwater port were renamed Hibiscus Harbour as part of an initiative by the island's Tourist Board; Victorian façades were put up on the fronts of the buildings and stores opened selling duty-free perfume and timepieces, T-shirts and batik sarongs, Cuban cigars and souvenir bric-a-brac: palm frond hats and seashell picture frames and bottles of local sand. The port was rebuilt with berthing facilities for fifty yachts and a jetty that could accommodate up to three cruise ships. Within a few years, the island became a popular stop on cruise itineraries; during the high season, Carnival and Celebrity and Royal Caribbean ships moored at the port daily and disgorged thousands of tourists, and as many as half a dozen competing steel bands waited on the jetty to greet them. Paradise Karaoke opened, then Papa Mango's, which became notorious for its thirty-two-ounce frozen cocktails.

The first of their friends to get a job at one of the resorts was Des's older brother Keithley, who became head of water sports at Salvation Point when they were sixteen and Keithley was twenty-two. The resort offered windsurfing and sailing. There were two speedboats for snorkeling excursions. If for whatever mysterious reason the guests wished to, they could cling to a bright yellow banana boat and get dragged back and forth across the bay. At night as the boys drank and smoked wherever they were drinking and smoking that night—at Paulette's Place, or behind Arthur's father's shop (for by then Arthur had given up his honor student ways and was drinking more than any of them)—Keithley regaled them with stories from work. He had watched parents chase young children across the sand for hours like fools, and a child turn inconsolable when his Shirley Temple arrived with only one cherry. His feet had been vomited upon by a middle-aged woman who drank four rum punches before she rode the banana boat. He had been told to "Take it easy, *mon*," when he insisted that a man wear a life preserver to go sailing, as the resort required. He had gazed upon the supine bodies of teenage daughters and honeymooning young wives as they worked on their tans in the tropical sun.

Keithley had been at the job a few months when he showed up at Paulette's one night with a small key in his hand. They waited until after midnight, then six of them piled into Keithley's car and drove across the island to Salvation Point. He killed the lights and the engine at the entrance to the service road and coasted down the hill to the parking lot. They hurried across the resort grounds.

"Shit, man, check this place!" Don said as they snuck past the main deck with its three swimming pools. When they reached the sand, they broke into a sprint. They pulled off their T-shirts and dashed through the soft waves of low tide with their shirts held in their hands above their heads, to where the speedboat was moored some twenty meters out. Des reeled up the anchor and whispered, "Now! Now!" Keithley turned the key and they sped away from the lights of the resort and out into the night.

For a few weeks, until they got caught and Keithley was fired, they spent their nights joyriding. (After Keithley was dismissed, he would work for a spell at the gas station on George Street before trying his luck in London returning three years later with a wife and a son, Jamie, who would die at nine, the freak consequence of a collision on the football pitch behind

Horatio Byrd Primary, one of those moments you could puzzle over for the rest of your life—the millimeters and milliseconds by which you had been given this fate in place of all others.) They cut through the placid waters off the coast and limed on one beach or another; they drank and smoked, tussled in the shallows, blasted Public Enemy and Run-DMC, and shouted up at the stars, which wheeled overhead so fine and bright it hurt to try to understand what they were. Just to be a little bad. During the day, the beaches belonged to the snorkelers and picnickers. At night, they became theirs.

From the boat, they discovered coves you couldn't see from land because they were hidden behind thick scrub. One night, they found a small crescent of sand surrounded on three sides by steep rock faces. They returned the next night with a rope. Keithley scrambled up the rocks and tied the rope to a tree at the top of the cliff. They returned to this spot often. They would climb the rope from the beach to the top of the cliff and stand, toes curled over the edge, the moon like a massive searchlight on the water.

"Do it! Do it!"

"Don't pussy out, bro!"

"Three-two-one, man!"

The fleeting infinity between when his feet left the edge and when the water sucked him under was the closest to weightless Clive had ever felt. Don, Des, Edwin, Damien, Keithley—each of them in turn left the world ever so briefly behind. You could hear cars from the top of the cliff; they were less than a five-minute walk through the scrub from Mayfair Road, and from there it was less than half a mile to Indigo Bay, yet nobody saw them, or knew this spot. It was a nameless place on an island where they knew the name of every last dog and dinky fishing boat—a promise that this world, these lives, could break open.

"Someday when I'm making mad cheddar in New York I'm gonna build a mansion right up there, so close to the edge when you look out the window you just see sea," Edwin declared one night. It was three A.M., and they were lying on the sand at the base of the cliffs with the radio turned down low.

"Cheddar," Don snorted. "Man, quit your Yankin'. You're not going to no New York."

"Up yours, Don. Anyway, is what you know about it? When I'm in

Brooklyn and you all still live with your mummies, you better not be expecting any barrel from *me*!"

"We'll be sure to keep that in mind," Damien said.

"What you want with New York anyway?" Don asked. "Why freeze your rod off doing shit work there when you can do it here where the weather fine?"

"And hang with we at Little Beach on your day off?" Des added.

"And with we youths," Clive whispered. He was so stoned his own words flew at his skin like wind.

"With we youths!" Don gasped, slapping his knee. "What the ass you talking about, man?"

"Nah, nah, he right!" Des shouted. "The Goges see it clear! All we liming in the shade with some Cruzan, and we wifeys making chat, and we sons playing windball in the sand."

For a moment they were quiet as the vision Des had painted seemed to take life above them in the dark sky.

"We wifeys nagging and we babies whining, you mean," Edwin said. "Anyway, I'm not gonna be doing no shit work in New York. I got plans, what you think?"

"Hear that, breds?" Don said. "Edwin gonna be a big man! What I think? I think you're full of shit. I think ten years from now you still living with your fat sisters. I think you gonna dead here, same as all we. Except the Doc here."

Damien smiled modestly. He was smart, so smart that he was able to lime with them every night while rising, quietly, to the top of their class at school. Though they teased him for his diligence, they were proud that he was theirs.

"The frig you know about it?" Edwin continued. "I'll swim off this island, come to that. Gogo will come with me."

"I'm shit at swimming," Clive said.

Edwin pinched the fat on his shoulder. "You buoyant." Edwin shrugged. "You'll float."

"Shit, it's late," Keithley said. "We gotta get back."

They gathered their things, waded through the shallows to the boat, and rode the calm waters back to Salvation Point. On the boat, Clive, too stoned to sit up, lay on the floor and let the wind blow over his open eyes as he stared up at the sky. New York was Edwin's dream, and though he spoke of it as a place they would go to together, Clive sensed the unlikeliness of this; instead, Edwin's desire for New York seemed to prefigure a future in which he would be left behind—on the island, and in the past.

For hours after that, until his grandmother woke him the next morning, he could feel Edwin's fingers on his shoulder as if they were still there, like the ghost of someone who was already gone.

"WE LIMING on Faraway tonight," Keithley declared as the boat sped away from shore one evening.

"We can't," Clive blurted out before he could stop himself.

"Why not?" Keithley asked.

Clive looked down at his hands. "You know why," he mumbled. In his mind he saw her—the long black hair hiding her face. Hooves for feet.

Keithley clapped his hands in delight. "Goges, man, don't tell me you still believe that old-folk fuckery."

"But my great-auntie disappear there!"

"Who don't have a great-auntie who disappear there?" Des said.

"Don't stress, Gogo. If she turn you into a goat, we'll set you up fine in my yard," Don said.

"Beside, if that sket would choose any of we to lure away with she, it would be me," Edwin said.

"Is that so?" Damien said.

"A lady all alone like that needs a man who can sort she out proper. Can I help it if all the ladies know I'm the only man for the job?"

As Keithley slowed the boat and guided it to shore, Clive was filled with an unease he felt helpless to counteract. The other boys climbed down the ladder and hopped into the shallows one by one. When it was his turn, Clive couldn't move.

Then he heard Edwin's voice in his ear. "It's okay, man."

"But my mum—"

He knew he should be past believing, but he couldn't rid himself of the story. It was what he had of her; it was the pocket watch, Bible, lock of hair she'd left behind for him.

"To hell with she. You don't need no mum. You have a brother."

Clive climbed down into the water, with Edwin right behind him. The moon that night was so bright they didn't even need the flashlights they'd brought. Beneath its light, the sand seemed to glow white—in his memory of it, it almost looked like snow. He hesitated again before he stepped ashore, shaken by the feeling that he was about to break something that could never be put back together. He glanced back at Edwin, who nudged him forward.

"Hurry up, you fools! We going to check out the goat lady's watering hole or what?" Don called.

"Wait up!" Clive shouted. Together, he and Edwin sprinted up the sand.

It was one of those nights whose every pleasure is multiplied by all the future moments when, you imagine, you and your friends will gather and reminisce about it. They tramped through the jungle in the moonlight, casting behind them a trail of crisps bags and still-smoking roaches. When they came upon a goat, they shouted and chased it into the bush, whooping with delight. At the waterfall, they peeled off their shorts and cannonballed in. They swam and roughhoused and pulled off stunts—leaping from the highest rocks, pratfalling into the water, swimming under the falls' churn and shouting "Fuck Daphne!" and "Fuck Joy!" and fuck all the other girls who wouldn't fuck them into the obliterating roar. As the night rose, growing wilder and wilder still, Clive felt himself sending it all away— the stories and the ghosts. His mum.

Later, they returned to the beach. Too drunk to make their way back to the mainland, they lay down on the shore, using their balled-up shirts for pillows and letting the soft sand love their stoned, tingling skin as the sound of small waves rocked them to sleep. That was the night they had everything. The night they brought friendship to the divine edge.

And the girl was already there. As they leapt and roughhoused and plunged into that cool, clean water she was beneath them, at the bottom of the pool, waiting to undo them.

Tuition for Jayson and Stasia at Porter's International School. A Manchester United jersey for Jayson. Stasia's pink dress for prom. A satellite dish with eight hundred channels. Life insurance. Jemma's salon visits. Her annual shopping trip to Saint Kitts. Bikes for Christmas. Our house in Crofton Hills. A loan to Don when he was hard up. A surprise trip to Kingston with Jayson to see Man-U play the Jamaican national team. Miss Verna to clean the house weekly. Jemma's smooth hands. Stasia's acne treatment. Jayson's club football fees. The headstone for little Jamie's grave, pure granite. The diamond on Jemma's finger.

I used to feel mad guilty over all of it. We never could have lived this way if I didn't start giving these tours. Pawning off my friendship with Edwin and Clive as secret insider information. Alison Thomas: Behind the Headlines, I call it. Ninety dollars a person, kids under twelve half price. On the tours, I'm careful to call it an unexplained death, not a murder. As if that makes what I'm doing any better.

I tried to stop once. I told Jemma it was dirty money and I had to put an end to it.

She took my face in her hands and made me look her right in the eyes. "Don't you ever apologize for providing for this family. You're a good man. You hear me, Desmond Phillips? You're a good man leading a good life."

I want to believe that.

If it weren't me, I guess it would just be somebody else getting rich driving Yankees past the houses where Edwin and Gogo came up, and the building where Paulette's used to be, and boating folks out to Faraway. But it's not somebody else, it's me. They were my brothers.

VOICES

My name is Alison Brianne Thomas. I am fifteen years old and this afternoon I ceased to be a virgin. I've been thinking that I should keep a record of my life so that someday when I'm completely bored with my suburban-lady existence, which I really hope I never have, I can listen to myself and remember what I used to be like and maybe I'll shake some sense into myself or something. Anyway, I figure today is the perfect day to start.

The first thing you should know is that this afternoon you cut dance rehearsal. You put on a fantastic performance for Mrs. Conyers about your horrible period cramps, which you obviously didn't have, and you went to Drew's house. The crazy thing is, after all this time, we didn't plan it. Today when I woke up I just felt different. I knew today was the day. Honestly? I didn't really enjoy it. The actual act was sort of uncomfortable. But that's fine. I'm not one of those idiots who thinks her first time has to be some perfect whatever. It's knowing I've done it that matters.

Anyway, when it was over Drew kissed my neck all over. I love when he does that. It just . . . gets to me in the best way. He kept whispering over and over, "You're so beautiful. You're so beautiful." Middle-aged Alison, wherever you are and whatever you're doing, I hope you have that. I mean, I'm not a dingbat, I know it probably won't be with Drew. But I hope you have someone who feels that way about you. The neck kissing. I love that.

IT HAD taken my mother several weeks to make duplicates of the tapes and send them to me. I imagined her hovering over them, fretting about whether to grant my request. When I returned home from work one evening in early November and saw the box addressed to me in my mother's handwriting in the building's foyer, it took me a minute to realize what it was. Opening it up on my bed, I saw that there were dozens of tapes, many more than I had expected. My mother had even taken the time to photocopy their labels, each one in my sister's bubbly teenage penmanship: "Frosh," "Sweet 16," "Seniorz," "Summah!" They were arranged in chronological order, beginning with "Fifteen" (the *i* dotted with a heart). At once, I put this tape into the dusty brown cassette player I'd purchased weeks earlier at a pawnshop on Flatbush Avenue and pressed play.

As soon as the first entry ended and Alison's voice faded to silence, I stopped the tape. With trembling hands I took the cassette out of the player and put it back in its case. For weeks, I had been waiting to listen to these tapes, to be held and soothed by my older sister's voice. But the voice on the tape was not what I had imagined at all. Alison sounded so much younger than I had expected, so shockingly girlish, and I was filled with shame. I was an adult listening to the private confessions of a child. Why on earth had I expected anything different? Then and there, I vowed I wouldn't listen to any more.

For a while, I managed it. I kept myself busy. I'd fallen terribly behind at work, and I endeavored to catch up—reading manuscripts, combing through the mixed reviews of the new Mann for phrases that, with a few strategically placed ellipses, might suggest positive endorsement. At night, I walked with Clive. Flowers outside of a bodega. Boys on playing fields. *Special! Persimmons!*

One night I had a work function to attend—one of our books was a number one *New York Times* best seller, and the whole office was going to happy hour at a bar in midtown to celebrate. I calculated that I could easily put in an appearance and make it to the Little Sweet in time to join Clive on his nightly sojourn. But the Q stalled on the Manhattan Bridge for over twenty minutes. It was announced that a rider on another train was in medical distress, and as I sat there, waiting with increasing impatience for us to move again, I decided this rider was a man who'd gotten stumbling drunk at his own happy hour, and I hated him as the minutes slipped away. When at last I arrived at Church Avenue, I dashed up the stairs and down the block. I arrived at the Little Sweet breathless, but I was too late. He was already gone. I would have to wait an entire day to see him again, an amount of time that felt no different than an eternity.

When I arrived back at my apartment, the man in the NASCAR hat was just coming in from walking Jefe, and he held the door open for me. Jefe, who had never paid me any attention, began to growl, a deeper and more menacing sound than I'd thought the poor animal capable of producing. "*Cállate*," the man said. The dog lunged at me. His little claws scraped at my tights. He bared his tiny yellow teeth. The man jerked the leash and scolded him, plainly shocked at his dog's behavior, but Jefe would not stop. He glared up at me with his milk-white eyes.

"I'm sorry," I said, though what I was apologizing for I couldn't explain—it seemed to me that I had been seen by this pitiful creature, naked right down to my soul. I fled down the stairs to my apartment. Quickly, before reason or willpower could creep back in, I plunged my hands under my bed, yanked out the package from my mother, and threw the cassette back in the player.

I just had this memory I haven't thought about in forever. When I was really young we had this tape of Irish folk songs I was totally obsessed with. I used to jig around the living room in my nightie. I remember singing along, trying to do this Irish accent which I thought was so romantic, and in my head I was one hundred percent prancing across the highlands in a tartan dress, which I guess is actually Scottish, but you get the idea. I was, what? Five years old? And I already sensed that there was this thing missing from my world. Like, depth. Or maybe, rootedness. I already got that I was from a totally superficial place. People do not exactly write books or make movies about their poignant childhoods in Westchester, you know? My family doesn't really have a heritage, or a religion, or any of that. Alison. What even is that name? I'm not named after anyone. It doesn't have some meaning. My parents just thought it sounded nice, as, apparently, did a million other parents, dooming me to a life as Alison T. At least they had the decency to spell it the good way. But it's like my entire identity from that first moment when they named me—it's not about anything. It's like our only culture is this very nice life we have.

Tonight for homework I have to fill out this career quiz for health class for whatever freaking reason, and the last question is, "What are you

*afraid of?" I'm honestly stumped. I mean, I can tell you the stupid things.
I'm afraid of being home alone at night because every time I hear a sound
I think there's a murderer. I'm afraid of mayonnaise because it's disgusting
and I hate how it gets on people's fingers. Loose teeth totally skeeve me out.*

*But real stuff? I guess the thing I'm most afraid of is that my life won't
be what it can be. I have everything, everything going for me. I have no
excuses. And what if I still blow it?*

When I broke my promise not to listen to Alison's diaries, I broke it fully.
There were so many hours of tape it seemed I would never get through it.
Much of it was rambling and not particularly illuminating. For twenty minutes she leafed through her high school yearbook and developed a ranked
list of the ten cutest senior boys. She sang along to the entirety of a Count-
ing Crows album. I didn't fast-forward. I listened to every word. She
talked about Drew a lot, about the romantic things he did for her, like
taking her out on real dates to restaurants and the movies while other boys
just took girls to the pond and parked. She talked about her friends. Lisa
was her "soul sister," Amanda was driving her "just bananas"; a week later,
Lisa had been demoted to "*okay*, I guess." She complained about her
teachers. Mr. Conti kept sticking her with the "chalk eaters" for group projects, which she had decided was a deliberate attempt to teach her some
lesson, and let him try. The more I listened, the less I considered whether
it was right to listen. What did it matter? I couldn't stop. I gorged on Alison until I could hear her voice even when I was away from it—her breath
hidden in the hum of a ceiling fan, her laughter tinkling within the piano
track of a song I was listening to on the subway home. She was with me as
she hadn't been in years.

*HEY THERE. Me again. Hahaha. You're so diverting, Alison. Jocular.
Convivial. Uproarious. Titillating. Winsome. It's March and as you
may have guessed, you took the SATs this morning, and let me just say,
the SATs are to actually being smart as having a pretty voice is to being
a talented musician. Analogies are to meaning as a puddle is to the
ocean. I'm pretty sure I did awesome, though. But that's not what I
want to talk about. This afternoon, Claire went to this birthday party
for some girl in her class. Stacy? Anyway, the party was at that Chuck E.*

Cheese–type place, and my parents asked me to pick her up when it was over. When I get there, all these kids are racing around together playing tag and some girls are pretending to be horses or whatever. I'm looking everywhere and I don't see Clairey. Finally I find her. She's in the ball pit by herself. She's holding a green ball and just turning it in her hands and looking at it like she's figuring something out about it. Then she started doing her writing thing, where she moves her finger around in the air like that? I wanted to run up and shake her and say, Just stop doing it, kiddo. Just stop, easy peasy. *But she can't. She can't change or she would change, right? Nobody* wants *to be the weird kid.*

But also? I feel terrible saying this because she's my sister and I love her, but sometimes I don't actually like being with her, because it's like her life—she's only six years old and I can already see every single way it's going to be hard. Meanwhile, for whatever nonreason, the same stuff that's impossible for her comes easily to me. I'm not trying to brag. It is what it is. When I'm with her, sometimes I feel so freaking relieved I'm not her, *and then I feel horrible for feeling relieved. I don't deserve anything I have, really. Then I took her out for ice cream even though she already had birthday cake, and the end.*

I remembered that day. Alison was close with "Stacy"—the party was Tracy Donofrio's. Our whole class must have been invited, otherwise I never would have been included. I remembered picking pepperoni off of greasy arcade pizza. I remembered that there was a My Little Pony cake with a buttercream flower border, and I wanted to get a flower on my slice, but other girls begged for them while I just silently hoped for one with all my might, so I didn't get one. What I remembered most vividly, though, was how excited I was as I sat in that ball pit, because soon, any minute now, my big sister would arrive and all of my classmates would see that she had come to pick me up, that she was mine. Could anything be better? But she had already been there, she had been watching me, and she had pitied me.

There was more. As I made my way through Alison's tapes, I discovered that there were many entries about me, more than there were about our parents, or Drew, or her friends. My sister had watched me. Analyzed me. Puzzled over me much as I was puzzling over her now, like I was a riddle to be solved and like maybe in solving me she would crack open some truth about herself.

There was this moment at the swim club today that totally killed me. Claire's going into second grade in the fall, which means she's officially old enough to go in the deep end of the pool. So the big thing for the kids her age is to jump off the diving board. Not the high dive or anything, and not dive, just jump off the low one, a few feet. Today was ridiculously hot, and we all went to the club together. All of Clairey's little peers are jumping off the diving board, and she's just watching them while she licks a Popsicle next to my mom. Then when my dad left to do his laps, my mom asks her, very calmly and low-pressure, if she wants to give it a try. Clairey nods uncertainly, and they go over together. My mom goes in the water so she's ready to catch her. When it's Clairey's turn, she steps up onto the board and walks really slowly to the end. I'm watching from my lounge chair. We wait and we wait and we wait. My heart was pounding out of my chest. My mom says, "Come on, sweetheart. You can do it!" Then some ten-year-old asshole waiting on line starts chanting that Jeopardy *song and the rest of the kids join in. Fuckers. Finally, Claire looks at my mom and shakes her head, and my mom tells her if she doesn't want to go she should get down. My mom got out of the water and Claire sort of fell into her arms. But right before that, I saw it happen. It was a tiny flash, so quick I've never, ever caught it before: My mom, just, swallowing everything of herself, just pushing whatever she was feeling down, and smiling really brightly at Clairey and telling her it was fine! Who cares? She'd do it later this summer! Which she can't possibly believe. Why is life so hard for her? What are you so afraid of, Clairey?*

It went on and on: Clairey came home early from the first slumber party she'd actually been invited to. Clairey refused to go up onstage when a magician chose her from the audience to be his special assistant. Clairey was too shy to order her own dinner at a restaurant. Clairey hid out in her room when Mom's college roommates came to visit with their kids.

What is there to say about listening to these entries? It was devastating, humiliating, awful. How I wished I could slip into the past and tell my sister I would not be that weird little girl forever. I would grow up to have friends, boyfriends, a cool job, a life. But what would she think if she could see me now, skulking in the shadows, collecting details about Clive Richardson like some eccentric hobbyist? What clearer evidence could there be that I was exactly who Alison feared I would be? The friends, the boyfriends, the job—these might have been things I'd managed, but were they really me? Who was I? Didn't you hear what Alison said? The weird kid. A coward. What if our situations had been reversed? *She* would have known just what to do. She wouldn't have been afraid, either. She would have done whatever it took. *What are you so afraid of, Clairey?* I sat on my bed, hugging my knees to my chest and hearing her words over and over as my eyes filled with tears. I rubbed my fingertips together, and for the first time in years I felt that old prickling feeling. I raised my index finger in the air. *A-L-I-S-O-N.*

I knew what I had to do.

IT WAS an evening of brewing winds, the Brooklyn night an inimitable hazel. I arrived at my post across from the Little Sweet earlier than usual and pretended to examine the shelves in the grocery as I waited for Clive. At the usual time, I saw him coming up the sidewalk. A few moments after he entered the Little Sweet, I crossed the street. When I reached the entrance, I hesitated. Then I opened the door and stepped inside.

My nights following Clive had not prepared me for this proximity. I took my place behind him in line, inches away from him. I could smell his aftershave. I could see where the cuffs of his windbreaker were worn thin. His hands—fingertips drumming lightly against his pant leg as he waited his turn. I couldn't do this. I was about to turn and run out the door when I heard a voice, clear as anything, in my mind. *Get a grip, Clairey. It's like this: He is just some dude who found your phone a few weeks ago and you are just some girl who digs authentic ethnic food and you're just going to get to know each other.* I stayed where I was. I forced myself to stare at his hands until I was able to convince myself that they were not *his* hands, not *the* hands, and as I did this, I felt my terror subside. In the coming months, I would play this game over and over. I split Clive Richardson in two: there was the man with whom Alison had spent the last night of her life on Saint X and there was this man in this restaurant in Brooklyn, and they were not the same.

When he looked up, I smiled at him politely and vaguely, then pretended to do a double-take, as if I'd just recognized him.

"Clive, right?"

"Yes . . ."

"Emily," I said. "You found my phone last month?"

He exhaled. "That's right. Nice to see you again." He squinted at me, and I could feel the question in his gaze: What was I doing here?

Come on, Clairey. You know the words.

"After I met you here I looked this place up on Yelp and saw the rave reviews. I figured I'd better come back and try it."

I was surprised by how convincingly this explanation came out. Who was to say I wasn't the sort of girl always on the lookout for the city's best arepas, curry, dim sum? Maybe I should have been alarmed by my facility for lies, by the ease with which I spun myself into someone else, but I wasn't. Alison beamed. *Well done, Clairey.*

"Pepper pot and Carib, my dear?" the woman behind the counter asked Clive when he reached the front of the line. She was short and heavyset, and her natural hair was close-cut.

"Yes, Miss Vincia," Clive said.

"Pepper pot and Carib, pepper pot and Carib," the woman clucked as she ladled crimson stew onto a plastic plate. "And who do you have with you tonight?" she asked, her gaze hardening as it shifted to me.

"Oh, we're not—" Clive began.

"I'm Emily."

She raised her eyebrows. "And what would you like, Emily?"

I looked up at the illuminated menu. I wanted to pick something quickly and confidently, but with the exception of jerk chicken, the items were mysterious to me, and I was determined not to order jerk chicken, which I was certain would mark me as a rube. Buss-up-shut. Roast bake. Souse. Aloo pie. Accra. As I scanned the menu, I could feel my face heating up and Vincia's eyes on me, and sensed (or perhaps imagined) her annoyance. Oxtails dinner. Doubles. Festivals. Sea moss. Peanut punch. "I guess I'd better trust the expert," I said finally, smiling at Clive. "I'll have a pepper pot and Carib, too, please."

Vincia filled another plate, and Clive and I slid our trays down the counter side by side to the register.

"My treat," I said when Clive pulled out his wallet.

He looked at me uncertainly.

"Please? You'd be doing me a favor. I've been feeling totally guilty you wouldn't accept any reward." I smiled my best silly-me smile.

"Okay," he relented. "That's very kind of you. Thank you."

After I paid for our meals, Clive lifted his tray from the counter and looked at me. He hesitated. "Won't you join me?"

By paying for his meal I had hoped to create in him a sense of obligation, and it had happened just as I expected.

"Oh, I don't want to disturb you," I said, looking down shyly at the floor.

"Please. I insist." He said this without conviction. He didn't want me to sit with him. That much was clear.

I smiled. "Okay, then. Thank you."

I recognized this turn as absolutely crucial. Because now, if Clive ever began to wonder about Emily, and why she was so interested in him, he would remember that he was the one who had insisted that she join him that first night. She hadn't even wanted to—had tried, at first, to refuse.

He gestured to the table beside the potted palm tree, and I took my seat across from him. He wiped the table clean of straw wrappers and grains of rice. The table was covered in a yellow oilcloth and adorned with a vase of artificial carnations. A mural on the wall depicted a party on a tropical beach. On the television mounted on the wall, a game show was on—people in costumes competed to win bedroom sets and Jacuzzis.

"You must come here often," I said.

He looked alarmed. "Why would you say that?"

"I mean, because she knew your order by heart."

He shook his head and chuckled at himself. "Of course. Well, it's a good place to pass the time." He picked up his fork and began to eat, and I did the same.

I swooned when I took my first bite. "Mmm. This is amazing." In truth I was too full of adrenaline to notice the taste. My reaction was a performance, and I could feel the falseness of it—the theatrical *Mmmm,* the big eyes.

"Vincia's food is the best in the borough." His manner, too, was performative. He was saying what he thought he ought to say to me.

What now? *Keep it simple, stupid.*

"So are you from the Caribbean?" I asked.

He nodded.

"Cool. Which island?"

He said the name and I squinted as if it were unfamiliar to me.

"It's small," he said hurriedly. "Most people here don't know it."

"How long have you been in the U.S.?"

"Seventeen years."

He'd left less than a year after Alison's death.

"So what made you decide to leave home?"

He rubbed his hand back and forth against his cheek. Guiltily, or merely uncomfortably?

"It became difficult to find work." He bent his head toward his plate, scooped a forkful of crimson stew neatly into his mouth, and chewed silently, mouth closed. Was there something off about these tidy habits? An attempt to distract, or to mask, or to convince oneself of one's own tidiness of character? I wanted to ask him why it had become difficult to find work and see what he would say, but I was wary of pressing him.

"You miss it?" I asked instead.

For a moment, a distant look came into his eyes. I imagined that in his mind he was back—the crystalline water, the sandy roads, a small white house that had once been his.

"You get used to things."

"Do you visit often?"

"Never." He said this quietly and definitively. He yawned.

"Long day?"

"I got a flat. I went to a garage downtown to get it fixed, but the nut was stuck and they couldn't repair it. I had to go all the way back to the fleet garage. It used to be any garage could fix this."

"Nothing works the way it used to, does it?" It was a false stab at commiseration, and I cringed inwardly. But he seemed to appreciate the comment. Or maybe he'd merely grown very good at appearing to appreciate comments like this from people like me.

I sipped at my Carib, and for a while we ate in silence. I wanted to move the conversation forward, but I understood that above all I must not do anything to make him suspicious. But why would he be? Wouldn't he just assume I was exactly what, in a way, I was—another white interloper in the new Brooklyn, my interest in his life motivated by a desire for self-assuagement, to prove to myself that I was a good community member, I cared about lives unlike my own, et cetera?

He cleared his throat. "What about you? Where are you from?"

"Nowhere. Well, pretty close to it. Indiana," I said with droll self-deprecation. "Starlight, Indiana, to be precise."

My response was not premeditated. The location rose to my lips by instinct. In the fourth grade we did a unit on the fifty states and, much to my disappointment, I had been assigned Indiana. (I'd had my heart set on Louisiana. Wild alligator swamps. Mystical voodoo.) I made a diorama on foam board with Crayola cornfields, brown sand for the plains, plastic cattle. I remembered Starlight because this name had seemed to me to be the state's single redeeming characteristic.

"Starlight. That's beautiful."

"Yeah, well," I said, rolling my eyes. I leaned toward him. "I don't visit, either." I conjured an expression of guarded sadness, designed to intimate some deep ocean of painful personal history: my childhood difficult, my reasons for leaving Starlight, Indiana, equally so, as if to say to Clive Richardson, *See? I have secrets, too. I, too, live in exile.* "It's funny. I've been in New York three years now, and it still feels sometimes like this is someone else's life I'm living."

It was only after I said this that I realized I really did feel this way. Though I didn't know it then, this was to become my method during these evenings at the Little Sweet. With Clive, I confessed to feelings I had not previously articulated even to myself. Yet these emotional truths were presented within a fictional architecture. My feelings of alienation from my own life, for example, were not caused by some banishment from Indiana. It was Alison's death that had cast me into the simulacrum.

"Just so." He tucked back into his food.

"I can't believe your partner left you with a flat. People," I said with a scoff.

"People." With his spoon, he gathered the last of the crimson sauce.

We stood in unison and threw away our trash, slid our trays onto the stack on top of the garbage bin. On the television, a woman dressed as a squirrel had just won an all-expense-paid trip to Bermuda. From behind the counter, Vincia watched us as we walked out of the restaurant and onto the street.

I'M NOT sure I will ever be able to explain what it was like to sit across from Clive Richardson at the Little Sweet. I had never felt anything like it before and I haven't since. I suppose it might best be called clarity—a sense, bestowed as if from some source outside of myself, that I was exactly where I was supposed to be, doing exactly what I was supposed to be doing. On my walk home that first night I was breathless, the danger of what I'd just done swirling with euphoria at how skillfully I'd managed it. I didn't delude myself that he'd especially enjoyed our interaction, but it was a beginning. I would figure out who he needed and I would become that person. I would gain his trust, insinuate myself into his life. And I wouldn't be alone. Alison had been with me that night, giving me words I would never have found on my own. The closer I drew to Clive, the more powerful her presence became, as if they were a unified system, the two poles of a closed circuit, amplifying themselves within me.

All of this sounds crazy, I know, and when I look back on it, on how far things went, it's difficult to understand how I allowed myself to be pulled under so deeply. But I had stepped into Clive Richardson's taxi. One can understand how such an unlikely occurrence could make a person believe she had a purpose, a fate, that transcended the ordinary realities of her world. Even all these years later, knowing what I do now, I cannot disabuse myself fully of the notion that forces were at work that season that defy easy explanation. At times I wondered, and wonder still, if Alison hadn't strung all of this together from some perch beyond this world.

As the city released itself from the showy burdens of fall and grew quieter and colder, my life steadily reduced until it revolved entirely around two intertwined rituals: I could not stop listening to Alison's diaries and I could not stop seeking out Clive. Her voice and his, that was all.

SO LAST night at dinner, my parents were having this totally riveting conversation about the dead patches on the lawn and my mom gets that Very Nice expression on her face that means exactly one thing, which is, I'm about to say something positive about a black person, and she goes,

"It's never looked the same since John died," and my dad says, "That man was a miracle worker." Then my mom turns to me and says, "You remember John, don't you, sweetie? You loved him. You were so sad when he died. You cried and cried." She smiled her sweet little smile. Whatever, it's not worth getting into with her because it's beyond her limitations to understand, so I just smiled a sweet little smile back, but in my head I was thinking, Wrong. Incorrect. That is not even remotely what happened.

Maybe you don't even remember John anymore, Old Person Me. I don't know what you still remember and what's been crowded out by the fascinating life I really, really hope you're living. John was our gardener when I was really little. He died when I was maybe four. Cancer, I think. I remember he had this pure white, lamb's-wool hair and extremely dark skin. He came once a week to mow the lawn and every week my mom took me outside to say hello to him. He always tried to talk to me, but I always hid behind my mom's legs. My mom would say, "She's so shy," which wasn't true, I was a really gregarious kid, and obviously my mom knew that. I remember being completely terrified of John but not knowing why. My fear of him was totally inexplicable to me. I just felt it.

I remember when my mom told me he died, and I wasn't crying because I loved him. I was crying because here was this really nice old man who had just wanted to be friendly to me, and on some level I got that my fear of him was bad, and maybe it hurt him, maybe I hurt him.

My mom just drives me crazy. Like, you do not get to choose to raise your family in a place with only white people plus a few Indian and Chinese doctors and then convince yourself that your kid desperately loved the black gardener who you took her outside for some beneficial interaction with, and that this love is proof that even though you made the choices you made, it doesn't matter, because your kids are good and you are good and you are all just so very, very good.

I RETURNED to the Little Sweet again a few nights later. Clive looked up when I walked through the door. He did not acknowledge me, and I pretended not to notice him. I got in line. I could feel him watching me. Vincia was curt with me, all business. I paid for my food. Then I turned and let my eyes fall on him as if I'd just spotted him. I walked over to his table.

"Back again," he said.

"You caught me. I think I'm officially hooked. May I?" I gestured shyly at the empty chair across from him.

My request flustered him. But I figured he wouldn't be so rude as to say no, and I was right.

"Please."

In the weeks that followed, I went to the Little Sweet many times. Each time I feigned sheepishness when I asked to join Clive, and each time he said yes. I grew quite adept at playing the role I had created for myself, that of a lonely exile in New York, a girl from far away, all alone. While Clive did not exactly seem to welcome my presence, it seemed to me that, gradually, he was warming to me, or perhaps I should say to Emily.

What did we talk about? We traded stories from work—a boorish passenger, a temperamental author. We commiserated over the various urban creatures making incursions into our apartments—silverfish in my shower, mice in his ceiling. I told him about my short-lived kickball career, and he told me he'd played in a cricket league until a shoulder injury a few years earlier sidelined him. But mostly, as New Yorkers are wont to, we talked about the city itself, which provided for us a language of common approval and disdain: De Blasio's carriage horse crusade—a lost cause. The MTA—abysmal. Pedicabs—a nuisance.

I told stories composed of inventions and half-truths about a childhood in flyover country, hoping that these confessions would elicit some from Clive in return. I would try—carefully, so carefully—to ask questions that might lead to a revelation of some kind. Did he plan to go home someday? Did he miss his family? What was he like as a child? Nothing. Often, I caught him telling small lies. For instance, take this exchange, from our third night together:

"Have you been driving a taxi since you moved to New York?"

"Yes. Though I only switched to the day shift a few years ago."

"I hope you won't think this is weird, but I looked up the island you're from online. It looks, like, ridiculously beautiful."

"Yes, it was quite beautiful."

"What's it like, like, living in a tourist destination?"

"New York is also a tourist destination."

"I guess that's true. Did you drive a taxi down there, too?"

"No."

"What did you do?"

"Odd jobs, mostly."

ANOTHER EXAMPLE, from a few weeks later:

"How was your day?"

"The traffic was terrible."

"This time of year must be the worst, huh? With the holidays coming?"

"There's always something. In spring, it's the parades. In fall, it's the UN summit. The tourists are quite bad now. Today I picked up a family at St. Patrick's that barely spoke English. They asked me to take them to Rockefeller Center. I tried to tell them it's just around the corner, but the mother kept saying, 'Skating! Skating!' Finally I just drove them there."

"I haven't been skating since I moved here."

"I've never been."

"Really?"

"We didn't have a lot of ice growing up, miss."

"Right, I'm sorry. That was stupid. We used to skate all winter long, as soon as the Wabash froze over. I remember my feet would turn so numb that when I took off my skates I'd cry." (Truths nested in lies nested in truths. The pain of numb toes warming after skating—a memory as visceral as any from my childhood. But the Wabash River? A strip of blue cellophane in my fourth-grade diorama.) "All the kids from my neighborhood would be playing some game together on the ice, and I was always just skating by myself off to the side. It was like I couldn't figure it out somehow. You know, I don't think I've ever really had a best friend?"

"Me, neither."

TONIGHT WAS my senior dance recital. I've been practicing for months. I choreographed the dance myself. I probably spent a hundred hours practicing. But as soon as I stepped onto the stage and went up for my first pirouette, I knew I would fall short. It was like it had already happened and there was nothing I could do about it.

I danced and it was fine. I didn't mess up or anything, but I wasn't inside the music the way I wanted to be. When the recital was over I put on my sweats and went out to the lobby and there's twenty people giving me flowers and accosting me with praise. "Oh my god, Alison, you're so amazing." "You're so talented." "That was so great." Blah blah blah fan-fuckingtastic.

Are most people so insensitive to what's going on that it all looks the same to them? I mean, how did everybody totally miss what actually happened tonight? I didn't make a single mistake, not one, and I still completely failed.

Flowers and white teeth. This was my image of my sister, taken from this very recital. She had seemed to float with happiness that night. What a shock to learn that she had in fact been seething with self-criticism and hostility. How well she had hidden it! I had not thought my sister capable of such deep dissatisfaction.

I FLEW to Pasadena for Thanksgiving. I resented this disruption to the progress I was making with Clive, but could see no way around it. It was the same small gathering as always: me, my parents, Aunt Caroline, and a man my mother referred to, in a tone that managed to sound simultaneously empty of and loaded with judgment, as "the flavor of the month." This time he was an acupuncturist of Argentine extraction. Aunt Caroline was in her sixties and skinnier than ever, her lips plumped to the edge of tastefulness with Restylane. The acupuncturist looked to be about forty-five. Aunt Caroline had been dating forty-five-year-old men since she was twenty and it seemed she had no plans of stopping now.

Before the meal we assumed our usual positions, my mother and me in the kitchen, Aunt Caroline, the boyfriend, and my father chatting in the living room. ("I promise I'll stay out from underfoot," Aunt Caroline said to my mother, as if she were doing her a favor by sitting on the couch getting tipsy on Cab Franc.) At the dinner table, things proceeded the same as always.

"The garden is looking magnificent. What's your secret?" Aunt Caroline asked my father, who launched into an animated discourse on his approaches to fertilizing, pruning, watering, pest control.

"And what's new with you, darling?" Aunt Caroline asked, leaning toward me.

Before I even had time to concoct a convincing reply, my father chimed in. "Em's getting into yoga."

"How fabulous!" Aunt Caroline said. "I have a friend who swears she grew two inches when she started practicing yoga."

"It's fantastic for your alignment," my father said. "And it transforms the way your body processes carbon dioxide."

"Is that right?" my mother asked.

"NPR." My father shrugged.

The conversation moved on to other subjects—the consulting project my father had picked up in his retirement, the dash of fish sauce my mother had added to the roasted Brussels sprouts this year, the half marathon in Huntington Beach my father had registered for and the nagging knee injury that would likely prevent him from running it.

As the meal progressed, its mundanity began to feel increasingly phantasmagoric. How was it possible they didn't realize something was happening to me? The conversation continued—my mother couldn't take this new contingent that had joined her book club, they never read the books, she was honestly considering defecting. I clenched my fists under the table, digging my fingernails into my palms. This, I now saw, was exactly how our family had maintained itself since Alison's death, by not squinting too closely at one another, not knowing one another too well.

As soon as we'd finished the pie, I announced that I was feeling terribly jet-lagged and headed to bed early, though I lay awake much of the night, staring out the window at my father's violets, which held perfectly still in the dry, windless dark.

ON SATURDAY morning I woke up early. Aunt Caroline and her boyfriend had flown home the night before. My flight to JFK wasn't until the evening. I found my mother in the kitchen.

"Coffee?" she asked, already opening the cabinet and reaching for a mug.

"No."

"Oh. Tea? Orange juice?"

I shook my head.

"How about some breakfast? I can make eggs?"

"Stop, Mom. I don't want anything."

I went to the dishwasher and began unloading the bowls.

She put a hand on my shoulder. "You spoil me."

I shrugged her off. She winced and shrank back from me with a wounded expression. Suddenly I felt nothing but revulsion for this fragile bird of a woman, my mother. I wanted to hurt her, and not like I just had, not with some minor daughterly rudeness, but to really hurt her, in a way she could not evade or dismiss.

"Do you remember Alison's last dance recital?" I asked.

She looked down at the floor. As a family, we were not in the habit of bringing up Alison without warning. I kept going. "The one where she danced to—"

My mother hummed a few bars of the song, then laughed quietly at herself. "Your sister was so beautiful that night." My mother never said her name.

"She hated it."

"Hated what, darling?"

"That whole night. Everything about it."

"What are you talking about, sweetie? She was on cloud nine."

"You're wrong. She was furious."

My mother hugged herself as if the room had grown cold. "You listened."

"How would you know? You said you stopped after a few minutes."

My mother held my gaze.

"You listened, too."

"Years ago. You were in college and your father was away on business for the week. I just—"

"Couldn't help it."

She nodded.

"Then you know what I'm talking about. You know how upset she was that night."

My mother sighed. "I know that's what she said, sweetheart. But I was there. I saw her. She was so happy."

"Apparently not."

"All I can say is I know what I saw."

I gritted my teeth. It was so like her, this aloof denial of an unpleasant truth.

"Honey, what was that?"

I stuffed my hand in my pocket. "What was what?"

"Your hand. I thought I saw . . ."

"An itch."

Strange, how something can lie dormant in you for years, so long you forget about it, and then it's back like it never left. It had been happening for a few weeks now, the need growing more difficult to suppress—words prickling in my fingertips, desperate to get out. *S-o h-a-p-p-y.*

"Sweetheart, are you getting enough fresh air?"

Fresh air? *Fanfuckingtastic.*

IT'S TEMPTING to paint my nighttime meetings with Clive retroactively with a shiny gloss, to suggest that after a while we achieved an easy rapport, and I want to be careful not to mislead in that way. Even after we'd spent hours together, our conversations remained stilted. Clive often gave only the most perfunctory answers to my questions before falling silent for long stretches. There was one topic, though, that he seemed truly to relish, and that was his job as a hack and the things he had seen, the stories he had to tell. He told me about the crazy conversations he'd overheard. The time someone left a two-hundred-dollar tip on a ten-buck ride. Getting held up in the nineties.

"I had a man once who started talking to himself," he began one evening. "He was talking about a heist he was going to execute with a partner. He said, 'Here's the plan. I'll go up to the teller, I'll show her the gun and tell her she has twenty seconds. When I put my hand in my pocket, you get the customers down on the ground.' He kept going like this, how they will get into the vault and what they will retrieve from it and where the getaway car will be parked. I began to worry that perhaps *I* was the getaway car. I was thinking about how I might drive to a police station without him realizing where we were going when he said, 'So? How did I do?' He was an actor. It was opening night of his first off-Broadway play."

"No."

"It's true." He grinned. "I've also driven three women in labor to the hospital, one of them in a blizzard. She told me she would name her child after me. I remember when I told my son that he said, 'But what if she had a girl?' If you ever meet a Clivette, I guess she has me to thank."

"You have a son?"

He appeared flustered, as if he hadn't meant to reveal this. He nodded. "He'll be turning twenty-one soon."

"He lives here?"

"Oh, no, no. He's back home, back—with his mother."

"Your wife?"

He shook his head. "She was a difficult woman. Troubled."

"Are you and your son close?"

He broke off small tatters from the napkin in his fist and collected them in a pile on the table. "I tried at first. She didn't permit me to be involved." He cleared his throat. "Here's another story for you: Would you believe I once picked up Mike Piazza two hours before a home game? His driver was stuck on the Bruckner. It was just after 9/11 and traffic was very bad. I got him to Shea just in time."

Clive had spoken the words "my son" like a kiss to a warm forehead. I hadn't known he had a child. If the boy was twenty now, then he had been two or three years old when Alison was killed. Bile rose in my throat. Clive had been a father when it happened. He should have looked at Alison and seen someone's child, not whatever she was to him instead: A way of injecting excitement into a life saddled with a kid and responsibilities he wasn't ready for? The unlucky victim of a man's anger toward another woman, a "difficult" woman? Had Alison known Clive had a son? As Edwin Hastie slid a cigarette between her lips in the sandy staff parking lot, had Clive told some precious story about his toddler, and had this story made her think these men sweet and safe?

"Wow," I said. "That's amazing."

"Only in New York. Before he got out I told him, 'Mike, I have a confession. Usually I'm a Yankee fan. But tonight I'm rooting for the Mets.'"

HAPPY BIRTHDAY to me. Woo-hoo. Today, old lady Alison, you are sixteen years old.

So I can drive now. Very exciting, blah blah blah. For my birthday my parents got me . . . drumroll, please . . . a new car!

That's right, my dad bought me a brand-spanking-new Audi. So inevitably we had a big fight about it. I wanted a used car. Something low-key. Because, come on. I'm sixteen. Why on earth should I own a brand-new Swedish or German or whatever . . . why should I have this luxury car that I'm inevitably going to fuck up because I just started driving and, news flash, I don't know how yet? When I told him that, he was all, "That's exactly why we want you to have a good, safe car."

I mean, he's right. On the one hand, I completely understand why if you could afford it you would buy the best car you can for your kid. On the other hand, I'm mortified. Not just for me. For my friends, too. On behalf of my friends, especially the ones who are, like, super-excited about their new luxury vehicles and see no issue here whatsoever. We're teenagers and people are just giving us these ridiculously nice cars. We should be embarrassed, right?

But being embarrassed only makes it worse, because if you're lucky enough to be given a nice, safe, fancy-schmancy car, isn't it brattier to yell at your dad about it than to just be glad you have it? But then—I feel like there's this really slippery slope between being glad you have something and thinking you deserve it.

WHEN MY mother had told me that, despite what Alison said in her diary, she was certain my sister had been on cloud nine at her last dance recital, I'd thought she was sticking her head in the sand. But the more I listened to Alison's diary, the more I began to wonder whether it could be trusted. I began to detect a self-conscious, performative aspect in the things she said. Take Alison's insistence that she did not want the new car my parents gave her. Are we really to believe that she did not, on some level, want it? Are we really going to accept that she didn't enjoy having it? Isn't it more likely that she loved the car—its new-car aroma, its elasticity around a sharp bend, its blue gleam in the school parking lot—but that her own materiality embarrassed her, or she thought it ought to—that she knew a purer person *would* be embarrassed by it, and she wished to believe she was such a person? Isn't it more likely that the extended diatribe on the subject that she recorded in the diary was an attempt to reassure herself of her own virtue?

Or let's return to the recital. What if my mother was right and Alison was simply giddy eating up compliments after her performance? That's how I remember it, too. You can see how a diary might become a useful tool, how it might be used to rewrite history, to recast the pivotal moments of one's life to suggest a humbler, more critical self.

At the same time, the urgency and raw emotion in Alison's words were unmistakable, her turmoil palpable. She was grappling with herself. I believe that. Alison at least *meant* to be honest with herself. Here we run up against yet another problem—the obstacle of her youth. How much does a girl of fifteen or sixteen really understand about herself? How accurate can she possibly be?

The diary was a slippery thing, weaving together confession with self-delusion, truth with distortion. No—the weaving metaphor isn't right. That suggests truth and distortion are strands and, therefore, separable. I think it would be more accurate to say that truth and untruth were present in Alison's diary as hydrogen and oxygen are present in water. The challenge is not one of separation—for what use are either hydrogen or oxygen in understanding the nature of water?—but of understanding these moments *without* attempting to separate them. I had to find a way to understand how truth and untruth make each other.

ONE DAY at work, a Facebook invitation appeared in my inbox. Jackie was throwing herself a birthday party: dinner at an all-you-can-eat-and-drink sushi and sake joint, followed by karaoke in Koreatown. I could no longer imagine attending such an event. How frivolous to be twenty-five and doing sake bombs, what a joke, what a cliché. What a cliché, even, to possess some ironic relationship to your own clichéd birthday party, as Jackie did, to affect a pose of self-mockery toward oneself and the basic things one loved. (*Yes, we're doing this. Bon Jovi non-negotiable,* the invite said.)

Before I set out for the Little Sweet on the night of Jackie's party, I texted her: *Sorry, I have a thing tonight, but have so much fun!*

Jackie texted back immediately: *You're bailing on my bday?!? Is everything okay??? I'm worried.*

Her worry opened something in me. For a moment I wanted to go to Jackie's party and have stupid fun there the way I would have just a few short months ago, but I knew I couldn't; it was simply no longer possible for me to get wasted and eat bargain-basement spicy tuna rolls and belt out "Sweet Caroline" like these things were somehow relevant to me, and there was loss in this, too. Briefly I considered telling Jackie everything. I typed and deleted half a dozen messages, but in the end, I gave up. I never replied.

I BEGAN sleeping less and less, and erratically. Night after night, through the dark hours, I listened to Alison. I had not experienced insomnia like this since I was a child, churning out fatal scenarios in the darkness, and the feeling now was familiar: I wanted to stop listening, to give myself over to sleep, but I couldn't. To press stop, to extinguish Alison's voice, seemed dangerous in a way I cannot explain rationally, but which felt absolutely inviolable to me. I was almost grateful when the man above me began his nightly guitar practice at two A.M., the music sifting down through my ceiling providing an alternate and utterly ordinary explanation for my wakefulness. For the first time in my life, I was sleeping through my alarm and arriving late to work.

I JUST got back from a trip to Becca's ski house. First of all, the trip was a freaking blast. I seriously think I have a six-pack from cracking up so much. I feel like I've been really, I don't know, blah lately, and this trip made me remember that I really, really love my friends. A few highlights: Matt and Andy losing a bet and streaking across the yard in the freezing cold. Staying in the hot tub for hours drinking beer and talking. Getting ridiculously stoned one night and taking all the blankets onto the deck and lying there looking up at the stars while it snowed. After a while I couldn't even tell if the snow was falling or the stars, it was just this beautiful mess. High stargazing is seriously the best.

Did I mention I broke my wrist? True story. It happened on the last day, otherwise the trip would have been a total bust. I fell coming off a big jump. Everybody else was in the lodge for a hot-cocoa break, and I went off on my own to get in one more run. I had a three-seater to myself on the chairlift. You know how sometimes the world just rips open and you find yourself in a moment that is totally sacred? This was that. The trees high up on the slope were coated in snow and glittering. The snow had that bluish glow, and it was like it was all here for me. I actually started to cry because I just felt so moved. I was still in that energy when I decided to take this jump on the way down. There was that moment when I was hanging in the air, that weightless, almost-flying moment when you start to realize your body is no longer under your control, then splat.

Ski patrol came and brought me down the mountain in one of those gurney thingies. Once my friends figured out where I was, they were all crowding around me in the med hut, and then at the hospital with me later for the X-rays and everything. I didn't cry. It hurt like hell but I was a total champ. I'm really proud of how tough I was. But then again, the only reason I didn't let myself cry is because I wanted the medics and my friends to tell me how brave and amazing I was, which is exactly what happened. So does that even count as toughness, or is it actually appalling?

I'm leaving for college next week and my parents said I have to sort through my so-called "junk" before I go. Today I was going through these boxes of old essays with my teachers' comments and school photos of my friends, and every stupid trophy and medal from swimming and dance. All of a sudden I was like, "Why have I held on to this crap? Why is it so damned precious to me?" I got these heavy-duty black garbage bags from the garage and I started filling them. I got into this rhythm . . . trance is too dramatic, but I got to this headspace where I couldn't see any reason to keep anything. The only memento I didn't throw away was my prom corsage from Drew, and I only kept that because I kept imagining he was in the room with me, and how hurt he'd be just killed me.

As I was throwing everything away I had this vision where I had pared down everything I need in life to a black attaché case, like people use to hand off dirty money in espionage movies. Then, like, what if you got rid of not just things but parts of yourself? Memories you'd been holding on to and random skills and knowledge and all the books you'd ever read that didn't matter? What if you pared yourself down to one essential part? What would that one grain be? It occurred to me that I have no freaking idea.

I broke up with Drew today. It was awful. He was crying in my bed and begging me to take it back. I know this makes me seem terrible but the begging actually made it easier for me. I kind of lost some respect for him, you know?

Now my mom is all concerned. "It was just so sudden, sweetheart!" Like sudden is this problem. But I did something that had to be done.

We're going to college, for one. But it's more than that. I am totally settled into Drew, and I can see how it could just go on and on, and something in me is saying, No, no, no. *Like, is that really where it's supposed to lead? But seeing Drew cry and knowing I did that really sucked.*

I had made my way through all but the final tape. I was terrified to reach the end, but I couldn't slow myself down. I called in sick at work. I stayed in my apartment and listened.

Do you ever wish something terrible would happen to you so the world could see how strong you are? People probably think I'm this delicate flower because nothing bad has ever touched me, but I'm not. This is fucked up to say, but I think I would be amazing in the face of a tragedy.

"Humiliation is purification, because it causes the most corrosive, the most painful awareness." We're reading Notes from Underground *in my World Lit Survey and Dostoyevsky is officially my new favorite writer. Dude gets it.*

I really shouldn't be recording right now, because I'm going home tomorrow for winter break and I need to pack everything I need for home and for the annual Thomas family vacation to a culturally devoid tropical resort, and I haven't even gotten my suitcase out yet. But this thing from last night has been bugging me and I have to get it down. So I was at this dorm party and this extremely hot junior from the lacrosse team was there. We went back to his room and we're sitting on the futon in that pre-make-out phase and he's touching my hair and everything's great. Then he launches into, "Have you ever wondered what if your green is my purple?" I told him I was really tired and left. Honestly, if I meet one more pseudo-intellectual, actually so stupid boy here, I'm going to lose it. Let me go on record and say that the number of dumbnuts at one of the best schools in the country is mind-blowing.

That was it. *The number of dumbnuts* and then the barely audible spooling of blank tape. Right away I took out the tape, swapped in the first one, and started back at the beginning.

Today when I woke up I just felt different. I knew today was the day.

She's only six years old and I can already see every single way it's going to be hard.

Fanfuckingtastic.

The more I listened, the more I felt that I was far out in the ocean, swimming down, down, down. I knew I should rush up to the surface for air, but I couldn't help myself. There was something at the bottom I was after, and I couldn't stop.

Maybe it hurt him, maybe I hurt him.

I didn't make a single mistake, not one, and I still completely failed.

Blah blah blah.

True story.

This beautiful mess.

It had grown dark in my apartment, but I didn't turn on the light. I listened to my sister's voice in the darkness until I could scarcely remember a time when I'd heard anyone but Alison. I had the feeling then that I was entering my sister. I stretched and filled her, head to toe. I opened my eyes and looked out through hers. Together, in our body that was Alison's body, we descended through lilac clouds.

THE REAL WHEREVER

THEY ARRIVE AT SUNSET, slipping beneath pastel clouds as the sun slips into the sea. For a moment it seems to Alison that the plane, too, will slip into the sea, but the tarmac rushes beneath them just in time. As the plane brakes down the runway, a ghostly whoosh fills the cabin. The minute it subsides, her parents and the majority of the white passengers unbuckle their seat belts and stand to retrieve their things from the overhead compartments: carry-ons, rackets, straw hats. Her dad edges out another dad in the aisle. A third dad edges out her dad. The pilot comes on the intercom and requests that everyone remain seated, but he is ignored. Heaven forbid their vacations start thirty seconds later. Once the plane door opens and people begin to move, her dad looks back at the black woman he had been seated beside on the flight; "Welcome home," he says to her, before hurrying along. When they get to baggage claim, the carousel is empty and motionless. Everyone prowls around it, staking out the most strategic position. Ten minutes pass. A guy with a winter coat unzipped to reveal a Hawaiian shirt walks past her muttering, "Unbelievable." She smiles. Let these dopes wait.

"You know that woman next to me on the plane was a lawyer?" her dad says to her mom on the walk to the arrival gate, once their luggage finally arrives. "She's from here. She was just in New York on vacation."

"Huh," her mom says.

"Imagine that, Dad. They have lawyers here," Alison says.

The shuttle to the resort is late, too. Alison's family stands on the curb with two other families, next to a white sign with gold letters that say INDIGO BAY, for quite some time. Everybody grouses and makes small talk. The other families are from the Upper East Side and Bedford Hills. The irony of traveling over a thousand miles to spend the week talking to other people from the New York metropolitan area does not seem to be dawning on anyone. The moms talk to the moms. The dads talk to the dads.

"How old are you?" Alison's mom asks a girl who must have changed out of her winter clothes in the airport bathroom—she is wearing bike shorts and a cropped T-shirt with a rhinestone heart.

"Twelve," the girl says wearily.

"She's on a birthday trip!" her mother says.

"Mom, why are we waiting?" the girl asks.

"I don't know, sweetie. Daddy booked this vacation."

When at last the shuttle arrives, the driver begins to load their suitcases.

"Is all of this going to fit in there?" a dad says, looking skeptically into the back of the van.

"Not a chance," Alison's dad contributes.

They are wrong, everything fits, and soon they are pulling away from the airport. On the drive to the resort, the small talk continues, but Alison doesn't hear it. Her face is pressed to the window. She sees scruffy dogs and houses with rebar sticking up out of the roofs. Three goats bite at the dirt outside of a small white building with a shingle out front: CENTRE FOR DENTAL AESTHETICS. Everywhere she sees piles of . . . *stuff*. Rubble? Junk? Supplies of some kind? There are houses with porches but no railings. A white concrete staircase ascends out of the scrub, the top step touching only air. As she watches the world pass by, she is filled with disquiet at her inability to parse the things she sees. Are the diminutive chickens pecking at the side of the road malnourished, or are they some breed of chicken she has never seen before, or is this what a chicken is *supposed* to look like? Do they belong to someone or no one? Is this place in the process of being built or unbuilt or rebuilt or none of these—maybe something is happening here that she lacks the experience to comprehend.

The van trundles past a girl standing in a yard along the road; she wears a purple T-shirt and yellow cotton shorts. When they drive by, she runs into the road and chases after them. Then she plants herself in the middle of the road, puts her hands on her hips, and thrusts out her tongue. The shuttle judders on over the uneven road and the girl disappears into the haze of dust and twilight.

Alison is mortified to be in an air-conditioned van with her family and her fellow resort guests driving past it all. In her Global Justice class, she learned that two billion people, more than a third of the humans on earth, live on less than two dollars a day. (Are the people on this island *those* people? Are the things out the van window poverty, or just people living their lives? She doesn't know how she would even begin to know.) Anyway, it's not like she didn't know people were poor before—she isn't a complete idiot. In high school she volunteered at a soup kitchen. But her lasting memory of that experience is not of bearing witness to poverty, or of any good she did; it's of the men . . . looking at her, calling her pretty with their ruined mouths. "You're coming home with me, little girl," a man in a giant tan parka told her one night. He pointed his index finger at her, then curled it toward himself and laughed madly. She felt afraid, though she was pretty sure he was messing with her, making himself into a caricature to mock her—like, *Boo!* The acrid smell of male bodies and the simultaneous unease and pleasure she felt in their gaze—this is what she has kept.

So the things she sees out the window do not *raise her awareness,* or whatever. They just mortify her. An old woman limping down the road. The accusation of that little girl's sharp pink tongue. That girl is really millions of girls. You cannot permit yourself to forget that. How is she supposed to square millions of these girls with her own life? And how, in turn, to square millions of girls with a trillion trillion stars? She has been born on the one temperate, unhostile planet in the universe, in the richest country on that planet, into a family whose wealth places them at the tippy top of that country. It is a disgusting amount of luck. You could never be forgiven for such good fortune. Sometimes, when she thinks of her teeny-weeny life and how *obsessed* she is with it, she feels physically sick.

She is also mortified that she will spend the next week darkening her skin on a chaise lounge alongside other oil-slathered tourists, while people whose skin is darker than hers will ever be (and darker than she wants hers to be) bring her beverages and fresh towels. And she is mortified that her parents see nothing wrong with the whole arrangement. No, that isn't exactly right. They do see something wrong with it, but they think something along the lines of, *We're fortunate, they're unfortunate, and it's neither our fault nor theirs because we are all part of something that is beyond any of us, and we just as easily could have been born them and they just as easily could have been born us, but we weren't, so here we are.* Welcome to paradise. Honestly? She doesn't even want to be here.

HER FIRST night at Indigo Bay, after her sister is asleep, she walks out onto the balcony to look at the stars. The warm breeze ripples against her skin. Venus burns a cold, clear blue. She unzips her dress. Just because she can. You can stand on a balcony and have an utterly ordinary moment, or you can let your dress fall to the cool terra-cotta tiles, unhook your bra, and offer yourself up to the night. Possibilities are everywhere, hidden in the fist of each moment, yet most people don't see them, or they see them but leave them untouched.

She wishes she could see the picture she makes with the white curtains billowing behind her, hair fluttering in the wind, breasts lit by a fingernail of moon. She surveys the resort grounds below her. No one. This pleases her, not because she would be embarrassed to be seen, but because it means this is a secret moment. Hers alone, then, *poof*! Gone. When she thinks of all the secret moments locked within this instant—of all the people on earth doing things no one will ever know—her heart feels so full it could crack.

She looks at the starry sky, the dark shimmering sea, and tries to savor the beauty of it all, but she can't get herself to really feel it. The view from the balcony bleeds together with too many other views on other vacations in other paradises. Which island had the pink sand beach? Which one had those zippy orange birds? Where was it you could wade out a quarter mile from shore before the water deepened? Somewhere she saw a sunset like a bloody sacrifice and a woman tossing white petals into the surf. She is eighteen and beauty already seems such a cheap thing. She can behold it and behold it without feeling a thing.

SHE SLEEPS late, then spends an embarrassing amount of time appraising herself in the mirror in the marble bathroom before making her entrance on the beach. When she finally emerges, her family is already set up, with a row of four chairs with white cushions in the shade of two white umbrellas. These resorts often have an obsession with white. White buildings, white floors, white linens, white uniforms. Like they're trying to convince you you've died and gone to heaven, or like you've arrived at some hedonistic sanatorium because you're afflicted by something and you didn't even know it but now you will heal.

Her parents start talking at her. Cruise ship, slide, something, something. She pulls one of the lounge chairs into the sun and lies down. She takes out her Walkman and lets "Big Poppa" drown her dad out. A minute later her father hails one of the beach waiter guys like he's a cab. Awful. But the guy doesn't seem to notice, or care, or something. She turns up the volume on her Walkman and pulls the headphones down around her neck, hoping he'll hear what song she's listening to. He introduces himself. He's Edwin. He is skinny and super-friendly with her parents, like all his life he's dreamed of meeting the Thomases of Westchester, who are totally eating it up. Her dad orders her a fruit punch, which . . . she guesses he can inhabit whatever alternate reality he wants.

When Edwin comes back, he's hunched under the weight of a tray of excessively garnished cocktails and she wants to disappear, because lying on this chaise lounge while he labors is so uncomfortable. The thing she can't figure out is, if she is honest with herself, she does not find this arrangement uncomfortable because a person is doing something for her, but because a black person is doing something for a white person. Which doesn't mean she doesn't want him to have his job. So what does it mean, exactly?

When he asks if she'll come play in the volleyball game in the afternoon, she shrugs, tells him maybe.

"More of a sunbather, are we?" he says.

Her entire body flushes. *Not me!* she wants to tell him. *I'm not just some ditzy sun worshipper.* But there is no way to convey this without protesting too much and coming off even worse.

He winks at her and continues down the beach.

Her fruit punch, actually, is delicious. The sun on her skin is delicious. Maybe she is wrong to have such a stick up her ass about the whole situation. Maybe she should, as a general thing, just shut up and be grateful. But lately she is beginning to suspect that gratitude (as an emotion, as an action) is a colossal scam. Rich, poor, it doesn't matter—everyone is expected to be grateful for what they have, whatever that is. Once, in high school, she snuck into the city with her girlfriends to smoke clove cigarettes in Washington Square Park and try to get invited to an NYU party, and on the way downtown from Grand Central they had a taxi driver who'd been a chemical engineer in Pakistan. When she asked if it frustrated him to do what he did now, he said no, just the opposite, he was grateful. It was a familiar story. In my country I was a lawyer, I was a doctor, I was a professor, but I'm grateful to drive this taxi in America, I'm grateful to bus these dishes in America, I'm grateful to clean up the vomit of fraternity brothers in this dormitory at an Ivy League university in America. Meanwhile, Alison is expected to be grateful for her Audi, and for she doesn't even know how much her parents pay for her college tuition, and for their beautiful vacations and the beautiful teeth she possesses after years of orthodontia. So what is gratitude, really, but reverence for a system that gives and deprives at random? No, not at random. The non-randomness is exactly the point, right?

THAT AFTERNOON when she hears Edwin yelling about the volleyball game, she pushes herself up from her chaise lounge. She will show him who she is.

"Want to come watch me play, Clairey?"

Her sister's face lights up at the invitation. Sometimes her power to make her sister happy terrifies her.

She's nervous when she pulls her tunic up over her head. Though she knows she's pretty, cute, arguably even sexy in a girl-next-door way, she is always nervous when she reveals her scar to people for the first time. She isn't insecure about it, exactly; it's more like the nervousness she feels at a dance recital just before she leaps onto the empty stage.

When her torso is exposed, it happens like it always does. Her teammates stare with the obviousness of cattle. When she catches them at it, they avert their eyes oh-so-politely. She loves catching people looking at her scar, shaming them with a glance.

As the players manage the ball back and forth over the net in sequences of sloppy bumps and sets, she imagines them imagining what happened to her. A wash of dark scenarios projects like a movie montage against the limpid blue sky. She sees herself thrown from a car onto one of those boggy meadows beside the highway, gnashed by a neighbor's Akita, cut open on a surgeon's table.

The real story is her favorite, but she guards it closely, not wanting to dull it by too frequent visitation. She was four. It was summer, and her family, which did not yet include Claire, was at a campground on a lake. They went every summer, and she never liked it. The bottom of the lake was soft, like stepping in dead things. It was night. She was sitting around a fire with her parents roasting marshmallows. Her parents turned away for a moment and when they looked back, she was in the fire. Her father dove in and scooped her out—she was in the flames for only a few seconds, just long enough to be marked by them forever. At the hospital, when her parents and the nurses asked her what happened, she just shook her head, unable to explain. As her parents tell the story, it is a mystery: whether she tripped and fell or whether, dazzled by the flames or propelled by some wild impulse, she jumped.

"I could have died," she told Drew the first time she let him see it. When he touched the smooth, pink surface of the scar gently with his fingertips, as if it might still hurt, she loved him. It's true—she *could* have died. In a way, her whole life grows out of that moment. Edwin will begin to see it now: she is a person to whom things have happened.

A woman on her team is talking through the earth-shattering conundrum of whether she and her husband should go on the excursion to the old sugar estate and rum distillery. "I wanted to go, but I've heard it's a drag. Apparently it's mostly about the history of sugar cultivation on the island, the plantation system and that stuff?"

That stuff, i.e., slavery? Alison purses her lips to indicate to Edwin that she does not approve of the woman's comment. She hears everything her teammates say twice—once as herself, and once as she imagines he hears it. The woman's husband, a man with dolphins on his pink swim trunks, serves the ball into the net.

"Almost, honey," the woman says. "I would just like to have a week here where I don't have to think about how awful the world is. I'm a defense attorney. I know it's awful."

Fair enough? Alison isn't sure. You don't get to decide, do you, when to care and when not to care, when to see the big picture and when to zoom in so super-close on your own life that your desire for a massage fills your entire field of vision?

There are a few other college kids playing, and they set about the unavoidable business of identifying the hall mates, teammates, bunk-mates that connect them. "Small world," remarks a boy who initially says he goes to school in Connecticut, and only when prodded lets "Yale" cross his lips, a confession he makes with an irreproachable mix of sheepishness and élan. *Small world. Small world.* Like it is some crazy cosmic coincidence, rich people overlapping with other rich people. If he weren't so cute—yellow-haired and tall, with a certain anemic quality she finds appealing—she would be done with him already. Instead, she flirts.

The other girl her age squeals when the ball comes near her. She adjusts her bikini top to maintain just the right revelation of boob. She says, "Did I do good?" in a baby voice when she sets up a spike for one of the guys. Alison doesn't get it. Okay, fine, she *gets* it. In a way you can hardly blame the girl, because it works. The boy with the hemp necklace is eating it up. But can someone please explain to her the appeal of a guy who can be reeled in by that kind of thing? What you want is a guy who is a little afraid of you. And you want to be a little afraid of him, too.

While the other girl swats the scary ball away, Alison leaps and spikes and pushes off powerfully from the sand. She can feel eyes on her—Connecticut boy's, Edwin's. A vacation is its own world, compressed and powerful, like a planet with stronger gravity. If you play it right, it can teach you things about yourself you can't learn the other 358 days of the year. It is her first day here and already it is happening. The vacation is finding its promise.

When the game is over, Connecticut boy approaches her. She can smell his sweat. It makes her think of Drew, salty and nice. He tells her about the bar in the white marble lobby where the liquor is watered down but where he'll be, anyway, tonight, around ten P.M. He touches his hand to her shoulder, then trots off down the sand.

I MIGHT have it all wrong. Maybe Alison did not stand naked on the balcony on our first night on Saint X. Perhaps she did not play volleyball with such vim and vigor in order to impress a boy from Yale, on the one hand, and a local employee, on the other. Perhaps the scar on her stomach was not her most sacred vanity. I'm trying to triangulate the truth, to inhabit my sister's mind. Impossible tasks, to be sure.

What I can say is this: While the details of this story may be products of my imagination, I trust its broad strokes and core themes. I believe that for my sister, our family vacation coincided with one of those brief, intense intervals of identity formation we all experience from time to time in our lives. She arrived at Indigo Bay at that critical moment when the girl cuts herself on the shards of her own reflection and watches, baffled and thrilled, as the blood begins to flow.

ALISON WEARS her pale pink slip dress. Her "fuck-me, I'm-a-baby" dress, as summarized by her friend Dan, who was in love with her but not *something* enough for her to consider a viable romantic option.

Connecticut is already there.

"Hey," she says, exquisitely low-key.

"Hey."

He is drinking a rum and Coke. He is even cuter than she remembered from earlier. He has one of those old-fashioned faces, the kind you can picture in black-and-white. For a moment she sees him in an army uniform and one of those little caps. The image excites her—a young man in the trenches, the secret personal sufferings of war, but also the part where she takes him and implants him in this scene while he sits here next to her in his button-down and has no idea that in her mind his face is smudged with dirt and he is living on rations of tinned meat.

She orders a tequila shot. She opens her throat and drinks it in one go, and though it burns she does not permit herself to react. She is a girl in a tiny pink dress, downing tequila like a champ.

They talk. In addition to playing cello in the Yale Symphony Orchestra, Connecticut is a German major.

"Why German?" she asks.

"I wanted to be able to read Rilke in the original." He rolls his eyes at himself, which she recognizes as the correct move. Nobody likes a snob, but everybody likes the discernment that allows for snobbery.

"How do you say, 'You must change your life,' in German?" she asks, raising her eyebrows like, *Of course I read Rilke.* Actually, she doesn't—she remembers this quote from a paper she wrote freshman year of high school comparing and contrasting Rilke and, for some reason, Keats. She got an A. Mr. Conti put the paper up on the projector as a positive example.

"*Du musst dein Leben verwandeln*," Connecticut says. "Or something like that. So what about you? Do you know what you're going to major in?"

"Probably something that will drive my parents crazy."

They talk awhile longer, letting the thing build. He asks if she wants to go for a walk and she says yes. He charges her drinks to his room, which would be romantic if his parents weren't obviously paying for it. They leave the bar for the beach. They kick off their shoes. The sand is soft and cool as cream. For a few minutes they walk along the water's edge, their fingertips brushing against each other's, letting their banter slow and the force of the night and this thing they are creating together fill them. When they reach a cabana he gestures at it, she nods, and he takes her hand and leads her in. Easiest thing in the world.

She has kissed quite a few boys since Drew, and Connecticut is particularly enjoyable. He does not use his tongue a lot, which she likes, because sometimes in the midst of making out with a boy she will think about what a tongue actually is and feel paralyzed. He kisses her neck a lot and she likes that, too. It is all very, very nice. But there is something about this niceness that doesn't sit right. She feels it like a cold gel applied to the moment. She is moving through this scenario the way she would work through a math problem she knows she will get right.

She knows why it is so easy for her, this and so much else. She knows the substance of the reserves inside herself that make the world a comfortable place to navigate. It is her mother and father loving her like crazy. It is the dappled lawn of her childhood home with its soft mown stripes of green and darker green. It is "fantastic insight!" written in a teacher's delicious cursive in the margin of an essay. It is the gothic magnificence of the Princeton campus, through which she strolled all autumn in mesh shorts and flip-flops and a messy ponytail. It is every witticism she's ever tossed off in a circle at a party and the impressed faces of the people who heard it. It is the people she knows and *their* reserves—their happy childhoods, their bright memories, their educations, all the beauty they have seen, out and out like ripples on the glassy surface of a pool in a secret glade they carry collectively within them. They are spinning it together, she and Connecticut, good fortune igniting on itself under the tropical stars. Is there anything more obvious in the entire world?

When he touches her thigh under her dress, she freezes. Not *actually* freezes. She keeps doing what they're doing. But inside. She is not very experienced, truth be told. She was with Drew forever, but she's learned in the past few months that all that experience is actually just one experience. They were babies when they started dating and they figured everything out together, and what if they figured it out weird? She hasn't had an orgasm with anyone else and she knows it's because she's afraid that if she does, the guy will look at her funny because her orgasms are weird and she didn't know it. She doesn't want to be here anymore. She wants to take the nice kissing with her and leave.

She presses a finger delicately to his lips. "I should go," she whispers.

"Are you sure?" He strokes her thigh higher up this time. It is the first thing he does that she doesn't like. He looks down at his lap, where his boner pushes against his khaki shorts. Her stomach flips. Back in her room with her sleeping sister—that's where she wants to be.

"I'm sure." She scrunches her nose, cute as a button.

He wraps his arms around her waist. "But I want to kidnap you," he says, and buries his face in her hair.

"Not tonight," she says.

"Tomorrow?"

"We'll see."

She stands, smooths her dress. He reaches for her hand, and she holds his for a moment, then lets it slip through her fingers as she turns and walks back toward the lights of the resort.

"TELL ME something," her father says the next day, as Clive gathers up the french fries he spilled in the sand. "Where do you recommend for some local food? You know, something authentic."

Alison winces. Her father asks this every year, at every resort, on his bullshit search for some local color, the Real Wherever. She can't stand how pleased he is with his question, like he expects Clive to be super-impressed by his desire to get off the beaten path. (Does he think Clive wants his favorite local spot to be invaded by hordes of tourists?) Her father wants to be able to say, *Now,* this *is delicious,* of the conch creole at some hole-in-the-wall, whether or not it is better than the conch creole served at Indigo Bay. Her mother wants to tell the cook on the way out, *You have a beautiful restaurant,* with her sweet little smile, when the truth is if she thought folding chairs and ceiling fans instead of AC were so great, she'd eat at places like this back home, too, which of course she doesn't. Then her father wants to take his mediocre photos of the place and blow them up and hang them on the living room wall so their friends will inquire about them at dinner parties and he can tell them about *this amazing little spot* he discovered.

That isn't fair. As parents go, hers aren't so bad. Isn't it better at least to have the inclination to leave the bubble? Well, maybe better for *them,* but shouldn't the people who live here get to keep some places to themselves? But maybe the people who live here *want* people like her parents to come to their restaurants; maybe her notion that they'd rather the tourists and their money stay away is just that, a naïve little notion. She could go around like this forever, trying to decide.

"People like Spicy's. Their roast crayfish is quite popular," Clive says.

"Roast crayfish," her father says. "Fantastic."

LATER THAT afternoon, Alison finds Edwin standing behind the open-air restaurant. "Hey, Mr. Carnival Sandcastle Champion."

"Watch out. The girl's feeling frisky today."

She snorts.

A cook calls out from the kitchen, "Order up!"

"Duty calls?"

"Nonstop till three."

"What's at three?"

"Break. I usually take it down there, past those rocks at the end of the beach."

WHEN THE hour comes, her parents are snoozing away. She tells her sister she's going to the bathroom. At the jagged black rocks that mark the end of Indigo Bay, she scrambles up and over, stumbling, then regaining her footing. She crests the rocks and sees Edwin sitting in the sand. He looks up.

"What are you doing here?" he says sternly. For a moment she worries she misunderstood. Then he tosses back his head and laughs.

"Ha ha," she says. "You're hysterical."

The beach here isn't groomed like it is around the resort. You can barely see the sand, it's so covered in stuff: green beer bottles, nests of odorous seaweed studded with cigarette butts. Three tires tied together with yellow rope. An old cardboard campaign poster with a picture of a woman in a blazer, the blazer still bright red, the woman's face so faded she looks like a ghost. She has to step carefully as she makes her way to him. He's eating fried fish out of a grease-spotted paper bag and smoking a cigarette.

"You know those will kill you," she says as she sits down beside him.

"Only if something else doesn't kill me first."

She nods at the cigarette with her chin. "May I?"

"I insist, miss."

She rolls her eyes at this word. *Miss.* She likes the way he calls her this with a subversive smile, like they're in on something together. He passes her the cigarette and she takes a slow, assured drag. As she exhales, she looks out at the water and tries to work her face into an expression that suggests she finds something very personally meaningful there. She passes the cigarette back to him.

"If you're looking for something more, me and Gogo usually lime in the car park for a bit after work. Smoke some herb, you dig?"

"Oh, I dig."

"Maybe we'll see you there sometime."

She shrugs. "Maybe. Anyway, I should get back before they send out a search party." She stands and brushes the sand from her legs.

"You're bleeding," he says.

She looks at her calf. She must have cut herself when she stumbled; a few long scratches bubble with red blood. She shrugs again.

"Tough girl."

"Oh, yeah. So tough."

"How did you get that?" He is pointing at her scar. She feels filled by a gust of bright wind. It is happening so right, his eyes riveted to the pink glaze on her stomach.

"I don't like to talk about it." It's like the words find her. She turns and walks back the way she came. She doesn't glance behind her once.

• • •

AT THE end of the day she makes her way to the parking lot. She finds Edwin and Clive leaning against a shabby, eggplant-colored car.

"Miss! What a fine surprise to see you here!" Edwin says.

She rolls her eyes. "Right. What a coincidence. What are you two upstanding gentlemen up to, I wonder?"

Clive stiffens.

Edwin slips a joint from his pocket. "Nothing much." He twirls it in his fingers.

"Mind if I do *nothing much* with you?"

ALISON'S FATHER summons Edwin to their chairs.

"What can I be getting for you this afternoon?" Edwin asks.

"How's the penne?" her father asks, which makes Alison want to crawl into a hole and die.

"Excellent, sir."

They place their lunch orders.

"And to drink, a Red Stripe for me and a rum punch for my wife. Girls?" her father says.

"Sprite," Claire says, then adds in a whisper, "with a cherry."

"Your wish is my command, little miss. And you?" he says to Alison. He doesn't use her name, as if he doesn't know it.

"I'd love a daiquiri."

"Virgin," her father says.

"Of course," Edwin says, at the same time as Alison says, "I thought that was implied, Dad."

When Edwin returns with their order, Alison takes a delicate sip of her daiquiri. It's full of rum. She looks at him. He has his eyes on her, steady. He puts her father's tip in his back pocket and continues down the beach.

"I NEEDED that," she says later, when she finds him beyond the black rocks.

"You're most welcome, miss," he says.

"Stop calling me that," she says, and leans her body playfully against his.

It's a clear day. Faraway Cay appears unsettlingly close.

"So how are you enjoying your holiday?"

"It's fun I guess," she says. "My parents are driving me nuts."

"Family's always that way. You need a break."

"Seriously."

"Come out tonight. With me and Gogo."

"Out where?"

"We lime at a place in the Basin. We can pick you up in the car park. Eleven P.M. Just make sure it's all right with your parents, okay, miss?" His eyes twinkle.

"Right. I'll be sure to secure their permission."

"You'll come, then?"

A hermit crab scuttles across the sand. She picks it up and holds the shell close to her lips, then blows gently across the opening, drawing its legs out into the air.

"We'll see," she says, with a sly smile she thinks irresistible on her lips. She stands and begins to walk away. When she reaches the rocks, she glances back. He has his eyes on her, watching her go.

ONCE HER sister is asleep, she changes out of her pajamas and into the outfit she decided on that afternoon, her yellow dress with the plunging neckline. She glances one last time at her sleeping sister before closing the door quietly behind her and stepping out into the warm night. The resort late at night is a vacant place—lounge chairs stacked six feet high on the sand, the fertile scent of washed clay rising from the tennis courts, everything dark save the dim illumination of lanterns along the gravel footpaths. The water has changed, too; the ocean is glossy and black as oil, the pool glows ghostly green. Every surface echoes her nervy energy back at her.

She can hear the distant sounds of chatter and merriment at the hotel bar. So *satisfied* with their margaritas and Marley. She imagines Connecticut sitting at the bar, looking over his shoulder frequently to see if she's coming. She feels his lips on her neck, dry and nice like warm stones. She sees his blue eyes under the thick fringe of his lashes. She shakes the image away. It is to be expected, this residue of desire, this lazy craving.

What does she want from tonight? She's not totally sure. She knows only that she wants these men to take her somewhere new, out past the familiar borders of her life. She is only waiting in the parking lot a few minutes when the eggplant-colored car pulls in.

"Look who decided to grace us with she presence," Edwin says.

"It was a tough decision. There are so many fun things to do at the hotel at night."

She climbs in the backseat. The car smells strongly of body odor and air freshener. The seats are upholstered, and the fabric is held together with tape where it has ripped open to reveal beige foam. In her head, she's sitting on her bed in her dorm room, telling Nika, *Then I snuck out with them and we went to this great local dive.* She loves the feeling that she is doing something she probably shouldn't with men who scare her a little. Life is about escalation: men instead of boys; a wilder wild night; more and more and more. In her mind, she sends the image of her in the car with these men to Drew. He sees her and is worried, and his worry makes her swoon and long for him. But the feeling passes quickly, and then she pities him. She has left him so far behind that he is nothing but a nice little memory. Besides, what could possibly happen to her on a tiny island where everyone knows everyone?

"What's this place we're going to?" she asks.

"Paulette's," Edwin says. "Best dance spot on the island."

"Do you dance, Clive?" she asks playfully.

Edwin palms Clive's head with his hand and rubs it. "Gogo's a fantastic dancer. Just you wait to see his moves. Isn't that so, mate?"

Clive turns to look back at her and makes an expression that is a smile but not really.

Paulette's is more of a shack, honestly, the exterior strung with orange Christmas lights. Inside, there is a plank floor covered in sawdust, speakers spitting tinny music, the smells of sweat and liquor, an old mutt sniffing the ground for scraps. There are maybe twenty people, some dancing but most just talking. Alison sees a woman she thinks she recognizes as a waitress at the resort restaurant, but she isn't positive—black people *do* look similar to her; it's embarrassing but it isn't her fault, is it, that she's been raised in a white place and made white friends and had sex with exclusively white men? Well, three of them, anyway.

Nobody seems surprised to see her here with Edwin and Clive. It occurs to her she is probably not the first girl from the resort they've brought here, but did she think she was? She did not. She isn't an idiot.

"I'll get drinks," Edwin says. "You keep the Goges company."

She stands with Clive at the edge of the dance floor, which isn't an actual dance floor but an area marked off with yellow electrical tape. She smiles warmly at him and he smiles uncomfortably back.

"Do you guys come here a lot?" she asks over the din.

"Quite often, miss."

"You don't have to call me 'miss,' you know."

"I'm sorry, m—" He looks down, shakes his head at himself.

"It's fine. Seriously."

He looks out at the dance floor, like it is an absorbing show he doesn't want to tear himself away from. She knows he's just trying to fill the time until Edwin gets back. He doesn't know how to talk to her.

"I brought you something special," Edwin says when he returns. He hands Alison a shot glass filled with something murky—it looks like the water in Claire's fish tank when she hasn't cleaned it in too long. "See if you can guess the secret ingredient."

Alison holds the glass up to the light. "What is it?"

"Do you trust me?"

Does she?

"Yeah," she says coolly. She snaps her head back and takes the shot in one gulp. "It just tastes like grass."

He claps his hands. "That's a fact. Vodka infused with fine Jamaican ganja."

"It's not bad," she says. She laughs. "It's actually pretty good."

"You going to drink any fool thing he hand you?"

She turns. A woman is standing a few inches away from her, looking at her critically. She wonders if the women here all watched her gulping down the mystery drink and thought, *Dumb, dumb, dumb.*

The woman breaks into a laugh. "I'm just playing," she says. "He's all right. He's real sweet."

"This is Paulette she self," Edwin says.

"Nice to meet you," Alison says reflexively.

Paulette smirks at her, amused. God, she feels clueless.

"She's bent all the time to messing up my game," Edwin says.

"Is this your game?" Alison says, eyebrows raised.

Paulette laughs. "She's a live one."

She is doing it. She is really doing it. *A live one.*

"Do you want to dance?" Edwin asks.

"With *you*?"

"Sassy."

She takes his hand and pulls him onto the dance floor.

I SEARCHED for Paulette's Place online but found no trace of it. It must have closed sometime in the intervening years. I do not know what the bar where Alison was seen with Edwin and Clive really looked like. I know only that it was in the Basin and that, according to several witnesses, Alison was there four nights in a row, including on the last night of her life. But I have a mental picture of the place to which, in this version of things, Alison reacts. When she sees my Paulette's, she is pleased by its shabby authenticity, which affirms that she's found the real fun to be had on the island, something better than the lame hotel bar where empty-nesters stay up past their bedtimes slinging tequila and laughing at their milquetoast naughtiness.

Is the bar I've created a terrible cliché? If so, how much does it matter? What happens if you replace the wood floor coated in sawdust with a proper dance floor? What if you nix the mutt and add a cocktail waitress, sub a sound system for the tinny speakers on the bar? Now what does Alison think, say, do? What quantity of truth resides within a story's details?

ALISON SITS on the putting green at Indigo Bay in her purple bikini and watches Connecticut drive golf balls into the lagoon. They are alone, at the far edge of the property. On the putting green there is a golf bag stuffed with clubs and a tin bucket of balls, special ones that float. At some later time, Alison assumes, a staff member will go out onto the water in a boat to collect them. So much effort so that they may have this moment.

The lagoon is a wide stretch of shallow water separated from the ocean by dunes and a thicket of sea grape. This spot feels private, secret. She understands this is why he has brought her here. She recognizes the strategy of this, but she can still feel the place working on her. It's quiet. The only sounds are the swoop of the club, the crack as it makes contact with the ball and, after the passage of an impossible number of moments, the distant plunk of the ball slipping into the water.

"You're good," she says. She sits with her legs straight out in front of her, leaning back and propped up on her elbows.

"I'm just okay," he says with a shrug that makes her heart skip.

She feels him taking in the inches of her. It's so easy it makes her want to wring the sky—his wanting and her not giving and his wanting more.

It begins to rain. The first drops cool her sunburned shoulders.

"Should we go back?" she asks.

"A little rain never killed anyone," he says. She can tell he likes how it sounds. He swings and sends a ball whooshing out over the water.

When it begins to pour, he slots the club back into the bag and sits down beside her. He tucks a wet strand of hair behind her ear. He leans in to kiss her, and she kisses him back. Then she pulls away.

What's wrong with her? Why can't she give this to herself? Ivy boy and Ivy girl, la-di-da, easy peasy, ashes ashes we all fall down. It makes her . . . what? Embarrassed? Ashamed? She could kiss him, and then they could have sex in a secluded corner of a resort on a tropical island as the rain falls around them. For a moment she wishes with everything she has that she were a different girl, one who would see this possibility as the pinnacle of something.

"I'm sorry," she whispers.

"It's fine," he says. "Whatever."

SHE SEEKS out Edwin and Clive more frequently. In the afternoons, she sneaks away to meet Edwin past the black rocks. She wakes at dawn and swims in the ocean while they set up the lounge chairs on the beach for the day. Before they depart in the evening, she finds them in the parking lot and they pass around a joint. She learns that they have a sideline keeping the guests of Indigo Bay supplied with marijuana and, occasionally, harder stuff—cocaine and Ecstasy, mostly.

"Sometimes we forget to pass on a small amount to our customer," Edwin says one afternoon.

"So technically this joint is the property of a stockbroker from Millburn?" she says.

"Maybe so."

"So are you, like, stoned all the time at work?"

"Not *all* the time, miss," Clive says with a grin—the first time she's seen him actually smile.

Her whole body feels charged with the delicious secret they've divulged. She has been chosen, brought to the other side of the wall that separates tourist from local. They tell her about the soca band that will be playing at Paulette's later that week; about the cup of spittle Nestor the bartender keeps under the bar, next to the maraschino cherries. When Clive asks, Alison declares college "pretty boring." When Edwin prods him, Clive recounts the story of a guest who crashed a Sunfish into a fishing boat in the bay.

"Tourists," Alison scoffs, then blushes.

Edwin asks her about New York. He tells her he has a cousin there, in Queensbridge.

"Cool," she says with an air of native authority, as if she has any clue where Queensbridge is; as if, when she was a kid and the school bus took them through Harlem en route to midtown for field trips—museums, Broadway—she didn't press her face to the bus windows with the other kids and stare at the spectacle of a world of black people. "I was born in the city," she adds after a pause. "My parents lived in this tiny apartment on the Lower East Side. It's this immigrant neighborhood."

Clive and Edwin nod blankly in response. Her face burns. She wanted them to know her family hasn't always been filthy rich, but it didn't land how she wanted. What's wrong with her, bragging about how her parents were poor for, like, five minutes, before she was even born? She's been doing this kind of thing at college, too. Just the other day she told Nika a story from last summer at her family's "cottage" at the shore, and now she's stuck, because she wants to invite Nika out there to visit this summer, but then not only will Nika see just how rich Alison's family is, she will also know that Alison is the kind of person who refers to a huge freaking beach house as a cottage, which is even worse than the huge freaking house itself. It's not just her, though. Every rich kid at college does this. They all have a "cottage," or forebears they seem very keen to talk about who came to America from some shtetl or Irish potato farm, or they're "from Chicago" when really they live in Winnetka. (In the past three months she has learned the fancy suburbs surrounding all of the major cities in the country.) They are pathological minimizers, telling their half-truths and hoping for some kind of credit.

"It drives me nuts that my parents moved out of the city to raise us," she says, changing tack. "I mean, you're in the greatest city on earth, and you leave for some lame suburb?"

"But isn't New York quite dangerous?" Clive asks.

She shrugs. "You just have to pay attention."

ONE EVENING when she is standing with them in the parking lot after work, Clive proposes they go down to the water for a swim.

"I'm game," Alison says.

"Nah, nah. My boy's stalling," Edwin says with a mirthful shake of his head.

"Am not. The water's just looking nice today."

"Gogo has to go see he baby boy and take the shit from he lady," Edwin says with a gleam in his eye.

"You have a kid?" she says. She's been hanging out with them for days and this is the first she's heard of any baby. The information tickles her. In her head, she tells Nika, *Then Clive had to go take care of his son,* as if it doesn't ruffle her at all.

Clive's face has gone blank. Maybe he doesn't care about the kid. Or maybe he does care about him and he's ashamed to be standing here getting stoned with Edwin and some girl while his child waits for him and he doesn't want to think about it.

"He'll make three soon," he says softly.

"Wait. Are you *married*?"

Clive shakes his head.

"Relax, Goges." Edwin claps a hand on his friend's big shoulder. "If Sara never consents to marry you, more time to lime with me."

Clive nods, his face empty. She can hardly bear it, and at the same time cannot look away from it, his gentle, pained way of being in the world; he reminds her, in a way, of Claire.

She touches his arm. "She don't know what she's missing."

"She *don't* know what she's missing. You're turning into a proper island girl, now," Edwin says.

. . .

EVERY NIGHT, after her sister is asleep, she crosses the dark resort grounds and meets them in the parking lot and they drive to Paulette's Place, where they drink and smoke and she and Edwin dance while Clive stands near them on the dance floor, bouncing his large body not quite to the beat. At times it seems clear to her what Edwin wants—he flirts, manufactures opportunities to touch her. One night, his crotch grazes her hip as they dance and she feels that he is hard. Her skin turns to gooseflesh. His erection scares her. Well, Drew's scared her, too, at first, didn't it? Connecticut's hand on her thigh scared her. But she knows it is not the same.

Suddenly she sees John the gardener's face—his soft lamb's-wool hair, his dark skin. Is that all this is, what she's doing with Edwin? An attempt to absolve her frightened child self? And she still can't do it. She feels him against her and she tenses.

But nothing comes of it. When the song ends, he buys her another round at the bar, complimenting Paulette on her dress while they wait. He is loose and jovial again, as if their pressed-together dancing didn't happen. She is starting to see something new about him, a controlled aspect simmering just beneath his charming surface. The moves he makes—letting her feel his hardness, then striking up a conversation with Paulette when she fully expected him to lead her off to some dark corner—seem, beneath the offhandedness with which he executes them, studied, like there is nothing he says or does that he hasn't thought through. Maybe this will go where she thinks it's going. Or maybe nothing will happen. When she considers this possibility she is humiliated but also, in some way, relieved.

ON A rainy day, after picking up a puka shell necklace for Claire at the gift shop, Alison finds Edwin taking his break behind the restaurant. "No beach today?" she asks.

"Can't." He points out at the black rocks. Waves crash against them, sending spray high into the air and blocking the path to his usual spot.

"We could swim there," Alison says.

"You crazy? Look at that water."

"Bet you two joints I can do it. Around the rocks, to the beach, and back."

"I'm not betting your death sentence, miss," he says with a laugh.

"Suit yourself." She walks down to the water. She peels off her tank top and shimmies out of her shorts, revealing the new bikini she got for this trip, blue with white flowers.

"What are you doing?"

She dives in. The waves are swollen, but it isn't as bad as it looks from shore; besides, she's a strong swimmer. She strokes through the waves, keeping her head when she sees them rise up above her. When she is out past the rocks she begins to arc around. She swims until her limbs are stiff with exhaustion and every part of her tastes salt. She loves this feeling, the rush of hanging off the edge of your comfort zone but still knowing you have a solid grip on it. When she returns to shore she hands Edwin a shard of green sea glass.

"Proof," she gasps, breathing hard but trying not to show it.

That afternoon in the parking lot, he gives her the two joints she has won. "I think I've been underestimating you," he says.

"Is that right?"

He nods. "You're a dangerous girl."

ON THE last night of vacation, she can't help herself. She goes looking for Connecticut. She finds him by the bar in the lobby. He wears khaki slacks and a blue-and-white-checked shirt. He is freshly showered. His blond hair still holds narrow ridges from the tines of a comb.

"Hey."

"Hey."

She reaches into the pocket of her jean skirt. "Want to?" she says, revealing the joint in her palm. Easiest thing in the world. Connecticut grabs one of the Indigo Bay matchbooks from the glass bowl on the bar. She leads him to the parking lot. She puts the joint to her lips. He strikes the match. When she exhales, she coughs.

"You okay?" he asks, a hand to her back, a show of rather than actual concern—he is a good guy and wants her to know it. It's nice, though, his hand there.

She nods and passes the joint to him.

"How'd you manage to get this?"

"Let's just say I have my ways."

He leans closer, whispers in her ear, "I like your ways." He kisses her neck. Her body shivers, but she shakes the pleasure away. When they have finished the joint, she drops the roach on the ground.

"You're really not going to tell me where you got it?"

"Well . . . ," she says.

"So secretive, Alison." He twists a strand of her hair around his finger.

"It's no big deal, really. Edwin gave it to me." She says it like it is the least interesting fact in the world.

"Oh," he says, stiffening. "Well, lucky us. We'll have to thank him." He pulls her hair away from the back of her neck and kisses her again.

"I have to go," she says. She pecks him, quick and delicate, on the lips.

"Come on, why don't you—"

"Shhh," she says. She is the star in a script she knows by heart. "Later. I'll find you."

She begins to walk away, but he holds on to her hand.

"Where?" he asks.

She smiles coyly. "I promise."

DOES ALISON seem awful to you? I admit that, as I channel my sister, I sometimes have an urge to shake her. I find her incessant judginess toward our parents and her fellow resort guests self-righteous and bratty, especially the judgments she renders on the blond boy, who is practically her double: bright, privileged, attractive, and tasteful enough to know to be self-deprecating about such things. Equally frustrating is the way she exempts Edwin and Clive from her judgment. How desperate she is for their approval, their special attentions, how badly she needs them to know that she is more than, better than, all the basically decent people from her world.

What I can't figure out: Was Alison insufferable in a perfectly ordinary teenage way, or was something darker at play? Was her behavior typical or troubling? What destiny lay ahead of her as she toyed with the blond boy and danced at Paulette's Place and swam out beyond the black rocks in the rain-swelled surf? Who *was* she?

AS THE eggplant-colored Vauxhall Astra (how she loves that name!) rumbles down Mayfair Road, she sees her last night on Saint X spread above her like a sky dense with stars. She feels the night's promise in the itch of the upholstery against the backs of her thighs and in "Boombastic" blasting from the radio. She wears a turquoise halter top and a short jean skirt; she is an island girl, flying away from Connecticut at the speed of light. *I think I'll stay in tonight. Honestly, Nika? These campus parties just feel very tame to me lately.*

It is hot inside Paulette's Place. Sweat gleams on skin. "Buy me a drink," she tells them. She takes a shot of rum, then another, and struts onto the dance floor. She sways her hips and presses up against Edwin, then spins away to uncertain Clive, back and forth. Irresistible. She sees herself from outside herself, from somewhere up in the mantle of stars, like the story of her life is already burned in light and she has only to navigate by it to make herself into herself.

Once Clive is a few drinks in he is not so hesitant. When she dances with him, he holds her hips.

"Check you out, Goges!" Edwin hoots.

Clive grins.

She winks at Edwin and moves in closer to Clive.

His hands, so clumsy and searching, stir something in her. As they dance, his eyes wander from her breasts to the floor to Edwin to the ceiling, never settling anywhere, as if looking at any one thing too long is just asking for punishment. An image comes to her, a baby boy with damp black curls and eyelashes to the horizon.

It's then she understands. It isn't only Edwin she wants. It is the two of them together, the power of two men so different from each other, and all eyes on her. They will dance a few minutes longer, and then she will say, "Let's get out of here." They will go to some deserted beach, or they will sneak into an unoccupied hotel room at Indigo Bay, or maybe they will only make it out behind Paulette's, to the scruffy patch of sand and grass at the edge of the parking lot, hidden from view by an old junked van. Things with Edwin will reach their natural conclusion. Even as she does it, she will be telling Nika, *It was pretty good. Not, like, earth-shattering or anything.*

Then she will turn her attention to Clive. She will push onto her tiptoes and kiss him on the mouth. He will surprise her. She will expect him to be timid and awkward, but he won't be. He will hold the back of her head and kiss her hard, so that the whole weight of him is contained in his kiss.

He will take her ponytail and squeeze it in his fist like a rag. He will take her hand and thrust it down his pants. The more afraid she feels, the more she will want it.

He will lay her down on the ground. The stars will wheel overhead, fine and white, and in them she will see herself, years from now, looking back at her as she is in this moment, beautiful and reckless as a young woman ought to be. She will have this night forever. She will carry it like her scar, a thing she can always feel, even when she isn't touching it. He will move over her like she isn't precious at all, like he is barely aware of her beneath him. She will feel so small in his arms, and she will like this so much it will suck the air out of her—the way she disappears, the way she becomes nothing at all. She will finally feel like she is in this place without herself, and maybe that is all she ever wanted, for her little life to vanish right out from under her.

She will stare into the sky. The stars will rush at her across time and space like spears. They will slash her up with their cold white light.

I didn't have sex for almost a year after she died. At first I didn't want to. Next to Alison, the girls at college were so mind-numbing. I'd go to parties and they'd be wearing all this makeup and this perfume or fruity shampoo or whatever makes them smell like that, and while they were talking to me they would pose and giggle like it was an audition, and it made me feel dead.

Later I wanted to, but I couldn't. I'd go back to a girl's dorm room and she'd light a vanilla candle or something, and all of a sudden I just had to get out of there. The girl would be embarrassed and hurt and insulted. She'd say, "Did I do something wrong, Drew?" I'd pull on my pants real quick and bolt. I'd go back to my apartment, which was a real shithole I shared with these guys I'd ended up living with, and drink beer and play *Mario Kart* until four A.M. I haven't kept up with any of those guys. I can't. I thought Alison was the love of my life and she was dead and that was it for me.

But things changed. Alison changed. With time, she stopped being this guilty conscience or this barrier or whatever she was. She became a way of . . . opening up, I guess. I told Shannon about her after two months, in the Sheep Meadow in Central Park. I told Anjali after only two weeks, when we snuck away from a friend's housewarming party. I'd tell the girls about Alison and they'd tell me about their mother's drinking, or their brother's depression, or being bullied.

I told Hayley after three months, on a road trip to her cousin's wedding in Cleveland. After I told her, she stroked my arm and said, "You poor thing." I drank too much at her cousin's dumb wedding. I got loud and obnoxious with her blowhard father. I spent the rest of the night puking into the toilet at the Best Western. Hayley stayed awake all night taking

221

care of me and the next morning she sucked apologies from me and I gave them to her, tail between my legs. I did behave badly. It would take a few more months for me to admit to myself that I hated her; I'd hated her from the moment she stroked my arm in the car like that.

With Rachel, I waited almost a year. I didn't want her to feel like she had to compete with my murdered high school sweetheart. When we got married, Alison changed again. She became a past I was ready to leave behind. A ghost I no longer invited inside. We're divorced now, but that was about other things. She wanted kids, I thought I did but changed my mind. "But don't you want to see who we'd make?" she'd say, like she thought it could only end well.

Sometimes I can't help it. Alison forces her way back in and I start litigating the whole thing all over again. She had a temper, no doubt about it. I think about how riled up she could get about things that were, I don't know, just the world being the world. Like when Nick cheated on Becca and Alison slapped him. Or that teacher, I forget his name, but he had this policy where if you were late he shut the door, and if there was a test, tough luck, you failed, and once this kid Paul, this poor fucking fat kid everybody gave a hard time, I think he was probably gay, too, and this was before you could be, he showed up late on test day and this teacher wouldn't let him in, and she went off on him. The star student challenging the teacher in front of the whole class. The rest of us sat there slack-jawed. She thought everything was her business, I guess is what I'm saying. I'll think about that and wonder if maybe it got her into trouble. Maybe she stuck her nose where it didn't belong.

But I don't spend nearly as much time thinking about this stuff as I used to. Alison's death is a mystery like God or Stonehenge or intelligent life in the universe—if you aren't careful, that shit will consume you, and in the end you'll still be no closer to solving it. I'm thirty-seven years old, and if I've learned anything it's that you can live a pretty decent life without unpacking life's mysteries.

SARA

IN HIS YEARS DRIVING A TAXI, Clive has observed that there are two kinds of passengers. First, there are those who ignore him. They spend the ride as if they are alone. They may make telephone calls about sensitive matters. A few times he has heard about the merger between two large corporations, or the resignation of the CEO of a Fortune 500 company, before the news appears in the papers; *I could have been a wealthy man ten times over with all the insider knowledge I've overheard, if I had any money to invest to begin with, hahaha*—he's heard this joke a few times around the garage. In his presence customers have called divorce attorneys ("I want him fucked, do you understand me? I want him fucked so hard his head spins.") and parents with dementia ("Mommy, I need you to listen to Nurse Jen, okay? Can you do that for me, Mommy?"). They may belch or pick their noses in the backseat, and they will not be surreptitious about it, for to these customers, the taxi is that rarest thing: a private enclave in the midst of the city. In his backseat he has seen grown men sob. A teenage girl hold up a small mirror to pop her zits and scowl hatefully at her reflection. A father slap a son across the face.

Then there are those who talk to him, seeking, he supposes, the wisdom that films and television shows have taught them to expect from taxi drivers. These passengers unburden themselves to him of their darkest shames. Affairs, addictions, a stepdaughter's birthday forgotten. To these passengers, the taxi driver is priest, the rider penitent.

Ultimately, though, these types are not as different as they seem. Both those who ignore him and those who entrust him with their most precious secrets do so because, in the end, he is no one to them.

It used to be that when he came home after his shift he could leave these people behind, but the neighborhood is changing. Last year, a white family moved into his building, a couple with a green-eyed, black-haired little girl,

Maeve. It won't be long before somebody opens a wine bar nearby. Before too long, one of those food halls might open in Flatbush, and maybe the Little Sweet will have a stall there. The white family in the building are polite and very friendly and at first it seemed there were some advantages to their arrival. When the boiler broke last winter, it was fixed within forty-eight hours. The white family, it turned out, had called 311 about it. He'd overheard them chatting with a neighbor in the vestibule, the neighbor explaining that in the past they'd gone as long as two weeks without heat, the white couple expressing outrage at the landlord's tenant treatment. But now his roommate Cecil calls the family the 311s, because they have also called on more than one occasion to lodge noise complaints, leading to police visits. "Why can't they just knock on a door?" Cecil grumbles, though he must know the answer to this question, as Clive does. They are afraid. Not afraid that their black, foreign neighbors pose a threat to their safety, but afraid that a confrontation will mean losing the approval they feel they've earned with their "Good morning"s and their "Let me get that for you"s. He remembers something Edwin used to say: *Nice is some real fuckery.*

So he knows what this girl, Emily, is doing at the Little Sweet. After all, she's not the only white kid who's become a regular recently. There is also the man with the sketch pad. (*What is he drawing?* Clive wonders. *Scenes of locals in their natural habitat?*) It's not enough for them to live here, to overrun every last space—they need everyone else to be happy about it, too. Every time he catches himself enjoying her company, he reminds himself that's what he is to her. Her local friend. Her badge of approval.

But the more time he spends with her, the more he forgets to remind himself. She is such an odd girl, so young to be so alone in the world. Some evenings, looking across the table at her pale hair, skin, lips, a disquieting notion washes over him: She is not real. She materializes each night so that they may speak, then melts back into the city, dissolving into the salt-whitened streets.

She may be trouble. Funny—from the time he was a child, he has always thought of himself as a person who avoids trouble and complication at all costs. Yet the facts of his life tell a different story. Sometimes he wonders if it is his fate to be controlled by people with the tug of stars, to let himself be pulled into their trouble again and again and learn nothing from it.

WHEN THEY were seventeen, Edwin and Clive and the rest of their class graduated from Everett Lyle Secondary School, all of them except Arthur, who had dropped out a year prior and who, as everybody save his sweet father knew, was into some serious shit by then. He could be found many nights loitering outside the bars and discos around Hibiscus Harbour, sometimes dealing to the tourists, sometimes looking to score. Damien continued his schooling; he would do well on his O-levels, receive a local scholarship, and go on to study biology at the University of the Virgin Islands. His picture would appear in the island newspaper, along with those of the other students from their form who would be attending college off-island, bound for Saint Thomas, Barbados, Miami, Washington, D.C.

"You better not come back all assified," Don would tell Damien when they gathered to see him off.

"I'm right behind you outta here, Doc," Edwin would say.

The rest of them found work. Don got a job in his uncle's auto repair shop. Des, good with boats like his brother Keithley, scored a gig aboard a party boat that took tourists—mostly American college students on spring break—for all-you-can-drink tours up and down the island's south coast. The boat had a dance floor, and the nightly tour included a dance competition in which a dozen or so girls vied for the prize of coupons for five free drinks at Papa Mango's. Often as they danced, the girls shed their clothes—flinging their tank tops into the crowd, sliding their panties down their legs. Des had been at the job a month when he confessed to his friends that there might be such a thing as too much pum pum. After four months, a naked woman was nothing to him. He would look at the girls flaunting their hips and breasts and feel an emptiness like water.

Despite his grandmother's disapproval, Clive joined Edwin in pursuing what Edwin referred to as his "business ventures." It was not uncommon for them to have four or five such ventures going at any one time. They started an agency doing paperwork for charter boats on the cheap. They went to Philipsburg, on the Dutch side of Saint Martin, stocked up on Guess jeans, and resold them in the Basin. They went out into the shallows of Britannia Bay at midnight and hunted sea crayfish, which they sold by the pound to the restaurant at the Oasis. "Nobody ever got rich working for somebody else," Edwin was fond of saying, as they hefted enormous trash bags filled with jeans through the streets of Philipsburg, or when Clive got his hand snipped by a crayfish at two A.M. They were earning a pittance, less than any of their friends, but Edwin was certain it was just a matter of time before they stumbled on the right idea, at which point they would finally have the cash to "make a big move," which Clive understood meant leaving—for the States, for New York, someplace with a stage grand enough for his friend's ambitions.

His life took on a familiar shape. He worked with Edwin. At night, they drove to wherever they were liming that night. (Officer Roy pulling them over with some regularity and tossing them in jail for the night to sober up.) When he arrived home, he stumbled into bed and slept until his grandmother swatted him awake, and then the whole thing began again.

He was nineteen the day Edwin did something that would change his life forever. It was Carnival. They had spent the afternoon with their friends at the Grand Parade along Investiture Boulevard, watching the revelers and passing a bottle of rum among themselves, cheering when their favorite local band went by on a truck with speakers blaring, catcalling Miss Island Queen with her silly crown. As the festivities wound down, they spotted Sara and her friend across the parade route.

"Your girl's looking fine today!" Des said.

"Check she out, dressed like a sket," added Don.

Sara Lycott was wearing a yellow dress that ended just below her ass, a thing that was altogether unlike the proper, innocent girl Clive had known all his life.

"You going to ask to walk she home or what?" Edwin said.

"Stop fooling," Clive mumbled.

"Who's fooling? This is your moment! She dressed like a sket because she's hungry for it."

Clive took a swig from the bottle of rum.

"Look at he, too puss to even try!" Don said.

Then Edwin grabbed him by the shoulders and looked at him with such conviction it shook Clive to his core. "You want to live your life or what, man?" He didn't wait for Clive to reply. "Go!" With that, he shoved Clive, who stumbled out into the parade. He hurried across the street and found himself standing before the tight female circle of Sara and her friends.

IT WAS over a mile from Investiture Boulevard to Sara's house. They walked along the side of the road. Sara wore peach pumps, her ankles wobbling on the uneven ground; she stopped periodically to brush the dust from her shoes. For some time, they walked in a silence that seemed to concern Sara not in the least, while Clive was desperate to break it but could come up with nothing to say, his mind at turns swirling and blank. He didn't understand how it had happened. She'd stood there surrounded by her friends, arms crossed, as he stuttered his invitation. "M-m-mmmay I walk you home?" Once he'd gotten the words out, he looked up at her, awaiting her rejection. But something had changed in her. It wasn't just the dress. Her eyes, usually so sharp and flashing, held a dull detachment, as if she were watching herself in this moment from some great distance. She opened her mouth and said, "You may."

"How did you enjoy the parade?" he tried finally.

"The parade is the parade."

They walked on.

"You look nice today," he said.

"No, I don't."

"Yes, you do. You always do. You're beautiful, Sara." He had wanted to say this to her for years, but had never believed he really would.

"You're the only one who thinks so." She paused to dislodge a pebble from her shoe. "Shall we go to Milk Queen?" She pointed down Tillery Street in the direction of the ice-cream parlor.

She ordered a banana split with peppermint ice cream. He got nothing for himself. He would have felt foolish eating in front of her. Sara ate her ice cream with the same weariness with which she'd responded to his compliments. She picked at it, licking tiny spoonfuls with a tongue like a cat's, setting the spoon down, then sighing and picking it up again, as if this were merely one more in an endless line of tasks she must complete before she could be dead. Why had she said yes to his invitation? He wanted to touch the secret world inside her. Instead, he watched dumbly as she ate. When at last she'd scraped the glass dish clean, she murmured, "You'd best take me home now."

They didn't speak on the walk from Milk Queen to her house. His throat felt clutched by a hand. He had not the faintest idea what had happened in the past hour, and he supposed that was what everybody meant when they talked about the mystery of women. There was some consolation, at least, in joining the ranks of mystified men.

Sara's house was a single-story cinder-block-and-plaster home like everybody else's, but the paint was fresh—white, with sunshine-yellow trim. The short front walkway was lined with purple flowers and there were no enervated donkeys or dogs cluttering the yard. All of this contributed to an air of gentility that Clive felt befitted a minister's widow and daughter brought down by circumstance. The only discordant feature was an old, tumbledown cookhouse out back, with a rusted galvanized roof.

As they turned off the road and walked up to the house, Sara's mother appeared in the doorway. Miss Agatha, like her daughter, was a meager woman, no taller than a child. Growing up, he had seen her at church every Sunday. But as she stood in the doorway, her stance slack and desultory, her eyes darting like a hen's, it occurred to him that he had not seen her there in years.

"G-g-good evening, Miss Agatha," he managed. The mother had the same effect on him as the daughter.

She did not respond, just continued to stand in the doorway with her arms at her sides. Past where she stood, he could see the parlor. There were piles everywhere, and dirty dishes stacked on a table. A framed painting hung askew on the wall; beneath it a planter held the brown husk of a dead plant. As he took it in, mouth agape, he thought of Sara's pristine speech and dress, everything that made the other boys call her *snob* and *prude*. He thought of his grandmother's house, its smell of bleach and not a thing out of place. He thought of his mother's house, and of his mother. When he felt Sara looking at him, he tried to avert his eyes from the scene, but he was too late—she had seen him seeing it. She bent her head. He wanted to tell her that her secret was safe with him. He wanted to tell her he understood how the shame came not just from being from a home like this, a mother like this, but from loving a home like this, a mother like this. But before he could do anything but fidget, Sara shook her head, and when she raised her eyes to meet his they were rinsed clean, bright and flashing as always. Miss Agatha turned and walked back into the dark house.

"Your mum vex?" he asked.

"My mum is nothing."

"I hope you did have a good time," he said pitifully.

Sara kept her eyes fixed on the ground.

Clive turned and walked down the porch steps, past the purple flowers that lined the front walk. He was about to turn back onto the road when he heard footsteps behind him. Then he felt Sara grab his hand. He turned, and she met his gaze. Her eyes were shining, he couldn't tell if there were tears or if it was the moonlight. She pulled him off the walkway.

"Where are we going?" he asked.

"Hush," she said. She led and he followed, around the house to the yard and into the old cookhouse.

TWO MONTHS later, when Sara told him that she was pregnant, Clive had the feeling that this eventuality had been waiting for him all along. He was scared as shit, but it had a rightness to it. Clive and Sara. He looked at her belly and tried to get his mind around the truth that a person who was half him and half her was inside, blooming into being day by day. It seemed like a thing that could not possibly have happened to anyone else ever before.

"I want you to know I'm going to take care of you," he told her. "Both of you."

"You don't even have a job," she whispered. Her voice was not angry or accusatory. There was nothing in it at all. She blinked.

"I'll get one. We can rent a place of our own. Buy a car. It will be okay. I promise."

"Didn't anybody ever tell you not to make promises you can't keep?"

"I will keep it, Sara. We can be married. We can be a family."

He did not stumble on the words. He had at last found something worthy of his conviction.

Sara looked right past him. "What kind of family would we be? You out all the time carrying on with your friends, and me . . . you've seen how I did grow up."

"It won't have to be like that. I'll stop all of it. We can give this child everything."

"I might be crazy like her. I know I might." Her voice was a whisper.

"Sara." He took her hands in his, but she yanked them away.

"You think because you did rut with me like a goat in a shed I must marry you?" she snapped.

He wanted to tell her he would weather any storm with her. He wanted to remind her that what happened in the cookhouse had been her idea; that as he emptied himself into her in the pitch-dark, breathing in the smell of must and rusted metal, he felt such sadness, because he didn't want to do it like this, that he would be angry with himself forever for letting it happen the way it did.

"I know you come from a good family," he said instead. "I'm prepared to set you up how you deserve."

She stared at the dirt. "If you believe I'm a minister's daughter, you're a fool for true."

"SWEET BOY LIKE honey. Always stick to the most venomous girl." His grandmother said this as if it could not be helped. Clive had waited nearly a month to inform her that he was going to be a father, telling himself he was withholding the news simply because it was none of her business.

"Sara is not venomous."

"Don't give me that backchat."

"You don't know anything about her."

She snorted, then released a laugh like vinegar. "I know she crazy mother. I know goat don't make sheep."

He slammed his fist on the table. "She's the mother of my child and I won't let you speak low of she!" he shouted.

For the first time in his life his grandmother averted her eyes from him. Looking back, he would realize this was the moment when she relinquished him to himself; never again would she pester him about his late-night liming or encourage him to enter a training program so that he might learn a vocation.

"Oh, you're a real man now," she whispered.

He wanted to press himself to her and weep.

HE BEGAN looking for a job the day Sara told him she was carrying his child, but found nothing. He was beginning to despair, and to think that

Sara was right when she'd told him not to make promises he couldn't keep, when Edwin announced he'd secured interviews at a new resort for both of them. "I thought nobody ever got rich working for somebody else," Clive said when Edwin told him.

"What you think, I'm going to abandon my bred in he hour of need? Beside, we gonna make mad service charge."

What would he do without Edwin? They were hired. The job came with a uniform, crisp and white, with *Indigo Bay* embroidered on the breast pocket in gold thread. When he went to Sara's house in the uniform after his first day of work and gave her the tips he'd earned, she smiled the secret smile he'd seen all those years ago at the Christmas pageant, the one he'd been chasing ever since.

Clive made plans. He spent a Saturday at the small island library, paging through a mildewed book about pregnancy. He brought Sara ginger candies to quell her nausea. He purchased bottles and diapers and a soft brown bear he imagined would become his child's favorite. He made sure Sara had the phone number for the back office at Indigo Bay so he could be reached when it was time.

But in the end, Sara went into labor at night, three weeks early. He was at Paulette's with his friends. He stumbled home that night the same as usual, woke from his hungover sleep the next morning like always. It was only when he went into the kitchen and saw his grandmother sitting stiffly at the table that he knew something had happened.

"You have a son," she said.

He could not square in his mind how, as he'd been drinking with his friends, elsewhere, he was becoming a father. He would never know exactly when it had happened. The moment he went from being one thing to another was lost to him forever.

When he went to Sara in the hospital that morning, she would not look at him.

"How could you?" she whispered. She held the baby, his son, asleep in her arms, swaddled in a pale blue blanket.

But how could he have known she would go into labor so early? Didn't she see all he'd done to prepare? Didn't she know he was not the deadbeat she seemed to want to make him into? He was about to say all of this to her, but the look in her eyes stopped him. It was not sadness, or hurt, but a brittle, impassive stare. The world had disappointed her once again, as she always expected it to, only this time he was the one who had done it.

The baby began to cry, a desperate wail that sucked the air out of Clive.

Sara turned away from him as she rocked the child. "Hush, Bryan. Hush, my sweet love."

When Clive told me I was beautiful, my heart cracked. All my life I had waited for a boy to say that to me, and now one had, and it didn't matter, because I could not let myself believe it. I had finally gotten what I wanted and it was no good because I was who I was and I always would be. Everything was like that, ruined just because it was me it all happened to.

Sara Lycott. So proper and well spoken, so devout at church, so obedient at school. How my friends would have recoiled if they saw who I became at home with my mum, how we yelled and yanked and scratched.

Behind its freshly painted exterior, our house was a wild place. We were not so much mother and daughter as two women suffocating together, breathing into one another until all the air in the house had been warmed by the insides of both of us. There was nothing in life we were not tired of.

Though we fought all the time, we only had a single argument, which we repeated over and over until I was insentient to it as stone. Our fight was like the walk home from school, marked by familiar signposts: the Scotts's orange front door, the pothole shaped like a heart on Underhill Road. I think there was comfort in knowing we would only hurt each other in familiar ways. I think I hoped each time that the argument would finally take us somewhere new, out beyond the hating and loving and hating that was all I had ever known.

It went like this: I would sass, or leave a mess, or be a disappointment to my mum in some other way, and she would scold that I should be better, for I was the daughter of a government minister and I could not afford to forget it. I would shout back, call her hypocrite. "When was the last time you did clean we house?" I would say, and off we would go, shouting about all the ways the other had failed to live up to the kind of family we both pretended we were.

On the morning of the Grand Parade, we had found ourselves deep in the mud of this same fight once again. She had come into the parlor to find me scratching at my scalp. She grabbed my elbow.

"Stop that. Where are your manners?"

"'You're a minister's daughter,'" I mimicked. I wrenched my arm free and went right back to sliding my fingernails beneath the irresistible dried skin on my scalp.

"Don't you mock me."

"And you're a minister's wife. Must be some other lady I saw in we house yesterday itching she pum pum."

"It's a good thing your father's dead. How ashamed he would be to hear you speak this way to your mum!"

How many times had she said this to me? A dozen? A thousand? But this time the anger I felt was different, feral and hopeless, sharp as teeth.

"You never tell me again whose daughter I be!" I shouted. "The only person I see I'm the daughter of is you. A sket like everybody say!"

I screamed so loudly my throat would be raw later that day, when I told Clive Richardson he could walk me home. I held my mother's gaze and sucked air through my teeth. I swear the whites of her eyes turned black.

Her hands fell to her sides. "You think I'm nothing but your mum," she whispered. "But someday you'll see." Then she turned and walked slowly to her bedroom at the back of the house and pulled the stained curtain across the doorway.

Oh, what a fine actress, my mum, playing the victim of my cruelty. Where did I learn how to lash with words if not from her?

I changed into the shortest dress I owned. I snatched my purse and slammed the front door behind me. At the end of the parade, when Clive Richardson stumbled up to me and mumbled his invitation, it was like God or fate or whatever thing I lacked the time or proclivity to wonder about then was handing it to me, just giving it to me for free: a chance to take my life into my own hands and spoil it before it could disappoint me; to break my mum's heart and free myself from our suffocating life together; to prove I was every bit my mother's daughter. Though in the end, the cost would be more than I could have imagined.

THE SECRET CITY

IN MID-DECEMBER, a food deliveryman on a bicycle turned the corner by my apartment too sharply and mowed down pitiful Jefe mid-elimination. I was at the other end of the block when it happened, returning home from work. I did not see bike and pup collide, but I heard Jefe's high-pitched yelp and witnessed the aftermath: The man in the NASCAR hat gathering Jefe in his arms like a baby. The deliveryman putting his hands up defensively and repeating, "Sorry," in heavily accented English as the old man berated him in Spanish and passersby craned their heads to watch, sometimes pausing as if they might intervene before averting their gaze and hurrying along. The deliveryman backed slowly away and got on his bike (plastic bags of takeout still hanging from the handlebars). He rode quickly around the corner and out of sight.

The old man carried Jefe to the front stairs, sat on the lowest step, and rocked him. I'm not sure whether the dog was still alive or whether he'd already departed this mortal coil. As I approached them, I thought I ought to say something, but when I reached the steps it seemed that to intrude in their final moments together would be obscene, so instead I walked quietly past them up the stairs.

As I disappeared into the vestibule, I heard the man whisper, "*Nos vemos pronto, viejito.*"

When I was underground in my apartment, it occurred to me that now there was not a single soul in the building whose name I knew. So began winter.

An entire season had passed since I found Clive Richardson. I had been conversing with him for several weeks, and an ironic reversal had transpired. In the beginning, our proximity had terrified me. Now it was just the opposite. When I was away from him I became unnerved, agitated, itchy, feelings that festered until I was sitting across from him again, our trays of stew and beer before us. I'd catch myself prolonging our evenings despite being aware that he was ready to leave, because once he was out of sight the dread would set in all over again, and I would face the long night hours alone with it.

When I was not with him, I was thinking of him. On the surface, I could be conversing with my mother on the phone about which produce it was most important to purchase organic (blueberries: essential; bananas: not), or racing past the travertine-and-glass grid of the Grace Building in the sleet on my way to work, or eating a lunch of anesthetized midtown falafel with my fellow bright young coworkers, and I might pull all of this off convincingly, but really I was with Clive, imagining hypothetical interactions we might have that would lead to his confession. I imagined, for instance, that there might be a fire at the Little Sweet, and that after making our escape I would dash back into the building to rescue Vincia; afterward, as I breathed through an oxygen mask in the back of an ambulance, Clive would be so stricken by my self-sacrifice and my goodness, and by his own shame, that he would prostrate himself at my feet and tell me everything. Another scenario found us at the Heidelberg on the Upper East Side, washing down käsespätzle and sauerbraten with steins of Dunkel. I would remark that the saying about the impossibility of stepping into the same river twice could be applied just as aptly to New York, a place as transient as it was eternal, the Germans of old Yorkville disappearing into the sediment and making way for new inlets and curvatures—Little Brazil, the Nepalese of Jackson Heights. This comment would strike Clive as so utterly insightful that he would decide that he had finally found a person worthy of being entrusted with his secret.

During this same interval, winter took firm hold of the city. It was the coldest winter anyone could remember, global warming be damned. Icebreakers turned the Hudson to shards. At crosswalks, pedestrians maneuvered around moats of frigid, gravy-colored slurry. The subway trains smelled of the particular sweat of overheated young financiers in puffer coats. That winter in New York was a period of collectively borne brutality, the sort during which it is possible for a passing glance between strangers on the sidewalk to contain an entire conversation about the awfulness of the season. Yet I had never felt more distant from my fellow urban denizens. As December wore on, I came to feel as if a pane of glass had slid between me and the rest of the world, a division so impregnable that when I collided with a man coming out of my office building one evening, I was so bewildered that I made my way to the subway at a near-gallop.

I SAID earlier that in general Clive did not speak about his life before New York and, in general, that was true. But there were a few exceptions to this rule, and I'd like to set those out here, because I can see now that they told me everything I needed to know, though I didn't understand this then. There were small things, mentioned in passing: I learned that Clive had worn a pink and maroon school uniform. I learned that he was raised by his grandmother, though he did not say what had become of his mother and father. I learned that when *Ghostbusters* came to the island's only movie hall, he snuck in at three forty-five every afternoon, just in time to watch the Stay Puft Marshmallow Man stomp through Columbus Circle (though he didn't know it was Columbus Circle then—New York, he said, had seemed to him a blur of traffic, graffiti, and crazy characters, an impression that remained unchallenged until he touched down in the city himself over a decade later).

Clive shared these stories with me in his reserved way. He chose his words carefully, set each scene with a minimum of detail. Sometimes he would begin to tell me something, then shake his head and stop. "Never mind," he'd say. "It's boring." I suspect he didn't think I would understand, and maybe I wouldn't have. Often, he paused for long stretches, during which I supposed he was reliving unspoken aspects of the stories privately, and I understood that these gaps were where it all resided, that my challenge was to parse these omissions, to decipher the negative spaces carved out by his stories.

One evening, after I told him a story about the late-night joyriding of my youth (a story lifted from the freeways of Southern California and transposed onto the streets of Starlight, Indiana, which were surrounded, in my telling, by endless fields of corn), Clive chewed his lip and said, "My friends and I used to take a boat out and party on beaches all around the island. Drink a bit, smoke a bit. I remember one night, we went to this cay called Faraway . . ." He paused. Smiled. "I used to know how to have a pretty good time."

He uttered the name of that place as if it were nothing at all.

In one of Ian Mann's novels, the private investigator explains to the parents of a victim that most murderers return to the scene of their crime, and this is how a surprising number are caught. They can't help it, the investigator explains. The place tugs at them and they can't resist. Was this what Clive was doing? Was saying the name of that place to me a way of returning to the scene? Did he reap some perverse pleasure from conjuring it indifferently, as if it were nothing more than the site of some fun party from his youth? For the first time in a long time, I felt afraid.

"That must have been super-fun," I said, forcing a smile.

"Super-fun," he repeated, laughing. "You've no idea."

THE GALLEYS of *The Girl from Pendeen* arrived. On the cover, a woman in a flowing white dress strode barefoot along a cliffside path, her hair in a long, windswept braid down her back. It was my job to compile a list of twenty or so authors at least as well known as Astrid, track down their addresses, and mail them copies for endorsement. My boss had also acquired a debut novel—a thriller set on a commune in the New Mexico desert—which we had agreed a few months earlier I would edit. When the manuscript came in, just before the Christmas holiday, she called me into her office. The manuscript sat on her desk, a stack of paper six inches high. She drummed the stack with her fingertips. "I wanted to be sure you feel up to this?"

"Absolutely!" I said too loudly.

"It's just—you're behind on things, Emily. The backlog is piling up. You seem . . . Is everything okay?"

"Everything's great! I'm super-sorry I've gotten behind, things have been a little crazy, but I promise I'm going to catch up."

"Okay, then," she said with a strained smile. She nudged the pile toward me and I carried it back to my cubicle. I opened my locker and placed the manuscript on the bottom, next to an umbrella and a growing accumulation of Tupperware that needed to be washed and taken home. I piled the early copies of *The Girl from Pendeen* on top of the manuscript and closed the locker door.

I ALWAYS went to Pasadena for Christmas, but this year I could not tear myself away from New York. I told my parents the only lie I could think of that was big enough to justify missing the holiday, but which would not cause them to book the first flight out to New York. I said I'd met someone, and we had decided to spend the holiday together in the city. Oh, my parents were so happy! *Yes,* I absolutely *must* stay in New York! We should enjoy Christmas just the two of us! How giddy they became, how altogether unable to conceal the things they hoped for: That I would marry, and give them grandchildren, so that they might enjoy the sweet pastures of old age. After all, I was their only hope. Their enthusiasm made it utterly transparent that they feared they would be let down by me, that they worried I would remain alone. I was furious with them, and yet my heart broke for them, for the ordinary happiness they still hoped would be theirs.

"Tell us about this guy," my father said.

"What do you want to know?"

"Throw us a bone, Em, what's he like?"

"I guess he's a lot like me."

I ate a hefty cancellation fee on my flight and bought a knee-high artificial tree, which only made my apartment even more dismal. Two days before Christmas, a package arrived—panettone and peppermint bark from Williams-Sonoma.

For you and your "special friend."
With love, mom.

CHRISTMAS IN New York: tinsel snowflakes on lampposts, holiday markets popping up like toadstools, infinite off-key renditions of "Silver Bells" on subway platforms—saxophone, mariachi, marimba. On Christmas Eve, I went to the newly opened Whole Foods in Gowanus and purchased the fixings for a Christmas dinner for one: a single filet mignon, a potato, sprigs of rosemary, a handful of haricots verts. A ruse, a performance for my own audience—I had no intention of staying home. I halfheartedly snapped the ends off a few beans, then grabbed my coat and headed out.

The Little Sweet was open, though nearly empty. Vincia stood behind the steam table as usual and a few men hunched over their regular tables. In the corner by the potted palm, Clive sat reading the *Daily News*.

I'd thought that seeing I had nowhere to be on Christmas might soften

Vincia to me, but I was mistaken. (*You do have somewhere to be, you just chose not to go,* I scolded myself, but I believed completely in my own sorry aloneness.) She took my money with the same cordial displeasure as always. Though I had been hoping for a reprieve from her surliness, I found myself grateful not to receive it. I took my tray, nodded my thanks, and made my way across the restaurant to Clive's table.

"You, too?" I asked.

"Afraid so."

We ate in quiet fellowship. When Clive finished his Carib, he bought two more, one for each of us. We smiled and bounced our heads when "Feliz Navidad" came on the radio, belched softly as we drank our beer. It grew late. Across the street, eerily quiet on this night, a man pulled the grate down over the storefront of the grocery. One by one, the other patrons departed the Little Sweet, until Clive and I were the only ones who remained. When Vincia began wiping down the steam table, Clive looked at me hesitantly. "Would you care to walk?"

We stopped at a bodega to buy tallboys of Bud Light.

"A toast!" I declared, raising my can with a wry smile.

"Happy bloody Christmas," Clive said.

We tapped our cans together and drank.

We walked without speaking, choosing our route by silent accord. Light seeped onto the street from every window: families and trees and carols sung in warm rooms. It was on that Christmas Eve walk I finally understood that I had begun to care for Clive Richardson. I don't mean that I had become any less suspicious. When I forced myself to imagine what he might have done, my blood ran cold. Yet when I did not force myself to imagine it, I was able to believe the lie that Clive was just a taxi driver with whom I'd struck up one of those unlikely urban friendships you hear stories about. (A hair colorist officiating at the wedding of a client who has become a dear friend. A manicurist and an Upper East Side mom brought together by a passion for mah-jongg.) A few months earlier, I had to exert tremendous mental energy to convince myself that the man before me was not the same man Alison had known, simply to bear being near him. Now that same process was effortless—the separation of one man into two was total, complete.

As we walked, it began to snow. The light from the streetlamps caught the falling snow in big, soft halos.

"Beautiful," I said.

He shrugged.

"But not home, right?"

He didn't respond.

"Why don't you go back? I can tell you miss it."

Clive's face tightened. "It's for the best."

"But not even once? Not even to see your son?"

He shook his head.

"You have secrets."

He stopped walking. "Pardon?"

I took his hands in mine. "It's okay. I just mean, you have your secrets and I have mine. That's why I know I can trust you. Because you understand what it's like." He started to protest, but I continued. "You don't have to tell me I'm wrong. We don't have to say anything about it. Not unless we want to."

ONE NIGHT I dreamed I was riding with Clive in his taxi. We were in New York, but it didn't look like New York. It looked like Saint X. We drove down sandy streets lined with palm trees, past fish-fry stands and pink motels; I understood that this was the secret city, a submerged place that existed beneath the city where harried workers and dithering tourists cluttered the sidewalks—if I listened, I could hear the shuffle of their footfalls filtering down from some distant, forgettable world high above. On a long straight stretch of road, we came upon a girl crossing the street. It was Alison, though in the dream this meant something different—my heart did not leap to see her, she had not been dead and was not now alive; she was simply a girl taking her sweet time in the middle of the road. Clive honked. She idled. He explained to me that this was always happening, that it was one of the primary aggravations of his job, these girls in the road. He honked again, but Alison was not the least bit concerned, and I started getting annoyed. I shouted, "Move! Move!" Clive honked and honked, and as I surfaced from sleep I realized that the honking was my apartment buzzer. It was eleven o'clock on a Sunday morning.

"Who is it?" I asked groggily.

"Emily, thank *god*. It's *me*. Please, please let me in."

Jackie. I looked around my apartment—it was a disaster, an easy visual symbol Jackie would be eager to latch on to, physical disorder as a sign of emotional disorder, and so on. "Wait there. I'll come up."

I threw on some clothes and met her at the vestibule, where she at once threw her arms around me.

My body went rigid. "What are you doing here?"

"Don't you know I would never, ever forget? I'm not just going to leave you alone today of all days, even if you have been a totally awful friend lately. You and I are going to a barre class that starts in twenty minutes."

I didn't move.

"Come on, Em, get your butt downstairs and get changed."

"No."

"No what?"

"I'm not going with you."

"Of course you are. I have a whole day planned. After barre class there's brunch at this amazing vegetarian place on Bedford. They do a homemade chai that is life-changing."

I tried to walk around her, but she reached out and put her hands on my shoulders.

"Excuse me," I said.

"What the hell? Are you seriously going to walk away from me?"

She held me firmly and our eyes locked. In that moment I saw many things clearly that had previously been opaque to me. Jackie was a basically good person, but I did not like her and I never had. It wasn't just Jackie. It was all of my friends. They were dramatic, self-absorbed, ridiculous people, and I had always thought so. I had cultivated friendships with them not for intimacy and connection but to be able to judge them, and to extract from our every interaction a sense of my own superiority. Look what I had been through! And still I was better than the lot of them. What was wrong with me? Why was I the way I was? Alison, Alison, the answer was always Alison.

"Excuse me," I said again.

Jackie's eyes filled with tears. She released me.

As I hurried down the street I heard her call after me. "I'm trying to help you! Can't you see I'm trying to help you?"

WHEN A person you love dies, the calendar becomes a minefield. Anyone who has lost someone knows this. There is the loved one's birthday. One's own birthday. Various national and religious holidays, if one is religious. All of these days are difficult in their own ways. The loved one used to call you and sing happy birthday over the phone, awful and tone-deaf. Cranberry relish was the loved one's favorite Thanksgiving food, they used to eat and eat. But the anniversary is different. On the anniversary of the loved one's death, you slip backward through time to this same day one, five, ten years ago. (Eighteen years . . . How could it be? She had been gone as many years as she was alive.) You live it all over again, minute by minute.

I made my way to Clive's apartment building just before noon. I was sitting under the faded blue umbrella then. We were sorting through the woman's basket of beads together, picking out purple and white beads, colors I had chosen not because they were my favorite but because they were hers. As I walked east on Cortelyou, I felt the brisk, delicate movements of the woman's hands braiding my hair.

The light was on in Clive's window. I walked to the end of the block and sat on a front stoop diagonal from his building to wait. I'd left my apartment in such a hurry, what with Jackie's unexpected appearance, that I hadn't even grabbed my coat. I wore jeans and a sweatshirt, and within minutes my ears burned with cold. Alison pecked me on the forehead. She walked down the beach and was gone.

More than two hours passed before the light in Clive's window finally went off. A few minutes later, the front door opened and he stepped out onto the sidewalk. He walked first to the bodega a few blocks away. He was inside for just a minute and emerged empty-handed. We headed south on New York Avenue, passing block after block of red-brick midrise apartment buildings, interrupted occasionally by a blip of row houses. Clive turned onto Nostrand at Avenue H. I expected him to loop back up after a few blocks as he often did, perhaps to stroll the lawns and brickery of Brooklyn College and then take Flatbush back to Farragut back to New York. But he continued south. We passed Avenues I, J, and K. At Avenue L we briefly left the city behind and entered a mirage-like stretch of Japanese car service centers—Acura, Honda, Toyota, Hyundai—which we exited to find ourselves deep in Jewish Midwood. Men draped in prayer shawls sporting enormous fur hats, girls in long dark dresses and black loafers crossing streets blanched white with salt. It was midafternoon. She was lying on the beach, sipping a Diet Coke in the sun. I wanted her to play with me, but I didn't want to annoy her, so I didn't ask, I waited. *My, you a patient child.*

We walked through Sheepshead Bay on Avenue U, then took Coney Island Avenue down into Brighton Beach. While the neighborhoods we traveled through each had their differentiating features—Hebrew giving way to Cyrillic on shop signs, Kosher then Georgian then Russian bakeries—it was the landscape's repetitions that began to take hold of me, the endless cycling of deli, slice joint, Key Foods, MetroPCS, and the thousands of thousands of brick apartment buildings. The farther we walked, the more disoriented I became by the *on* and *on* and *on* of the borough, by its vast peripheries and the impossible number of people living their lives out past anyplace I had ever wondered about. We passed Avenues X, Y, Z. Neptune. We had been walking for nearly two hours. It seemed the brick apartment buildings would go on forever, and when we turned onto Oriental Boulevard and, after a few more minutes, found ourselves standing on the sand of what I now know to be Manhattan Beach, the sight of the ocean stretching before me was like stepping into a dream. I clung to the perimeter of the beach while Clive walked forward. The sand was a gray crescent, the sea a sheet of shale. A man in a parka sat on a bench, tossing shards of bread to the gulls. The sun was already beginning to go down. We were in the water, one last swim before the flight home the next day. The salt water stung then soothed the bites on my legs. Alison dove into the waves, surfacing and disappearing again and again. Clive stood at the water's edge for a long time, staring out at the ocean.

Before he turned to go, he pulled something from the pocket of his jacket. From where I stood, it took some squinting to discern that it was a chocolate bar, which must have been what he'd purchased at the bodega. He removed his gloves and unwrapped it. The sun set without fanfare, its weak light spilling briefly and colorlessly across the clouds. Clive ate the chocolate bar slowly, never turning from the water. Then he crumpled the wrapper, stuffed it in his pocket, and headed home.

How did I pick Saint X? Easy. I knew not a soul there and not a soul knew me. I had two suitcases and Sara. She was four months old, a scrawny babe with a head of dewy curls and an aroma like boiling milk turning to caramel. I wore the prettiest thing I owned, my floral dress and ivory pumps. The pumps had cut up my feet before Saint Kitts was even out of view, but so what? They would heal somewhere else, and that was all that mattered. I was seventeen.

When we debarked at Bendy Harbour, a gentleman in a linen suit offered to help me with my luggage. When he asked my name, I told him I was Agatha Lycott, which wasn't true. All my life I had been Agatha Hodge, but over my dead body would I be her here, too. Lycott was the surname of a girl in the form above me at school. I always thought it elegant, the sort of name that, of course, belongs to somebody else. From that day forward it was mine and, above all, Sara's. To anyone who asked, I told the story I had dreamed up awake and alone and growing bigger in the dark in my father's house, about how my husband, a government minister, had died in a tragic automobile accident just weeks before our daughter's birth. To make the story more convincing I told everyone I was twenty-four, though I was such a small thing I could more easily have passed for twelve.

But this one's cousin on Saint Kitts knew that one's friend on Saint X, and so on. I had been on the island less than a month the first time I told my story and was met with suspicion rather than compassion. The rumors trailed me even here, to this sand-and-rock speck where they make their curry with vulgar quantities of allspice and where not even the teachers speak properly.

You can never start over. They will not permit it, neither the ones who shun you nor the ones who are kind to you so they may lord their kindness over you. In the end they are all after the same thing, all so very curious to know the truth about the origins of the daughter of that skinny little Kittitian sket. I will not give them the satisfaction, though the truth would make them beg for my forgiveness. I will carry the secret of Sara's paternity to my grave.

Before Sara was born, I imagined that my love for my child would be a sweet blooming inside of me. I was desperate to have someone to love this way, desperate for love to swoop in and soften my sharp edges. But there are other kinds of love. What I got instead was a love that filled and terrified me, a love I knew as intimately as my own body; it was my mother's love for me, a thing I never, ever wanted.

When Sara told me she was pregnant, I knew I had been naïve to think a new name would be enough to put an end to the passing down of this broken mother's love. I never should have let her leave the house so angry that day, the day she brought Clive Richardson home. *Wait! Don't go! Sara, I love you. Sara, forgive me. Sara, my child.*

At night, I plead into the darkness, hoping with the force of my love to undo the past so she may begin again.

But answer me this: If I'm such a sket, then why have I been lonely every day of my life?

SNOW

AFTER THEY FOUND THE GIRL, Clive became untouchable. When he was released from prison he tried to return to his life, but Don and Des closed ranks. Even Arthur wouldn't touch him. He couldn't find work, not cutting grass, not even scrubbing toilets at Papa Mango's. He and Edwin kept their distance from one another. As far as he knew, Edwin had also been shut out of polite society, but it was different for him. He hadn't been to prison, for one thing. He didn't have a family to support, for another.

For weeks after his release, Clive went to Sara's house and begged to see his son. But Agatha wouldn't let him past the front door. Finally, one day, he waited down the road until he saw Agatha go out. Then he went up the front walkway. "Please, Sara! Let me talk to you!" he shouted as he pounded on the door. He didn't care who saw.

The door swung open. "Hush," Sara scolded. "You'll wake him."

He told her everything he had planned during his time in Her Majesty's Prison. He was sorry. He would do whatever it took to make it up to her. He would quit drinking and smoking. He had messed up and he knew it, but he would fix it.

"And what kind of mum would I be if I let you into my boy's life after this mess?"

"But I'm innocent! I swear it! Don't you believe me, Sara?"

"It doesn't matter what you are," she snapped. "Innocent, guilty, can't you see? It's all spoiled."

"I know it must seem that way right now. But with time, maybe—"

She shook her head. She had her hand on the door, ready to close it.

"Please," he begged.

She paused. She smiled a small, sad smile. "You know, I think you're the only person who was ever really sweet to me," she said. Then she closed the door.

• • •

GROWING UP, Clive had known more than a few people who had returned to the island from abroad, and it was from them, long before he ever thought their stories would be relevant to his own life, that he learned what it meant to leave home. Almost all of these people had gone either to New York or London, though he knew a few who'd gone elsewhere—to Glasgow, Birmingham, Toronto, Miami. A few years before he left, a boy who'd been three forms above him at Everett Lyle Secondary flew off to Houston, but last Clive heard he, too, had washed up in New York.

For most of his childhood, New York and London were roughly interchangeable to Clive, big, gleaming cities, more Dominicans and Haitians in New York, more Jamaicans in London. But when Keithley returned from London with his wife and the baby boy who was destined to die on the soccer pitch behind Horatio Byrd, he began to understand that the people who returned from New York and those who returned from London had changed in distinct ways. Though Keithley had left home determined never to return, he appeared relieved to be back, and this seemed the case for many people returned from London. It was true they had failed to do what they had set out to do, to build a big life *away*. But in London it had become plain that this plan was naïve and misguided. The city had taught them that the big life was nothing but the delusion of a person from nowhere who didn't know any better. They rarely spoke of their time away.

The New Yorkers, too, appeared relieved to be home. New York, like London, had been drab and crowded and unforgiving, and the winters were colder and the summers hotter and more humid than in London. But their relief was thin, a skin covering the flesh of longing. They spoke of New York constantly, as one turns over a riddle one has not managed to solve. They seemed convinced they had missed the big life by inches. It had been there, set plainly before them, but some narrowness of vision had prevented them from grasping it. Now New York was over. They had not grasped it and they could not figure out why.

Clive knew he was not like these men. He did not want to leave home. New York had been Edwin's dream, never his. He arrived with no grand plans, no conviction that in New York the world would finally recognize his special deservingness. He hoped only that his time away might make it possible, someday, to go home and reclaim the only life he'd ever wanted, a quiet existence with Sara and his son. Mates and a drink after work. Picnics and cricket in the sand at Little Beach on the weekends. Perhaps another child eventually, a daughter, chubby like him. People did not forget, but they might decide, eventually, that they no longer cared.

Most of the people he knew who had gone to New York had settled in the Bronx, but he did not want to run into people from home. He chose Flatbush because it was the largest Caribbean neighborhood in the city; a place, he hoped, he could get lost in. He found a room in an apartment on Farragut Road, in a building whose dim hallways smelled of mice. The apartment had four small bedrooms, each shared by two men, and a common space with a kitchenette against one wall. When he moved in, a bunch of rotting bananas atop the fridge cast off a sickly sweet smell. In the bathroom, toothbrushes balanced precariously on the rim of the sink, which was lacquered with a pale blue chalk of hardened toothpaste; the floor around the toilet was littered with cardboard tubes. He could hardly believe this filthy apartment was New York, and he was thankful that it was he, not Edwin, who was here to see it.

The unwritten rule of the apartment was that the men pretended not to see one another. In such close quarters, it was the only way to keep the peace. They took wordless turns in the bathroom, slept and woke and pretended not to overhear one another's phone calls home.

Only two of them disrupted this dreary concord. The first was Ousseini, Ouss for short, the youngest among them at twenty-two and the only one not from the Caribbean. He was short and sprightly, with the simultaneously curious and sleepy countenance of a child. On Clive's first night in the apartment, as he unpacked his suitcase in his bedroom, Ouss stood in the doorway in his mesh shorts and undershirt, elbow against the doorjamb, and confessed he'd been socially and sexually deprived ever since he arrived in Brooklyn from Burkina Faso three years before.

"I desire a wife with such ardor I can think of nothing else."

Clive was hot and tired and wanted only to lie down on his thin mattress and sleep. On the opposite side of the room his roommate Charles was flipping through a sports magazine, diligently ignoring Ouss and eyeing Clive every so often with a glint of warning.

"You're young," Clive said succinctly.

Ouss shook his head sadly. "This is what I thought, but it was an error.

I have five brothers in Ouaga, and all have children. When they were marrying I thought they were foolish to start families. I thought I was so smart to remain free to pursue my dreams. Now I fear I am too late. I want a woman who will be my partner. I want to start a business. But what woman in New York will love me? We need women. All of us here. You, too, Charles!" Charles kept his eyes on his magazine. "You see! You see! We are becoming dysfunctional. To live in this world of solitary men is not natural."

Ouss talked on and on and Clive, not wanting to be rude, nodded politely and offered small words of comfort. Later, he understood that this had been his critical mistake. The other men ignored Ouss absolutely. This was how Clive became the recipient of Ouss's laments, a position he found somewhat irritating, though ultimately not as disagreeable as he supposed he should, because, as Ouss had said, theirs was a solitary existence, and it was nice to have company.

Then there was Sachin, as surly as Ouss was talkative and romantic. Sachin left his briefs on the bathroom floor, his old food in the fridge, was often drunk and prone to picking arguments. (Those were his bananas rotting atop the fridge when Clive moved in.) He took an immediate dislike to Clive, who found himself on the receiving end of much of the man's vitriol. "It's not personal," Ouss assured him. "He possesses a lot of anger. He had a wife and daughter back in Trinidad who died in an accident after he left. I think he should go home and begin again, but he's afraid. Jean-François says he speaks to them in his sleep."

In New York, with these men, he became Clive again, as he hadn't been since Edwin christened him in the schoolyard at Horatio Byrd Primary. Gogo. That name, that world, that life. At times it seemed to him like one of the stories his mother used to tell him, vivid and vaporous as a dream.

NEW YORK surprised him. He expected a rough, gritty place, and while this vision was not exactly inaccurate, there were things it failed to capture. The pleasure of a nine P.M. summer sunset. In spring, in the parks, the quiet grace of what seemed like all the people in the world spread across the lawns. He had expected a place where there were a million things to see, but also where what you saw was what you got. Instead, New York seemed to tremble with the unseen. Subway tunnels whooshed people through the earth, the warm steam rising from street grates the only sign of this subterranean world. He had heard that the layers of the city went down ten meters, that below the city of today were buried houses, streets, and cemeteries, and he could sense this past beneath his feet. Walking at night, he sometimes feared someone would grab his elbow, and he would whip around to find himself staring into the eyes of his dead father.

IT TOOK him three months to get his hack license. He submitted the dozens of pages of paperwork for the application. He got a medical exam from a Dr. Khutsishvili in Midwood. He took defensive driving at Safe Taxi Academy and sat for the six-hour exam: *What landmark is located at the intersection of 33rd Street and 5th Avenue? Which of the following streets runs parallel to Adam Clayton Powell Jr. Boulevard? How many roads cross Central Park, and where are the transverses located?* When he found out he had passed, the first thing he did was call Sara.

"I'll be making decent money," he told her happily. "I'll be wiring some home to you and my gran as soon as I can."

"My mum needs new tires for her car," she said bluntly.

"Your mum?"

"Yes, she needs new tires for the car I use to take your son to the doctor and to do the shopping. Although you cannot see us, Clive, we are living every day down here, and every day has its expenses."

He took a deep breath in. "Can I speak to him?"

She sighed. "It would only confuse him."

For a moment neither of them spoke.

"Clive?"

"Yes?"

"Be careful on those roads."

HE LEASED a night shift because he heard it was more profitable.

"Last chance to change your mind," said the manager at the fleet garage, a middle-aged man named Larry in an old, beat-up Mets cap calcified by sweat and grime, before he took the money for Clive's first night's lease.

"You'll never see him without that filthy thing," the driver behind Clive in line said, gesturing at the hat.

"Don't even take it off to screw my wife," Larry said proudly.

Clive handed him the money.

"Don't say I didn't warn you," Larry said with a smile. "I've got hacks getting mugged on the regular. Half these guys have diabetes, and you can say sayonara to your kidneys unless you want to piss in a bottle all night."

In the months that followed, Clive found that the things Larry said were true. It was the most punishing work he'd ever done. Customers ran off without paying. He was regularly accused of taking a slow route on purpose. (How was it that these people, these *New Yorkers,* didn't know he made less, not more, the longer each fare took?) Some nights, his first fare found him stuck in gridlock on the FDR bound for JFK, where he waited another hour in the holding area for his next fare, and when this happened he knew the best he would be able to do on his shift was to break even, and he would spend the next ten hours laboring simply not to lose money, after which, bone-tired on the bus home, he might see a white woman seated next to him clutch her handbag and smile kindly at him; at first he was perplexed by this sequence of behaviors, but he came to understand that these women did not trust him, but they also did not want to appear distrustful.

In spite of all this, the work also had its pleasures. The drivers inhabited a secret shared world. He liked to linger after his shift in the garage, where men played checkers and polished off takeaway containers of curry and jollof rice in the break room, retreated into the prayer room with its three threadbare rugs, groused about the new weekly lease rates in Punjabi and Urdu and Haitian Creole. He found comfort in the ritual details of the garage—its smell of motor oil, the rainbow slicks on the concrete floor, the clouds of yellow dust cast off as the mechanics touched up paint. He learned a hidden archipelago within the archipelago of New York: the Pakistani curry-and-chai cafeterias on Lexington, the Haitian spots in Harlem, the dwindling gas stations, the bodegas that carried meter paper. He learned to feed himself in New York from the examples of his fellow drivers. Deals: two plain slices and a can of soda; egg roll and sesame chicken combo. Egg and cheese on a roll from a bodega, scarfed down on the sidewalk, gone before he tasted it. Foods from home, too, peas and rice and pumpkin soup and fish stew with dumplings, though none of it satisfied him; the scent of island food carried on cold air delivered a sense not of nostalgia, but of error. So much of New York was like that, not-quite-memories and almost-evocations that slapped him with his distance from home . . . the sonorous coos of the turtledoves of his youth emanating from the filthy iridescent throats of pigeons in the streets.

There was something about the night shift. He discovered that his favorite New York was the one you could only know at four A.M.: The darkness, which was never true black but a trembling blue, as if the city exhaled the residual light of day all night long, and against which the vivid green of traffic lights on the avenues—block after block of them to the edge of sight—was that rarest thing, beauty as pedestrian as it was exquisite. New York was the city that never sleeps, but it did, and as he drove its empty, witching-hour streets and sailed across its starry bridges, he sometimes felt that the city had been abandoned to him, that every other living soul had vanished into the air.

He left the garage around six in the morning. On his walk to the bus he watched the sun come up behind the buildings. The oystershell light of dawn. How it tugged at him, reminding him of his old bike ride to work at Indigo Bay. Even this daily sadness he did not mind, exactly. The ache of it was its own pleasure.

Be careful on those roads. He heard Sara's voice all the time. *Be careful,* when a car cut him off on the BQE at sixty miles an hour. *Be careful,* in the pouring rain and when his eyes yearned for sleep. Her words were the most meager of gifts, a small seed of hope that he had not been completely forsaken, and he held fast to them.

ON A night in December of his first year in New York, he picked up a man in a suit outside of an office building in midtown. Once the man had hefted his briefcase onto the seat beside him and closed the taxi door, he declared, "We're going to Westchester." The man told Clive the name of a town at the northernmost edge of where he was required to take passengers, and proceeded to spend the ride alternately reading documents and directing Clive. Up the Henry Hudson, the river a black abyss, the cliffs of Jersey twinkling across the water. On to the winding ribbon of the Saw Mill. After nearly an hour, the man directed him off the highway. A few minutes later, Clive found himself on a narrow road driving through what could only be described as the country. It was his first time this far out of the city. He drove up steep hills from the crests of which the villages below glittered like something from an old movie. In a moment of wonder and terror, a silvery deer leapt out from the woods into the road; Clive slammed on the brakes and narrowly missed hitting it. "Jesus," the man in the backseat muttered without lifting his head from his papers.

Clive wondered if this man had ever vacationed on the island that had once been his home, or if he would be going soon, this Christmas, even, or to celebrate a promotion or anniversary.

"Sorry for dragging you up here," the man said when they arrived at his house, which was huge and had a turret on one side. In the illuminated square of a window Clive saw a pretty wife in jeans and a sweater. The man handed him a generous tip. "Right, right, left will get you back to the highway," he said. As Clive watched the man walk up his front steps, and his pretty wife open the door and push onto her tiptoes to kiss him, he felt himself fill with anger he didn't like and didn't want.

Right, right, left did not get him back to the highway, and soon he was hopelessly lost. He passed a silo beside a barn, a hillside where pine trees hugged the curve of the earth. Then the sky filled with white. His first snow. In the beginning, the flakes melted as soon as they hit the windshield, so he hardly saw them. He pulled off the road at a park to piss and pull out a map. The parking lot was beside a pond surrounded by trees and hills. He urinated into the gravel of the parking lot, studied a map for a few minutes before giving up. (Half an hour later he would stumble, mercifully, upon an elderly woman walking a dog, and she would direct him back to the highway.) The snow picked up. He was shocked by the lightness of it; it fell faster than it seemed a weightless thing should be able to fall. He stood and watched the snow melt into the pond. As he looked at the snow on the water, the blue hills beyond, he saw his own sadness stretching out in tandem with the landscape, as if the land knew his affliction, as if it were weary with the burden of human secrets. Suddenly the colors of home struck him as flat and cheap, a prettiness like white sugar. (And it was really only the water that was pretty at all. The land was dry and covered in gray scrub. The towns were overcrowded with concrete houses.)

The girl was from here, or a place like it. Any one of these big houses might have been hers. Standing in the snow in the middle of who knows where, he tasted the berry of her lips. He saw her dancing; she raised her arms in the air and her shirt lifted to reveal that touchable, touchable scar. He heard her say again all the disparaging things she'd said about the place she was from. She had lied to him. They all had. All the vacationers who went on and on about how beautiful his island was, how lucky he was to live there, how jealous they were. What bullshit. They had *this*.

EVERY SEASON in New York had its indignities. The stink of urine on pavement in summer. Trash cans stuffed with the corpses of umbrellas during the rainy, blustery days of early spring. By his second winter in New York, Clive saw the season as yet another thing to be gotten through, the clang of the radiator at night, the black snowbanks that uglied the city (or rather, that revealed the ugliness that was always there). Their landlord kept the building like an icebox. This was illegal, but so was everything about their situation, so what could they do? The shower did not get truly hot; the water came so close to warming him without actually doing so that he came to dread bathing, the *almost*ness of it, comfort held just out of reach.

Roommates had come and gone by then, Ouss and Sachin and Charles the only ones who remained. Sachin was as volatile and Ouss as earnest as ever; he'd recently been promoted to assistant manager at the hardware store where he worked, and was convinced this would turn out to be his "big break." The others had been replaced once, twice, three times over, the men different in their particulars, though these differences hardly mattered to Clive. Jean-François kept a laminated picture of his father back in Dessalines in his jeans pocket. His father was ill, and Jean-François would be stuck in New York until he died, paying his medical bills. After four months he was replaced by Dennis, a bachelor who had sent home enough money over a decade in New York for his sisters' weddings and houses and schooling for his nieces and nephews. He went home once a year, for a week.

Clive had begun to wonder by then if Ouss hadn't been correct on that first night—maybe this temporary existence was changing them in ways more permanent than they could fully comprehend. He thought of Hamid, another night-shift driver, who loved to brag about the accomplishments of his four children back in Pakistan, but whose plans to bring them over to join him always seemed to get pushed back to the next year, and the next. He thought of Neer, a baby-faced driver who had returned to Gujarat for the month of December for years. When December arrived that year and Neer was still at work, Clive asked if he would be going home at another time, and Neer told him he would not be going at all. Had something happened, Clive asked, was something wrong? Neer shrugged evasively, and Clive was frightened to find that Neer didn't need to explain. He understood. The family Neer had longed for, eked out this lonely existence for . . . it had been too long. The noise and chaos of children early in the morning, a wife's hopes and desires and disappointments—these things were too much now. He had grown too accustomed to a life he'd never wanted in the first place to give it up. That December, the sight of Neer—gazing impassively at the television in the break room, smoking a cigarette on the curb in front of the garage after his shift as the sun tried uselessly to break through the clouds—was enough to bring tears to Clive's eyes. He missed Sara and his grandmother, missed being in the company of and under the care and brusque direction of women. He was determined not to let what had happened to Neer happen to him. He would not become one of those men for whom family became too difficult, a thing better surrendered than reclaimed. Yet he could feel it happening to him, bit by bit, as seawater erodes rock. He wired money to Sara monthly, but he called less frequently now. Sometimes he asked if he could speak to Bryan, but sometimes he didn't try, even when he could hear cartoons in the background, punctuated by his son's airy giggles.

Sometimes, he could never predict when it would happen, he would be plunged into Bryan's life. He was stuck in traffic on the Major Deegan. He was trudging through the snow on an unshoveled stretch of Forty-seventh Street. Then he was in the yard at Horatio Byrd, invisible and watching, as a pack of boys (all much bigger than Bryan—in his imaginings his son was a small and delicate child) shoved him and called him bastard. He watched his son curl into himself and cry. Then Bryan turned and looked at him. He was not invisible anymore. His boy ran to him, and he gathered him in his arms, taking Bryan's small, heaving body into his large one, absorbing the tears and the runny nose and the brave trembling lip into himself, and in that moment he understood, finally, what his too-big body was for. There had been a reason for it all along: to take into himself the suffering of his child.

Then he was back—the taxi inching along the asphalt, the snow soaking into his shoes. And he felt emptier than it had been possible to feel before he'd had a child to be absent from his life. He should never have left. He should have found a way to stay. If he had not been able to regain Sara's trust he should simply have demanded it, so that he could remain on the island and in his son's life. No, he had done the right thing. Sara needed space and time. Eventually she would soften. It might all work out in the end. He felt better, except sometimes he didn't. Could you ever undo it when a father and son became nothing to one another but voices? He could never decide—he would wonder for the rest of his life—whether his departure was his single most courageous act or just one more example of his cowardice.

IN BED at night, he closed his eyes and sent himself home. His grandmother's house, white curtains in the kitchen and the oleander tree in the yard. The potholed streets, Mayfair and Gould and Princess Margaret and Underhill. The three-legged goat in Daphne Nelsen's yard. The secret, nameless cliffs from their nights joyriding with Keithley. Conch fritters and limeade at Perry's Snackette. The gas station on George Street and the salt ponds with their pleasant stink and clotheslines on which school uniforms crisped in the sun. The spots where the buildings, the hillocks, the scrub parted to reveal flickering glimpses of the sea. The sea itself. He sat on the sand at Little Beach and looked out at the water. He was not alone. On the beach were all the people he had ever known, the old and the young, the living and the dead. They, like he, sat still and solemn with their eyes on the sea, waiting.

For what?

Then it began to snow.

IT WAS January of his third year in New York when Clive stopped for gas at the Shell on Hudson Street and the man at the next pump said, "Clive Richardson? Is that really you?"

He looked up and saw a man standing beside a Range Rover, and after a moment he realized it was Ron Rawlins, who had been in his form at school and who had gone on to attend university in the States. In school Ron had been a square, mercilessly teased for his eczema and acne. He looked good now. His skin had cleared and he wore a gray suit with a lavender tie.

"I heard you left for here, and here you are!" Ron said.

He could feel the weight of what Ron hadn't said. Surely Ron had heard about everything that had happened to him in the years since they had last seen each other.

"What are you up to these days?" he asked Ron, who happily accepted this shift of focus to himself.

"Real estate. The market's hot right now, my man."

How he and Edwin and their friends would have laughed and mocked Ron if he had dared to call any of them "my man" back home.

"You know Berline's up here, too," Ron said.

"Bery?"

"I set her up working in the same optometry office as my girl. She's saving for art school."

Clive forced a smile.

"Hey, man, good on you for making an honest living here," Ron said, gesturing at the taxi. "Keep it up, you hear?" He pulled out his wallet and flicked a business card at Clive. "You need anything, call me."

Early next morning, when Clive got back to the apartment and flipped on the light, Sachin leapt off the couch.

"The fuck, man? I'm sleeping here," Sachin shouted, his eyes crazed. Drunk.

"Sorry. I didn't know you were out here."

Sachin spread his arms before him. "Well, here I am. Trev's driving me mad. I can't stand to sleep where I can hear that joker breathing."

"Sorry," Clive muttered again, and fled to his bedroom. He had to piss, but he didn't want to go out and face Sachin again, so he relieved himself into a Big Gulp cup from the day before, his urine swirling with the inch of flat cola at the bottom. He lay down, but though he was tired he couldn't sleep. He imagined Ron Rawlins and his girl and Bery sitting together in a diner. Ron had his arm around his girlfriend, who was small and pretty and American. "You'll never believe who I ran into," he would say to Bery, swiping a fry through ketchup and tossing it in his mouth. After he said Clive's name, Ron and Bery would tell Ron's girlfriend about him: an illegitimate child, drugs, jail, the girl. Then Bery would snort at a thought in her head. "You know, he punched me in the face once," she'd say, without bothering to explain the circumstances.

• • •

IN FEBRUARY, his roommate Charles returned to Saint Thomas. Three days later their landlord came to the apartment with his replacement. Fazil was a diminutive man with mantis-like limbs and a tidy beard dyed with henna. He was much older than the rest of them, in his fifties at least, and he kept nearly silent. He prayed five times a day, and Clive liked this about his new roommate, though he had no interest in religion himself. It seemed to him that Fazil had released himself to the universe in a way that made him, not happy exactly, but reconciled to his life. He had a habit of picking his nose and flicking his excavations into the corners of their small bedroom, but other than this he was unobtrusive (in his sleep he was completely soundless, so that Clive sometimes worried he was dead) and fastidiously neat, and Clive accepted his one vice as the cost of a roommate who was much better than he might have been.

Not long after Fazil arrived, Clive was working on a Monday night when, barely an hour into his shift, he pulled over on Amsterdam and vomited a salmon-colored froth onto a hardened gray snowbank. He was so suddenly and intensely ill it was all he could do to drive the taxi back to the garage, stopping periodically to be sick again, and then struggle home. He thought he'd eaten something bad and figured he'd be back on his feet the next night; instead, he awoke drenched in sweat and delirious with fever. The illness lasted for days. Fazil moved his mattress against the wall to create as much distance between them as possible. Ouss cared for him to the extent possible when he wasn't at work, bringing him soup and medicine and washing Clive's sheets at the Laundromat.

Just an hour before he fell ill, Clive had paid his weekly lease, six hundred dollars he now had no chance of recouping. When he was finally well enough to return to work, he showed up at the garage only to have Larry tell him he'd found another driver for his shift. He would have to wait until a spot opened up. Two weeks passed.

Sara called. "I expected you to wire us something last week."

"Things are hard up here at present."

"Well, down here at present your son is growing like a weed and needs new polos and trousers and shoes."

"You think I don't know your extensive list of demands, what with how you do remind me?" he snapped.

For a moment Sara didn't speak. He could hear her breathing into the phone slowly and deliberately.

"This is not about me and you. It is about your son."

He hated when she called Bryan *your son*—as if Clive didn't know, as if he needed reminding.

Rent was due but he couldn't pay it. Their landlord came to the apartment and told him in front of Fazil and Trev and Sachin that he had a week to pay. That night he took Ron Rawlins's business card from his wallet and turned it over in his hands. He walked to a pay phone. He dialed the first digits. Then he heard Ron's voice, *Good on you,* in his head. He hung up. He tore the card in pieces and tossed them in the rubbish bin on the street corner. He did not trust himself with it.

Two days later, he returned to the apartment after a day spent fruitlessly walking the city looking for HELP WANTED signs, his feet aching, and found Sachin sitting on the couch. Sachin looked up at Clive, his green eyes sparking. "Where is it?"

"Where is what?"

"You know very well."

"Please, Sachin. I'm too tired for this today. If you're vex with me, say so and be done with it."

"You bet your dick I'm vex. This morning I had four hundred dollars in an envelope under my mattress. Tonight, I don't."

"You think *I* took it?"

"I know you owe rent."

"But I've been gone. I've been out since this morning."

"Says you," Sachin spat.

Clive heard the sound of a key in the lock. Fazil stepped inside. When the small old man saw the two of them, frozen and glaring at each other, he hunched his shoulders and disappeared quickly into the bedroom.

"I'm giving you a chance to make it right, Clive. You give me what you did take and we'll be cool."

"I didn't take your money, Sachin. How would I even know where you hide it?"

Sachin clapped his hands and released a dark, amused laugh. "How would you know?" He was wired; he spoke with a red-hot smoothness. "Clive, even you could find a stack of cash in a room that's nearly empty."

"I don't know what else to say," Clive whispered. "We've lived together a long time. You know me. You know I would never—" He heard the floorboards creak in his bedroom beneath the light weight of Fazil's body settling onto his mattress and he knew. Small, silent Fazil who never bothered anyone. He also knew there was no point in accusing him to Sachin, who would never believe him, blinded as he was by his anger. "I wouldn't," Clive said finally, uselessly.

"You have until tomorrow night." Sachin stalked off to his bedroom and closed the door behind him.

He should not have thrown away Ron Rawlins's card. It had been exactly the wrong thing to do. What else was new? The next evening, he went to the Little Sweet. He planned to stay there until closing, then remain out until two or three A.M., by which point, he hoped, Sachin would have blown through his anger and turned in for the night. He ordered his pepper pot and Carib, then another beer and another. Vincia pursed her lips but did not comment. The radio was on; the local Caribbean station was broadcasting a cricket match, Barbados Pride versus Leeward Island Hurricanes. By his sixth beer, he could feel the grass on the pitch like velvet beneath his fingertips. He closed his eyes and said a silent prayer that when he opened them he would be sitting in his grandmother's kitchen. She would be rinsing dishes in the sink. She would swat a mosquito and scowl, and how happy he would be.

When he opened his eyes, he was in the Little Sweet, his empty plate before him. He looked through the storefront at the street. Sachin was standing on the sidewalk, staring at him through the glass.

ONE AFTERNOON when he was fourteen, during the boys of Everett Lyle Secondary's brief love affair with boxing, Clive took a punch to the gut so powerful it knocked the wind out of him. His mouth opened and closed like a fish's on land as he waited what felt like an eternity until the air rushed back in. It was Thomas Hinton who had walloped him that time, a shy, handsome boy, well liked by the girls, who would go on to become the landscaping foreman at one of the resorts on the south coast. Clive remembered the intensity of the punch, but he did not recall feeling any pain at the moment of impact. This must have been partly because of the adrenaline of the fight, his body thrumming with it as he tried to get off

Alexis Schaitkin

his best shot to a chorus of cheers and jeers. But mostly it didn't hurt because
Thomas was his friend. So were Damien and Des and Don, and because
they were his friends, his body seemed not to believe the physical seriousness of their blows. Those matches in Don's yard never hurt. It was the great
irony of their contests. They administered injury to one another in order
to teach themselves something of the violence of manhood, yet each blow
was carried on the wings of fraternal love; you could feel it as plainly as
you tasted the tang of blood seeping from your split lip. Because of this,
those afternoon sessions were no preparation at all for what finally did come,
on a frigid February night in New York. As he understood very quickly
after he left the Little Sweet and followed Sachin around a chain-link fence
to a vacant lot (broken glass glistening like jelly in the moonlight), it was
not the physical power of a blow but the contempt which fuels it that makes
it so terrible.

Why did he go with Sachin? That's what he would ask himself after, leaning against the fence and spitting blood onto the sidewalk, his face man-
gled and swollen. He could not explain it. Sachin had stood on the sidewalk
outside the Little Sweet, staring at Clive through the glass with such coldness. He curled his index finger, gesturing for Clive to come out as if offering an invitation. Clive felt his body rise from his chair. He had the feeling
that he was walking toward something he'd been trying to avoid for a long
time, that Sachin had something to show him about himself, and that it
would be the truth.

When they entered the vacant lot, Sachin stumbled on the uneven
ground, then swung his arms wildly to steady himself. He was very drunk.
"This is your final chance," he slurred. His voice was brittle and ironic, as
if this were a poorly acted performance they were both in on, as if his own
anger were hilarious to him.

"I didn't take your bloody money," Clive grunted through clenched teeth.
He was suddenly furious, because he understood now that Sachin didn't
even really believe he'd taken it, but it didn't matter. He was hated.

The first sloppy blow glanced off Clive's jaw. Sachin spun on his own
momentum, regaining his footing just in time for his chin to meet Clive's
fist. Clive heard the gnash of Sachin's bottom teeth smashing into his top
teeth, saw his head snap back.

Well, Clive thought, he'd given Sachin his chance. It wasn't his fault if

Sachin had shown up too drunk to put it to use. He turned and walked over the uneven ground toward the sidewalk. He was almost at the fence when he heard the pounding of feet behind him. Then Sachin was on him. An arm hooked around Clive's neck, the crook of an elbow crammed against his windpipe. He fell to the ground and Sachin sprang on him. Clive felt every blow—on the rim of his eye socket, his throat, his chin. Finally, he was able to grab hold of Sachin's shirt and shove him off. Sachin flew backward. Clive heard a crack. Skull hitting concrete.

The night filled with a terrible stillness. Sachin lay on the ground, motionless. "No," Clive whispered. "No, no, no."

Then Sachin raised his arm. Clive had never felt such relief in his life. Sachin brushed his hand against the back of his head, held it up to the moonlight to confirm a gummy swipe of blood. He pushed himself off of the ground and rushed at Clive. Clive let Sachin pummel him, too terrified of what he'd almost done to retaliate.

Sachin began to laugh. "Is the big man scared?"

He punched Clive in the gut. Clive did not respond.

"Does that make you angry? Does that get you going, big man?"

Sachin's pale eyes never wavered from Clive. He was a father whose child had been taken from him; his loss was black magic, allowing him to see through Clive and know the things that he had taken. When Sachin delivered a swift, fierce kick to his groin, Clive fell to his knees, spat into the dirt. The world began to swirl. Sachin kicked at his ribs like he was trying to dislodge a stubborn flat tire. He kicked and kicked—he was moaning, Clive realized. The sound had been going on for some time. It filtered down from far above his body like the voice of God.

Then footsteps, stumbling away. He caught a fleeting whiff of berries. Tinkling laughter. A final howl: Sachin's? His? Hers? Clive sailed away on it.

HE COULD not stay in the apartment. It wasn't just Sachin. After that night, he could find within himself only pity for Sachin, whose family was gone and always would be, no matter how he tried to batter the truth of his life out of existence. But he hated Fazil. (Where would the money he'd stolen end up? Clive wondered. He imagined grandkids in Guyana opening a package of Nikes and CDs. Or maybe Fazil had no one back home and would spend the money in small morsels on himself; he saw him hunched over a large slice of red velvet cake in a café, scraping every last bit of frosting from the plate.)

Ouss loaned him the money for his back rent and the deposit on a new place. He found an open bed in an apartment shared by five roommates just a few blocks away. Not long after that, a shift opened up at the garage, and Clive returned to work. His first night back, in early March, was the first warm night of the year, a promise of spring. When he got off in the morning, he decided to walk. He crossed Manhattan on Forty-sixth, Times Square so early in the morning empty, his. When he reached First Avenue he turned south. He walked past the United Nations, its sweep of flags snapping in the wind, past the brick projects of the Lower East Side, quiet and softly lit at this hour. At Delancey, he turned onto the pedestrian ramp for the Williamsburg Bridge. He crossed the bridge, pushed forward by westward winds and fanned, at intervals, by ephemeral breezes from bikes whizzing past. When he reached the bridge's apex, he stopped. At the edges of the panorama, the silver tip of Manhattan and the brown façades of Brooklyn aproned the river; the water was a rich, indeterminate color, as if the essence of the city had been condensed into a dark, sparkling broth, and here he was above it, catching its cool upward breezes.

Things would get better now. He would be able to wire money to Sara and his grandmother soon. His cuts from the fight with Sachin had scabbed over. His whole body felt tight and new as a bud. At the foot of the bridge, he got on the B44 and rode Nostrand all the way down to Snyder. When he got home, the phone was ringing. He picked it up just in time. It was Sara.

"I was just thinking about you," he said.

"Oh?"

"I'm back at work. It's all sorted out. I'll be wiring money in a few days." She said nothing.

"Sara?"

"That's wonderful." She paused. "I want you to know I'm proud of you, Clive. I know it hasn't been easy there." Years later, the memory of it was enough to pull tears to his eyes. "I'm calling because I have something to tell you." Her voice sounded neither happy nor sad.

"What is it, Sara?"

"I'm married."

For a moment he couldn't speak. "You're—Sara, did you say y-y-y—"

"Yes," she snapped. "I said I'm married. I got married. Last week."

"No."

"I'm sorry, Clive."

"You should have told me. You should have given me a chance to—"

"To what? To try to stop me? I'm sorry, Clive, but I couldn't do it anymore. I've been here, all this time, raising our son alone."

"While I'm up here slaving away for that boy."

"And how do you think it's been for me? You don't have to take the stares when all you want is to buy groceries."

"Please, Sara. Listen to me. I love you. I—"

"It's Edwin," she said. "Do you hear me? It's Edwin." Her voice seemed to study the words, as if she only half believed them. "I married Edwin."

Bery Wilson, Sculptress. That's what it says on my business card. These days every actress wants to be called an actor, every waitress wants to be a waiter. But I'm a woman and I want every last person who sees my work to know it. My artist friends scoff when I show them my card. They think it's vulgar, like I'm an electrician or an accountant hocking my services. But I'm making a living doing what I love, and I want the world to know that, too.

In my twenties, when I was new to New York, my love affair with the city just beginning, I salvaged my materials from its streets: twisted bike rims, concrete, pigeon feathers, lots of metal. My latest pieces are different. In this place of my adulthood, I resurrect the spaces of my youth.

Rubbish Day went up last year in a pocket park in the West Village. If you're not from where I'm from, you'd see it and think it was just a sculpture made of castaway items, but anyone from home would see the bottle of Maggi and the box of Sazón Goya, the Ivory soap and Crix crackers wrappers, the bottles of D&G pineapple soda and Vita Malt and the canister of Nestlé Klim and know it was a love letter.

School Girls was installed in front of the Adam Clayton Powell Building in Harlem a few years ago. A circle of straw-and-plaster girls with painted-on skirts and blouses, maroon and pink. On the opposite edge of the plaza there was another girl, alone, looking back at the others and flaying them with her eyes. The piece was up November through March. The decay of the materials over the course of the winter was part of the project from its inception. I used to ride up there to see how people interacted with my work. Hardly anybody noticed the lone girl. I would watch her as if held there by something. Watch the snow settle on her shoulders, pigeons peck at her straw, sleet lash her wide-open eyes. I wanted to take her home and make her cinnamon tea and tell her, *Just you wait.*

Faraway Woman will be my next project, on Governors Island. I've only done sketches so far, but I know she will be larger than life. A woman twelve feet high with locks of black hair six feet long and bright white haunches thick as tree trunks. Hooves for feet. I want people to fall in love with her. I want her to give them nightmares.

When that girl died on Faraway, I knew it was the woman who took her. You might expect me to believe it was Gogo Richardson, on account of the afternoon he punched me so hard my legs flew out from under me. But that afternoon wasn't what I thought about when I heard that he and Edwin had been taken into custody. Instead, I thought of a morning many years earlier, the first day of second grade, when Gogo's terrible stutter almost caused him to wet himself in front of the entire class. I felt such rage at him then. Rage for allowing something so humiliating to happen to himself. Rage that he couldn't just *fit in*. I know, I know. Irony is a live wire. It seems to me now that for years of my life, rage is all I was. It lived in my skin and crackled in my teeth. I would have followed it anywhere.

STARLIGHT

YOU GET FAR ENOUGH INTO winter and you no longer believe it was ever warm or ever will be again. The trees seem as unalive as the other fixtures of the city's sidewalks: newspaper boxes, abandoned bicycles, hydrants (their tops covered now in little ushankas of snow). During the day, the light seems filtered through a dishrag, and by late afternoon, day is gone; the surrendering blue of a four o'clock twilight becomes your whole world.

When I try to get myself back into that winter, to reenter my psychic state during those frozen months, I find that I can no longer do it. I can remember that period in an external way, using the things I did and said to reconstruct what I must have felt. But I can no longer inhabit those memories as I can inhabit even more distant ones: Sipping espresso with Aunt Caroline in the Place des Vosges. My skin peeling in the days after Alison's death. *Me say day me say day me say day.* The best I can do is to describe how the world around me seemed altered. Before that time, the city was for me what I believe it is for most people: a commons, all of us grazing together in its glass-and-steel meadows, a place the most salient feature of which is not, in the end, its skyscrapers or its cacophony, but the excruciating and ecstatic demands it places upon our empathy. To push through the crowds in the Times Square subway station, zigging by tourists with suitcases, zagging around bankers in suits, brushing past people hawking churros, EPs, God, veering around a troupe of young men performing backflips above the hard tile floor, and squeezing onto a train so packed your chest compresses in the crush of bodies, and to know that every one of these people is in the thick of a life every bit as complex as your own, that you are all extras in one another's dramas—isn't this the quintessence of urban life? But during those months, it was different. The city seemed not public but private, a place created for me and the things that were playing out in my life. New York was mere backdrop, a screen painted with buildings and delivery trucks and dog-walkers and children on scooters, in front of which I enacted my life. I did not care what people around me thought of me because I did not entirely believe they were real. On the subway I bit my nails with impunity; I traced words in the air without bothering to disguise my behavior.

The significance of Clive's pilgrimage to Manhattan Beach was clear to me. He had been marking Alison's death. It had been months since I had entered his life, and I knew it was time to move things forward. Either I'd gained his trust or I hadn't, and it was time to find out. Every night before I stepped into the Little Sweet, I promised myself this was the night I would press him, the night I would bring the conversation around to the secrets of his past. But these were false promises; even as I made them I don't think I believed them. Instead, I spent our evenings lamenting the hideous condo tower rising on Fifty-seventh Street. We groused about the disastrous snow removal after the most recent storm. Clive explained to me the workings of cricket and the Windies' tumultuous history of shame and glory. On the walk home afterward, I would excoriate myself for my cowardice, though I knew it wasn't really cowardice preventing me, but something else, something I wouldn't be able to fully understand for a long time. In truth, I had altogether lost sight of the purpose of my time with Clive Richardson. The winter, these nights, this man—it stretched on and on. I could see no end in sight.

I GUESS what happened next was inevitable. On a Tuesday in early February, I called in sick at work. Clive was off on Tuesdays, and I spent the day trailing him as he ran various errands. The next morning when I arrived at work, my boss called me into her office. As I sat across from her, she proceeded to describe to me the events of the day prior. Astrid Teague had come in for a marketing meeting. When she was ready to leave, it was sleeting, but she didn't have an umbrella. My boss took her over to my cubicle, hoping to lend her one, and in my locker, amid an accumulation of dirty Tupperware, they discovered the stack of copies of *The Girl from Pendeen* which I had never mailed, along with the untouched manuscript by the debut novelist, which my boss would now have to edit herself in a hurry.

I was told to pack my things. I did so quickly. I removed the pushpins that had for the past three years affixed my photographs and decorations to the wall. I gathered my belongings from my locker. Everyone around me was very quiet. My coworkers avoided walking by my cubicle, except for the few who made a point of it, stealing pitying glances at me as they passed. I think this was when I understood that I would lose things in pursuit of the truth that I could not get back, that my life might be derailed in ways I could not recover from.

I COULDN'T tell my parents I had been fired. How on earth would I explain it to them? I couldn't tell Jackie. She had given up on me—there had been no texts, no attempted interventions, since the morning I brushed her off at my apartment. The only person I could talk to was Clive. That night, when I told him I had lost my job, he said the usual comforting things. It happens to everyone at some point. I would find another. That old chestnut: "Everything works out for the best."

"You can't actually believe that," I said.

He cocked his head back. "I guess not." He furrowed his brow, chuckled.

I began to cry, tears that were at once utterly genuine and a command performance. "What should I *do*?" I reached for his hand, and he took mine in his. He stroked the inside of my wrist with his fingertips. When our gazes met, it seemed they were both filled with the same question. I leaned toward him. I closed my eyes.

It is impossible to say how much of this action was strategy and how much of it was desire. These two tracks had collapsed in on each other. I had reached a level of cognitive dissonance that seems almost impossible to me now, but of which I had only the most submersed, peripheral awareness then: I simultaneously trusted and distrusted Clive Richardson absolutely. I loved him and loathed him. I wanted to destroy him and was terrified of losing him.

Clive dropped my hand. He leaned away from me.

"I'm sorry," I blurted.

His eyes darted from the floor to the television to the table, looking at anything but me.

"God, I'm a shit show tonight," I said, wiping the tears from my eyes. "Can we just pretend that never happened?" I attempted a lighthearted smile.

"I'm sorry if I—" His gaze had fallen on my hand.

I shoved it under the table. "A cramp." I'd been doing it without even realizing, tracing a finger through the air: *N-e-v-e-r. N-e-v-e-r. N-e-v-e-r.* He looked warily at me, and a rush of embarrassment flooded me.

"I think we could both use a drink," I said. I got up and went to the counter and bought two cans of Carib.

When I turned to walk back to our table, Clive was gone.

HE WASN'T there the next night, or the next. I sat at the Little Sweet alone, lingering until closing in case he should appear. By the fourth night, I was in a panic. I had pushed things too far, driven him away with the very expressions of intimacy with which I'd hoped to pull him closer.

"Clive hasn't been around lately," I said casually to Vincia on the fifth night of his absence, as if I were merely making conversation. She pursed her lips and continued scooping rice onto a plate. "Do you know if he's, like, away or something?"

"I know if he didn't tell you, it's none of your business."

After that, I didn't go inside the Little Sweet. I spent hours every night walking the streets, looping past his building to see if he would emerge, which he never did. Back in my apartment, I occupied the liminal space between sleeping and waking all night long, and in the mornings I couldn't say for sure whether I'd slept at all. I had nowhere to be during the day. I returned to Alison's diaries, searching her voice for some hint of where to go from here. I roamed the streets of Manhattan, looking in every taxi for his face.

As the days without Clive wore on, a vision of who I was and would be from then on began to sharpen in my mind. I was not one of the city's bright young things after all, but one of its invisibles. You know the kind of person I mean. You see me hauling myself up the subway stairs in the summer heat, or down them in winter with bags of groceries banging against my knees. You see my brown parka, which is not even utilitarian but actively—intentionally, it seems to you—ugly, and if you are a person with a full and busy life, you cannot even understand the logic behind such a sartorial choice, and the life behind such logic, except to feel sorry but also, well, irritated—all the lonely people clogging the world, making you see them when all you want to do is take the subway home and deal with your own problems and engage in your own small pleasures. Don't you deserve that? Well, sure, you do.

. . .

A WEEK later, when I looked in the storefront at the Little Sweet through a light snowfall and saw Clive sitting at his usual table, I thought I was imagining it. He looked up and spotted me through the glass. He smiled and waved.

"You were gone," I said as I took my seat across from him.

"I had some things to take care of. Did you miss me?" He smiled jokily.

"With all my heart."

"Did you hear about that flasher on the J?"

"It's always something with the J, isn't it?"

Just like that, we slipped back into our normal conversation. There had been a coyote sighting in Hamilton Heights—apparently it had scavenged a carton of General Tso's chicken from a trash can. An abandoned Mickey Mouse suitcase had led to the evacuation of Times Square and snarled traffic all afternoon.

When we finished our food, he proposed a walk. The halal butcher. Immaculee Bakery. The fruit stand (KUMQUATS FRESH!). Winthrop Hardware. The bookstore. (*The mother puts the children to bed. He waits for the bus. They say goodbye.*) What a relief it was, passing these familiar places with Clive again. When we came to a bench, Clive gestured at it, and we sat. It was a frigid night. Our breath left white contrails in the air. Clive said he'd heard on 1010 WINS that the Gowanus Canal had frozen over.

"I guess now we know the freezing point of whatever the hell is in the Gowanus Canal," I said.

He laughed. Then his face became serious. "There's something I've been wanting to tell you, Emily, and I don't want to put it off anymore. If I put it off I'm afraid I'll never say it."

My chest tightened. "Yes?"

"It's about what you said on Christmas Eve. About how we both have secrets. I think I'm ready. I want to tell you. I want us to tell each other."

"I want that, too," I whispered, half afraid that if I spoke too loudly I might shatter the moment. My eyes filled with tears. *Bravo, Clairey.* "I want that very much."

"I trust you. I know you would never do anything to hurt me."

"Never."

"But I'm afraid," he continued. "It's not easy for me, what I have to tell you. Maybe you could begin? With what happened to you in—what was it called, again, the town you're from?"

"Starlight."

"Where you skated all the time on the Wabash River."

I nodded.

"That's a lie, Emily."

"What are you talking about?"

"I looked it up. The Wabash River is all the way across the state from Starlight."

I looked down at my lap. Snow had gathered there, and I brushed it off automatically. "I'm sorry," I whispered. "I've wanted to be honest with you for weeks now. For months, really. The truth is I'm from California. Pasadena. That's where I grew up. You have to understand—when I talked with you that first night I had no idea you'd become part of my life the way you have."

He didn't reply.

"I said I'm sorry, and I am. But I told you I have secrets. So I tell people I'm from one place when I'm from another. Does it matter so much? Are you going to sit here and tell me everything you've shared with me is the whole truth?"

He shook his head.

"Please don't be angry with me. We can still tell one another our secrets, just like you said. Forgive me?"

He held me in his gaze. "Who would I be forgiving? Emily, or Claire?"

SOMETIMES YOU close your eyes and you are back at the beginning. You are walking down the beach. The sand is warm beneath your feet. The water is aquamarine, a wonder, yet when you cup it in your hands it is clear, and this is the biggest mystery you know. Your hand is in her hand. You see the apricot freckles crowding her milky skin, her hair in its messy bun with the yellow elastic band, the billowy white tunic that hides her secret. She looks down at you and smiles. She is yours, a beautiful sister made only to receive and return your love.

Somehow you understand that if only you can hold this moment firmly enough in your mind, if only you can plunge deeply enough into it, the two of you can break off from the world. You can erase the future through an act of will and live together with your sister in this moment forever, see the blue sea stretching before you forever, walk forever down the warm sand, the black rocks up ahead receding at the pace of your approach so that you never reach them. You can remain here until the world forgets you.

But you can never quite manage it, can you? In the end, you always let the world back in. You could have everything you ever wanted, but you spoil it. You spoil it every time.

"HOW DID YOU KNOW?"

Snow continued to fall. Steam rose from a grate in the street. I kept my eyes fixed on the interface where the steam and snow melted into one another to keep me from slipping off the edge of the moment.

"The thing you did." He traced a finger through the air. "You used to do it then, too."

"I could never help it," I said softly. I pressed a fingertip to a snowflake on my coat and felt it melt away to nothing.

"There was a night a few months ago. I was walking home and I thought I heard—did you follow me? Did you call my name?" He bit his lip and squinted down at the sidewalk as if he could scarcely believe what he was asking me. Then he looked up at me, his eyes so full of foreclosed hope that for a moment all I wanted was to be able to tell him I hadn't and have it be the truth.

I looked back down at the sidewalk. "Yes."

He shook his head. "I thought I was losing my mind." He was facing away from me, speaking to the sky, the snow, the brittle February night, and I understood that these words were not meant for me, but for someone else.

"I don't know what to say."

"I'm sure you'll think of something. You're so good at thinking up things to say. All these nights. I hope you did have a fun time."

"No."

"Bullshit," he whispered.

"You think I *wanted* to do this? I've given up everything. All I ever wanted was the truth. For Alison."

"For Alison," he echoed back. It seemed to me that his mind was far away, only the most gossamer of threads tethering him to this bench on this sidewalk here with me. He looked around—at the shop fronts across the street, the snow on the sidewalk, the black sky overhead. "Fuck," he shouted, punching his fist into his open palm. His shout echoed down the deserted street.

"I'll go," I said. I stood. "I'm going."

He grabbed my arm. "Sit."

"I'm sorry. I shouldn't have—"

"Sit."

"Please let me go. Please don't—"

"Don't *what*?"

"I'm sorry. I just wanted—"

"The truth, *Clairey*?"

I nodded.

"The truth is you're a fucked-up girl."

"I know," I whispered.

"Just like your sister."

"Please don't do this."

"The truth is Alison destroyed my life, and from what I see, she destroyed yours, too."

"Please just let me go."

"No. You want the truth, Claire, and I'm going to give it to you. You're going to sit here and listen to every word of it. And then I never want to see you again."

THE GIRL

EVERY WEEK THERE'S A GIRL. Every week she's pretty. Some weeks she's tall, some weeks she's short, some weeks her hair is blond and silky, other weeks it's red curls. She has big tits or flea bites, it makes no difference to he. He does like them with freckles.

He picks this one straightaway. I see it happen. She gallivants down the sand to the volleyball game and when she arrives she takes off she shirt. I was some distance away, but I saw it. He went still. I followed his eyes to she belly, where she has a big pink scar. Edwin and me have been breds since second grade. I know his mind and how it turns. He likes them with some twist to their pretty. He picks her then. I know even before he.

On the sideline, the girl's pale little sister spectates. She does something funny with she finger, waving it through the air. She's burning, but it's not my place to say so.

AFTER WORK, me and Edwin smoke in the car park. We count up we tips on the hood of Edwin's car. Me, twenty dollars. Edwin, thirty-four.

"Figure," I say.

"What I tell you? You're too serious. *Yes, sir. Yes, ma'am.* Yankees want to be your friend."

He's right, but so? When I try to make chat, the guests' faces go crooked. When Edwin tells a wife she looks lovely, her husband smiles because he loves to hear how his wife is pretty. When I say the same thing, the husband thinks it's none of my business how pretty his wife be. I can't do the job the way he does it. But I'm polite. I'm prompt. Some days, anyway.

After, I bike to Sara's house to see my boy. When I arrive, Sara's standing in the doorway with Bryan in she arms and displeasure on she face. Agatha is on the sofa in the parlor, scratching at she scalp.

"You're late," Sara says. I feel annoyed, though she's right—I am late.

She tries to hand Bryan to me, but my boy clings to his mum. When I take him he cries. I stroke he ringlets. My boy is handsome, and I'm not just saying so because he's mine. His ringlets have light in them. "There, there, my Bry," I say.

THE NEXT morning I wake up to pounding on my bedroom door as usual. Gran.

"What's wrong with you? You late!"

Shit, woman.

I don't say this. I get up and stumble to the toilet. How sad is it for a man to look forward so much to his morning piss? When that relief may be as good as his day will get? But it's such a good feeling. It could have gone another way. God could have made a world where good things feel bad. Pissing, eating, banging. Maybe he would have been doing us a service.

I bike Mayfair to work. I'm hungover as usual from liming at Paulette's last night. My bike is old and rusted and squeaks with every pedal. When cars pass, they stir up the dust and leave me in it, and I hold my breath until it settles. But this hour, the streets are mostly quiet. The only sounds are roosters and women sweeping and cartoons inside houses. I feel myself on the bike, a big thing on a little thing. I'm of two minds on this ride, always. It's a mortification, but so peaceful. When I set out, as long as I'm not running too late, the sky is still smoky blue, like something far away. As I ride, it turns the color of an oyster shell. The breeze still possesses some coolness. Dogs wake. The skinny black hound with the white belly trots alongside me sometimes. Early morning feels like church, when I did go.

When I pass Arthur's father's store I'm close. I ride past the gas station on George Street where Keithley used to work, past the three-legged goat tied to a post in Daphne Nelsen's yard, past the clinic where the antimen go when they're deading. Past Prosser's School Uniforms—pink for Horatio Byrd, yellow for All Saints, blue for Sir Northcote. Past the scrub that leads to the nameless cliffs. Past the house where my father was born. It's abandoned now. The roof is more sky than galvanized. Chickens roost there. I crest a hill and the ocean appears, a color nobody can describe. Damien once told me science says mankind came up in the sea—we started as lizards with fur or some shit. It's only recent we left the sea for land.

Maybe that's why the sea feels so, like a house in a dream you wish so badly to enter, but where's the door?

Indigo Bay is the last resort on Mayfair Road. When I look at it, I see it twice at once: the white buildings and the clean sand, but also as it was when we were boys, with wild pomme-serette trees and needles and condoms in the seaweed and the antimen who loved this spot. With its stink and sand flies, nobody bothered they. Well, nobody but we.

Morning is morning. Edwin and me carry the lounge chairs out from the storage house and arrange them in a crescent, just so. Next, the chair cushions. I carry them four to a stack on my shoulder. Finally, the umbrellas. A bit later, the early birds arrive. By nine, the beach is crowded. Then it's towel, bottled water, adjust umbrella, drag chair, fresh towel, fresh water, all morning long. Today, a man with dolphins on his swim trunks and a pretty Asian wifey orders a Red Stripe.

"Peace, *mahn,*" Edwin says when he sees the bottle on my tray. Edwin thinks it's fucking daft how Yankees love to order Red Stripe here. But Jamaica's not so far from here. I see their point. Later, Edwin will chat this daft fucking Yankee up to see what else he likes. Guests who order a drink in the morning often turn out to be good customers.

When I bring his drink, the man reaches in the pocket of his swim trunks, pulls out five dollars, and says, "Get yourself one, too." He smiles.

"Thank you, sir," I say. His smile goes flat. He wants me to make some chat, but chat is Edwin's thing.

Midday, the girl's daddy asks me where the locals eat. I'm glad he asks me and not Edwin. It pisses Edwin off when guests ask for recommendations for authentic island food. A few weeks ago we had a guest order only curry goat and conch creole for lunch all week.

"Fucking dolt," Edwin said to me one day after he took the man's order.

"Last week you say the same about the lady who only ate burgers and pizza. What would you like they to eat? How can they do right by you?" I thought I had him then.

He shrugged. "Maybe they can't. What I care about it?"

"That sounds fair." I rolled my eyes.

He snorted. "Gogo, man, you so soft it get you someday."

When he takes break past the rocks at the edge of the beach I see she, gallivanting down the sand toward he.

• • •

THIS JOB'S not so bad. The Yankees who go to Papa Mango's and stay at hotels near the Basin and shop in Hibiscus Harbour where the cruise ships dock act like they're royalty because they bought some budget Caribbean cruise package. The guests here are so rich they can relax about it. They're polite, mostly. The food trays are heavy, the chairs are heavy, the umbrellas are heavy, but that's just usual job shit.

One thing I do mind. While I walk the beach, I feel the guests' eyes on me. It's like I'm onstage, but at the same time, the audience is not even interested in me. I feel so big under their gaze, like if I open my mouth I may swallow the world by accident and leave myself alone.

Everybody knows Yankees are fat, but at Indigo Bay, most of them are thin. All day they eat and drink and sleep like babies. I walk back and forth carrying trays heavy with they cheeseburgers, coconut shrimp, and conch fritters. Food so oily it shimmers. So how are they thin? It seems like someone somewhere just decided it.

Not all the guests are beautiful, but they all have a certain something. A wellness, maybe. Terrible things may happen to any person, rich or poor, white or brown, and I'm sure terrible things have happened to some of they, but they don't appear so. They appear like they believe the universe loves them, and maybe it does.

A few guests are not so well maintained. At present, we have a fat woman with skin like cottage cheese and a Frenchie man with a hard round belly. They don't cover up; they lie out like everybody else. When we're waiting at the bar for our orders to be ready, Edwin says, "You check the belly on the old fucking Frenchie?" and puts a finger in he mouth like he's gagging. I laugh. But when I'm not with him, laughing at they, it's different. These fat people, almost naked under the sun—I'm amazed by they.

FLEET. I learned this word from Jan, the old Dutchie we used to lime with when we ditched school. One day when Edwin and me were walking to Paulette's, it started to pour. Edwin took off he shoes and sprinted through the rain and I followed behind, panting all the way. When we arrived inside, all soaked through, our school polos stuck to we, Jan said, "Edwin, how fleet you are!"

English was not Jan's first language or he second; first came Dutch, then German, then French, then English, but he still knew this word I didn't.

I never looked it up, but I have the idea of it. *Fleet*. A thing I'll never be.

WE HAVE a customer. The man with the dolphin swim trunks. Edwin chats he up after volleyball one afternoon. Turns out his lawyer wifey needs to relax. This morning, after my daily highlight morning piss, I reach under my bed and pull out the lockbox. The combination is Bryan's birthday. First, so I don't forget it. Second, to remind me I do this under under business for he. When I open the box, the ganja scent rushes out. Gran must smell it, but she's given up being up in my business. This is why the lockbox stays at my place. Edwin's sisters are nosy as shit.

The lockbox is how I do my part. Edwin chats up potential customers. Edwin makes the sale. I keep the lockbox under my bed. We split the profits even. I weigh out ten grams. Most I put in one baggie. Enough for two spliffs, I put in another. This bag's for we.

I wait in the car park, and when Edwin arrives I hand he the big baggie. In the afternoon, the man with the dolphin swim trunks has a rendezvous with Edwin by the tennis court. The wifey's there, practicing she serve; she pauses in she little white skirt and watches. The man gives Edwin sixty dollars. Edwin gives me thirty.

Sundown is sundown. Insect coils with their sweet fake smell, last call, a posse of children chasing Edwin around the sand. Girls and boys tug at he legs and tickle he, and finally he lets them take him down. The girl's pale little sister doesn't join. She watches. Her finger turns and turns.

When the guests leave the beach we collect the towels, hundreds of they—damp and sandy and smelling of salt. We take down the umbrellas. We drag the chairs across the sand and stack them up. After a day trudging in the sand beneath the hot sun, we uniforms have the same strong, mothy smell as the boys' P.E. changing room at Everett Lyle Secondary, full of sweaty plimsolls and pinnies. We change out of them and throw them in the bin for the wash lady. In the car park, we roll a spliff with the extra herb we skimmed from we sale.

Evening, I give Sara my tips plus the money from the sale. If she suspects where the extra money comes from some days, she never says so.

• • •

TODAY, WHEN we're smoking in the car park after work, I see the girl coming up the path, swaying she hips before she even spots us. "What the ass?" I whisper to Edwin. He shrugs, as if her arrival is unexpected for he, though we both know it's not so. When she asks what we're doing here, Edwin takes a spliff out of he pocket, twirls it in he finger, and says, "Nothing much."

She raises she eyebrows. "Mind if I do *nothing much* with you?"

This girl appears cunning.

WORD GETS out from the man in the dolphin swim trunks. A few newlyweds purchase from we. Some retirees also. We sell some pills to the girlfriend of the actor on holiday. She has a body like a porn star. "That man have it made," Edwin says. "So old he balls must sag to his knees and still the women line up to be fucked." The actor appears shy to me. He touches his girlfriend's body, but he doesn't appear to enjoy it. That's some Yankee shit right there—rich, famous, porn-star girlfriend, and still he's so low.

One day I arrive at Sara's with fifty dollars, and do you know what she says?

"Look at you, high as a kite! How can I leave him with you now?"

"I'm not high as a kite, Sara."

She places she hand on she hip. "You smoked before you showed up here. Do you deny it?"

"Don't be like that. I'm out there breaking my back ten hours a day for you."

"You think I'm not breaking my back all day, caring for this child?"

"Me and Edwin just smoked a bit. A man needs his breds."

"What about me? When do I get to see my friends? As if I have any left, anyhow."

Here's some words of wisdom for you: Don't ever try to out-talk a woman. They store the right language up so it's ready to throw down when the time comes. Her face goes bitter, but then she changes it—she crinkles she eyes and gives me this injured look, like she's a gentle woman without a nasty bone in she body and in the face of all the poor treatment I dole out she feels only this soft, pretty sadness. Such fuckery.

"All I ask is one hour's reprieve from taking care of him, Clive," she says. "One hour. So that I might bathe and, heaven forbid, lie down and put on a little perfume and listen to the radio." She's crying now. I can't tell if it's more pretty acting or if she's crying for true.

I look past she. Through the window I see the dead yard, the clothesline, and the old cookhouse. We were together there, in the dark. She led and I followed. What was I thinking? Only one thing: Sara. It was Sara pulling me through the dark yard. It was Sara opening the door, and Sara unbuttoning me, fast and urgent like she would combust if she didn't manage it soon, and it was Sara's small, narrow hips I was pulling the yellow dress away from with my shaking hands. It was Sara pulling me against she, Sara I entered, Sara who I had loved for so long. I look at the woman before me, her eyes so tired it's like she's been watching this life since the beginning of time, and I wonder how we got here.

"I'm sorry," I whisper.

"I'll see you tomorrow, Clive," she says. Then she closes the door.

NIGHT, EDWIN picks me up. When we get to Paulette's, Don and Des are already there. Edwin buys two rums, one for each of we, though we know I'm going to drink both. Edwin hardly drinks, though I'm the only one who notices. He holds he glass, then when I finish mine, we switch. It's been this way so long I don't recall how it became so.

"Tonight's spliff brought to you by the Yankee in the pink dolphin swim trunks," Edwin says.

"You shitting we," Don says.

"Antiman?" Des asks.

"Nah. Hot Chinese wifey."

"Women in America must be desperate," Des says.

"Man must be filthy rich," Don says.

"Man be nice," I say. I don't know why. Maybe because it's true. He tipped nice, too.

Edwin grabs the spliff from me and takes a puff. "Nice," he snorts, "is some real fuckery."

THE NEXT day I arrive at Sara's sober and on time. Bryan's toddling on the floor. I sit beside he, make some silly faces. My boy gurgles when he laughs. His eyes are big and round like his daddy's.

While I entertain he, Sara takes a bath. She comes out looking refreshed.

She wears a scarf around her hair the color of grass on a cricket pitch. Sara has parts of she so small sometimes I wonder how God did manage it. She tiny toes, all lined up. She leans down and tousles Bryan's ringlets. He gurgles. Her small small feet carry her to the kitchen. She takes the lids off the pots on the stove and ladles food onto a plate.

"Dinner, Mum," she says.

Agatha stops she scratching in the parlor and trudges to the kitchen. She sits down at the table in such a way. I can't explain how she does it, what it is she does with she eyes or she back or she jaw or she hips, but she manages to sit down at a table in a way that says that she—she! scratching lady in the parlor!—is too good for this, and that it takes all she has to abide she daughter, who falls so far below she expectations. Here's the thing about women: If the world was only women, there wouldn't be language at all. They don't need it.

Sara pretends she doesn't notice the way her mum sits. Her pretending pains me.

Agatha takes a single bite, then sets down she fork and says, "There's grit in the callaloo."

I lose it a bit then. I walk to the table and stand over she. I pick up the fork and hold it out to she.

"Eat," I say.

Agatha looks at me with she black beady eyes of a hen.

"Sara does everything for you! She cooks and cleans and tends to Bryan while you sit around with your feet up like some grand woman you never was, scratching at your nasty head. Now, *eat*." For a moment our eyes lock. Then Agatha takes the fork. She eats.

When I leave, Sara walks me to the door. "See you tomorrow, Clive," she says. She smiles.

TONIGHT, WHEN Edwin turns left onto Mayfair instead of staying straight on to Paulette's, I feel the evening congeal like old porridge.

"Edwin," I say.

"One stop." Like the stopping's the problem.

"You promised."

"Relax."

When we pull into the car park the girl is there, waiting pretty against a palm tree. So many weeks the girl waits against this same tree. Women always know their best angles.

"How would you like to stick your cock in that?" Edwin whispers to me as she walks toward the car.

"Girl decked out for you." I never know how to stay vex with he.

"Ten dollars say she decked out belowdeck, too."

We laugh at this, at she, as she approaches. He loves to laugh at they.

"Look who decided to grace us with she presence," he says.

This one is perfection when she rolls she eyes, and she knows it. She climbs in. This is happening, no stopping it. Though Edwin promised how many times this shit be finished, we're driving to Paulette's with somebody's daughter in the backseat.

THIS WEEK'S girl keeps appearing. When we arrive at the beach in the morning she's in the water, stroking. I've never seen a pretty little thing swim with such power. She stays in the sea a long time and never pauses to look at we.

"Oh, hey," she says, back on land, like she's surprised to see we. Who does she think she's fooling? We know she's performing for we. For he. The girls always do so. Sometimes they do it by sunning themselves in their tiny bikinis. Sometimes they do it by getting drunk and crazy at Paulette's. There was a girl a few months ago, Callie, who climbed onto the bar and danced, and when she was up there you could see straight to her pum pum because she wasn't wearing any panties. Edwin and me lost it. I think he still fucked she in the end, but he fucked she like it was the funniest thing in the world. Sometimes, if they're shy, they even do it by pretending to ignore him, but the way their gaze keeps flicking back at him gives them away—their walk, their pretty dresses, even the way they read their book on the beach like it's so interesting they can't spare a moment to look up at he as he passes—it's all for he.

Volleyball, she's there, flashing she scar. Everybody watches she. Edwin, the Yankee boys. On the sideline, her sister spectates and does she tracing with she finger in the air. Poor little girl—such an odd child, and she sister so pretty.

Sundown she's there, too. She comes around the car park and shares we spliff like this is she usual routine. People see she with we, and I don't like it. Waitresses arriving for the dinner shift. Gardeners departing. Sometimes women shake their heads as they walk past us. Sometimes they do nothing, but still I know they disapprove. Let me take this even further for you: Women don't even need bodies to tell us exactly what they think. They could be ghosts, all air, and still men would walk through this air and know just how vex they be with we.

Night, she's waiting in the car park for we, in she little dresses with she little sweaters over she little shoulders for the chill. This girl can hold she liquor, and when Edwin compliments her on this, she says, "The value of a college education," and rolls she eyes. When the dancing begins, I stand to the side and watch she motion. How does a body know and choose everything it does like that?

Sometimes in the afternoon I see she gallivanting down the beach after he. She flashes over the black rocks and gone. What they do there, just the two of they, I don't know. He's not fucking she yet. At least, I'm pretty sure, though this is the one thing my chatterbox friend doesn't speak about much. Don't get me wrong, he makes plenty of big talk about banging these rich-daddy girls. But when Don or Des bang a girl, they go into the particulars . . . this girl smells like fish down there, that one knows how to work she teeth, another one has nipples wrinkled up like walnuts. Edwin stays on the surface, no matter how we pump he for details. Still, I gather he waits for the last night to fuck they. He likes pursuing them even more than he likes fucking them. Fucking is easy for he. Waiting's what he loves, and making them wonder: Did their pretty little performance work?

Another thing: I think he waits because this way, if the girl regrets it, by the time the feeling sinks in, she's on the plane to Chicago or in she pretty purple bedroom in Boston, and what's she going to do then?

A few months ago, a girl almost made everything go bad. Julie. A California blondie, pretty pretty. Julie was quieter than the ones Edwin usually picks. A good girl. She barely touched her drinks at Paulette's, and when we offered her the spliff in the car park, she said, "No, thank you," like she was declining a fresh towel on the beach. I thought she was a lost cause, but then she spirited Edwin away one sundown to she room. With Julie, he didn't wait; he went right along with she. When she bled, he knew it was a mistake. Virgin girls are not a thing to mess with. They think they know what they want, but how can they? And a virgin Yankee girl who decides this is how she wants to lose it? Holy shit.

After that, Julie started acting funny. Her daddy wasn't stupid. He knew something was going on. One sunup when we arrived at work, he was waiting for we in the car park. He marched up to Edwin and grabbed his shirt and told us to stay the hell away from his daughter and threatened to get both our asses fired and to beat the shit out of we if he found out Edwin had laid so much as a hand on his little girl. First time I ever heard a guest threaten to beat the shit out of someone. We were lucky. Julie was so embarrassed she kept she trap shut about what happened. Ever since, Edwin waits. You never know when a girl will get vex. You never know what a vex girl will do, or say.

These girls have a danger to they. He likes that, too.

WHEN WE meet the girl in the car park after work today, she appears troubled. Restless. Maybe it's the rain. It fell all day, constant. Her fingers keep moving like they're not ruled by she. She drums she fingers on the hood of Edwin's car. Then her fingertips circle she scar, around and around. Maybe something happened between she and Edwin. Maybe with this one, so pretty, he failed to wait. Shit.

Then she furrows she brow and says a thing I never expected.

"When I was swimming today I saw a woman on Faraway Cay."

For a moment nobody says a word. I look at Edwin. I expect him to grin and brush her off, but his face is dead serious, even a bit afraid. I shiver.

"Jesus, Mary, and Joseph," he whispers.

"What?" she says. "Do you know her or something?"

"Woman you say you saw—she have long hair, black black?" Edwin asks. The girl nods.

"White white skin?"

She nods again. "She was, like, staring at me."

I'm thinking, it can't be. But this girl freaks me out a bit. She fingertips never stop tracing she scar. A silly notion comes over me that this scar is the source of she power.

Edwin looks across she to me. "Tell her, Gogo."

I tell her about the Faraway woman's hooves for feet and her wildness. I tell her how she lures people to Faraway and leads them across the cay, how if you follow the woman to the waterfall and see the stars reflected in the water you will lose all sense of up and down, earth and sky, you and she, and they say that's how she takes you.

"I saw her," she says when I finish.

I shiver again.

Edwin snorts. He claps his hands, tosses back his head, and laughs.

"Check you two," he says. "Girl, only thing you did see was a goat. Faraway's overrun with they."

I should have known he wasn't being serious with his Jesus, Mary, and Joseph.

"It wasn't a goat," the girl says. "She had black hair and white skin, just like you said."

"Old nanny goat, probably." He shrugs.

"Why you think Faraway is overrun with they in the first place?" I say. I turn to she. "Every time someone vanish on Faraway, a new goat appears. She turns they."

Edwin cracks up. "Goges here's the only one under sixty who believes that nonsense. Tell me something: What you ever see a goat do beside eating, shitting, and rutting? How do *you* think that cay became overrun with they?"

"How you explain the planes, then?" I say. I can't tell anymore if I'm defending she from Edwin's ridicule or fucking with she, too. Maybe it's some of both.

"Oh, yes!" Edwin says, grinning. "Let it be known that there are not one, not two, but three downed planes on Faraway Cay."

"And they form a triangle," I say.

"Three things *always* form a triangle," Edwin says.

He's right. Shit.

The girl appears nervous.

"But the triangle's not the point," I say. "Guess what's at their center? The waterfall. She lures they. How else you explain it?"

"Drug runners. In shit prop planes."

The girl chews she lip and looks down at the ground. "Maybe I didn't see it as clearly as I thought." I'm pretty sure she only says this to please Edwin, though, because she gazes past the parking lot in the direction of the cay with this dreamy look, like something legit is happening to she. Like she thinks she's special now because we local folkloric creature has taken an interest in she. I feel so annoyed then I wish I didn't argue with Edwin on she behalf. Anyway, he's probably right. Must be a goat she saw.

We change the subject. We smoke we spliff. We pass around a bottle from Edwin's car—hot, unpleasant liquor. We're ready to leave when the girl asks, "Why is it called Faraway Cay anyway, if it's so close? Is that supposed to be, like, a joke or something?"

"No, miss," Edwin says. "This is a deadly serious matter. This name protects us from the cay's proximity." He snorts. "Typical superstitious island shit, thinking if we call it so, it will be so, when that goat-infested cay is staring we right in the face. Better take care, now, girl. The Faraway woman has she eye on you."

TODAY WHEN I arrive, Sara opens the door with a basket in she arms. "I thought I'd take him to Little Beach," she says.

"Oh," I say. "I guess I'll see you tomorrow, then?"

She looks at me with softness in she face. "Come with us."

We stop off at the food mart on Hopper Lane and I buy three Cadbury bars, one for each of we. We arrive at Little Beach at that magic hour just after sunset when everything is veiled in blue—the sky, the sea, the sand. The guests at Indigo Bay miss this hour. They take their photographs of the sunset and then they go inside and they miss it. Little Beach is quiet, but not empty. We choose a spot a bit away from the others. Sara takes a cloth from the basket and spreads it on the sand. I set out the Cadbury bars. Bryan pets the sand beside the cloth like it's a living thing. Sara lies down, closes she eyes, and lets the remains of the day warm her.

In the distance, one fishing boat is still out, a small dinghy with a fishing pole planted at the bow. The boat is a black silhouette. The fishing pole appears to lance the clouds. At the water's edge, a shirtless man in track pants sprints down the sand. A few strays follow after him, yapping and so happy. Boys scamper onto the pier, then dive into the sea. Not long ago this was me, and someday it will be Bryan. The lampposts on the pier are rickety and their white paint is nearly all flaked away. The lampposts have no lights and they never have and I've never known why, and I like this.

"Should we draw shapes, my Bry?" I say.

He doesn't reply. A shy day. I hoist myself from the cloth and squat in the sand. I trace a balloon with a squiggly string. A bird. A sailboat. Bryan looks at the shapes with interest and also some wariness. "Do you know what that says?" I ask, pointing. He shakes his head. "*B-R-Y-A-N*. That's you, Bryan."

He murmurs something.

"What's that?"

"A nana."

"You want me to draw a banana?"

His lips part and release the faintest, "Yes."

I do my best, a thin shape that looks more like a crescent moon. "Like so?"

He nods. "Thank you, Dada."

It's not me who taught him *thank you*. It's Sara. Already she's showing him good manners. I didn't even notice it happening.

Bryan is still shy with me when I tear the corner off a Cadbury wrapper and show him how to press out the melted chocolate. My boy accepts the chocolate I squeeze onto his finger like it's something holy. He licks it off with his small pink tongue. Sara's tongue.

Sara sits up. "Should we go in?"

I undress Bryan and take off his nappy. My son's skin is dark and even and supple. His belly button is a small sweet nut. Sara removes her shirt and her skirt to reveal her swimming suit. I take off my polo, so I'm down to my shorts and singlet. I'm a bit embarrassed for Sara to see me, but she doesn't stare.

With Sara beside me, I take Bryan in my arms and carry him into the sea. At Indigo Bay, the guests pause on the sand before they walk into the water, as if some sort of preparation is required. It's different here. We walk into the sea as easily as taking our next step. We are not alone in the water. I see a father with a daughter. A woman in a pink bathing cap. An old man holds an old woman by the arm and guides her through the soft waves.

We wade out until the water comes to Sara's waist, Bryan nestled in the crook of my arm. The water is warm, almost the same as the air. Then I feel something warmer on my arm. At first I think it's the last of the day's heat, but the warmth is moving, flowing. I look at Bryan. My boy is laughing—big laughter, full and free. Sara and I look down at my arm at the same time. Urine, trickling in a small channel. We laugh, too. Then Sara closes her eyes, leans back, and floats.

I see us then, a family together in the sea. And something happens to me that maybe I can't ever explain. On this evening, I am a father. Later, Sara and I will tuck Bryan's sleeping ragdoll body into bed. Later still I'll lime with Edwin. For the first time ever, my life feels like my life.

ISN'T IT the fuck of it all that tonight of all nights, when all I want is to lime with my mate, to feel my life being my life, we're saddled with the girl? We're in the car on the way to Paulette's. Engine sputtering, chicken in the road, and she. Tonight's she last night. Edwin knows what this means and from the way she's dressed in a short skirt and a top that ties with a string around she neck, she knows it, too.

"You ready for a wild night, girl?" Edwin says.

She scoffs. "Paulette's is not exactly the pinnacle of wild."

"Maybe we'll take you out to Faraway," he says with a grin. "See if the goat lady take an interest in you."

"I'm down for whatever," the girl says, like it makes no difference to she. But I see she hidden smile, so pleased to think we're going to do something big for she last night. What is it about this one, so convinced she's special? I want to tell she there was Julie and Callie and Lisa and Lauren and Molly before her, and there will be plenty of pretty pretty girls after her. She may be a bit sharper than most, she may be quicker with her tongue, but in the end she wants what they all want: to take home the story of how she fucked the man who brought she towels on the beach. But so what? She's using him, but he's using she, too. They get their story and he gets them.

At Paulette's, Edwin buys all of we a round of ganja shots. Next, rum. At some point I must switch glasses with he, because soon both of ours are finished. I buy another, and another. I'm getting good and gone now. Music playing, bottles clinking, mutt begging. Sounds of Edwin and the girl.

I watch them dance. She does have a nice sway. Together they move so right. You can't learn this. You want to know the secret of life? You will never be they. *They* is always someone else.

We're at Paulette's an hour or so when the girl says, "I'm bored. Let's get out of here."

"Where do you have in mind?" Edwin says.

"I thought we were going to Faraway?" she says with a glint in she eyes.

He laughs. "You mad, girl?"

"But I thought you said—"

"I was just messing with you. Anyway, how you think we would get there?"

She looks down at the floor. "Whatever," she mumbles. "Forget it."

"Relax. Plenty of wild places to go."

Next thing we're in the car. Edwin drives fast. Windows down, radio blasting. The potholes give a good *bump*—the girl bounces so high she head hits the roof, hard, and she laughs. We're all good and drunk. Ready for the night to take we.

When Edwin pulls off the road at the spot where the scrub leads to the nameless cliffs, I turn a hard gaze on he. I don't want to take some Yankee chick to this place. But Edwin pretends not to notice. He turns off the car and climbs out. He grabs a bottle of rum from the car and says, "Follow me."

We walk single-file, Edwin then she then me. We've limed here pretty regular over the years since we found the spot in the boat with Keithley, and there's a path carved into the scrub, so faint you have to know it's there to find it. But the ground is uneven and the path is narrow and the scrub is so thick sometimes you have to shield your face as you walk. I see the girl turn around and look behind she. The road is gone.

"Where are we going, anyway?" she asks. She tries to make her voice calm, but she's nervous, and I feel a bit pleased to see this cocky one brought a little low. She stumbles as she walks. This is she drunkest night yet.

"This wild enough for you, miss?" Edwin replies.

She wraps her arms tight across she chest like she's cold. She's scared for true now, and just when I'm about to break and tell she everything's fine and where we're going, the scrub parts and we're here. The stretch of smooth, flat rock that leads to the edge. The ocean lit up by the moon. The girl doesn't hesitate. She dashes right up to the edge, so fast for a second I think she's going to go right over.

"Shit, girl, watch yourself!" Edwin says.

She turns to us. "This place is amazing." She kicks off she sandals and we do the same, leaving we shoes in a pile. She walks the edge like a high-wire walker in the circus, up on she tiptoes with she hands out to she sides.

Next, she stands with she toes curled over the edge, looking out. In the distance, Faraway is a black shadow against the black sky.

Edwin nudges me. "She ripe to be fucked or what?"

Then he runs at she, his bare feet soundless against the rock. When he reaches she, he puts his arms around her and she shrieks. He scoops her up. He twirls her around.

"You scared the shit out of me!" she says, laughing so hard she's gasping. She hits him, but not hard; she's not angry, she's flirting. She leans back in Edwin's arms and looks up at the stars and kicks her feet like she's swimming through the air. He puts her down and we sit together on the rocks.

Edwin passes the bottle of rum around. He pulls a spliff from his pocket. We're having a real bacchanal now, the three of we. The rocks are smooth and cool. The sky offers we everything: crescent moon, stars so bright it's like they're fucking with we.

She tips the bottle back and lets the liquor flow down she throat. She blows smoke into Edwin's face and he breathes it in. I reach for the spliff. She shakes she head, wags she finger.

"Not yet." She takes another hit, brings she face close to me, and exhales. Then her mouth is on my mouth. I'm so gone I don't wonder what or why. Her tongue twists around my tongue. I take she hips in my hands. She berry lips. She little tits pressing against my chest. I feel myself going hard.

She pulls away. There's a twinkle in she eyes. She turns to Edwin. Then her mouth is on his mouth and I watch she kiss he. Her ponytail tosses in the wind. He unties the string around her neck. He runs his hands up and down she sides and groans.

She pulls away from he, same as she did from me. I look to see if something's wrong, but she still has the twinkle in she eyes. She twirls her ponytail with her finger, like she's alone here, amusing herself. Then she looks at we. "Your turn."

I laugh.

"What's so funny?" she says.

"You shitting we," Edwin says.

"You scared, boys?" She makes a big show of tying the string around her neck again, though she's so drunk she does it sloppy. "I thought you were up for something wild. Never mind, I guess."

Edwin shakes he head. "Fucking girl." He grabs me and pulls me toward him. Next thing I know, his lips are on my lips. His tongue pushes into my mouth. Quick, he pulls away. He wipes the back of his hand across his mouth and I do the same. We spit onto the rocks. He kissed me hard, like a smack across the mouth. At first I want to laugh. Can you believe what we just did? Can you believe how far my bred will go to fuck a girl? But then I look at he and he looks at me and something in his face stops me. For the first time in we life, Edwin appears afraid.

I hear the girl clap, slow slow. I hear she say, "Bravo." We don't move. "Guys?" she says. "Hey, guysss." Out of the corner of my eye I see she stumble. She falls to her hands and knees like she's going to be sick. Then she lies down on the ground, curled up like a baby.

Edwin snaps back into the moment then. He turns away from me and faces she. "You satisfied, *miss*?" he says.

"Shhh. The stars," she mumbles. Her eyes are closed.

Edwin goes over and sits next to she. He takes the string of her shirt in his fingers and pulls. She lets him. She shirt falls down to she waist. She's not wearing a bra. Her tits are like Sara's, small small, the kind that remind you a woman was a girl. He unbuttons his trousers. He runs his fingers up she leg, she thigh, under she skirt.

"Mmm." She says it so faint I barely hear it.

I go off to give them space. I walk to the edge of the rocks and lie down and listen to the sea crash. I close my eyes and for a moment I'm falling, weightless. Then I hear Edwin.

"What the fuck?" he says.

I look over.

He's wiping his hand on his trousers. "Girl, quit slobbering!" he says.

I laugh. "Edwin, man, she passed out!"

He groans and shoves she away. In the starlight her scar glistens like a thing that could slither away. He lifts she arm and lets go. It flops.

"Typical," he spits.

Edwin leaves her there and walks over to me. He lies down near me, right at the edge, so close he hangs one arm over it and swings it back and forth through the abyss above the sea. We look up at the stars. A memory comes over me like a breeze, of lying like this back in this same spot in secondary, when Keithley would take us out in the boat and sometimes, amid the bacchanal, the night would find its stillness. I'm drifting off now. Ground cool and smooth. Air cool and smooth. Sound of waves far below.

Then I feel Edwin's hand on my hand.

He turns and looks at me. I don't laugh or pull my hand away. It all happens fast. He unbuttons himself, then me. I make my mind go empty. I make myself all body. Not because I know what I want or don't want, but because this night has taken us to a place we may never find again, and I need to be there with him before it's gone. I don't believe we're doing this until he places my hand around him. He's warm, like my own self. It's he or me or we—I don't bother to understand, just touch and rub, touch and rub, until the world goes tacky with we. We're together beneath the cold stars, and then the stars groan and unleash their white light and the night goes so thick and sweet with our chlorine I swear that perfume will last until the stars are dead.

Then I'm on the ground. Shoved off by he, hard, and at first I don't know why, but then I sit up and rub my eyes open and see she looking at we.

"The fuck you staring at, little girl?" Edwin says.

Her eyes open wide. Her mouth makes an *O* and a sound comes out so small the wind takes it.

She stands, gathers she sandals, and runs.

FARAWAY

"AT FIRST, I believed she would turn up."

People disappear and are found. A mother at a department store plunges into panic until she hears a muffled giggle coming from inside a rack of clothes. A husband is late on a rainy night, but eventually the headlights come up the driveway. The girl is sobering up somewhere. She is swimming in the ocean, in the pool. She is a bit late, is all, to the breakfast buffet. For a time, the missing person is everywhere. Then, sometimes, just as quickly, she is nowhere.

Clive and I sat on the bench on the sidewalk. Snow had collected on our coats and on Clive's gray wool hat. The traffic light at the end of the block bathed us in its shifting light—green, yellow, red. It was after midnight. I felt as if I had been walking for days, for years, and now that I had finally arrived at my destination, this faraway place the reaching of which had been my sole object for so long, I didn't want to look around. I didn't want to take in the sights or know anything about what kind of place this was. I was only tired.

I said nothing and he continued. "When she ran off, I started to go after her, but Edwin said to let her go, and I did. We were only half a mile from Indigo Bay. We weren't abandoning her in the middle of nowhere. I figured she'd find her way. On the drive home, we got pulled over and the police officer took us in to sleep it off. You must know about that, I guess. We were in a cell together all night, only the two of us, but we didn't talk. We just sat there together. But it wasn't a bad silence. It felt like we had time, is what I mean. We didn't have to say anything to each other yet about what we'd done. Then the next day we found out she was missing and everything changed."

"What did you do?"

"When he heard the news, Edwin came up to me on the beach and said,

'Listen. We limed with she at Paulette's and then we drove her back here. That's all.' So when the police questioned me that's what I told them. I knew how it must look. The two of us with her all night, and now she happened to be gone? They knew I was hiding something, but what could I do, tell them what had happened?" He shook his head. "The police came and searched my grandmother's house. They were looking for drugs. I don't know how they knew. Edwin—he wouldn't have done that to me. I still believe that. My grandmother watched me get taken away, with all the neighbors out in the street." He ran his hand over his face.

Clive told me the rest of his story, and I did my best to listen, though I confess I found it difficult to focus on the details of a life that I saw now had very little to do with me. He told me about his time in the eggshell-blue prison, where he and the twenty or so other incarcerated island men did nothing much as they waited out their sentences. At night, he was troubled by dreams. In them, he was back at the cliffs with Edwin, together beneath the stars. He looked up and saw everyone he knew standing in a circle around them, watching. *We have found you, we know, everybody knows*. He woke from these dreams soaked in sweat. Then he reminded himself that the girl was the only one who had seen them together, and she was dead. He felt so relieved, and right on the heels of this emotion came the next one—filthy, gut-twisting shame that he was relieved that a girl was dead, and in these moments it seemed to him that they must have willed her death somehow, that their desire to protect their secret had made it happen.

In prison he had time to think. Mostly, he thought about Edwin. They had not spoken since Edwin instructed him on what to say to the police, so Clive was left alone with the mystery of that night and what it meant—a mystery that cast its shadow back to the beginnings of his boyhood. He went over it and over it, sifting through the smallest moments and details of their shared life. He thought of the antimen on the beach before Indigo Bay was Indigo Bay, when Edwin orchestrated the ambushes to chase the men away. He thought of Jan sitting in the stifling afternoon air of Paulette's, his eyes bloodshot with drink, his thumb beating like a heart against the sticky bar. *Fleet*. What was Jan's interest in them, in Edwin, really? He thought of Alison and Julie and all the rest, the whole parade of Edwin's pretty American daughters. Edwin always said he went after them because the local girls were either prudes or skets or gossips, and Clive had always been impressed with himself for knowing better than to believe this. He had thought Edwin pursued these girls because they came from the places he dreamed of going, because he hated them for their stupid good luck even as he tried to draw himself closer to his dreams through their sweet-smelling skin. And maybe that was part of it. But what if there was something else, too? What if he chose these girls because whatever happened, or didn't, they were leaving, gone?

No matter how much he thought about it, without knowing what that night had meant to Edwin, it was impossible to determine what it had meant to himself. What would have happened next? What future was thwarted because that girl went off and got herself killed?

Edwin did not come to see him in prison. His grandmother did, every Sunday. She sat stiffly across a folding table from him in the visitors' room, beneath an overhead fan that ticked as it uselessly stirred the warm air. It was from her that he learned that Edwin was looking in on Sara and Bryan in the evenings. He had been fired from Indigo Bay, of course, but recently he had started a new venture silk-screening island-themed apparel—T-shirts with palm trees, neon sunsets, a pineapple wearing sunglasses, slogans: I'M ON ISLAND TIME. WHAT HAPPENS ON THE CRUISE STAYS ON THE CRUISE. His merchandise was already in a few of the souvenir shops in Hibiscus Harbour. He was giving Sara money. Clive was grateful. Edwin had always helped him, and he was helping him now, as Clive still believed he always would.

Two months after his release from prison, he flew to New York. He thought Edwin might come to say goodbye, but when the time came to drive to the airport in his grandmother's church friend Verna's car and Edwin had not come, he was not surprised.

He made his way in New York, as he had already told me. He built a life passed in the fellowship of other solitary men. He had been gone three years when Sara told him she had married Edwin. That was over fourteen years ago, so long that it was difficult to believe it wasn't always true, that there was a time before the mother of his child married his best friend. He had been through so much. He had lost his father and been abandoned by his mother, gotten a girl pregnant and become a father too young, been a suspect in a murder, gone to prison, started over in a new country, had the shit kicked out of him in a vacant lot in Brooklyn. Yet it seemed to

Clive that the man who lived through all that was still an innocent, for he had not yet lain awake at night imagining his son walking between Sara and Edwin, one hand in each of theirs. His boy, laughing with delight as they lifted their arms and swung him into the air.

Why had Edwin done it? Did he love Sara, or had he only married her to hurt him, to reject the love that had hung in the stars like an open question on their last night together? Or maybe marrying Sara had been a way of holding on to the only part of Clive that Edwin could have— Bryan; maybe Edwin's most wounding action was also his greatest act of devotion.

Two years after Sara and Edwin married, Clive received a letter from his grandmother. It was autumn. He remembered because just before he found the letter in the metal mailbox he shared with his roommates, he paused on the stairs outside the apartment building to scrape the tacky samara wings from the bottoms of his shoes. He read the letter in the dark hallway. Buried in updates about the renovation of St. George's, about the local election and Verna's nieces from Toronto, was the news that Sara had given birth to a son, Edwin Jr. Eddie for short. Clive saw his son and Edwin's growing up together. More than mates, more than breds. Brothers. The thought of it was so sweet to him his chest ached. He knew that to feel this way after what Edwin had done made him a chump. Edwin had stolen the only life he had ever wanted, a quiet existence with Sara and children and not-so-bad work and Sunday afternoons at Little Beach. Yet he was grateful. It seemed to him that this life was better off without him in it, for surely he would have spoiled it with his clumsy touch.

What if he had known everything that was waiting for him? What if, when Edwin approached him in the schoolyard on the first day of second grade, back when he was only Clive, you had shown him all that was going to happen and said, *Will you take this life?* What is there to say? He would have walked right up to Edwin and joined the game. Because of Edwin he'd lost everything, but without him, he would not even have had these things to lose. He needed Edwin. He could make no sense of his life without him.

Years passed. He was thirty-five. One summer evening he was walking through Prospect Park—the air redolent with charcoal, laughter and music wafting into the huge night above the lawns—when he heard his name.

"Gogo? Clive fucking Richardson, is that you?"

It was Bery Wilson. She marched right up to him and wrapped him in a tight embrace. "I've thought of you," she said. That was as close as she came to talking about the past. She told him she was an artist now—something about the city as canvas, pain as art. She wore her hair in a Mohawk, shaved on the sides and natural on top. In the purple twilight, he could make out tattoos of birds on her arms. An Asian girl and a white guy ambled over and said hello. Bery introduced them to him as members of her collective.

"Join us," said the guy.

"We have veggie dogs," said the girl.

"Yes, please, come sit," Bery said with a smile. How had she managed it? The anger seemed to have evaporated out of her altogether.

He told her he was running late, though the truth was he had nowhere to be.

"I understand," she said. Then her face turned serious. "You've heard about Edwin?"

Clive spent the months after Bery told him that Edwin was dying waiting for his friend to reach out to him. ("Cancer," she'd said, and when he asked what kind she said she wasn't sure, she only knew that it was everywhere now.) He imagined it so many ways. He would be getting out of the shower, or paying for dinner at the Little Sweet, when his cell phone would ring. "He's asking for you," Sara would say. Clive would fly home, arriving just in time. The house would be dark and quiet, Bryan and Eddie having been sent out to occupy themselves despite their protestations, for they knew their father was dying and did not want to leave his side. Clive would walk through the kitchen and the parlor to the bedroom. When he first saw Edwin in the bed he would gasp. His friend would be unrecognizable—his skin ashen, his cheeks sunken, the sockets of his eyes alarmingly prominent.

Hey, Gogo, Edwin would say, as if it had been only hours since they'd last seen each other.

They would talk. About the boys. About their own boyhoods. Remember the time we climbed the radio tower? Remember sneaking into *E.T.*? Remember, remember, remember. Edwin would close his eyes, as if drifting off to sleep, and for a minute Clive would think he was gone. Then

Edwin would open his eyes again, and when he did they would be glazed with tears. He would look up at Clive with that old grin.

Will you miss me? he would say.

Clive would take Edwin's trembling face in his hands. He would lower his head and kiss his best friend lightly on the forehead, and they would know without having to say it that all was forgiven.

But Clive did not hear from his friend, and one day his grandmother called and told him that Edwin had died. He tried to wrap his mind around the truth that Edwin was not still down on the island, away from him, unseen for years, but still there, still *here*, but he couldn't. It was only then he recognized that all these years he had held on to the buried belief that someday, somehow, they would be brought together again, and that in their new, shared aftermath they would have all the time and words and silence they needed to understand together everything that had happened. Now this would never be. He had moved into another chapter of his life, one in which he would have to live without the possibility that the central mysteries of his life would be demystified.

Ever since, his days passed like walking downhill. He drove his taxi, moved from apartment to apartment. He kept apprised of the news in the lives of his friends and acquaintances. There was a gallery in Fort Greene where from time to time he saw Bery's sculptures on display. He and Ouss still got together once or twice a year for a meal. Ouss and his wife owned a hardware store on Tremont Avenue. They had four girls; the eldest was on a full scholarship at Exeter.

At night, he walked. Every evening when he set out, the details of the neighborhood were overwhelming—a lover's quarrel on the sidewalk, blinking lights in the windows of an electronics store, peaches at a fruit stand so ripe their perfume made him woozy. But the longer he walked, the more the city receded, until the world around him rendered itself invisible and he began to hear water lapping against the edges of the metropolis, which became water lapping at the edges of another island, and then he was not walking through New York anymore, but through the landscape of that other world, that other life. He would stop at a basketball court or a playing field to watch the boys at play, and he would see them all there, shouting and tussling on the pitch, Edwin and Des and Damien and Don. Sometimes a boy left the raucousness of the game behind to sit in the grass, or to hum a song to himself, and Clive knew that he was Bryan; his boy was beautiful and sweet and everything good. And once a year, he walked to Manhattan Beach with its gray sand and its mangy gulls swirling overhead and ate an American chocolate bar that tasted all wrong but was the best he could do, and in this way he marked the day he lost all of them forever.

If only Alison hadn't found it so necessary to stir up the shit between him and Edwin, to intrude in things she didn't understand. If only she hadn't gone off and done whatever she did. It wasn't just her own life she was risking—had she thought about that? Had it occurred to her for even a moment?

And if only . . . if only they hadn't taken her out with them. If only they hadn't been taking pretty white daughters out with them for months like the world was a place it most definitely wasn't. If only he had gone after her when she ran. If only he'd called out to her. "Wait, don't go," and maybe he wouldn't be sitting here now, with his hands numb and the snow falling on his coat.

"But I never would have. He told me to let her go and I did." He put his head in his hands.

"You couldn't have known," I whispered. I placed a hand on his back, but he jerked away from my touch. He stood and brushed the snow from his windbreaker.

"What are you doing?"

"What does it look like?"

"You can't just leave! There's so much more I want to ask you. I know there must be more you want to ask me, too. We can be open with each other now. We don't have to hide."

"You wanted the truth and now you have it. What more could you want from me?"

I understood then what I did want, what I had wanted for months. There was a version of this story in which two lost souls whose lives had been irrevocably altered by the same long-ago night found each other in New York and, in one of those unexpected turns you hear about with surprising frequency, built a new life together. It was the best version of the story, one with the power to salvage everything that had happened. At the same mo-ment it became clear to me that this was what could have happened, I also understood that it would not happen, and that from then on I would be living in a different aftermath—no longer the aftermath of Alison's death, but of this winter in New York with Clive Richardson. For, whether we're aware of it or not, we are always living in the aftermath of something.

"It has to mean something that I got into your cab. Don't you see? All of this was supposed to happen. Please," I said uselessly.

He looked up at the sky and shook his head. "The crazy thing is I knew. I must have, right? That something with you wasn't . . . You just seemed so lost and lonely."

"I am lost. I am lonely. Clive, please. It's still *me*. I was just a little girl." My eyes filled with tears.

For a moment, as he looked at me, he seemed to be peering into the past, seeing the strange sunburned child I once was. He nodded. "I know." Then he slipped the wool hat from his head and stuffed it in the pocket of his coat. "Goodbye, Claire."

He walked down the street and disappeared into the falling snow.

FOR WEEKS after that I circled the Little Sweet hoping to find him. Maybe we could reconcile. Maybe it wasn't too late. But he never came back.

One night when I was walking past, Vincia spotted me. She left her post behind the counter and came outside.

"He's gone," she said.

"Gone?"

She nodded. I expected her to be angry. Instead her expression was sharp with loss. It occurred to me that I might have misapprehended her prick-liness toward me; maybe Vincia had harbored her own ideas about two lonely people in this city who might have found happiness together. "I heard he left in the middle of the night."

"Where did he go?"

"As if I would tell you if I knew!" She turned and marched quickly back inside.

I suppose that in the days before he confronted me, Clive must have been settling his affairs in New York and making plans for wherever he was heading to begin again once more. I stopped returning to the Little Sweet after that. It was as Clive had said: I'd wanted the truth and now I had it, as much of it as I would ever have. It was enough, wasn't it? There are many versions of the Alison Thomas story and I suspect there always will be. The police have theirs. So do the interweb conspiracy theorists and *Dying for Fun*. Now I had my own. One I could accept. One I could, perhaps, move on from.

ALISON WAKES from her stupor on the cliffs to the sounds of lovemaking. She turns and sees them, these men for whom she has performed her spectacular self all week.

The fuck you staring at, little girl?

Suddenly she feels very young and very foolish. How impressed she had been with herself! How pleased their approval had made her and how convinced she was of her appeal to them. How clearly she had seen it: she would get their groans of pleasure, their black skin against her white skin, the night a souvenir to remind her who she has the capacity to be. How humiliated she is to realize this night isn't about her and it never was, to see Edwin and Clive together beneath the stars and to know with corrosive, painful clarity that there is not a thing in her own life as true as this moment between them.

She gathers herself up and she runs, sandals in her hands, through the scrub. When at last she breaks through to Mayfair Road, she continues to run along the ditch on the road's shoulder, not caring how the rocks cut her feet, wanting it, even. Up ahead, she sees the lights of Indigo Bay. The illuminated fountains and the perfect lines of palms. She smells the floral air, feels the road turn smooth and loving beneath her feet. And then?

Some months after my last night with Clive Richardson, a package arrived from Philadelphia, a slender bubble mailer addressed to Claire Thomas.

I'm sorry it's taken me such a ridiculously long time to send this to you. I hope it's helpful. Sending you all my best.

Inside was a color copy of a poster for the Princeton Modern Dance Ensemble's "Winter Extravaganza." Polaroids from parties. Messages scrawled on scraps of notebook paper: "12:15, just left for dining hall. C u there?"

"Free ice cream at student center tonight. Let's do this!" A postcard. On the front, a consummate sunset, lilac infinity over a tropical sea. On the back:

> *Nika Nika,*
> *Greetings from paradise! Haha, not exactly. Hope your parents*
> *aren't driving you as crazy as mine are. On the bright side, I met*
> *the <u>cutest</u> boy. Guess we'll see!*
>
> > *Love ya,*
> > *A*

Where does she turn after everything with Clive and Edwin falls apart? Isn't it obvious? She finds him at the bar doing tequila shots as "Redemption Song" is piped in over the speakers, or sipping a Red Stripe on a lounge chair by the pool, or participating in a game of beer pong on the Ping-Pong table off the lobby, his enthusiasm changing to cool boredom the instant he spots her. Better than nothing, she tells herself. Even before it's over she knows it isn't enough, not even close. It is worse than nothing. It is all wrong. This boy whose baby-blue eyes match his baby-blue polo shirt match her baby-blue manicure. It only makes her feel more acutely the exact problem of her life: No matter what she does, no matter how she tries, she cannot get out beyond herself. She can only ever be Alison.

But suppose you told her she could have a different life, swap out hers for one she'd deem more acceptable as an offering to this beautiful, brutal world? Though it would be pretty to think she'd say yes, she knows what she would really do: She would snatch up her cute dresses, her A's, her orthodontia-sleeked teeth, the many dappled lawns of her life . . . the gothic dormitory washed in eventide bells, flip-flops in autumn, fresh powder on the mountain. She would take it all and she would run. There it is, her most shameful secret: She loves her life. Oh, how she loves it.

It is very late now, and she is desperate for something, anything, with which to salvage this night, this vacation that has gone so awry from her carefully cultivated plans. It's then that she looks out into the water and sees Faraway, a black silhouette etched against the sky. She hears the soft wash of waves. She walks across the beach to the water's edge. She unties her halter top, unzips her skirt, shimmies out of her panties, and lets them fall to the sand at her feet. She considers moving her clothes higher up the beach in case the tide should rise and carry them away. Instead, she leaves them. Let the sea do what it will. What a story it would be, what a thing to be able to remember. She steps into the water.

Maybe, as she strokes through the sea to the cay, she believes she is being lured there by a black-haired woman with hooves for feet who has chosen her, and into whose wildness she can finally lose this self she loves and hates in equal measure. Or maybe she does not believe any of that. Maybe her strokes are powered by a desire she can't name, a need going unmet and unmet and unmet. Maybe she simply wants to give herself her wildest wild night; proof, to some older, duller version of herself, that she was young once and didn't squander it.

She follows the starlit path inland, her feet sensing their way over roots and rocks. In the darkness, the spray cast off by the waterfall is a vaporous fog, soft as a caress on her skin. Maybe she slips on the moss-slicked rocks close to the water and falls in. Maybe she dives, the water appearing deeper than it really is in the dark, and hits her head. This version, too, has its blank spaces. Things I'll never be able to know. These are the secret moments. Hers alone.

BUT FIRST . . .

In the dead of night, a little girl opens her eyes. As she surfaces from dreams, she smells the tang of blood. She has been scratching in her sleep. Then she hears rustling. She calls her sister's name and her sister comes to her.

"Where were you?" she asks.

"Shhh."

Her sister crawls into bed with her and wraps her arms around her. When the little girl is on the edge of sleep, her sister kisses her on the back of the neck and slips out of the bed.

"Where're you going?" the little girl mumbles.

"Far away."

"But—"

"Shh. Don't tell." She pads across the room, opens the door, and is gone.

The little girl doesn't tell. Not when her parents ask. Not when the police question her. At first she doesn't tell because it's a secret, and she is good at keeping secrets. She is patient. Later, when her sister has been missing too long, she doesn't tell because she is scared she did something wrong by not telling and everyone will be angry with her. Later still, when they tell her that her sister is dead, she knows she will keep the secret forever, because it is the last thing she has of her sister and she wants to keep it for herself. She keeps it so long, unspoken, that it becomes difficult to believe it happened at all.

Don't go.

If she had said this, maybe her sister would have listened. Her sister would have rubbed aloe over her itchy skin, and in the morning she would have woken to her sister's warm body beside her in bed.

Feeling better? her sister would ask.

Don't go. That was all she had to say. But what kind of thing is that to know, really? Because to have said those words, she would have had to be a different person altogether. So, in the end, what is the tragedy of her life if not being, again and again, the person she is?

"It will feel good."

I actually said that to her. Like I knew better than she did. Like she was under some naïve misapprehension that sex might be unpleasant and here, let me clear it up for you. She had found me at the bar and we had gone out to the beach. We were alone, it was late, and we were pretty drunk. We were doing what, for lack of a better term, I'll call making out. She was taking the lead and I was just happy to be taken along for the ride. At Yale, I was not exactly a Casanova or a Vronsky. I was a German major in the orchestra; I played the cello, for Christ's sake—these are not cool things now and they were not cool things then. But sometimes when you go someplace where people don't know you, they get an impression of you that's different from who you are in your regular life. I remember thinking that this girl was way out of my league, but lucky me, she hadn't figured that out yet. I'm not talking about the night she died. This was before, on her first night at Indigo Bay.

I wouldn't call her aggressive, but she was forward. There was no coyness to what was happening between us, no game being played. When I put my hand on her thigh and she pulled away from me I was genuinely confused. I thought we'd both been pretty clear where this was leading and, like I said, she was the one doing the leading. I was moving my hand up beneath her skirt, and she stopped me. She said she should go. She looked nervous, which threw me because until then she had seemed so confident. That's when I said it. I stroked her hair and said, "Are you sure? It will feel good." Then—Christ, this is embarrassing—but I sort of, not sort of, I *did*, I nudged her hand toward the crotch of my shorts, toward my boner, if you want to call it that. I hate the language we have for this stuff: *boner, horny, making out, feeling up, eating out*. It's so crass and graceless. Hanna teases me; she calls me a prude because I can't say these words out loud. I'm not a prude. But these words make me feel like I'm an animal.

After I said that, I was actually relieved when she didn't give in to me, when she said good night and left. Turns out all I really wanted was to go back to my room and jerk off and pass out. But there's this script, a script all boys know, and I didn't write it and I didn't even really want to say it, but there we were, and it's not like I was some player with a stockpile of great lines, so that's what I said. It scared her. *I* scared her.

For months after she died, I was terrified something would surface and my life would be destroyed. When everyone thought those men raped and killed her and I knew they didn't, I felt terrible. But what could I do? When the police came to question me, it wasn't even a conscious choice—I simply told them she'd been doing drugs and who gave them to her. When I told them I saw her early on the night she disappeared, and only briefly, and they asked if I was sure I didn't see her again, I nodded my head and said, "Yes, I'm positive," so decisively I almost believed it. It was not a choice, but something I knew I must do. To tell the truth, to tell them she had been with me after those men had already been put in the drunk tank, would have been unthinkable, tragic, foolish. It would have yanked me into this horrible mess, and for what? My life wasn't meant to be derailed by one night on vacation.

It was late, and I was making my way back to my room from the bar, scuffing my Top-Siders against the pool deck, when I saw her. Her hair was a mess. Her mascara was smudged around her eyes.

"I promised, didn't I?" she said. She smiled that sly smile that had teased me all week. Something was different, though. She was agitated, I might even say frantic. I was pretty sure she'd been crying. She grabbed my hand and I let her lead me to one of the beach cabanas. She wasted no time. She pulled off her top, her skirt, and her panties with a pragmatism that both chilled and aroused me. She pointed at my khakis with her chin. I unbuttoned them.

It was unlike any sex in my admittedly slender library of experience. She pinned my arms above my head and held my wrists so hard they still ached the next day when the police questioned me. (There were faint bruises there, which they would have found if they'd looked.) Then I moved on top of her. She placed my hands around her neck. At first I jerked them away, but she grabbed them and wrapped them around again. I squeezed. She closed her eyes and smiled faintly, like I wasn't even there. So I squeezed harder, and her eyes popped open. I'll never forget it. The violence she unearthed so easily in me, like she knew it was right beneath the surface.

It was about something other than pleasure for her. Something was wrong but I didn't know what and I didn't ask. When I remember it, my dick goes limp, but I was twenty years old—capable of enjoying all kinds of misguided sex. When it was over, she dressed and ran off so quickly I was still dribbling cum into the sand when I lost sight of her.

At first I felt horribly guilty. Maybe if I'd asked her what was wrong, or if I'd done something different, then . . . I played that game over and over until it nearly drove me crazy. Back at Yale, I paid penance in all kinds of ways. I tutored a low-income New Haven kid. I called my parents more. For a brief period during my senior year, I seriously entertained joining the Peace Corps. But with time, I grew comfortable in my life again.

I've never thought of myself as a secretive person, but I am practical, and practically you can't tell this story, and I never have. I lead a good life. It is not as grand as the life I assumed would be mine when I was young— I haven't changed the world with my goodness or brilliance or bravery. I haven't made a giant splash with my existence, but I'm well respected in my field. I'm an architect. Hanna and I own a boutique firm together. She's Dutch. We met during a summer studio in Budapest in graduate school. I love her frankness, which can come off as arrogance to those who don't know her because she is beautiful, tall and slender and erect. I love the space between us, the gap our different native tongues and cultures opens, and the privacy this affords.

I read somewhere—okay, not somewhere, I saw it on this fairly lowbrow pop-psychology website—that each of our lives is anchored to a single moment, whether disturbing or traumatic or euphoric or inscrutable, from which we never move on, and that the age at which this moment occurs is our Eternal Age. This strikes me as true. Hanna's Eternal Age, for instance, is twenty-eight, when she gave birth to our son. But mine isn't thirty-two, my own age when he was born. My moment came years before I met my wife, and maybe that explains the distance between us: I shared her moment with her, while she doesn't even know mine exists. My eternal age is twenty. I see him, this lanky kid I was, with a mop of unruly hair, so erudite and charmingly, forgivably assured, and I'm a bit in awe of him, to be honest.

"It will feel good." Sometimes I wonder whether this thing I said, this juvenile horndog pressure I put on her at the beginning of the week, is to blame in some small way, like it set her on a course. Then I scold myself. I tell myself that it's vanity, thinking something I said was powerful enough to do all that. I tell myself that just because I didn't behave perfectly doesn't make me responsible. I remind myself, finally, that I barely knew her. Still, sometimes I wake up in the middle of the night and the darkness is full of her.

REMEMBER THIS

I ONCE READ THAT EVOLUTION has predisposed us to see ghosts and spirits, to find signs and omens in the ordinary: a sudden swell of wind, answers revealed in dreams. This impulse toward the mystical has its basis, so I read, in neurology. Our brains hunger for order. The early man who could make sense of the patterns of deer, the migration of birds, the movement of clouds, lived. From the beginning, our survival has hinged on our ability to look at the miscellany of the world, to sift through its deluge of details, and find the story. Stories, this article claimed, are the essence of human endurance.

But on the radio last week another expert, a neuropsychologist, explained it differently. Stories, this woman said, are our Achilles' heel. Our desperation for them leads us to live in a perpetual state of delusion. Early man, at the mercy of animals, weather, each other, invented Artemis, Ra, Vishnu. Our hunger for stories leads us to mistake a distracted spouse for an unfaithful spouse, an earthquake for divine punishment. A death for a murder.

Aren't they both right? Stories lead us to the truth and they lead us astray, and how are we to know the difference?

SLOWLY, THE city began to thaw. The air turned wet and clean. Trees unfurled vivid newborn leaves. The man in the NASCAR hat sat on the front steps with a fluffy white puppy beside him.

"Isabella," he told me with a grin.

I took Jackie out to brunch to apologize for my recent behavior. She forgave me quickly, and over mimosas and eggs Benedict she updated me on her drama of the week.

My parents flew out for a visit. We did the things we always did when they came to New York—the Met, brunch at Sarabeth's, a show. One afternoon my father had plans with an old college friend, and my mother and

I found ourselves in Central Park. Lines of girls in powder-blue pleated jumpers and sneakers followed teachers onto the park's muddy fields. The last gray snowbanks were almost gone, and the melt from them darkened the footpaths. We bought ice-cream bars. ("Naughty us," my mother said with a conspiratorial smile.) We sat on a bench to eat them. We talked about the television show everybody was watching that spring. About the vacation my parents had planned for October, a two-week river tour, Basel to Barcelona. Then we fell into the uncomfortable silence of a mother and daughter who know that mothers and daughters ought to be able to speak to one another endlessly.

"Mom?" I said finally.

"Yes, sweetheart?"

"What happened when I went to Paris with Aunt Caroline? When I came back everything was different, but I never knew why."

My mother pursed her lips, and I feared she was going to give me the kind of evasive nonanswer I was used to from her.

"I told your father it had to stop. Not just him with the police. Me, too. Both of us."

"But why? Why did you just give up?"

"We didn't give up, sweetheart. But we had to leave it behind. Because we had you, and you were everything. You *are* everything. We wanted you to have a life."

I think Alison was wrong about our mother. I was, too. We thought she was a fragile, timid woman. But as I looked at her on the bench, a smile flickering in her eyes as a young boy toddled unsteadily past us holding a small pink ball, I saw her differently. It took strength not to allow oneself to be subsumed by a thing that loomed so large.

(NOT LONG after my parents' visit to New York, a Hollywood agent would drive out to Laurel Canyon, let himself into a mid-century modern house nestled among eucalyptus trees, and find the actor, dead in his bed. Foul play not suspected. Oxycontin, Ativan, and cocaine found on the nightstand, according to an anonymous paramedic. Most of the articles about his death were accompanied by the same photograph, a recent paparazzi shot in which the actor gave the impression of abundant unwellness: long unruly hair, a too-big suit and sandals, gin-glazed eyes and coffee-yellow teeth. I would stare at that photo, looking him in the eyes across time and space, life and death, and he would seem to look back at me.)

IT HAS been several years since I stepped into that taxi. I live in Charlotte now. I work in ad sales. My condo is spacious and bright, the walls painted an institutional peach I don't really mind. I drive a little red Honda that gets great mileage. A few weeks ago, a coworker sent me an old article from *The Onion*, "Horrified Man Suddenly Realizes He's Putting Down Roots in Charlotte," and I laughed because it reminded me of me. I go by Claire here. At first hearing that name on the lips of my coworkers and new friends unsettled me. But I've grown used to it.

Clive Richardson has disappeared from my life as completely as he entered it. I find comfort in not knowing where he is. Sometimes I close my eyes and send messages to him. I tell him I hope he's found a place beyond the grip of his past. I tell him it wasn't all a lie. I ask him not to judge me too harshly. The winter I spent with Clive is a locked room inside myself, one which, I'm reasonably certain, I will never open again. (Though still, now, when I find myself back in the city, I will climb into a taxi and hope that when the driver says hello it will be Clive's voice I hear. And when, inevitably, it isn't, I summon that voice, those nights, the city as it was that winter, and I tell myself, almost sternly, *Remember this.*)

I can see now that during those months, I fooled myself into believing I was after closure, when all I really wanted was never to let go. Because, as Alison's scar was her most sacred vanity, her death was mine. Because I needed a murder mystery. Without one, what choice did I have but to be angry at Alison for making herself so indispensable to me, to all of us, and then being so careless with herself? (Drinking and drugs, a reckless swim, a stupid accident. The police had suggested this basic scenario from the beginning, but my parents had refused to accept it. Why would they have? Why would anyone accept such a sad and pointless story, a tale that was not even cautionary but simply tragic, a shame?) What choice was there, finally, but to admit that I hated Alison every bit as much as I loved her? I hated her while she was alive for the way her dazzling, spectacular self took up the entire spotlight, and I hated her even more for the oppressive shadow she cast with her death. How could I ever be enough? How could I possibly compare to someone who never had to grow up?

Had she lived, perhaps in her twenties Alison would have been like Jackie, a person who might say to her friends, over craft beer or picklebacks or whatever beverage would have been de rigueur then, "I need to find time for my *dancing*," in a way that suggested that her dancing was something the world needed. If I was visiting her, in Williamsburg or the Mission or Silver Lake, say to celebrate my sixteenth birthday, then I would have rolled my eyes when she said this, and I would have gotten to experience the wrenching, liberating moment when your idol becomes just another person. She might have grown to be a woman like Nika, preoccupied by her children's homework assignments and video game habits. Perhaps she would now be living a life not so dissimilar from our parents'; maybe she would take her own children to Caribbean resorts and reflect, as she read a memoir beneath an umbrella's shade, on the trade-offs she had made for a life that was, it turned out, more than enough.

I still haven't told my parents—not about Clive, or Alison, or what happened to me that winter. Maybe someday I will. The thing is, I haven't decided if telling them would do them any good. For so long it was all I wanted. The truth! The truth! Good, fine, but for what? With the truth we will do what, become what? And in gaining the truth, what do we lose? It seems to me now that some truths will never be enough to seal the mysteries that precede them. I think in her own way my mother understood this all along—that there is nothing the truth can give you that you cannot give yourself. That in the end, you just have to decide. To live. To continue.

SAINT X

LOOK DOWN UPON SAINT X from above and it will appear as if little has changed. In the Basin, children in pink and maroon uniforms still run and shout through the yard of Horatio Byrd Primary. Her Majesty's Prison, eggshell-blue, still stands beside the bank. Along the winding ribbon of Mayfair Road there are now billboards for Digicel and FLOW broadband, but the white stucco churches remain, as does Perry's Snack-ette, and the radio tower with its flaking red paint, houses with galvanized roofs and sandy yards. Float up and over Devil Hill and there it is—Little Beach. It is late afternoon, and everyone has gathered here. They have their umbrellas and picnic baskets, their coolers filled with cola and Carib. Constellations of families float in the sea. Children clamor out of the water and run onto the pier, not even pausing before leaping off the edge back into the water, again and again in an unbroken loop.

Search among the faces and you will see a woman seated on a blue and white cloth, a point of stillness amid a lively family gathering. Her eldest grandchild dribbles a football down the sand. The youngest is curled asleep in the shade cast by the woman's own body. Her daughter-in-law hushes and soothes and doles out kisses and tamarind balls. Her sons, Bryan and Eddie, laugh together as they let the workweek's troubles lift from their shoulders. Sometimes she cannot quite believe that all of this is hers. Sara Lycott is neither as young as she once was nor as young as she still feels sometimes, until she catches herself in a shop window, startled by the silver flash of her own hair. It has been years since she first laid lisianthus on her mum's grave. Remarkable, isn't it, that a woman her age, who has not been anyone's daughter in a long, long time, still, hearing a funny story on the news, or picking the first ripe sugar-apple in the yard, opens her mouth to call out, "Mum"? On some nights, she is still laid low by a longing for her mother's house. She longs for bedding that smells human and that has grown soft as oil with unwashing. The plink of a sink that leaked throughout her whole childhood. The odors of old fruit in the refrigerator, of her mother's urine in the bathroom. In her own house, she washes and presses the sheets on Tuesdays. She keeps the bathroom scrubbed and smelling of bleach. When a thing breaks she fixes it. When a thing is empty she disposes of it.

The best thing she ever did was to behave in front of her children. If all she could give them was to contain the dark, squalid rooms within her, then that is enough. If to other people it seems like very little, well, she knows that it is everything. She has freed them from a burden they do not even know exists, that of being tormented by a deep, unsolvable ache for all the wrong things.

She has outlived them all. Her mother. The father whose name she never knew, whom she assumes must be long dead. Edwin, whom she nursed until his last breath but who never, not even then, truly let her in. (Yet did two boys ever have a father who adored them more?) Only Clive is still out there somewhere. Rumors reach the island. Last she heard he'd left New York for the West Coast someplace. According to a friend of hers, he got married out there and has a daughter. But this is secondhand knowledge at best. She does not think of him often. A difficult chapter in her life, from when she was very young. It has been so long since any of them were here with her that her own endurance confounds her. Lately, she has the oddest notion that she might go on living forever.

The baby beside her on the blanket stirs and cries. Before she can reach out for him, Bryan is there, scooping the child into his arms.

"There, there, my boy," he whispers. "You're all right. You're just fine."

TRAVEL TO the edge of the island's south coast and you will find yourself on a different beach, where the sand is soft as cream. At the water's edge, children turn cartwheels and bury one another in the sand. A boy lifts a conch to his ear and hears the secret sea. A mother considers grabbing her phone to capture this moment; instead, she just watches him. A cruise ship glides soundlessly across the middle distance. Somewhere, in another world that is also this world, it is snowing.

Farther up the sand, a little girl sits beneath an umbrella as a woman braids her hair. In the sea, brothers on boogie boards ride the gentle waves.

A teenage boy picks up a girl and threatens to dunk her, and she squeals with delight.

A woman pauses on her walk down the beach and watches them all. This place is much as she remembers it. The pool in the shape of a lima bean, the open-air restaurant where last night she ate conch carpaccio and drank rum punch on the veranda and felt the cool ocean breeze. As with all places remembered from childhood, it appears smaller now, more ordinary. The domed ceiling of the marble lobby is not quite so high, the sand not quite so white, as they are in her memory. They've changed the name, too. Indigo Bay is the Royal Hibiscus now, and has been for years; a rebranding effort after the things that happened.

One more thing is different: Several years ago, a French conglomerate purchased the development rights to Faraway Cay. Now it is a private island resort and spa with bungalows built on stilts in the shallows. According to the resort's website, the restaurant is helmed by a celebrated Nordic chef who "marries his farm-to-table ethos with the local Caribbean bounty." The spa's offerings include a hot volcanic-stone massage, a local salt scrub, and a two-hour "Arawak Ritual" that promises "complete purification of both body and spirit." The downed planes on the cay have been preserved. There is a picture of one in the website's photo gallery, a yellow wing choked in sea grape. *Stroll past the island's mysterious relics en route to your own private waterfall.*

The goats are gone. Exterminated, one assumes.

When the woman reaches the black rocks that mark the end of the beach, she sits in the sand and looks out at the cay. The white beach. The cliffs tufted with growth, a vivid green unlike any she has seen before or since. She can make out the bungalows that ring the shore and, if she squints, people on the beach—husbands with wives, parents with children. The woman stands, brushes the sand from her legs, and walks back in the direction from which she has come.

On the volleyball court, a game is under way. The players are newlyweds and retirees, thirty-somethings and teenagers. They bump and set and spike. When a girl who is a bit of a weak link serves up a winner, both sides cheer. After a teenager takes a running dive into the sand to save a point, a retiree slaps him five. "Appreciate those," the man says, and points to the boy's knees. "They'll betray you someday."

The woman watches, as she watched years ago. It occurs to her that this game is always under way; that, in a sense, it never ends.

In the shallows, two pairs of legs poke out of the water—a handstand contest. A moment later, two sisters surface.

"I win!"

"No, me!"

"First one to the buoy!"

They are off, swimming away from shore.

AUTHOR'S NOTE AND ACKNOWLEDGMENTS

From New York City's John F. Kennedy International Airport, it is possible to fly direct to nearly twenty Caribbean islands. One can reach Jamaica, Haiti, the Dominican Republic, Cuba, Turks and Caicos, the Cayman Islands, Saint Martin, Saint Thomas, and Puerto Rico in under four hours; Antigua, Saint Lucia, Barbados, Saint Kitts, Grenada, Trinidad, Aruba, and Martinique in under five. Some 15 million American tourists visit the Caribbean each year. The islands are so close, American tourists visit them so frequently, and yet most of these visitors know so little about them. For a long time, I have been fascinated by the place the Caribbean seems to occupy in the mind of the American tourist as an "escape," or, as I put it early in the novel, a "lovely nowhere."

This phenomenon was at the heart of my decision to create a fictional, unnamed island, Saint X, for my setting. Building the world of Saint X was a process I undertook with a great deal of questioning about what it means to invent a fictional island within a place that is not fictional at all. In a region where every island has a rich and distinctive history, culture, dialect, cuisine, flora and fauna, and on and on, how does one approach creating a fictive space that embodies without simplifying, that is none of these places, exactly, but is also never pure invention? I have done my best to create in Saint X a cohesive place that, I can only hope, will inspire readers who don't know much about the Caribbean to learn more.

In this process, I am especially indebted to the wonderful series of Caribbean histories and guides published by Macmillan Caribbean in the nineteen eighties and nineties, in particular: *Nevis: Queen of the Caribees* by Joyce Gordon, *Anguilla: Tranquil Isle of the Caribbean* by Brenda Carty and Colville Petty, *St. Kitts: Cradle of the Caribbean* by Brian Dyde, *St. Lucia: Helen of the West Indies* by Guy Ellis, *Grenada: Isle of Spice* by Norma Sinclair, and *St. Vincent and the Grenadines* by Lesley Sutty. To the

Dictionary of Caribbean English Usage and the *New Register of Caribbean English Usage,* both edited by Richard Allsopp. To *Island People: The Caribbean and the World* by Joshua Jelly-Schapiro (see also the beautiful map "Archipelago: The Caribbean's Far North" created by cartographer Molly Roy in *Nonstop Metropolis: A New York City Atlas,* edited by Jelly-Schapiro and Rebecca Solnit). To *Caribbean Folklore: A Handbook* by Donald R. Hill. And to Jamaica Kincaid's seminal work, *A Small Place.*

When it came to rendering Clive Richardson's life in New York City, some key sources included *Taxi!: A Social History of the New York City Cabdriver* by Graham Russell Gao Hodges, *Taxi!: Cabs and Capitalism in NYC* by Biju Mathew, and *Islands in the City: West Indian Migration to New York* edited by Nancy Foner.

I am incredibly grateful to those people on Anguilla who gave so generously of their time when I visited the island for research. Thank you to Josveek Huligar for being such a fun and helpful guide. My deepest gratitude to Anhel Brooks, Trevon Liburd, to M., to A., to M., and to J. for sharing your stories with me. Thanks also to Scott Kircher for the introduction to Trudy Nixon, and to Trudy for sharing her experience as an incomer on the island.

Thank you to Melissa Borja for sharing her knowledge on conducting oral histories and interviews.

To Stephanie Stokes Oliver and Crispin Brooks for reading the manuscript with such brilliance and care. To Graham Gao Hodges for so graciously reading the passages about Clive's working life in New York.

To wonderful friends who shared geographic and linguistic expertise with me: Margo Levin, Kate Rubin, Dave Serafino, Geraldine Shen, and Erin Zimmer. To Marisa Reisel for . . . everything.

To the brilliance and generosity of Greg Jackson and Lulu Miller, who read this book when it was a mess and saw so clearly how it could become less of one. To my teachers: Christopher Tilghman, Caroline Preston, Ann Beattie, Deborah Eisenberg, Chang-rae Lee, Joyce Carol Oates, and Wendy Phelps.

I thank my lucky stars daily that Henry Dunow is my agent. He is the wisest reader I know, and he worked with me patiently over many years and many, many drafts to help this book find its footing. Thank you also to the wonderful Arielle Datz and everyone else at Dunow, Carlson & Lerner.

To my fabulous editor, Deb Futter, who sees everything so clearly and who made this process more fun than I could have imagined. To Rachel Chou, Anna Belle Hindenlang, Randi Kramer, Christine Mykityshyn, Jaime Noven, Heather Orlando, Clay Smith, Anne Twomey, and everyone else at Celadon: I feel so fortunate to be in your capable hands. Thank you also to David Cole, Elizabeth Catalano, Cheryl Mamaril, and Jonathan Bennett for their wonderful work on this book, and to the incredible Callum Plews at Macmillan Audio for his work on the audiobook.

Our son was born a year before this book was completed, and I never would have finished it were it not for the people who cared for him so lovingly in his first year. To Meg Sweet, Cate Nowlan, Roberta Sweet, Carly Knight, Allison Haley, Maria Mastrandrea, and Molly Egger: Thank you.

To Shawn, Walter, Charlie, James, and Kelsey: I'm so lucky to be able to call you my family.

To Dona, Keith, and Brian: my rocks, my favorite people, from the very beginning.

To Emerson, our baby, our big boy. We are the very luckiest to have your light and spirit in our family.

And, always, to Mason, whose faith in me is the most profound thing I've ever known. I love you.

SAINT X

BOOK CLUB GUIDE

Reading Group
Discussion Questions

_____

Author Alexis Schaitkin on
What She Did—and Didn't
Do—While Writing _Saint X_

_____

DISCUSSION QUESTIONS

1. What does the island setting contribute to the story? What about the juxtaposition of New York City?

2. What do you think Claire's habit of writing words in the air with her finger demonstrates about her?

3. What does Claire's name change to Emily signify to you?

4. What does Clive's nickname, Gogo, indicate about his personality? About Edwin's?

5. Did you ever think Clive might pose a threat to Emily when he found out who she was?

6. What's the symbolism of Faraway Cay and the woman with hooves for feet? What does that mythology add to the story?

7. Emily's world in New York becomes very small after she encounters Clive. Do you think that was intentional or unintentional on her part? What might have motivated her to turn inward?

8. What do Alison's recorded diary entries reveal to Emily? Was Emily right to listen to them, or do you think it was an invasion of privacy? Do you feel differently about their mom listening?

9. What are the similarities between Emily's life in New York and Clive's? What are the differences?

10. What do you think about Edwin's relationship with Sara?

11. Alison witnessed a pivotal moment in Clive and Edwin's relationship. How did that shape the rest of the narrative— Clive and Edwin's relationship, their futures, Alison's tragedy?

12. When Emily learns the truth, and remembers the night before Alison disappeared, what do you think is her primary emotion? Grief? Relief? Guilt? Something else?

13. Do you think Emily coming into Clive's life was ultimately a bad thing or a good thing for Clive?

14. Emily speaks about the loss of a sister and different milestones they missed out on. What do you think their relationship would have been like in present day?

    Submitted by Pittsford Moms Book Club (Pittsford, NY)

15. Why do you think the author chose to intersperse the voices of minor characters, such as the movie actor and other vacationers, throughout the book? What effect does this achieve?

    Submitted by The NYC Wine and Dine Bookclub (New York, NY)

16. How did Emily's perception of her sister change from viewing her from a seven-year-old's perspective to listening to her audio diary as an adult? How did this change her assumptions about the events leading up to Alison's disappearance?

    Submitted by We Book and We Brunch Bookclub (Tucson, AZ)

17. How do you think the story would have changed if Emily had been honest about who she was with Clive from the start?

    Submitted by Peter's Book Club (Charlotte, NC)

AUTHOR ALEXIS SCHAITKIN ON WHAT SHE DID—AND DIDN'T DO— WHILE WRITING *SAINT X*

Avoiding true stories that could influence the plot and traveling to the Caribbean for in-person interviews was just part of the process.

What inspired this story?

The setting of a tropical resort. I wanted to tell a story that would bring the reader into the lives of tourists there on vacation and the people who live on the island and work at the resort. To me, the Caribbean resort is such a fertile, interesting setting because people of very different backgrounds are sharing this confined place and interacting in ways that can be quite intimate; there are complicated dynamics and tensions just beneath the beautiful, serene surface. Alison was there from the beginning: this teenage girl who touches down at Indigo Bay and immediately starts searching for the cracks in this surface, for a way to get around it, beneath it, beyond it.

Did Natalee Holloway's 2005 disappearance during a trip to Aruba influence you?

I was certainly aware of the Natalee Holloway case, but once I knew I was writing a story about a pretty American girl who disappears on vacation in the Caribbean, I wanted to be careful not to tread too closely to the Holloway story. People who followed her case may find it interesting to see where her story and Alison's connect and diverge, but I don't think Natalee's story informs *Saint X* very much beyond basic similarities in the events.

A much larger influence for me was the JonBenét Ramsey case, which I followed closely as an eleven-year-old, and which taught me at a young age that society cares about some murdered girls much more than others. Natalee Holloway, JonBenét Ramsey, Hannah

Graham, all of these girls and our society's obsession with them, are the air this novel breathes.

You write from several different perspectives in this book. How long did you spend developing each character?

I developed them all simultaneously; I wasn't working on one character at a time. To me, characters are part of an ecosystem—they're all contingent upon each other. I also had a very clear sense from the beginning that I was working with two pairs of main characters: Alison and Claire, Edwin and Clive. Each pair has a dazzling, charismatic character, with the other living in that person's shadow. A lot of the story is about how these passive characters, Claire and Clive, learn (or fail to learn) to make sense of their lives independently after their worlds are upended.

Tell us about your writing process—how did you create Saint X, a fictitious Caribbean island?

I knew from the beginning that I was not going to set the story on a real island. It didn't feel like my place to do that. Creating a fictitious island and not naming it, but leaving it anonymous, is an ironic nod to the way tourists interact with these islands—as an escape, a paradise without context, a "lovely nowhere" as I refer to it early in the novel. Yet, I also knew that I wanted Saint X to be every bit as detailed and nuanced as the sidewalks of Flatbush—I didn't want New York to be rendered minutely and Saint X to be a hazy tropical dreamscape. I wanted specificity, images and details that take hold for these characters in both places.

I began by reading histories, guidebooks, and contemporary Caribbean fiction. Linguistic guides to Caribbean dialects and creoles. Books about flora and fauna. Cookbooks and books about religious practice. I traveled to Anguilla and conducted interviews. One of my readers, who grew up in the Caribbean and now lives in the United States, looked for anything that rang false. We got down to tiny things, like picking the best of three names to use for a food that gets mentioned once in the book.

How did your image of Saint X transform from your first draft to the time you finished the book?

The biggest change was capturing Saint X not as a static place, but as a place that transforms over the timeframe of the book. In early drafts, Saint X was basically the same from the time Clive and Edwin were small boys to when Clive leaves the island in his early twenties. The resorts were always there. The tourists were always there. But when I went to Anguilla for research, I had the opportunity to speak with several men about the same age as Clive and Edwin. I learned that the island wasn't fully electrified until they were ten or twelve years old, and there was no refrigeration when they were growing up. The first big resorts didn't open until they were teenagers. I decided to bring that basic arc to Saint X.

Telling the story of Saint X's intense and rapid transformation created a powerful parallel with Clive and Claire's Brooklyn neighborhood: two places where an influx of money, and people with a lot of it, changed everything.

You weave in short recollections by some of the people who crossed paths with the story's main characters on the island or in the United States. Why did you add those?

It's interesting that you say "add," because I did literally add them. The short recollections weren't in the early drafts of the book. They did slip in at times for a few pages, most notably in the voices of Sara (the mother of Clive's child) and her mother, Agatha. At a certain point, I cut them out because I thought it was just too oddball and confusing to have the narrative deviate like that out of the blue.

But those scrapped pages kept haunting me, even though Sara and Agatha aren't main characters. Those brief glimpses into what this all meant for them and their lives felt vital to the story. I also liked the intrusive nature of their voices—this insistence on having their own stories listened to. That's how the idea of threading short recollections from many different characters throughout the novel came about. Once I thought of it, it seemed so obvious.

NANCY BOROWICK

ALEXIS SCHAITKIN's short stories and essays have appeared in *Ecotone, Southwest Review, The Southern Review, The New York Times,* and elsewhere. Her fiction has been anthologized in *The Best American Short Stories* and *The Best American Non-required Reading.* She received her MFA in fiction from the University of Virginia, where she was a Henry Hoyns Fellow. She lives in Williamstown, Massachusetts, with her husband and son. *Saint X* is her debut novel.

CELADON
BOOKS
———
NEW YORK

Founded in 2017, Celadon Books, a division of
Macmillan Publishers, publishes a highly curated list
of twenty to twenty-five new titles a year. The list of
both fiction and nonfiction is eclectic and focuses
on publishing commercial and literary books and
discovering and nurturing talent.

MOVED
MY
LAUNDRY?

A day-by-day
guide to your
first year
of college life

WHO
MOVED
MY

From keeping up
your grades to dropping
the freshman 15,
**WHAT EVERY FRESHMAN
REALLY NEEDS TO KNOW**

LAUNDRY?

Susan Fitzgerald, MA
and J. Lee Peters, EdD

▲adamsmedia
AVON, MASSACHUSETTS

Contains material adapted and abridged from:

The Everything® College Survival Book, 3rd Edition by Susan Fitzgerald, MA, and J. Lee Peters, EdD, copyright © 2010 by F+W Media, Inc., ISBN 10: 1-4405-1207-8, ISBN 13: 978-1-4405-1207-0;

The Everything® Healthy College Cookbook by Nicole Cormier, RD, copyright © 2010 by F+W Media, Inc., ISBN 10: 1-4405-0411-3, ISBN 13: 978-1-4405-0411-2;

The Everything® Guide to Nutrition by Nicole Cormier, RD, copyright © 2011 by F+W Media, Inc., ISBN 10: 1-4405-1030-X, ISBN 13: 978-1-4405-1030-4;

The Everything® Guide to Ayurveda by Heidi E. Spear with Foreword by Hilary Garivaltis, Dean, Kripalu School of Ayurveda, copyright © 2012 by F+W Media, Inc., ISBN 10: 1-4405-2996-5, ISBN 13: 978-1-4405-2996-2;

The Everything® Personal Finance in Your 20s and 30s Book, 2nd Edition by Debby Fowles, © 2008 by F+W Media, Inc., ISBN 10: 1-5986-9634-3, ISBN 13: 978-1-59869-634-9;

The Everything® Guide to Meditation for Healthy Living by David B. Dillard-Wright, PhD, and Ravinder Jerath, MD, copyright © 2010 by F+W Media, Inc., ISBN 10: 1-4405-1088-1, ISBN 13: 978-1-4405-1088-5;

The Everything® Guide to Study Skills by Cynthia C. Muchnick, MA, copyright © 2011 by F+W Media, Inc., ISBN 10: 1-4405-0744-9, ISBN 13: 978-1-4405-0744-1;

The Everything® Guide to Stress Management by Melissa Roberts, copyright © 2011 by F+W Media, Inc., ISBN 10: 1-4405-1087-3, ISBN 13: 978-1-4405-1087-8;

The Everything® Green Smoothies Book by Britt Brandon with Lorena Novak Bull, RD, copyright © 2011 by F+W Media, Inc., ISBN 10: 1-4405-2564-1, ISBN 13: 978-1-4405-2564-3;

The Everything® Guide to Food Remedies by Lori Rice, MS, copyright © 2010 by F+W Media, Inc., ISBN 10: 1-4405-1100-4, ISBN 13: 978-1-4405-1100-4.

ISBN 10: 1-4405-4267-8
ISBN 13: 978-1-4405-4267-1
eISBN 10: 1-4405-4289-9
eISBN 13: 978-1-4405-4289-3

Printed in the United States of America.

10 9 8 7 6 5 4 3 2 1

This publication is designed to provide accurate and authoritative information with regard to the subject matter covered. It is sold with the understanding that the publisher is not engaged in rendering legal, accounting, or other professional advice. If legal advice or other expert assistance is required, the services of a competent professional person should be sought.

—From a Declaration of Principles jointly adopted by a Committee of the American Bar Association and a Committee of Publishers and Associations

Many of the designations used by manufacturers and sellers to distinguish their product are claimed as trademarks. Where those designations appear in this book and Adams Media was aware of a trademark claim, the designations have been printed with initial capital letters.

Parachute and Swim icons © 123RF.com

This book is available at quantity discounts for bulk purchases.
For information, please call 1-800-289-0963.

FOREWORD

As university administrators with almost sixty years of experience between the two of us, we are longtime observers of and participants in the life of the college campus. Sue received her undergraduate degree from a small private liberal arts college while Lee received his from a large state university. Sue has had broad experience at the University of Hartford, where she has held positions in four different divisions of the institution, while Lee's breadth comes from having held positions at seven different institutions of higher education over the past thirty years.

What we have found through working together and sharing notes, memories and perceptions, is that large or small, public or private, young institution or old, the life of a student, especially in the first year, does not differ much from school to school. You will have ups and downs, both intellectually and emotionally. You will need to adjust to a different kind of schedule, and will need to study harder and more strategically than you did in high school. You will make new friends, try new experiences, and for residential students, you will adjust to a new kind of living arrangement that you have probably not experienced before. The biggest adjustment for most students is the increase in their responsibility for themselves and their well-being. Making all of these adjustments can be exhausting. Just like students who study abroad and have to learn a new language and different lifestyle, you will be in a totally different environment and culture than you are used to.

It seems to us that the more you can anticipate these changes, the better prepared you will be to handle them. In college life we tend to mark time by the week ("seven weeks to mid-terms . . . only three weeks till spring break!") so we thought that it would make sense to lay out this guide in week long chunks of time, giving you something to think about on each day of the week as you roll through your first year. We hope that you will use this guide as a way to think about the adjustments you will need to make, and how you will handle them.

We were talking about this book during a basketball game we were watching last week, in which freshmen, talented enough to be playing at the division one level, were making silly mistakes that you would not expect from a player of that caliber. But as we talked, we realized that they are just like you. They are playing a game they know well, and excelled at in high school, but they are playing against players far better than they have ever faced, at twice the speed they played the game before. The thing is, they are getting better and gaining more confidence in their abilities with each game they play, just as you will get better at negotiating life on campus every day that you live and study there. Enjoy the book and get ready to give your college experience a full court press!

Best of Luck and Enjoy,
Sue Fitzgerald, MA and J. Lee Peters, EdD

INTRODUCTION

Your bags are unpacked, your parents are weeping (and maybe cheering a little on the inside), and your head is spinning. You are at college. Um, now what?

It's cliché as anything, but know that these will be the best years of your life so far. You will make lifelong friends and perhaps meet your soulmate. You will try new things, learn valuable skills, and be challenged to figure out who you really are and what you stand for. You will fall in love with some of your classes (and perhaps classmates), deeply discuss serious issues with peers and professors, and enjoy many moments of quiet reflection.

You'll read thousands of pages and process dense information for class discussions and presentations. You'll also write hundreds of pages in essays, reports, and exams. There will be more concerts, parties, and cultural events than you have time to attend. You will have a full range of athletics to watch or participate in, a new community to explore, nearby exercise facilities to work out in, and perhaps even natural resources such as hiking trails, beaches, or ski mountains to enjoy. You will meet and live with interesting people, some from places you have never visited, with very different backgrounds and experiences than yours. By developing these new friendships, you'll learn more about yourself and what you want out of life.

By the time you finish college, you'll be prepared for a job in a field that may become a career. You'll also be prepared to change jobs if necessary, and you will still have college resources available to help you make that change. Your education in the classroom will be represented by your degree, but your education outside of the classroom will shine on your resume and in job interviews. Leadership experiences, internships, and semesters spent abroad will all help shape your approach to life and your contribution to the adult world.

This book was written as a guide for you, as an incoming college freshman, to take you through your first year of collegiate life. The topics covered will help you think about and prepare for the remarkable experience that is college. Each day from September to May is broken down into themes:

Mondays: Be Smarter

You may think you know it all, but get ready for college to change your mind pretty quickly. These entries have tips and techniques you can adopt to be a smarter, more attentive, and successful student—from making use of office hours to researching to acing the final exam.

Tuesdays: Be Financially Savvy

Unless you're rich, college will be a wonderful whirlwind of ramen noodles and paying for things with pocket change. These entries will help you learn ways to make extra cash, make your money last, and turn it into more money—all while staying out of the dreaded debt cycle.

Wednesdays: Be Healthier

Pssh, forget the Freshman 15! From avoiding fatty foods in the dining hall to exercise and taking care of your body, these entries will teach you to be a healthier, happier, and fitter college student.

Thursdays: Be Aware

As awesome as college can be, it can also present situations that can be dangerous, awkward, or difficult. These entries will provide tips on how to stay safe (on and off campus, at parties, and on the town), make careful decisions, spot warning signs of trouble, and be a well-rounded, responsible, and accountable college student, roommate, and person.

Fridays: Be Active

Contrary to popular belief, friends and activities won't come to you. Fridays are for getting up, getting out, losing the headphones and the slouchy walk, and getting involved in campus life. From how to join clubs to making friends to widening your social horizons, these entries offer ways to rise to the challenge of your college experience.

Saturdays: Be Adventurous

College is about breaking out of your typical comfort zone. Saturday entries encourage you to try new things, strike up conversations and friendships, experience new places, eat new foods, and stretch your wings. Let go of the ridiculous fears of "being uncool" and break the mold!

Sundays: Be More Relaxed

College is a busy and stressful time, between classes, friends, activities, and clubs. Making time for yourself is not only important, it's essential. With entries on deep breathing, simple meditation, coping with homesickness and other issues, and taking care of yourself, Sunday entries are all about staying calm, healthy, and happy.

College is whatever you want it to be, so wake up every day and make the best of it. Regardless of your background or future plans, you are about to embark on a priceless journey. Good luck, and enjoy every minute!

FALL SEMESTER

Well, you made it here in one piece. You're officially a college student! Whether you're standing in your dorm in a sea of boxes, staring at your new roommate like he's an alien, making a friend in your hallway, agonizing over your courses, wondering where you can get something to eat, or calculating exactly where your parents' car is on the freeway home, it's time for you to step up and explore your new college life. Get going!

Build Your Schedule

At most schools, upperclassmen and honors students usually get first choice at class selection each semester, so odds are it will be slim pickings for you at registration. But consider your personal patterns and preferences when it comes to selecting—and keeping—a schedule.

Are you a morning person or a night owl? You should have an idea of what time of day you have the most energy, when you do your best thinking, and how you prefer to work. When registering for courses, try to pick sections that are available when you are naturally most alert. You may find that the introduction to psychology course that you need is only offered at (*gasp*) 8 A.M., and you generally roll out of bed around noon. Keep in mind that if this class is offered Mondays, Wednesdays, and Fridays, that's about **forty-five class meetings** that you are responsible for attending this semester. Can you do it?

Unlike high school, your college professors won't chase you if you miss class; it's on you to show up on time and do the work. If you're typically a late sleeper, either try to find a later class, or ask Mom and Dad to tuck a fully loaded Starbucks card and extra-loud alarm clock in their next care package.

Get Extra Credit in Class, Not in Your Wallet

When you get ready for college, the issue will not be so much *how* to get a credit card as *which* credit card to get. Even though most colleges now prohibit credit card solicitation, advertisements may be stuffed in your bookstore bags, companies may send solicitations to your dorm mailbox, and fliers may be posted around campus. There are good, practical reasons to have a credit card—namely for emergencies, for travel, and to keep from carrying large amounts of cash. However, there are a number of pitfalls as well.

If you have thought it over and decide that you do need a credit card, it's important to compare credit card offers carefully and read all of the fine print before making a decision. A 0 percent annual percentage rate (APR) looks great, but may only last for a limited time. The lower your fixed APR, the better it is for your budget. In addition to APRs, you should look at annual fees. Many cards charge you for the privilege of using their services, even if you don't make any new purchases!

Remember that all things have their price. As sure as the sun will rise, that credit card bill *will* come, so make sure you have some income or savings to keep your charges in check. Bad or damaged credit will follow you for a very long time, way beyond college, and someday you'll wonder why you spent hundreds of dollars on Twizzlers and bobblehead dolls.

Snack Smartly

You'll probably want to keep snacks in your dorm room for late-night cravings or just something to munch on while you study. Try to resist the temptation to buy sugary or fatty foods like cookies or potato chips. Instead, keep snacks such as fruit, raw veggies, granola bars, microwave popcorn, and protein bars around. You'll stay more alert and focused if you limit your fat and sugar intake.

When it comes to keeping munchies in your room, here are a few good tips that will keep you from going straight for the junk.

- Talk to your roommate about keeping food in the room. He or she might want to share communal snacks, which is good because it stops you from eating what isn't yours, and cuts down on the amount of food you have within arm's reach of your bed.
- Invest in those snacks that have smaller "100-calorie" packs in the box; you'll eat less if you get an automatic portion size.
- *Never, ever* go grocery shopping when you are hungry. Eat a meal at the dining hall before you shop to avoid coming home with the entire chip aisle.

Another thing to keep in mind is that you may have already paid for a college meal plan that allows you to have three square meals a day at your dining hall (which is also a great way to get out and meet new people, *hint hint*). Why spend more money on becoming a food hoarder in your room?

Party Down Responsibly

Alcohol, despite its popularity, is connected to more student problems than any other single factor. If you drink alcohol irresponsibly, you can find yourself in dangerous situations or in trouble with
law enforcement, get lower grades, and experience poor relationships. And if you drink irresponsibly *in your first week*, you're
setting yourself up for a bad first impression and a potentially
downward spiral into some serious bad habits. It goes without
saying, but if you're not twenty-one years old, you're not legally
allowed to drink alcohol, and many schools have very strict alcohol policies—consider your actions carefully! There are plenty of
ways to have an active social life that don't involve alcohol, so
never feel like you *have* to drink to get a real college experience.

If you're new to drinking, you are at a greater risk in social
situations, particularly at the beginning of the school year when
everyone is trying to make their mark socially. Peer pressure can
lead "newbies" to drink too much and too quickly, resulting in
their getting sick or becoming dangerously incapacitated. Always
go to social events with a friend whom you trust, preferably more
than one—**and when you arrive together, you leave together.
Period.**

This should also go without saying, but under no circumstance
should you drive after drinking, nor should you get into a car with
someone who has been drinking—regardless of how many drinks
have been consumed. Many schools have safety transportation
vans that run at night and can bring you where you need to go on
campus. Program their number into your cell phone before you
go out!

Run for Public Office!

As you begin your college career, you may want to investigate student groups. These groups often hold events during the first week of school to attract new members, so be sure to visit any new student fairs being held around campus. One of the most popular and active organizations at the college level is the student government.

Running for a seat in the student senate can be a lot of fun. At most schools you must begin by having a set number of students sign a petition to get you on a ballot. After you achieve this, you must start your election campaign. A few schools will have a budget available for candidates, but most of the time you will have to do this on your own. It's a good idea to ask friends to help you think of creative slogans and post fliers around campus.

Of course, being elected to the student senate comes with responsibilities. You must attend the meetings, take information to and from your constituents, and be active in discussions and projects. But you also get a chance to get involved and make a real difference on campus for your classmates, plus you have the chance to make some great connections with the faculty. The more you put into your senate activities, the more rewarding they will be.

Take a Road Trip!

If you have a car on campus or know someone who does, organize a road trip to explore your new community. Is your college near any cool landmarks or attractions that you have always wanted to see? Are you close enough to a nearby city to take a trip and see the sights? Check with your local student life office for information on nearby places.

This is not only a great chance to get out of your dorm and see the world around you, but it's also an opportunity to spend some time with your roommate, new friends, or fellow freshmen. Many schools sponsor a trip early in the semester for freshmen to mingle and get to know each other, like cruises or skiing trips, so keep your eyes peeled.

Some basic travel etiquette: if you go on your own and someone else drives, offer to pay for gas or snacks, and play navigator with a map or a GPS if needed. If you don't have access to a car, check out local transportation like trains or buses. For other travel tips, check out:

Lonely Planet
www.lonelyplanet.com

Travelocity
www.travelocity.com

Expedia
www.expedia.com

Meditate on Your First Week

Your first year of college is full of changes: a new bed, new faces, a new schedule, and new opportunities. It can be very exciting but also very overwhelming. The coursework is much heavier, you miss your family and friends, and you are having difficulty slipping into a solid routine. Rest assured you will find your natural rhythm as time goes on, but all the initial stress and pressure can really get to you.

Today, take some time for yourself. Turn the lights off, put on some relaxing music and lay on your bed. If your roommate is in the room, put on some headphones and go for a walk. Let your negative thoughts come out, give yourself permission to feel stressed about them, and figure at least one possible solution to each one:

I feel like I can't keep up in my science class.

I can ask my professor for help and see what he suggests.

I miss my parents.

It's okay to miss them. I will see them over break, and will make sure to call them later.

I am worried about getting hurt or sick and being so far from home.

The school has a great health center and can take care of me.

Our fears can be so big because they are unknown. If you face a problem and provide a possible solution, you feel more prepared. Try talking with your roommate if you feel comfortable. You may be surprised to find that you're not alone.

Plan to Plan

Even if you have a memory like an elephant and never missed one class assignment in high school, you need a planner or portable calendar in college. You'll be juggling at least four or five classes (including in-class projects, homework assignments, and scheduled exams) in addition to any other activities or jobs that you have on your plate. Mom and Dad are not here to remind you about soccer practice or your French test next week, so it's up to you to keep up.

Office supply stores and your college bookstore sell an array of planners that could be helpful to you. Initially, the variety may seem overwhelming: daily, weekly, monthly, pocket-sized, desktop, portfolio, and wall-mounted are among the available options. Just look closely at each style and consider how you want to manage your time. A pocket-sized planner, for example, is handy to carry with you, but does not offer a lot of space to write your plans. Most students choose notebook-sized planners that they can take to class along with their other books. These planners make it easy to write down the dates of upcoming exams and deadlines as soon as you get the information.

Your phone may offer a calendar app, but its effectiveness really depends on how you use your phone. Is your phone attached to your hand? Do you get several texts a day? Do you regularly go over your monthly minutes? If so, really consider if another notification on your phone will help—or just get ignored in a sea of texts and calls.

Juggle a Job and School

Being a hip and popular college student can be expensive. Between meals out and buying books—plus your daily coffee— the costs can add up. It can be tempting to pursue a part-time job to make some extra cash to fuel your social life, but there are many factors to take into consideration.

You're not alone. Many college students have jobs to help them pay for incidental needs, tuition, or books, doing anything from brewing coffee at a nearby café or working the cash register at the local supermarket. Whether your job is on or off campus, your employer is going to give you a set schedule. If you fail to abide by this schedule, you may lose your job. A job is a very important commitment and it should be treated as seriously as your classes. However, if a job becomes so stressful or time-consuming that it takes away from your study or class time, you may need to search for a less demanding position. Remember, at this point in your life that you are a student first.

Classes aside, consider this: Does your job allow for you to devote enough time to your classes, but no time for anything else? Do you spend every waking minute when you're not studying at your job, working, leaving you with no time to pursue any clubs or activities? This is no way to spend your college years, so it's best to find a job with reasonable hours or just go without some extra pocket money. It will be worth it.

Join Your School's Gym

You've heard of the "Freshman 15," right? This mysterious term applies to the amount of weight new college students typically gain when they get to school; unlimited food at the dining hall, lounging around in your dorm, and unrestricted access to snacks are the usual culprits.

The best way to take care of your body is to engage in moderate exercise regularly. You'd be surprised to learn (unless you studied your tuition bill) that you've probably already paid a fee for use of your school's gym or athletic center. Find out when it is open and visit it three to four times per week. Also, make a point to learn when the center's peak hours are. Some people prefer to go when the gym is empty so they have a greater selection of machines and free weights at their disposal. Others enjoy the sense of community and motivation that comes with working out in a crowd. Whether you prefer to work out in an empty gym or a bustling one, you can plan your schedule around the peak hours.

A regular exercise regimen is an integral part of a healthy college lifestyle, and if you set this in motion during your first weeks of school, it will be easier for you to maintain a set gym schedule. A great tip is to recruit your roommate or a friend to be your gym partner; you'll be a lot less likely to skip a workout if you have someone there motivating you.

Make a Date

When you start school, you'll be swamped with new people. New friends, new roommates, and new classmates—to name a few—but you will also meet new people whom you are interested in romantically. This is completely natural and healthy, but there are a few things you should always remember when you enter the college dating pool.

When you first start dating someone new, you may not know what his or her true intentions are. This being the case, you will have to take certain measures to protect yourself. Here are some tips for your dating safety:

- Never go someplace unfamiliar with someone you don't know well.
- Meet at the date location instead of riding in an unfamiliar person's car.
- Tell a friend where you are going, with whom, and when you will be back.
- Carry a cell phone and a small amount of extra cash.
- Never do anything that makes you feel uncomfortable.
- Stay in public places with someone you don't know well.
- Don't drink alcohol until you know your date well.

These may seem over the top, but it's better to be safe than sorry. Besides, if the person you're dating is truly genuine, all these worries will become moot.

Find Your School's Activity Fair

The activities fair was mentioned earlier, but it's definitely worth it to check it out. At the beginning of the fall semester, many schools offer an activities fair, in which clubs and organizations set up tables in one large area to teach new and interested students about what they do and how to join. It's rare to get all the clubs at your school in one room, so this is a golden opportunity for you to browse them all and see what fits your interests best.

Go to the activities fair with your roommate and a few friends from your residence hall. Take the time to walk around and see everything before you start to sign up with groups. Ask a lot of questions and find out what each group stands for, what is included in the membership, and what kinds of events the group sponsors. After you have seen all of the organizations that are available, go back and sign up with those you find most appealing. Consider the activities you participated in during high school, but also learn about new opportunities—things that were not available to you before but that you find interesting.

Many groups will have sign-up sheets where you can write your name and e-mail address. If you choose to sign up with a group, be sure to ask what you are signing up for. Are you volunteering to organize an event for the organization, promising to attend the group's next meeting, or simply requesting more information? Talk to the representatives and get as many details as possible.

Join a New Club

It may be intimidating to do something by yourself; after all, you're coming from high school where all activities were planned out for you and were done as a large group. But take a chance in college and find a club or organization that you've always been interested in—even if none of your friends or your roommate are interested.

Are you interested in student government? Speak to your local student government office about joining. Do you like to write? Visit your school's newspaper office and inquire about job opportunities. Are you a science enthusiast? Your school may have a club for you. This goes double for intramural activities; see if your school has a pick-up basketball group or a running club.

It's always nice to do things with a friend, especially someone you know well. But when you join an organization in college, the people in it will soon become your friends as you bond over a common interest. Don't be afraid to get out there and try new things, even if you have to start them alone.

Be as Homesick as You Want

Transitioning to a new environment is stressful. You may find your-self missing the familiarity of your home, your family, and your high school friends. If you do, you are certainly not alone. Homesick-ness is one of the most common ailments among first-semester college students. So, if you look around your classroom, prob-ably at least a third of your classmates are experiencing some degree of homesickness. It's completely justified; you've spent about eighteen years of your life doing the same thing every day and having instant access to your family and friends, and this is a big change.

It can be tempting to call home every time you feel a pang of sadness. Resist these urges, because constantly calling family or friends will not help if you are homesick. Doing this won't allow you to make the transition to your new life. Call people about once a week and be sure to discuss positive as well as nega-tive experiences that you are having. Instead of complaining to your mom about how you hate your roommate and want to come home, talk about the interesting psychology class you're taking or the organization you're thinking of joining.

If your homesickness is becoming worse or you are feeling extremely anxious all the time, visit your school's counseling cen-ter. Many students like you have been through their doors, and they know how to help you manage your distress. Your conversa-tions with them are confidential, and your student fees usually cover these services.

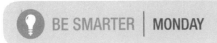

WEEK THREE

Form a Study Group

Studying with a group of friends is not always an effective method of learning material for an exam. While with friends, you may be more tempted to tell jokes than focus on your studies. However, if you exercise discipline, working closely with a small group of others can greatly advance your understanding of a topic and enhance your performance in a class. It's up to you to control experiences when working in groups.

When your group meets, you should always have a specific purpose in mind. You may want to review the last few lectures, discuss the readings, or figure out how certain concepts are related to the focus of the class. The purpose can change as the meeting proceeds, but it at least gives you a starting point for your conversation.

As far as where to study, choose a location that is comfortable and accessible to everyone in the group. However, be sure that your location isn't too comfortable. If you choose to study on your bed, you may get drowsy and lose your concentration. Your residence hall lounge may be a better place to work. Everyone can gather around a table or grab a spot on the floor, spread out notes, and have a robust discussion. The library is also a good place to go, but you may not be able to have a loud discussion there. Try to find a place where you can bring a lot of materials, where you can speak loudly and candidly, and where you can remain for several hours, if needed.

Find a Local Bank

Especially if your school is far from home and you typically do a lot of banking, you should look into starting an account with a bank in the town where your college is located. It makes it easier for you to have access to your money without incurring ATM fees from other banks or mailing checks home for your parents to deposit.

If you are going to start an account with a new bank, you need to understand the various account packages offered and how they fit with your banking needs. For example, you are unlikely to need unlimited checking if most of your spending will be done with cash or credit. Here are a few questions to ask before opening an account:

- What is the interest rate for each account?
- Is there a charge for writing checks?
- Do you have to maintain a minimum balance on each account?
- What is the charge for bouncing a check?
- Can you link checking and savings accounts for overdraft protection?
- How often will you receive statements?
- Is there an extra charge for getting or using an ATM card?
- Where are other branches of the bank located?
- Where are the bank's ATMs located?

If possible, schedule some time to visit a bank while your parents are moving you in. They can help with any additional questions you or the bank may have.

Keep a Healthy Weight

While at college, you may decide to try to lose some weight. The best weight-loss plans are managed through a responsible diet and healthy exercise. Fad diets and juice cleanses are typically overrated and can even be dangerous. Any diet that promises fast results with minimal effort should be viewed skeptically. If you don't know how to begin a healthy weight-loss program, talk to your campus health center staff or your physician, or ask your RA to sponsor a program for your floor. Remember, too, that your body is still changing. As you grow into a mature adult, you are inevitably going to look and feel differently than you did in high school. You should only choose to go on a diet or join a specific weight-loss program if you have your health in mind. Don't do something drastic or dangerous just to gain the approval of your peers.

The fear of the "Freshman 15" or some initial weight gain at the beginning of the year can scare new students into diving into crash diets that can jeopardize their health. If you want to avoid gaining weight or lose some new pounds that you gained at school, just watch what you're eating and get into an active exercise routine. Remember also, if a diet promises fast results in a short amount of time, it's probably not safe. If something seems too good to be true—it probably is!

Watch Your Laundry

This may be your first time doing your own laundry, but even if it isn't, doing laundry in your dorm is vastly different than doing it at home. Although it may seem that nobody could possibly be interested in taking your clothes, students report theft from college laundry rooms every year. Not only are clothes stolen, but students sometimes find that laundry baskets left in the laundry room get taken as well.

The most important thing is not to leave your laundry unattended. Nobody will take your clothes if you're there watching the machines. Read a book, do some studying, or text or call your family and friends while your clothes are in the washer or dryer. You and a friend might even choose to do laundry at the same time and keep each other company. At the very least, stay in the building.

A point of laundry etiquette—and another reason for you to stay put while your laundry washes and dries—dictates that you should never leave your clothes in the washer or dryer after the cycle has been completed. Security reasons aside, your fellow residents may be waiting their turn while your clothes sit there, finished, taking up space—this can be a big pain, especially on busy laundry days or weekends. Be polite and attentive; remove your laundry when it is done or an impatient resident may remove it for you.

If you pop your laundry in and go out for a few hours, don't be surprised to see your wet clothes sitting on top of the washer for all to see. Keep your underwear private and monitor your laundry!

Make a New Friend

You often roll your eyes at your science professor's crazy hand motions with the girl sitting beside you. The people across the hall in your dorm always say hello when they see you in the laundry room. The guy working at the coffee shop is in your communications class. As you proceed in your college career, you'll notice how easy it is to meet new people and find some common ground.

Go out today with the sole motivation of making a new friend. It's not difficult; in fact, you probably already have several candidates from your classes, your activities, and your residence hall. The easiest way to do this is to start a conversation with a question about something you have in common. Ask someone in your class a question about the coursework or if they have any experience in the subject. Ask what music someone you usually see at the gym is listening to. Invite the person across the hall to have breakfast or dinner with you.

Forget about looking "uncool" or being shy. If a friendship doesn't stick, it doesn't stick and you both move on. But when it does, it can last a lifetime.

Get to Know Your RA

Too often RAs are stereotyped as cruel enforcers of college policy. Though they do have the unpleasant responsibility of keeping order in raucous residence halls, your RA is just a student doing her best to complete requirements and graduate with a degree. In fact, most RAs take the job so that they can help new students adjust to college life; they aren't trying to ruin anyone's fun. A big part of an RA's job is organizing activities and programs for the residents on her floor or in her building. Some of these programs will be educational in nature, but they can also be very interesting and exciting. Your RA might arrange for a singer to put on a show in your hall or invite a martial arts expert to teach you and your peers some new moves.

Visit your RA today and introduce yourself. If you have ideas about floor activities or methods to get residents more involved, don't be afraid to offer these suggestions to your RA—in fact, she will probably appreciate your insight. You should talk to your RA about activities that you would enjoy, or ask your RA about campus programs that you have heard about. She will probably work that much harder to meet your needs because you have expressed an interest in her efforts. Sometimes your RA will even ask you to help organize a program you suggest. This is a way for you to get involved and gain more control over your life. And if you think that you may want to be an RA in the future, working with your own RA will give you insight into the position.

Sometimes all it takes is one conversation to make a real difference. Be brave and go knock on that door!

Manage Your Anxiety

General feelings of stress and anxiety will also plague you periodically throughout your college career. Stress will result from academic and social pressures along with managing your transition to independence and adulthood. Most stressors will dissipate with the passage of time, but the feelings associated with stress can be overwhelming.

The good news is that there are a variety of readily available resources for managing stress and anxiety. If you are a resident student at your college, you can start with your resident assistant or hall director. If you are a commuter student, you might also make an appointment with your counseling center or heath center. Many colleges have centers for health education and wellness, and if your college has one, this is another great place to start.

College students experience a number of other mental health issues. As a rule of thumb, if you don't feel like yourself and are behaving, thinking, or reacting differently than you used to, you should seek the advice of a counselor at counseling services.

Make Use of Your Professors' Office Hours

You should never be intimidated by your professors! In truth, college professors are an undergraduate's best allies. They have gone through many years of college and thus know what you are experiencing. They are excited when you are genuinely interested in learning, often enjoy questions and an exchange of ideas, and have interesting lives outside of the classroom that can sometimes intersect with your life. Professors can help you navigate the waters of your major, help you find internships, write letters of recommendation, and are wonderful professional connections down the road.

On your syllabus, your professors should have listed a few hours each week when they make themselves available for students to come to their offices. Make a point to go by early in the semester and chat with your professor about the subject matter, any questions you have about the course, or latest developments in the field. A professor will be thrilled to see that you are interested, engaged, and ready to work with what he's teaching, plus he will remember you in a sea of freshmen faces.

If you can't make the professor's office hours, e-mail him and ask about other possible times to meet and be sure to show up at the agreed time! Nothing annoys a professor more than a student who does not value his time—and this is a sure way to guarantee he'll remember you, and not in a good way.

Get a Job at the Writing Center

If you enjoy writing, you might look for a work-study job in the writing center. After some training, you'll be able to use your skills to help other students become better writers. In addition to the satisfaction that comes from helping someone, you'll make some money. You may also get good topic ideas for future papers and make friends with the students you assist.

Keep in mind that as a freshman, your odds of getting hired over an experienced upperclassman are not very likely, but you should still approach the center's director and ask for an interview. If she is not prepared to hire you until you have more experience, inquire as to which classes she recommends you take to become a more solid writer. You may walk out with a job offer!

Working in the writing center is wonderful because you are on campus, in the thick of students wanting to become better writers, which can help you become a better writer, too. On-campus work is ideal for freshmen because you have limited hours, don't have to leave campus or work into the night, and have the chance to meet new people who share your passion—all while making some spending money!

Find a Workout That Works Out

The quickest way to give up on regular exercise is to overdo it or force yourself to participate in an activity that you don't enjoy. If you try and run ten miles on a treadmill without ever having run so much as a half-mile before, you'll get frustrated when you can't do it. If you hate tennis but sign up anyway, you'll start to resent the activity before you eventually quit.

Before you hang up your sneakers forever, check with your health or fitness center to see what else is offered. College is the ideal time to try new kinds of exercise. Alternative sports, like racquetball or squash, are often available. You might also want to ask a friend to be your jogging partner. Consider taking advantage of local natural resources, such as hiking and biking trails. Or you can join an organized sports team or athletic club, like crew, field hockey, swimming, or soccer.

Forcing yourself to become a runner might not work out, but your school's weekly yoga classes might just be the perfect fit. Explore and try everything to find out what works for you.

Don't Broadcast Your Life

Social media sites like Facebook and Twitter have made it easy to connect with people in an instant. You probably used Facebook to find your roommate before school, or "friended" some people on your floor. It can be a great way to expand your social circle, but you have to realize that some of your social media "friends" are not really your friends!

If, in whatever social media context you happen to be accessing at the time, you tell everyone that you are, say, "out and about the big city," or "locked up in this classroom until 10 P.M.," then you tell everyone who is listening that you are out of your room. If they also know, say, that you routinely leave your door unlocked while you are away, then you have become easy pickings for a burglar.

This is not to say you can't make posts like these out of fear that someone is going to take advantage of you; but realize that when you friend every person you meet, you are sharing access to a lot of personal information.

Choose Your Clubs Wisely

When you start school, you can see a ton of organizations that you would love to join, but remember that your commitments to classes come first. You certainly don't want to wear yourself out by spreading yourself too thin. Because you won't have time to do everything, you will need to make difficult choices. When you are considering an organization, ask yourself the following questions:

- Do you feel comfortable with other members of the group?
- What time commitment is involved?
- What are the requirements of membership?
- What does the group offer you, other than a fun group to hang out with?
- What financial commitment is expected from you?
- Will membership support your academic or career goals?
- Are there leadership opportunities available for you?
- Do the organization's goals and values match your own?

As you examine each organization and ask these questions, discuss your options and thoughts with friends and family. The people who know you best will sense any reservations you have and are familiar with your goals and values. Sometimes you will disagree with friends and family, but be certain to listen to their feedback. Be sure to pay the most attention to those who have known you the longest. After careful consideration, you can choose the group that's right for you.

Shake Your Groove Thing!

One of the latest fitness crazes to sweep the nation is a dance-aerobics class called Zumba. Invented in South America, this dance involves a combination of cardio moves and salsa, mambo, and other Latin dances. It caught on in the United States, and now instructors everywhere are getting certified to teach Zumba in gyms, studios, and other fitness centers. Zumba is a great way to burn calories, get a good workout, and have a great time.

Check if your school's gym offers a Zumba class; if not, search your local community for one. If you don't have luck finding a class nearby, invest in a Zumba DVD or look for videos online. Even if you've never danced before or have two left feet, Zumba is a really fun experience. Have your roommate join you, and if you can, make it a regular weekly activity.

Reduce Your Screen Time

Current estimates state that, between your television, your phone, your computer, and other electronics, you are subjected to as many as *nine* different screens throughout the day. These screens by their very nature can stimulate your mind and make it hard for you to relax, particularly at night when it's time for your body to unwind. Excessive screen time before bed can make your sleep uneven, restless, and ineffective.

It's unreasonable to ask a college student to avoid screens all day long, but today, try and cease any screen time at least an hour before you finally go to bed. It may be hard, but you will notice how much easier it is for you to fall asleep. Some mellow things you can try while unwinding instead of playing on the computer or watching television:

- Study for your classes. Use your books and your notes— no laptop!
- Read a book for pleasure.
- Invite a friend to go for a nighttime stroll.
- Visit a friend in another dorm for a chat.
- Brew a cup of tea and check out the latest edition of your school paper.
- Make a craft.
- Play solitaire—with a real deck of cards.
- Make a list of things you need to accomplish this week.

If you can throughout the week, try and turn off your screens before you hit the sheets for the night. Your quiet mind will thank you!

Prepare for the First Exam

Tests are a huge source of anxiety for college students, particularly freshmen who are not familiar with exam protocol in college. Your first exam should come sometime in the first month of your course, and will usually cover everything you have learned so far. If you have attended class, taken notes, and completed your assignments, you should be in good shape. If not, you have your work cut out for you catching up.

With very few exceptions, there are no make-up tests in college. Usually, if you skip and miss a test without a good (and real) excuse, you get a big fat zero, which can spell disaster for your final grade depending on how much the test is worth. So mark it on your calendar, store it in your phone, or write it on your hand—whatever you need to do to be there that day.

It will help if you know what kind of test you will be taking. If it is going to be a short-answer test, you need to be able to explain concepts briefly. If it is a multiple choice or fill-in-the-blanks test, you need to know names, dates, and vocabulary. Usually the professor will tell you the format of the test ahead of time, but if not, feel free to ask. Even if the professor denies your request, he may offer some other helpful study tips.

Once you have identified what you need to study, review your notes and pertinent readings. Make summary sheets of important information, flash cards of dates, facts, and people, and then shuffle them and quiz yourself.

Know What You Paid For

Few things are less exciting than a bill, and few things are more important. Keep all the financial papers you receive from your college in one place so that you can keep track of and review them as necessary. You will probably leave all this paperwork at home with Mom and Dad when you go, but it might help if you take copies with you to reference when you need to.

Take a good look at the final, itemized bill that your school sent you or your loan organization. There may be some charges on there that you may not be familiar with, and some that you are. Feel free to visit your school's billing office and ask questions about amounts and dues and what certain payments are applied to. You should know what you are spending your money on. The billing office can show you where your money is going. You'll see some obvious charges like tuition, room, and board, but there may be charges that you aren't sure about, like "student fees." This can include many different things.

Things that you've already paid for as part of your yearly student fees by the time you get to school can include your daily meal plan, a health insurance program, and access to your school's fitness center. There could be opportunities that you are missing (and money that you're wasting) because you didn't take a close look at your bill, so take some time to give it a good read.

Have a Healthy Plate

Healthy eating involves quantity, variety, and frequency of meals. While your cafeteria may offer a variety of appealing foods for every meal, you will need to exercise some self-control. Fruits and vegetables are important to your body's ability to function and are readily available in the cafeteria. Fill your plate at least halfway with veggies in the dining hall, and don't overeat. Take one serving of food and if you are still hungry when you're through, go back and get more. The cafeteria isn't going anywhere.

Don't neglect the other basic food groups, either. Grains and dairy are also important in a balanced diet. Take time to read the nutrition information posted in your cafeteria and try to select meals that hit all of the recommended nutrition points listed.

Plan ahead with your meals. If you know you're having pizza with your study group that night, partake in a big salad for lunch. If you're attending a rush party and you know they'll be serving fried foods, eat some healthy snacks before you go so you aren't starving when you get there.

Create a Roommate Agreement

During your first few weeks of college, you and your roommate may get along perfectly. But before long, academic stresses, conflicting schedules, boyfriends and girlfriends, or a lack of space may begin to complicate things. You may start to feel uncomfortable in your room, or you may be making your roommate uncomfortable. The best time to start working on conflict is before the conflict actually occurs, and this proactive approach can begin with a roommate agreement.

Your RA may approach everyone on the floor about completing and posting formal roommate agreements. If your RA does not provide a form, sit down with your roommate and write down issues that are important to each of you. Some items may include:

- Sharing CDs, DVDs, books, and electronics
- Sharing clothing
- Sharing food
- Using items that are off-limits
- Using each other's computers
- Taking phone messages

After you have come to a consensus about these smaller points, you need to address more personal issues like privacy, sleep schedules, and visitor guidelines. These points will be harder to negotiate because they affect each of you more personally. Be honest about your desires and listen carefully to your roommate's views. If you are unable to come to agreement on an issue, ask your RA for guidance.

Join a Club Sport

Many colleges have club sports available, either to meet a special interest or to fill a gap where an intercollegiate team is not available. Sports clubs often compete with other colleges and sometimes with community groups. Examples of club sports might include fencing, crew, and rugby. These clubs give you the opportunity to play a sport you love or learn a sport that is new to you. The one drawback to club sports is that colleges often don't fund them. In these cases, club members have to work hard to organize fundraisers and collect money to keep their sport going.

If you love a sport but aren't interested in the idea of trying out for your school's competitive team, this option is perfect for you. Club sports are less time-consuming than other athletic endeavors, and you can easily miss a practice or even a competition if your academic or work commitments are particularly demanding at a certain point. You can also leave a club sport if you find it just isn't working out. However, it's worth it to stick with a club sport for a while. Too many students quit early because they aren't doing as well as they hoped or they don't seem to be fitting in. You should give yourself at least half a semester to truly evaluate your experience with a club.

Many times college club sports will be devoted to an alternative sport. Some clubs include Ultimate Frisbee, croquet, and lawn bowling. If this strikes your fancy, join up and have fun!

Bring a College Friend Home for the Weekend

If you find yourself going home for a long weekend in your first semester, invite a college friend who is unable to go home to come with you. (Check with Mom and Dad first, though!) Bring him around your town, introduce him to your family, eat at your favorite hometown restaurant, and hang out with your local friends. Your college buddy will get the chance to experience a nice weekend at home and see where you came from, and your home life will have a bit of college added to it.

If there is anything your college friend would like to do while you're in town, oblige him and make a real weekend of it. You'd probably like to go out and paint the town red every second, but be sure to spend some time at home with your family. They've missed you and you've missed them, and it might be nice for your college buddy to have a quiet evening in with a set of parents, even if they aren't his!

Breathe!

Is it possible to breathe incorrectly? Well, not exactly, but it is possible to breathe in a way that better nourishes your body and relaxes you. These techniques are a great way to relax and calm down before a big test, so remember them for those stressful moments throughout the semester!

Standing Breath

Stand with your feet slightly apart to balance your weight. Focus only on your breathing for three minutes. Do not attempt to control or direct your breath; just observe it.

Now take three "good" breaths, not necessarily deep or long but comfortably filling your lungs as you inhale and exhale. As you take in each breath, raise your arms; then lower them as you exhale. While inhaling, think of the air also entering your body from the ground upward to your head. Try to allow each breath equal time in duration and quality. Try to keep the rhythm the same as your "normal" breathing, especially in the beginning.

Sitting Breath

Sit in a comfortable chair, making sure that you are as upright as possible and your feet are comfortably on the floor. Place your hands on your lap or palms down on your thighs. Focus only on your breathing for three minutes. Do not attempt to control or direct your breath; just observe it.

Next, lower your head to your chest, and inhale while slowly raising your head. As you exhale, lower your head back to your chest. Do this for three "good" breaths. Try to do it as slowly as possible.

Check Out a Learning Community

If your school offers membership in a learning community, you should definitely investigate the option. In general, a learning community strives to move formal learning beyond the classroom. Most learning communities are organized as living-learning areas and involve a residence hall, suite, or house. In addition to living together, you and your colleagues in the community will take a class or series of classes together and/or participate in seminars, lectures, or retreats outside of class time.

The term "learning community" can be defined very differently from campus to campus. At some schools, they are founded on an academic component. At other schools, a learning community is more of an affinity group, composed of students who choose to live together because of a shared interest. Not only will you further your education, but you will also build a group of friends with whom you can enjoy discussions and activities. Additionally, you will probably get to know professors beyond the classroom. This can be a lot of fun, and it will help you when you need advice or letters of recommendation as well.

Some students find that learning communities are too focused on academics and cocurricular activities and lead to the exclusion of extracurricular activities. If you are not able or willing to devote the necessary time to being a member of a learning community, you may want to avoid this commitment.

Make a Budget

Now that you're in a consistent routine, you should make a solid budget to follow so you're not constantly building up debt or borrowing money from your parents or your friends. You probably don't need a detailed budget; just think of general categories of spending and set an amount for each. After you have listed each category, total the amount you anticipate spending and compare that with your income and savings. If you're spending everything you're making (or spending *more than* you're making), you need to find places where you can spend less. Some categories you should consider for your budget are:

- Travel to and from home and around town
- Car maintenance and gasoline
- Eating out and food deliveries
- Entertainment, such as movies and concerts
- Clothing purchases
- DVD/CD purchases
- Phone bills
- Laundry
- Toiletries and medications

Keep track of where your money is going. Be prepared to say "no" to some activities. You can't go out to eat every night, go to every concert, or do other things that drain your budget. Finding no-cost entertainment won't be hard once you decide not to spend more.

Get a Good Pair of Flip-Flops

Your dorm is regularly cleaned by a trained housekeeping staff, but you still probably shouldn't go traipsing around in your bare feet—especially when you're taking a shower. How many people used your shower at home? You, your parents, and your siblings, probably, and you had no reason to believe that you could contract any number of germs or infections from them. But when you share a limited amount of shower stalls with an entire floor of college students (who may not be as hygienic as your folks), it's better to play it safe and invest in a good pair of open and durable flip-flops.

If a football player on your floor has a case of athlete's foot, which is a very common and nonthreatening ailment, and this person showers barefoot . . . pretty soon your whole floor could be running to the drugstore for Tinactin. Same goes for other communicable diseases.

It may seem odd at first, showering with shoes on, but you'll get used to it. Remember, just because you shower in them doesn't mean your shower shoes are always clean. Stagnant water and soap scum can build up a residue or even turn to mold after a while, so be sure to give your shower shoes a good washing every now and then.

Set an Alcohol Policy with Your Roommate

Did you know that if your roommate sneaks alcohol into your room and gets caught you may also suffer the consequences, even if you had nothing to do with it? Or if you bring beer into your room your roommate can also get punished? Unfortunately, colleges cannot always trust one roommate over the other, and both are punished for alcohol possession. In fact, many campuses are "dry" and have a zero-tolerance policy for alcohol in their residence halls.

Talk to your roommate and set an alcohol policy. If your roommate likes going out every Thursday and getting drunk with her friends, that's her choice, but when she begins to bring that behavior into your living space, it becomes your business and potentially your problem. Be clear about your wishes, and let your roommate be clear about hers. Some points can include:

- No alcohol in the room. This includes open containers and sealed containers in the fridge.
- No coming home drunk and making a mess.
- Be considerate of one another. If the presence of alcohol makes one of you uncomfortable, discuss and remove it.

Getting caught with alcohol in your room can lead to a monetary fine, a warning, and at some schools, expulsion from the residence halls, which for some of you essentially means expulsion from school because you have nowhere to live. Don't blow the college opportunity for a few drinks, and don't ruin it for your innocent roommate either!

Learn More about Potential Majors

Sometime in the summer before you begin classes, usually at orientation, you should be assigned an academic advisor. This may be a professor who will be teaching a required first-year student course, a professor who teaches courses in your major, or a member of the academic advising staff. Your advisor is your personal expert on academic matters and should be the first person with whom you consult about course selections. Typically, you don't have to select a major until your junior year, but it's never too early to investigate possible options. Set up an appointment to talk to your advisor to discuss the different programs.

Another good source of advice is other students. If you know students who are already attending your college, get in touch with them and ask for suggestions about classes you should take in the future. Keep in mind that their advice will be coming from a much different perspective. They can tell you which professors are approachable, which buildings are close to your residence hall, and what class combinations were overwhelming for other first-year students. You can also go online to *www.ratemypro fessors.com*, but be cautious about not taking a class simply because one or two students gave the professor a poor rating. More often than not, these students are bitter about bad grades they received from these professors.

As a freshman, you're in a wonderful position to take, in addition to your general education requirements, any classes that you think are interesting as electives. Try everything that interests you and see where you land.

Visit a Friend at Another College

Your core high school group of friends may have gotten separated when you all ventured off to college. Take the time this weekend to visit one of them!

It's easier if your friend is close, but don't be afraid to jump in the car or on a train to make a longer trip. See your friend's dorm, meet her roommate, and explore her campus. Sit, drink coffee in her local coffee shop, and share any personal experiences that either of you have encountered as you navigate college. Try not to let the conversation steer back to your old high school topics and focus on the new stuff.

You may feel strange and even a little upset when you see your friend interacting in her new life: inside jokes with new friends, new tastes in music and clothes, or even a new boyfriend. She might not even resemble the same girl you've known since kindergarten! Your feelings are completely normal, and remember that your friend may be viewing you differently, too. College is all about change and embracing new experiences.

Thank your friend at the end of the weekend for taking you in and showing you around, and invite her to come visit you one of these weekends. She can see how you've changed, too.

Spend Some Time Alone

As you go through college, you'll find between classes, activities, meals, and even studying that you are rarely by yourself. This can make for a welcoming, involved atmosphere, but it can also be exhausting. Take some time for yourself today and be completely alone. This may alarm you after having spent so much time in the company of others, but you deserve some time to yourself, to think about everything that's going on in your life. And spending time alone means *spending time alone*, which means no laptop or Facebook or Twitter. Tell your roommate where you are going before you leave. Bring your phone in case of an emergency, but don't surf the web or send text messages. Some ideas:

- Grab a book and head over to the coffee shop nearby to read.
- Study at your own table in the library.
- Put on a pair of headphones and go for a long walk.
- Hit the gym alone.
- If you have your room to yourself, stretch out on your bed and listen to music.
- Take a drive to a local scenic area.
- Visit your college town's public library.

When you return, you'll be surprised how relaxed you are after spending some time alone.

Schedule Your Core Classes

You may have a set of basic classes, or core requirements, that you must complete in order to earn a degree from your college. These core classes often include subjects like history, math, writing, and science (often with a lab). Often you can fill a particular requirement by choosing one course from a list within a particular category. For example, in order to complete a cultural understanding requirement, you may be able to choose from several history courses. Take a look at your required general education requirements and core classes today and start a plan to schedule them.

You'll have to make a decision about when to complete your core requirements. One strategy is to complete all core requirements as soon as possible in your college career, leaving your final years to focus on courses in your major. Another approach is to do things in the completely opposite order, focusing on your major initially and completing core requirements in your final semesters of college. For most students, the sensible choice rests somewhere in the middle. Taking one or two core requirement courses each semester keeps you on track for graduation and allows you to take other courses for your major, minor, or personal interest. It's also nice to have one or two less-challenging classes while you're taking the toughest courses in your major. As a senior, you may not be overwhelmed by an introductory course, even if the freshmen in your class are.

Get Every Penny Out of Your Education

As with your college meal plan, you have already paid for your schedule of classes this semester. The college has your money already, and is holding up its end of the bargain by providing access to the classes you registered and paid for. Whether or not you make use of them is not your college's problem—it's yours. Think about it economically, and understand **that this is your money**.

A typical undergraduate class is worth three credits at any given school. Depending on your status as either an in-state or out-of-state, resident or commuter student, the cost per credit can be a wide range of figures. The basic in-state cost for a state college is usually a little more than $300 per credit. So at three credits, your English class can cost you about $1,000 for the semester. If your English class costs $1,000 for the semester (and this amount is on the *much* lower side) and meets every Monday, Wednesday, and Friday, that's forty-five classes or thereabout.

Divide $1,000 by forty-five class meetings and you get about $22. So every time your class meets, it is worth $22. And if you sleep in or go to the mall instead, you're wasting that $22 that you have already spent securing your place in this course.

Your professor, your college, and your classmates will not lose any sleep over you not going to class. Your professor will still get paid, the college already has your money, and the only one losing out is you. Go to class—you paid for it!

Take Your Vitamins

Your college diet is likely to be inconsistent, even when you are vigilant about it. This being the case, you might consider one of the many multivitamins that are available over the counter. It's important to make sure your body is getting the nutrients it needs on a daily basis, and multivitamins offer a one-stop solution for people who aren't necessarily health-conscious. Consult your family physician, pharmacist, coach, or college health center staff for advice on a good multivitamin or other dietary supplement. But remember: only treat your vitamin as a supplement and not a substitute for healthy eating. If you are taking prescription medication, check with your physician to make sure that the multivitamin you choose won't create any unwanted side effects.

Another good tip is to try and see what nutrients you get from your vitamins, and research foods that have those nutrients. Try and find them at your dining hall. If your vitamins are high in iron, opt for a spinach salad. If they are high in fiber, try some whole-wheat pasta instead of regular pasta. Try and get your nutrients from your plate as well as your pill.

Take a Self-Defense Class

Everyone wants to be as safe and secure as they possibly can. You will be able to concentrate better and enjoy yourself more if you feel secure. In the United States it is common to take safety and security for granted, but you really should be vigilant in matters of your personal security, especially on a college campus.

Most colleges offer self-defense classes, either for academic credit or as special seminars. Such classes are a good opportunity to learn some new skills and meet other people. If your campus doesn't offer such courses, ask your RA to bring in an instructor to teach the residents basic self-defense tactics. You can also check with the local YMCA to see if they have a self-defense class you can take.

However, self-defense is only useful when you are being attacked, and your goal is to keep from being attacked in the first place. You should take advantage of such classes, but don't mistake your new skills for invulnerability. As a rule, always be alert and aware of your surroundings, avoid risky situations, and trust your instincts.

Learn to Multitask

In high school, your life was pretty much laid out for you: school was organized into class periods, then sports practice, then home to eat the delicious dinner your mom or dad prepared for you, then time for homework, TV, and bed. In college, you still have a set schedule, but you are responsible for a lot more in the same amount of time.

You will have many opportunities to combine tasks while at college, but you have to be selective about which tasks you combine. Writing a term paper while eating dinner will leave a mess on your keyboard or food all over your notes. However, catching up on your reading while you wait for your laundry to dry may be a very efficient use of your time. Multitasking is a common time management strategy among college students. The challenge is to find tasks that can be successfully combined.

One of the best opportunities to multitask is while doing your laundry. Laundry takes up a lot of your time and there is no way to avoid it. So, while your clothes are in the washer or dryer, do some reading, get ahead on an assignment, or review the notes you took in class that day. If you are already caught up on your studies or the noise of the machines distracts you, use laundry time to write your family a letter, fill out birthday cards for friends, or plan your holiday shopping list.

Whenever you find yourself waiting for something, this might also be a good opportunity to combine tasks. Whether you are waiting to see a doctor, waiting in a long line at the grocery store, or waiting for a bus or train, you can always use the time to your advantage.

Rush a Greek Organization

Fraternities and sororities are among the best-known social organizations on any college campus. Choosing to join a Greek organization is a big decision and one that you should consider carefully. You will have to separate fact from fiction and let go of your preconceived notions about these groups in order to make the decision that's right for you. Consider the following advantages and disadvantages of Greek membership and speak with friends and family before choosing to join. Talk to friends and other students about joining the group that makes the most sense for you.

You may have heard quite a few stories about what goes on inside fraternity and sorority houses. You may also have seen movies and TV shows that put a certain spin on these groups. Very often they are portrayed as places where members do nothing but throw wild parties, and some think Greek involvement means you don't have to pay attention to schoolwork. However, these extreme stereotypes are rarely true. Greek organizations have persisted because they are valuable to their hosting colleges and to their members.

The most immediate benefit of joining a fraternity or sorority is the camaraderie and friendship that exists in these organizations. These men and women choose to unite based on shared values, goals, and interests. They get to know each other well and learn to depend on each other through good times and bad. While participating in the full breadth of Greek activities, students develop a deep bond with their chosen brothers and sisters, and for many students this bond lasts a lifetime.

Catch Some Zzzs

The big schedule item most often neglected by college students is sleep. Now that you dictate your own bedtime, it is tempting to stay up half the night talking with friends, watching movies, or eating take-out. The truth is that your body needs a minimum amount of sleep each night, and this amount must be kept relatively consistent. This can be particularly difficult if you have an 8 A.M. class on Mondays, Wednesdays, and Fridays, but can sleep in on Tuesdays and Thursdays. If this is the case you need to find a happy medium and do your best to go to bed at similar times every night. Your body will function better if you have a regular routine. It is also important to allow yourself seven to nine hours of sleep each night.

Today, make yourself a sleep schedule and stick to it as best you can. Create a calm environment by turning your computer monitor away from your bed, setting your alarm for the same time every morning, and loading up your iPod with soft, calming music to lull you to sleep. There are some herbal teas out there that are meant to help drinkers mellow out before bedtime, so look into those, especially if you are having trouble winding down.

Show Up to Class and *Participate*

Whether or not attendance is a requirement for your class, it is best to attend every day. Some college professors have attendance policies, but many don't. Even those professors who don't keep track of attendance may still grade you on class participation, and you can't participate if you are absent, if you didn't do your homework, or if you are asleep at your desk.

You should try to arrive at your classroom five or ten minutes before the class begins. This allows you to get a good seat and briefly review your notes from the last class meeting. Reviewing your notes in this way primes your brain to receive new information on that topic. And whenever possible, you should try to sit in the first three or four rows of the class. This will ensure that you can see and hear everything that happens in class and will reduce the number of distractions you have to contend with. Some students prefer to sit near the middle of a row to get the best view of everything, but in lecture halls students with long legs often prefer aisle seats so that they can stretch out.

If you know that you are going to miss a class, speak to your professor ahead of time. This will let your professor know that you are interested in the material and are not showing disrespect by your absence. And after absences, never ask your professor: "Did we cover anything important in class?" You should consider all of your classes equally important.

Play the Textbook Game

You probably already spent a whopping amount of money on your textbooks for this semester, but you should start making a plan for spring semester now to avoid dropping all that money on a book you barely use.

Your bookstore may offer used copies of books for classes. These are texts that students who had taken this course previously sold back to the bookstore at a discounted rate. Used copies are cheaper and, if they are not heavily marked, work just as well as new copies.

Set up a sharing system with a classmate or friend in which you both pay half for one book and share it. This can be great for your wallet but terrible for your coursework since your friend may need the book the same time as you do, but if you can make an arrangement that works for both of you, go for it.

Some online booksellers will have your textbooks, too, but when figuring out the cost of the text be certain to factor in shipping and handling. Sometimes what looks like a cheaper book is actually just as expensive as the one you can purchase at your bookstore. Don't purchase your books online the first week of class; you'll miss out on readings while you wait for them to ship. And be prepared to pay a significant amount for college textbooks; no matter what the subject, they don't come cheap.

Keep Track of Any Medicines You Are Taking

You may come to college while taking medication for a chronic medical condition. It's important you continue doing so while you are at school. Keep track of how much medication you have and when you'll need to refill your prescription. If your health services cannot refill your prescription, they should be able to point you in the direction of the closest pharmacy and tell you how to get there. Some pharmacies deliver to college campuses. Give yourself plenty of time to find out this information so you don't run out of your medication at a time when health services or pharmacies are closed.

If you take a prescription medication that might be tempting to other students, you should keep it in a drawer under personal items and take it when no one is in the room with you. It's unlikely that a roommate or friend would steal your medication, but it's best to be as discreet as possible.

Know Your Surroundings, and Bring a Friend If Possible

One of the first things you should learn at college is that you are not invincible to crime. When you are walking around campus, it's a good idea to walk with a few friends. As you are walking, be aware of your surroundings and the people nearby. Stay in well-lit areas and know where you're going before you leave your room. Always make sure that a roommate or friend knows where you're going and when you expect to return. Don't carry a lot of cash, and only take credit cards with you if you know you'll need them. Today, take a look around your typical walking paths and note what is pretty standard; it will help you notice if anything unusual is happening at a later time.

If you have to travel across campus alone after dark, call ahead and tell the person expecting you that you are on your way. Also, check with your security office to see if an escort is available. Many colleges will hire students or other staff to work as escorts for students. These staff members or professional security officers can walk with you across campus and report any suspicious activity they see on the way. The escort will probably be wearing a uniform, but if not, ask for an ID if you are at all suspicious of the person. Sometimes an escort service will give you a ride to your destination, and in cold or rainy weather a dry, warm car is a much better alternative to walking.

Join a Club in Your (Potential) Major

It's important to choose a major that interests you, but it should also lead you to a career or graduate program once you graduate. If you only have a general idea of a career that you might enjoy, declare a less-specific major such as business or communications. This will prepare you for a wide array of jobs and still allow you to further shape your education in graduate school. Interested in English? Check out your school's poetry club or honor society.

Many majors will have an associated club or interest group. Many times you will be a member of this organization by virtue of being a major in the field. Your initial impression may be one of disdain. How much fun, for example, can the history club really be? In fact, these organizations are valuable to you during your time at college and perhaps beyond. The group will consist of students who share at least one of your interests and will have the attention of faculty in the department. You will have a built-in resource for forming study groups as well as learning about professors and classes you hope to take. These clubs will also sponsor speakers or take trips that might help you further define what you want to do with your life. Finally, your participation in club activities might help connect you with alumni or professionals in your field who can help you network to get an internship or a job after college.

Look Into Study Abroad Opportunities

While you are a college student you can take advantage of the opportunity to visit, study in, and perhaps even live in other parts of the world. Studying in another country or away from your home campus is referred to as studying abroad, and it sometimes includes programs on another domestic campus. Some programs allow you to study the language or culture of another country and others help you study your major from the perspective of another environment. Students who study abroad report significant changes in themselves. They see the world differently, have a new understanding of what can be done with a particular major, and often develop a new sense of self. Though going abroad can be scary, it can also enrich your life in ways you never thought possible. Visit your study abroad office and get some literature and information!

When planning a trip to study abroad, be certain to visit your financial aid office, too. Your aid package may not be acceptable to some programs, and if you are going abroad without aid you need to ensure that your assistance package will still be available when you return. Be sure to speak with your financial aid officer early in the planning process. One advantage of using a program sponsored or approved by your campus is that your school has already accredited the classes you will take while abroad. That is, the classes you take away from your campus will transfer back and count toward your degree and graduation requirements.

Give Yourself a Spa Treatment

You're a broke college student, yes. But if you can scrape together some funds, treat yourself to a nice treatment like a manicure or pedicure or a massage at a nearby spa or salon. You work hard all week and deserve a special hour or two to be pampered.

If your wallet can't make this happen, rustle up some nail polish from your makeup bag or from a friend and paint your nails yourself. Visit your school's fitness center and ask about massage therapy availabilities. If that doesn't pan out, take a nice, hot shower in your dorm to relax your muscles. Opt to do it in the afternoon when the showers are less likely to be crowded.

Learn How to Take Notes

You may think that you will remember everything your professor is saying in class, but you won't. Learning to take effective notes is one of the keys to college success.

To begin, your notes must include a few basic components, such as the date and overall topic of the lecture. This will help you keep information organized when you need to review later. Also, when you're working with study groups or attending review sessions, you can quickly reference a particular day's lecture notes. If your professor titles his lectures, make a note of that as well.

Another major thing to keep in mind is that lectures usually have a definite structure, just like the papers you write. There will be an introduction, several main points and illustrations, and a brief summary. When your professor begins her lecture, you want to listen carefully for the structure. Try to identify and write down the focus of the lecture. Listen for key words such as "first" or "for example" that indicate important points or transitions. Another thing to do is watch and listen for nonverbal clues about what is important. Your professor's hand gestures, facial expressions, and pauses will add to the material that you are receiving. Some of these clues will help you take notes, indicating which points are more significant than others. Other clues may indicate items that will be on a quiz, related to a paper assignment, or represented on the final exam.

Be a Frugal Eater

Some nights you'll crave a certain food that you can't find in your dining hall. When ordering food for delivery, find out which restaurants are the cheapest in the area. Some places may charge a delivery fee, so take that into account when ordering. You can also look for restaurants that offer specials or discounts for college students. Another way to save is by splitting delivery orders with friends. You don't need to eat an entire pizza by yourself, and sharing the cost with friends will save you money. This can also be a great opportunity to socialize with other students on your floor. And keep track of which restaurants offer weekly or nightly specials. For example, if Thursday is "wing night," you might be able to get a standard order of chicken wings for significantly less money.

You should tip the person who delivers your food. Their job can be pretty thankless, especially on those cold and rainy nights when you don't even want to go out. This person may be a college student, like yourself, or a parent working hard to support a family. Either way, you should always include a few extra dollars when paying for your food. Tipping makes delivered food more expensive, so if you're trying to save money, consider picking up the food yourself.

Learn Healthy Recipes

Don your chef's hat every now and then and cook your own meals. Odds are you are not allowed to have any cooking appliances in your dorm beyond a microwave, but don't let that stop you!

Look for a kitchenette in your residence hall and consider cooking an occasional meal there. You may be able to prepare a family favorite, such as lasagna or tacos, which can be nutritious as well as comforting. You may also impress your new friends with your cooking prowess, even if the recipe is actually very simple. Invite your roommate and some friends over to sample your delicious delicacies, and use the opportunity to make new buddies. People may want to contribute with their own recipes, so plan these nights in advance so people can get the ingredients they need.

Pack up the leftovers to reheat in your room for lunch the next day to get an added bonus meal.

Get Connected to Your Campus Emergency Notification System

Since the shootings at Virginia Polytechnic Institute and State University in 2007, many colleges have implemented a campus emergency notification system. If there is an emergency on campus, you will get a text message telling you what to do and where to go. Some colleges also use this system to inform students about other news, such as weather-related school closings.

At some colleges, everyone is automatically enrolled in this system; in others, students must opt in. If the latter is the case at your college, you should register for these notifications as soon as you can. Speak to your RA to learn the procedure for registering; it can usually be done online.

Many colleges will also have "low-tech" emergency warning systems, such as alarms or building intercom systems. It is important for you to know what to do if one of these systems is activated. If you are not told what to do in the event of a campus emergency during orientation, ask your resident assistant or academic advisor as soon as you can. If you hear a siren or intercom warning and do not know what to do, try accessing the college website. Usually in an emergency situation the college will post relevant details and instructions prominently on its home page. Unless otherwise instructed, the best idea is usually to stay where you are and pay careful attention to what is going on around you.

Get Involved in Community Service

You will find it very meaningful to engage your spirit through serving others.

Check out these community service organizations that have ties on college campuses:

- Alpha Phi Omega
- Circle K
- Habitat for Humanity
- Best Buddies
- Amnesty International
- Big Brothers Big Sisters

You may be interested in doing other types of service work through local agencies. Your community service and religious life offices will have a list of such agencies. These opportunities often include:

- Literacy programs
- Food banks
- Domestic violence shelters
- Public libraries
- Homeless shelters

If your preferred volunteer opportunity is not represented on your campus, consider organizing a group of students and pursuing resources to help you engage in that service. The service you provide will greatly enrich your college experience, have a positive effect on your community, and leave you with many fond memories.

Overcome Your Shyness—in Your Hallway

Make a point to walk up and down the hallways of your building and look for rooms with open doors. Walk by these rooms slowly and look for an opportunity to start a conversation with the people you see. They may have decorated or arranged their rooms differently than yours, so something intriguing may catch your eye. You will also hear music or see decorations that match your interests. When you see a person sitting in a room, make eye contact with him, smile, and say hello. If he invites you in, take a few minutes to stop and talk to him. You may find that those few minutes turn into a couple of hours and, before you know it, you could be making plans to have lunch with this new acquaintance.

Even if you have trouble initiating conversations, you still need to be out and about, giving other people the chance to approach you. If you experience a lull in a conversation, ask the others about their residence halls, homes, or hobbies. People enjoy having a chance to talk about themselves, and this will give you insight into their personalities.

Trim Your Busy Schedule

You've fallen into a steady routine of classes, studying, organizations, and clubs. You've joined everything you're interested in and every minute of your day is jam-packed with activities and tasks—and you're completely pooped. If you think you've taken on too much, use today to examine your weekly schedule and see what you can cut out to keep your sanity.

It is important to be active on campus, but it is also easy to overdo things. Students who are over-involved too early in their college careers, or students who work too much on the social part of college life tend to be struggling academically at the end of the first semester. Keep in mind that you have several years of college to do everything that you want to do. Pace yourself and build your involvement in activities slowly. Stick with the three or four activities that are the most fun for you, spend time making new friends, and focus a lot of your energy on your schoolwork. After your first semester, you will have a good idea of how much you can do outside of class and will be able to increase your involvement if there is free time in your schedule.

Try to gracefully leave any clubs that your heart isn't in, or ask if you can scale back your commitment. Just clearing up your schedule a little bit can make your week seem so much more relaxing.

Plan a Research Paper

While a test is usually completed in one class period, a term paper can seem to last forever. From developing your topic and doing research to writing it out and having it handed back to you full of red marks—the process can seem endless and disheartening. But the ability to do research and present findings in a professional manner is a foundation of the modern college education. The skills you gain during the research and writing process will serve you well for the rest of your life. Picking a topic and planning your paper can be half the battle, so do it early.

Your first task will be deciding on a topic for your research paper. Sometimes this will be assigned to you, but most of the time you'll have to propose one to your professor. You may also have to determine a particular viewpoint to pursue for your paper. Your research must be unbiased, but your professor may want you to examine the available material and reach your own conclusions.

When choosing a topic you should consider several important factors. The advantage to picking a topic that is related to ongoing course work is that you may have more resources available to you. Your textbook, syllabus, and even lecture notes may help you throughout the process. You can also choose a topic that is not directly covered by your class, which may be more interesting for you, but it still must have some connection to the subject matter of your class.

Ask Your Old Boss to Take You Back

Winter break is coming, and you'll soon be faced with some free time. Today, give your old boss a call and ask if he can use you over break. If you worked in retail or at a restaurant, your boss will likely be looking for extra holiday help anyway.

Remember to point out that you are experienced in the job and offer to work flexible hours. During the holiday rush, your experience will certainly be an asset, and you may be more marketable as a seasonal employee since you will likely be able to work daytime hours once high school students have returned to school. Don't assume that you automatically have a job, even if you parted on good terms.

If your former employer does not need help during your winter break, you could try finding work through a temp agency. These companies specialize in finding work for students, people who are between jobs, and those in other special situations. If this option doesn't work, you could try baby-sitting or shoveling snow for neighbors. These activities may not yield large profits, but the money will come in handy and your neighbors will appreciate your services.

Either way, make your winter break job plans now, because soon everyone will be home and looking for work. Get ahead of the game!

Lose Your Sweet Tooth

You probably eat about 150 pounds of refined sugar every year, even if you don't realize it. And at college? There is sugar in practically everything you find in your dining hall, at campus events, and even in your yogurt.

Refined sugar causes your body to crave more refined foods, suppresses your immune system, and causes your energy levels to spike and then crash. (So if you eat sweet stuff, you trick your body into craving more sweet stuff.) There are more than twenty different names for sugar—most being refined—in our sweet but poor national diet.

Whether you realize it or not, sugar is in almost everything you eat. Sure, you know it's in the obvious stuff, such as soda and cookies and candy. But it's also in ketchup, mayonnaise, salad dressings, fruit juice, bread, cereal, soups, pizza, pasta, yogurt, and cheese.

Make a habit of checking the labels of the food you eat. This will be hard in a dining hall, but once you do it enough with your own food and at the grocery store, you'll be able to recognize which foods have sugar without a label. Unless a product is specifically labeled sugar-free, chances are it will have sugar in it. But be sure to look carefully. Sugar goes by other names, including dextrose, glucose, fructose, lactose, corn syrup, sorghum, galactose, invert sugar, and malt or maltose.

Be Careful of Big City Livin'

Many college campuses are located in or near a large town or city. Students living on campus can easily become complacent about safety because their campuses tend to be very safe places. If this is your situation, it is important to remember that most cities and towns do not have anywhere near the police protection that you will enjoy on campus. You will need to take heed of the precautions mentioned previously in the personal and group safety sections—as well as some other considerations—when you venture off campus.

If you find yourself alone and separated from friends when off campus, and you cannot reach anyone by phone, then take a bus or a cab back to campus; you should not walk through unfamiliar territory or try to flag down a ride with a stranger.

Always leave yourself an out when traveling off campus. A great idea is to keep a $10 bill folded and stashed away in your wallet or purse somewhere so that—in case of an unforeseen need to get to campus—you always have cab fare with you. Do not spend this money on anything else unless it is an emergency. If some crisis forces you to spend the money, replace it as soon as possible so you always have your emergency fund!

Offer a Helping Hand and Make a Real Difference

Studies show that, typically, when people are in a group and see a robbery, assault, or injury, they are not likely to help out because they expect someone else in the group to know more than they do. Everyone else in the group thinks the same thing, and no one does anything. Without putting your own safety at risk, be the one in the group who does something: un-prop a door, help someone who falls . . . make a difference!

Look out for your friends and for your fellow students to increase safety for everyone. For example, do not prop residence hall doors open and put others at risk. If you see a propped door, un-prop it and throw away the prop; do not leave it there to be used again. If you see a strange or threatening person who looks like he does not belong on campus, tell your RA or call the campus police or public safety department.

You can make a difference in the safety of your campus by being an engaged and responsible member of your community. Too often, people let bad things go because they think it is "someone else's" responsibility. If you think of campus safety as *your* responsibility and do your best to watch out for yourself and others, you can truly make a difference in the safety and security of your campus home.

Look Into Auditing a Course

Your schedule is probably jam-packed, but if you have the time and are open to it, consider auditing a course you find interesting but don't necessarily want to pursue as part of your degree program.

Auditing a course is usually something students do before they formally apply to a program, sometimes before they are even considered official students at a school. It gives them a taste of what the course and subject field offer, and they can decide if they would like to keep going. If you're leaning toward an English degree but are interested in the stars, audit an astronomy course. If you're into psychology but math piques your interest, audit an accounting course.

When you audit a course, you still may have to pay for it and it may not count toward your program, so really consider it before you commit.

Do Some Self-Examination

It's pretty easy to get down on yourself in college. One bad grade or a few pounds gained can ruin your day, and you can start to really beat yourself up over it. But you're a human being, not a robot, so it's okay to slip up every now and then.

You are the result of millions of repetitive thoughts and actions. You do not come into this world finished; you are always in the process of becoming something more and someone else. Within this stream of growth, there are also millions of choices you are making and will soon make that will affect who you are and what you will be.

Now is the time to pause and look at this process. You can initiate this with an exercise in self-inquiry. Write the following questions on separate pieces of paper, and reflect on each one in turn.

1. What am I now?
2. What should I be?
3. What do I want to be?
4. How can I be all of that?

Look into yourself and make a plan. You'll feel better if you take control of your situation rather than just knocking yourself down.

Consider a Minor

Most colleges offer you the opportunity to declare a minor area of study, and some actually require such a declaration. The idea is that you can develop a concentration of knowledge on a particular subject, in addition to your major area of study. Many students who declare minors try to pick something that complements the major they have chosen. An education major, for example, may choose a history minor to help prepare him for a career teaching social studies. Other students choose a minor that seems completely unrelated to their major; a chemistry major may choose an English minor to help improve his writing ability. Unless you're involved in a specific preprofessional program, such as premedical or preveterinary, you are best served by choosing a minor in an area of personal interest. The more you enjoy the learning process, the more you will gain from it.

Your minor will show up on your college transcript, and perhaps your first resume, but after that it is of little interest to potential employers. So treat your minor as a chance to explore a subject you really enjoy. Try biology or art even if your major is political science. You may discover a lifelong pursuit outside your career.

Look Into Work Study

Work-study aid is money from federal, state, and/or college sources that is available to you if you work on campus. These jobs can pose a great opportunity because they are convenient and you can learn more about a particular department that interests you, form relationships with professors and other administrators, and earn money to fund your education.

Your campus probably has a work-study office, often located in the financial aid office or career center. Contact this office to find out how to secure a job on campus. Be sure to ask if your campus guarantees jobs for students with a work-study award. Students with special skills, such as lifeguard certification, may be able to secure a desired job quickly. Other students will have to work hard to find lucrative positions on campus; the sooner you get started, the better chance you have of finding a position.

Don't rule out working for the college food service or maintenance programs. It may be hard work, but you'll meet some great people—students as well as staff—and have a lot of fun at the same time. Working for these offices can also have some nice perks, such as getting free leftover food or learning valuable skills that you may use in the future.

Many colleges need more student positions than can be filled through work-study awards alone. Even if you do not receive federal work-study aid, check with career services, human resources, or in the student newspaper for these openings. Local business owners close to campus may also desire seasonal student help. Look for advertisements on campus, and again, check with your career services department.

Let's Talk about Sex

By this point in your life, you have probably received lectures about sex on several occasions. You're not confused about where babies come from, you're probably aware of the many reasons to use contraception, and you're familiar with family and religious views on premarital sex. How you approach sex while at college will be one of the most important decisions of your college career and perhaps your life.

If you choose to have sex while at college, you need to protect yourself physically and emotionally. You should start by deciding what circumstances will lead you to having sex. How long do you need to know your partner, and what do you need to know about him, before you have any form of sexual contact? Also, what type of sexual contact are you willing to engage in? Know your limits before you get involved in a sexual encounter. If you don't want to do something, be certain to express that clearly early in the encounter.

If you decide to have sex, use some form of protection. You want to avoid getting a sexually transmitted disease as well as preventing pregnancy. Latex condoms are the most popular and widely recommended safe-sex devices. However, even condoms can't provide 100 percent protection from diseases or guard completely against pregnancy. For this reason, it's wise to use two forms of contraception when engaging in sexual acts. Your health services center can help you out here; they often hand out free condoms and can answer your questions.

Keep Your Drink in Your Hand

Rohypnol and gamma-hydroxybutyrate acid (GHB) are two insidious drugs that are very popular among sexual predators, and they are indicative of the hidden dangers that exist in college social scenes. Rohypnol and GHB are typically dissolved in a drink and are difficult to detect. The person who consumes these drugs may appear to be okay; however, she is somewhat sedated and may be more open to suggestion. These drugs also create a memory gap for victims. Victims may wake up in a strange place and not remember what happened in the preceding hours. Ketamine, an anesthetic used mostly by veterinarians, and gamma-butyrolactone (GBL), an industrial solvent, are also used by predators to disorient and disable their targets. Certain prescription drugs that have similar effects when mixed with alcohol may also be used. While you should not let this information frighten you to the point of never leaving your room, knowing about these drugs and their effects will help keep you safe.

These drugs are often found at parties where people don't know each other well. Sexual predators don't want to get to know their victims; they only want to have sex or have control over another person. So when you're at a party and don't know some of the people there, be extra vigilant. Never accept a drink from someone you don't know or only know casually. Don't leave your drink unattended; if you must, abandon that drink and get a new one. Talk to your friends before going to a party and let them know your intentions for the evening. And make a pact to leave as a group no matter what.

Cheer On Your School's Team

Most colleges have a full range of intercollegiate teams, so you can attend sports competitions year-round. At larger schools, more popular sports like football and basketball may attract fans from all over the area. Smaller sports will also attract a group of fans. While being a spectator does not provide you with much exercise, it is a great way to show school spirit, to have fun with friends, and to cheer your school's team on to victory.

Attending sporting events is more than just an opportunity for you to express school spirit or support your friends. A soccer or football game offers a chance to get out of your residence hall and away from your studies for a few hours. If the weather is nice, a football game is a great outdoor event. And if the weather is cold or rainy, a basketball game could be a great way to get out of your comfort zone while still being involved on campus. By attending sporting events you may also end up in some photos featured in a local newspaper, on the school's website, or in the college yearbook, providing you with a fun memento of your college years or something you can send home to your family. Whatever your motivation, take advantage of these opportunities and support your teams.

"Friend" Your College

Many colleges have developed Facebook presences where incoming students can connect with one another even before arriving in the fall. Utilizing these and other Facebook pages will help you meet students at your college. Plus you'll see upcoming events and activities that you may be interested in.

Make sure to go beyond the Internet, though. If you meet someone on Facebook who is in the same major as you and takes many of the same classes, find a way to meet and get to know each other; maybe you can form a study group. Do not be "face-less" on the web! Once you have met some other students, you will be texting and tweeting up a storm—just remember not to do this in class. Using social media in class distracts you and others around you, and is very disrespectful to your professor.

Host a Movie Marathon

Either watch alone or invite guests, but today is meant for watching your favorite movies. Pop some popcorn and grab some snacks, because your dorm room is officially a movie theater today. You can either watch a series of movies, like *Lord of the Rings*, or just a collection of your old favorites with a theme, like chick flicks or comedies like *Clueless* or *The Hangover*.

Ask around on your floor and invite people to come by and bring their favorite movies to add to the collection. You'll probably see a few films for the first time and get some new favorites. Watching movies, having snacks, and laughing with your friends will take the edge off any bad week and put you in a really good place to start the new week tomorrow.

Your college also may offer a DVD swap or rental system, so be sure to look into that.

Skip the All Nighter

All-night cramming sessions seem to be a rite of passage among college students. Every year students use this method when studying for final exams, but in truth this strategy is usually far from effective. When you arrive for your exam, you may have trouble keeping your eyes open, focusing on the page in front of you, or writing coherently. As a rule, don't rely on cramming. But if your time-management strategy has gone awry and you need to fit a lot of studying into a short period of time, try to at least get a few hours of sleep and eat breakfast before your test.

In most cases, cramming can be (and should be) avoided. The problem may be that you cannot focus on your studies because your residence hall is too noisy or your neighbors are being inconsiderate during exam periods. If this is the case, your RA can seize control over the situation. If you have simply overloaded your schedule and don't have time to complete your assignments and study for tests, your academic advisor should be able to offer assistance. And if frequent headaches interrupt your study time, causing you to put it off until the last minute, you may need reading glasses or some kind of medication. Your health center staff may be able to identify such a problem and suggest a solution. Whatever your trouble, you won't have to work through it alone. Ask for help when needed and heed the advice you receive.

WEEK TWELVE

Start Looking Into Scholarships for Next Year

It's never too early to think about paying for the next year of college! Scholarships and grants are defined amounts of money that the college or another source gives to you for your educational expenses; these don't have to be repaid. Scholarships are the most sought-after type of aid for most college students. Scholarship eligibility is normally based on student characteristics, including one's academic merit, declared major, alumni relationship, and extracurricular involvement. Grants are different in that eligibility is usually based on the financial need of the student and family. Institutional grants are more common at private colleges than at public institutions.

The federal government is probably the largest single source of financial aid for college students, typically focusing on need-based grants. But a surprising number of private organizations offer some sort of scholarship support as well. Take the time to search the Internet for possible financial aid opportunities. A quick search for "college scholarships" will turn up a wide variety of choices and possibly a lucrative award for which you are perfectly qualified. Also ask community agencies, such as churches and civic groups, if they have money available for students heading to college. Additionally, your family's employers may have grant programs for children or dependents of employees.

Learn about Hunger, Cravings, and Just Eating Because You're Bored

Is it a craving, or are you really hungry? You first need to understand the difference between a physical food craving—or actual hunger—and an emotional food craving. Cravings can be caused by either physical or psychological needs. Emotional cravings or eating triggers are usually caused by psychological needs, whereas hunger is a biological function of the body's real need for food. Emotional cravings can lead to binging. Learn to listen to your body and understand what it is trying to tell you.

You can use many techniques to distinguish between biological and emotional cravings. A physical craving has the following qualities:

- You are physiologically hungry.
- The craving does not go away if you try to wait it out.
- The craving intensifies over time.
- Nothing you do will take away the craving except the craved food.

An emotional craving, on the other hand, looks like this:

- You are not physiologically hungry.
- The craving goes away if you wait it out.
- The craving does not intensify over time; the emotion does.
- Doing something else satisfies the real need, and the craving disappears.

College is a time where you are literally surrounded by food, so it is best to learn when you want to eat because your body needs nourishment and when you want to eat because the cookies are just sitting there.

Keep It Locked Down

In addition to keeping your room locked, you should also keep cash and valuables well hidden in drawers or secured in a small safe or lockbox. Items that are left in the open are easily seen and make prime targets for thieves. Even textbooks are sometimes stolen; they can be sold to other students or returned to the campus bookstore. This information is not meant to scare you into locking up all your belongings and giving your roommate the stink-eye, but to warn you to be vigilant.

You will likely feel safe in your residence hall because RAs and security staff do regular rounds and the front door of your building is locked or monitored. However, you are partly responsible for the safety of your residence hall. Never prop exterior doors open, never let someone into the building if you don't know him, and always report suspicious activity or safety hazards to your RA as soon as possible. These simple things will significantly contribute to the safety of everyone who lives in your residence hall.

Experience Some Diversity!

Student organizations also sponsor parties. These are usually very well attended because students want to support their organization or their friends. It can be great fun to see your new friends show off their culture's music, food, and traditions. Your friend in the Middle Eastern club may teach you native dances and a little bit about his culture. And many clubs will combine efforts to cosponsor dances designed to appeal to all students. The African American club may cosponsor an event with the Latin American club, bringing a great deal of diversity and energy to the event.

Some events will attract everyone—students, faculty, and staff. Most campuses have fall and spring festivals that consist of live music, games, vendors, demonstrations, and other activities. Often the campus food service will have a cookout in conjunction with these activities. These all-day events are a great chance to get out and have fun while meeting a lot of people. You are likely to converse with lots of other students, whether you're waiting in line for food or enjoying the live music.

Redecorate Your Room

You've been at college for a while now, and may not have had the time to decorate your living space. It is important to make your residence hall room feel a little bit like home. You will be sleeping, eating, studying, hanging out, and talking with family and friends on the phone all in this one room. You need to be comfortable here and make your guests feel comfortable as well.

Posters have long been a staple for college students. If you have some favorites, bring them along. If not, your college bookstore is certain to have some on hand and some colleges invite poster vendors to set up shop on campus during the first few weeks. You will also learn from the bookstore or housing office how to best affix posters to your walls; housing officials frown on punching holes in walls, and some kinds of tape will remove the paint or stain walls. Keep in mind that posters cover a large section of wall and make a statement about you. Only display posters you don't mind friends and family seeing.

Many colleges have restrictions on the use of wall hangings. Few schools allow you to hang things from your ceiling and none permit you to block smoke detectors and other safety equipment. Make sure that you review your college's policies before affixing anything to your wall.

Take a Blackout Day

Your days are going to be pretty full with final exams coming up, so you better take some time to relax now. Take a blackout day starting in the morning. Let your family and friends know what you're doing in case they need to contact you, and give them your dorm's landline if there is an emergency.

A blackout day is when you forgo any electronics for one whole day. This includes cell phones, computers, and televisions. Be reasonable and try doing it for the full day, but don't neglect any previous commitments to do so.

Invite your roommate or some friends to go for a hike or visit a local museum. Leave your phone at home or turn it off. When you get back to your room, you'll be refreshed and ready to face your exams.

Polish Your Studying Skills

Final exams are coming, and you need to be ready to fill your brain with all the information you learned this semester. There are a variety of little things you can do to learn the material you are studying. One longtime favorite has been the use of mnemonics and acronyms to help students remember things. For example, students who took music lessons as children may remember trying to memorize the lines on the treble staff in music. Many children were taught, "Every Good Boy Deserves Fudge" to remember that the lines are E, G, B, D, and F. You can create similar mnemonics and acronyms for the material you are studying.

An easy and yet often neglected learning tool is recitation. Going over information several times increases the likelihood that you will recall it when you need to. When you're reading a chapter, stop frequently and recite what you think you've just read. Then go back and read it again to see if your understanding was correct. This works with textbooks, articles, and even class notes. By making your studying an active process, you have a better chance to learn the material.

A final trick for superior learning is rest. There will be times during your college years when it is impossible to get a good night's sleep—you can count on at least one fire alarm at 3 A.M. But for the most part, you should be able to get enough sleep to allow your brain to function at the high level necessary in college courses.

Cut Back on the Caffeine

Health issues aside, there is one other reason why you shouldn't be blowing your pocket money on the expensive café mocha latte every morning. That creamy delicious caffeinated delight gives you the energy to power through your classes (although it has a lot of calories and the high only lasts until late morning), but it can also leave a big hole in your wallet. Those expensive brand-name coffees can run anywhere from $3 to $5 per beverage, and that adds up pretty quickly over the year.

If you absolutely need a coffee every morning, there is usually a generic brand coffee in your dining hall, with takeout cups nearby. Go for that instead, because you already paid for it and it probably has a touch less caffeine. Splurge every now and then on the brand-name stuff (it makes a great reward for a good grade!), but otherwise keep your coffee simple.

Don't Use Naps to Supplement Bad Sleep!

Don't plan to make up for lost nighttime sleep with daytime naps; the two are not equivalent and sufficient naps are hard to achieve in noisy residence halls. Every now and then you can take a cat-nap in the afternoon, especially if you're not feeling well or you had a busy week, but do not rely on that two-hour snooze to make up for you staying up all night to play video games.

Sleep patterns are extremely important, and you don't want to get into a cycle that involves you taking a nap as part of your regular sleep schedule. College schedules change, and breaks happen, and you don't want to be home for Christmas yawning at 3 P.M. because you need a nap or stuck with afternoon classes in the spring semester that fall right when you usually nap.

If you are tired during the day, consider giving yourself an extra hour of sleep each night or exercising more often to boost your energy.

Deal with Roommate Conflict

No matter how well you get to know your roommate before arriving on campus or how well you design a roommate agreement, some kind of conflict will undoubtedly arise. This may be something trivial that simply annoys you or something much more serious. Whether the conflict occurred because someone put an empty milk carton back in the fridge or one roommate stole the other's stereo, every issue needs to be resolved.

If the conflict is minor, sit down with your roommate as soon as possible and discuss the issue—talk about why you are concerned and listen to what she has to say. After you have each had a chance to speak, work together to find a solution. If your conflict is more heated, you might be best served by stepping away for a while and calming down. Instead, take a walk, call your family to vent (and explain that you are only venting, not asking for solutions), or go work out at the gym. Leave immediately if your roommate becomes extremely agitated, violent, or threatening.

Your college will also provide you with a great resource for working through roommate conflicts: your RA. This student has lived through what you are experiencing and has taken the RA job in order to help others. All RAs receive formal and informal training about roommate conflicts. So when you are having difficulty with your roommate, knock on your RA's door and ask for some time to talk privately. Be completely open with your RA—she will keep your problem confidential. If your roommate problem is too big to overcome, ask your RA about switching rooms in the spring.

Gross, Clean Your Room!

Yes, the semester is nearly over, and no, you probably haven't cleaned your room thoroughly yet. With break approaching, why not do it now so you can come back to a clean area?

With all the studying you have to do, you won't have time to keep your room immaculate. This is okay, but keep in mind that friends are more likely to hang out in your room if it is relatively clean and there are places for them to sit. You can leave study materials out on your desk and a sweatshirt draped on the back of your chair, but if you have piles of dirty clothing on the floor people will not feel comfortable in your room. You don't have to empty your trash every day, but perishable food will begin to smell if left in the garbage for too long.

There are a few specific items that you should have in your room to keep it looking and smelling clean. First, it's a very good idea to have a can of air freshener on hand. This can help you mask the odor of takeout food that may remain after you've eaten it, or you can spray it into your garbage can every time you change the bag. A spray bottle of glass cleaner or all-purpose cleaner will also be helpful. If you spill juice on the floor, this will get rid of any stickiness, and you can also use these products to dust the surfaces of your desk, dresser, and mirror. Remember, though, that certain cleaners should not be used on your computer or other electronic devices. Check with your school's technology help desk for information on cleaning and protecting these items.

Explore Student Leadership

Colleges often have scholarships designed to recruit or encourage student leaders. Eligibility criteria will vary but often includes some demonstration of leadership in high school or your local community. However, colleges tend to think of leadership broadly, so don't rule yourself out if you were not the president of an organization or the captain of a team. Leadership is about making a difference, and that is exactly what the college wants you to do upon coming to campus. Some leadership awards will be based on your list of activities, some on an essay or application you complete, and some on interviews with college staff and students.

One of the best examples of leadership development aid is through the Reserve Officer Training Corps (ROTC) program. Students who choose to pursue this route for scholarship aid often find generous assistance for their education costs. However, if you receive money from an ROTC program, you'll be obligated to complete some sort of military service upon graduation. Most ROTC programs want to train the best leaders for today's military branches, and if they invest in helping you become a leader they will expect you to use that leadership to their benefit for a few years.

Drink a Mug of Hot Chocolate

Depending on where you are in the country, the weather may be getting colder. If not, enjoy this calming drink anyway.

SWEET DREAMS HOT CHOCOLATE

Hot chocolate is a classic comfort beverage to wind down after a long day. Good old-fashioned milk eases muscle tension, anxiety, and grumpiness. Try a new twist on an old classic, chili powder, for double the comfort and warmth. Digesting chili, even in small amounts, boosts production of endorphins, neurotransmitters that increase pain tolerance.

Serves 1

1 cup milk
1–2 tablespoons flavored chocolate drink mix such as Nesquik
Ground chili powder, to taste

Warm milk in pan or microwave. Add chocolate drink mix and dash of chili powder to taste. Enjoy slowly, in pajamas, in absolute coziness and comfort.

Begin the Preparations for Your Finals

If you want to truly succeed on your final exams, you need to know more than just the subject matter covered in your courses—you need to know what type of exam your professor will give. This will determine how you study and will tell you a lot about what your professor is looking for from your final exam.

Cumulative final exams, covering the entire semester of material, are relatively common. While this is often intimidating to new students, this format can work in your favor. A cumulative exam generally covers more material, but cannot cover it deeply. You must understand the general concepts covered in class, how they are interconnected, and be able to tie them to a few specific examples. Contrary to popular belief, cumulative exams don't necessarily require more studying; they just require a different approach. If you've regularly attended classes and completed all your assignments, you're in good shape.

If you have been a lazy student all semester, skipping as many classes as you can get away with, not turning in assignments, and ignoring your syllabus, please don't put all your eggs in the basket of the final exam. It's rare that you'll ace a tough exam in a class you've ignored, and even rarer that you'll pull your lagging grade up enough. Your professor will not have much sympathy for you, but if you insist on visiting him and asking his advice, be prepared to try and learn one semester's worth of work in one week. Don't ask for extra credit projects at this stage in the game.

Avoid the Delivery Trap

This week is going to be busy for you, studying for finals and keeping up with your regular activities. Leaving your dorm or the library will be tough, and the temptation will be there to order in with your study group for almost every meal. This can quickly add up to a large hole in your wallet.

Take regular breaks to visit the dining hall and eat. It's healthy for you to take a step away from your books for at least a half-hour and eat, but if you can't tear yourself away, opt for a wrapped sandwich and bottled drink with a bag of chips that you can take right back to your study station with you.

Another option is to make a large meal in your dorm's kitchenette and save several small Tupperware containers of it in your fridge. That way you can just pop them in the microwave when you're hungry.

Prepare Physically for Your Exams

Think of a test as a performance for your mind. You already know that your body does not perform as well when it is worn out. Whether you are an athlete or an actress, you know that you need to exercise your body appropriately in order to be prepared when it comes time to take the field or go on stage. Similarly, when it is time to take a final exam, your mind must be appropriately prepared for the challenge.

The first and most obvious thing you need to do is get a good night's sleep prior to your exam. If you have been studying diligently and intelligently, you can set your books and notes aside in favor of a good seven to nine hours of sleep. You may find it hard to turn off your brain, with thoughts of key concepts or important dates running through your head. But getting enough rest will pay off when you arrive in the classroom for your test. A rested mind will be able to create better essays, pick up on key words more quickly, and adapt to any surprises that appear.

It's also important to avoid burning yourself out. Though it may sound contradictory, deserting your study materials from time to time is a good idea. An evening of intense studying should be interrupted with several breaks that involve thoroughly relaxing activities. Take thirty minutes to watch a sitcom, or a little bit of time to take a walk around campus. Find a few friends to join you for a quick meal or snack and talk about anything *except* your exams. When you return to your studies, you'll feel refreshed and your mind will again be prepared to absorb important information.

Get the (Caffeine-Free) Rest You Need

We talked about cutting down on caffeine to save money before, but there are a bunch of health benefits to dialing down your dose, too. As finals week rears its ugly head, the temptation to stay up and study all night becomes easier and easier to succumb to. Sleep is important, and without it, you're a zombie with a No. 2 pencil in your hand. Pounding coffee after coffee might give you a bit of a rush, but it's not doing you any favors.

When abused, caffeine causes anxiety, stomach irritation, headaches, and insomnia. What's worse, it is addictive. People who consume more than 300 milligrams a day (about three cups of coffee) will suffer withdrawal symptoms when cut off from their supply, so when exams end and you no longer need your constant coffee fix, you'll have a tough time. Symptoms include fatigue, depression, irritability, jitters, and headaches as blood vessels in the brain dilate. Additionally, caffeine is a diuretic, flushing your body of fluids.

Take better care of yourself and create a more sensible study environment by getting regular sleep, switching over to tea, and saving the java for when you want it, not when you need it.

Schedule a Review Session

After all the reviewing you have done on your own, why bother with a review session? And aren't review sessions really meant for the students who haven't studied? Actually, these misconceptions can lead you to miss out on one of the most valuable study tools available at college. Beyond your individual study time, review sessions are the best way to prepare for your final exam.

Many review sessions will be organized or approved by your professor. Sometimes review sessions will be arranged independently of the professor, and if your professor hasn't scheduled a session, you could be the person in charge—send her an e-mail and ask permission to set one up. Depending on her schedule, your professor may volunteer to run the session; if not, you're on your own with your classmates.

These professor-free sessions can be either very helpful or a big waste of your time. If a group of students is gathered to talk seriously about the class material, you are likely to benefit from the session. On the other hand, if a group of students meets with no set purpose, you probably won't benefit much from the experience.

After the review session has ended, make a list of the items that were covered. Compare that list to the outline or list that you created based on your notes and textbooks. If the two lists are very similar, you're in good shape. If several of the topics covered in the review session don't appear in your own private study notes, you should spend extra time on these areas. Finally, combine the two lists to create a master list that can serve as the basis of further studying.

Consider Making Arrangements to Stay on Campus

If you just can't tear yourself away, consider staying on campus over winter break. There are times when your school will be closed but residence halls will remain open, and others when the entire campus will shut down. If travel is prohibitive because of cost, your academic workload, or family travel conflicts, you might consider staying in the residence hall for a break period. Be warned that this is a lonely time on campus. However, you can use the time to complete some of your coursework, watch some movies you have missed at the theater, or just relax. This is always a good time to catch up on your sleep or further explore the area around your campus.

Although your residence hall may be open during a break period, your housing office will almost certainly want to know if you are remaining on campus. As with any good bureaucracy, it probably has a form you need to fill out in order to officially remain on campus. Staying on campus for a break will rarely cost you any extra money, so filling out the form is a good idea. In addition to staying on the housing staff's good side, you will remain undisturbed by the facilities, housekeeping, and security staff. While on campus during a break, be extra vigilant about security. Be sure that your room door is locked when you are asleep or out of the room, and watch for unfamiliar people around the campus.

Stop Worrying—It's Nearly Over!

You've finished or very nearly finished your final exams, so you should be relieved, right? No! Now you're fretting about what your final grades will be, and whether you answered question three correctly, and did you answer the essay questions fully? Your friend reported that he answered the true/false portion with a completely different set of answers? Hello stress!

Learning is potentially stressful. Besides understanding new material and organizing it in ways you can recall, there is always competition and the high expectations that go along with it. Altogether, these things do little to inspire confidence when you are faced with turning points like taking a test. And afterward, you can be filled with agony over what you did incorrectly and what your final grade will be.

Read this, say it to yourself, and understand it: *"There is nothing I can do about my final exam now. I studied the material and did the best I could. Now I just have to wait to see the results. There is **nothing** I can do about the test now."* Today, go and have a good time with your friends. Splurge on a nice lunch at a restaurant or go see a movie—anything to take your mind off your finals.

Worrying won't change what answers you handed in, and it's a waste of your energy. Don't be tempted to contact your professor to ask when you can expect your final exam grade. Many campuses offer a final date for grades to be posted, so just assume that date is when you will receive your grade. If you find yourself unable to shake the anxiety, consider visiting your health services center to speak to a counselor.

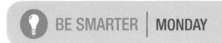

Pick Your Classes for Spring Semester

Now that your first semester of college is under your belt, you're ready to move into the spring semester as a wiser, more knowledgeable freshman. Reflect on your experiences in your first semester when building your course schedule for the spring.

Did you find that you overbooked yourself by taking too many classes in the fall? If so, consider dropping to the minimum amount of classes you need to retain your full-time status. If you found yourself twiddling your thumbs, bored with all your free time, add another course to your schedule—you can always drop one if you find it's too much in the spring. If you had to sprint across campus to make it to your next class, don't schedule back-to-back classes in buildings so far apart. If your psychology class really interested you, think about taking a similar course in the spring or another course taught by that professor—you may be on track to picking your major!

Early in your undergraduate career you have the opportunity to be creative with the classes you take. If you are intent on majoring in biology, then you might select a course in pottery or dance as an elective. You will have the opportunity to think in new ways, meet a different group of students, and gain a well-rounded education by experimenting in this way. You will also gain an appreciation for the type of work involved in other disciplines and a vocabulary that will help you communicate with a wider variety of people.

WEEK FIFTEEN

Go Easy on the Holiday Shopping

As a college student, you may find yourself without money more often than you find yourself with it. Around the holidays, this can be a real bummer.

You may be tempted to blow your meager budget on gifts for your family and friends as the holidays approach, or even look into opening a credit card account to afford the presents you want to buy before you go home for break. Don't! Your family and friends know you're in college and not necessarily rolling in the dough, so odds are they won't be expecting a blue box from Tiffany's from you this year. If you're nervous about not having top-shelf presents, have a talk with your parents and let them know your situation. Since they've been with you every step of the way, they'll understand.

Get creative with your gift giving. Consider making crafts to distribute this year, such as homemade tea bags or candles—the supplies are cheap to buy in bulk and the effort will be appreciated. Your college bookstore will have small gifts that your family would love: a decal for your parent's car, a college coffee mug for your grandmother, or a school T-shirt for your younger brother— all at a price that fits your wallet.

Try a Vegetarian Diet

If you often eat red meat and think of chicken wings as its own food group, it may make sense for you to take a break and adopt a vegetarian or vegan diet for a week or so. A plant-based diet offers many health benefits; however, it can be challenging to sustain a nutritionally complete diet without eating animal products if you don't plan ahead, so you really need to do your research and determine your individual goals. Which foods do you choose to eat? No meat or fish? No animal products of any kind? Lacto-ovo vegetarian? Vegan? Macrobiotic? Perhaps there isn't a term that fits you exactly, and that is okay! What's important is that you feel comfortable and confident with your food choices. Consult your doctor or health services before embarking on the diet if you feel it may compromise your health.

As most experts agree, eating the vegetarian way can provide all the necessary nutrients. But there's no single diet and no single source for every nutrient. The key to your success is combining foods from different groups and then getting enough calories to meet your age and activity level.

To get it right, say the experts at the Oldways Preservation Trust, you'll need several daily servings from the food groups—fruits and vegetables, whole grains, and legumes—at the base of the pyramid. But you should be sure to eat moderate servings from all the food levels and drink enough water each day to stay healthy. Make sure your diet contains the appropriate balance of carbohydrates, fats, and proteins.

Be Extra Vigilant as the Semester Ends

As you get closer to the winter break period on campus, be sure to use extra caution. Many predators see college breaks as opportunities to assault, mug, or otherwise take advantage of isolated students. To help protect yourself, always keep your cell phone charged, avoid walking alone at night, and keep all valuables safely stowed in your locked residence hall room.

If your exams are scheduled later than other students, you'll notice that campus will begin to empty out as students complete their fall semesters and head home. Your school may track your final exam schedule and assign you a date to leave your residence hall based on the date of your last exam, so you may find yourself alone in your room, alone walking to class, and alone at the dining hall.

Unfortunately, this puts you in a vulnerable position, so always be aware of your surroundings. You'll never be completely alone in your residence hall, so notify your RA if you see any suspicious people or behavior in and around the building. Your school's library will likely increase its operating hours to accommodate students studying for finals, so if you find yourself studying late into the night, call the school's transportation van to bring you back to your residence hall rather than walking alone.

Make Friends Beyond Your Residence Hall

Even if you do plan on going home for break at some point, you can find other opportunities for some company on campus before you go. Perhaps a professor will invite you to her house for a meal, or you and the international students who can't travel home will get together to see a movie at some point. If you have developed a good relationship with your custodian, he may bring you a home-cooked meal during the break, or a commuter student that you have a class with may invite you out with some of her friends. Look for opportunities to be social during this time. Though it's important for you to get ahead in your studies, small social events will keep you from getting too bored or lonely.

Remaining on campus during a break period also gives you the chance to earn some extra money. Perhaps one of your professors is going to need a babysitter for a few days around the holidays. Or maybe the local pizza place will need some extra help since all the regular student employees will be out of town. To make sure you avail yourself of all possible opportunities, do your best to make these arrangements well in advance of the break.

Visit a New Friend Before You Go Home

If you will not be working, have finished your finals early, or are looking for ways to fill the time during winter break, you should consider taking a trip to visit some of your college friends. If you have friends who live in a different part of the country, this is a wonderful opportunity to see places you have never visited. You might also have the opportunity to try new experiences. For example, if you are from the South, consider visiting a friend who lives up North. You could try skiing, ice skating, snowmobiling, or snowshoeing for the first time.

If you have a week or so before the holiday, visiting a college friend on their home turf is a great way to end your semester before venturing home to spend time with your own family. Visiting your new friends will allow you to maintain your independence while furthering your life experience. You can strengthen a new friendship, travel to a new place, and make great memories. When visiting friends at their homes, always be polite and express your appreciation for the hospitality you receive.

Make Sure Your Room Is Ready for Break

Many students—like you for example—don't begin packing their rooms until exams are finished, and many parents—like yours for example—are frustrated when they arrive and find a room that is completely unpacked. In addition to taking things home through-out the semester, use study breaks during finals week to pack items you don't need anymore. The more you have done before your family arrives, the better. Packing can be quite stressful but you need to do it right—you will not have access to your room until the new semester begins, and you don't want to spend your break fretting over something you left behind. So take a deep breath, sip some water, and dive into packing.

You'll find as you pack that you've acquired a ton of extra stuff over the semester: books, clothes, gadgets, school supplies, etc. See what you can ship home or send home with friends. You may find that many of the things in your room won't be needed again until you return to college for your second year. Why take them home just to leave them in boxes? Inquire with your housing office about storage companies in the area around your college. Just be careful that you don't store too much—when you graduate you will have to move it all home, put it up for sale, or donate it.

You will also be responsible for unplugging all electronics and appliances, securing your windows, and preparing your room for break. Your RA will usually do a sweep to make sure everything is okay before you go. The building will be locked with no access until the new semester, but security is never guaranteed; if you can and you have space, take home your valuable electronics to keep your mind at ease over the holidays.

WINTER BREAK

So, you're officially off the clock as a college student. Whether you stayed in your dorm or are
home eating your mom's home-cooked meals,
you survived your first college semester and are
ready for some time off to relax and reconnect with
yourself and your friends. But break is no excuse
to stop all the good things you've started doing
for yourself! Here are some helpful tips for keeping your break as productive as possible without
interfering with your relaxation time.

Prepare for the New Semester

So you're all registered for your classes next semester. Consider purchasing some of your textbooks through your college bookstore or online sites like Amazon.com or Half.com, or borrow them from your local library over break. This will give you a chance to peruse the content and get a leg up on the subject matter. Sometimes professors will post their syllabuses before the semester begins. If so, print them out and take a crack at reading the first few assignments. If not, don't contact the professors asking for them; many times professors finish their syllabuses closer to the semester's beginning to ensure everything is included. But you should have access to your booklist either through your professor's website or your college bookstore's website.

Save on Green by Staying Home

It's winter break, and your old high school crew is back together! You may be tempted to hit the town and spend your holiday gift cards and money at restaurants and local haunts. Don't do it. This may be the last income you see until you start working again, so hold on to it and stay home. Chill at each other's houses and have home-cooked meals—besides, your parents and your friends' parents would like to see you, too, and ask about your semester.

Also, remind yourself—or Mom and Dad—about filling out financial aid forms for next year after January 1st!

Stay in Fighting Shape

The holidays are a prime time to overeat, stay sedentary, and snack on junk food. Don't fall victim to this trap and undo all the positive work you've done over the fall semester. Of course you should help yourself to your mom's special mashed potatoes and have seconds of your grandmother's classic pumpkin pie—it *is* the holidays, after all—but don't overdo it and keep active. You might not be able to play flag football with your team and your jogging partner might live across the country, but there are simple ways to keep in shape over break. See about joining your local gym; many of them offer day passes or short-term memberships. Take a walk with your mom. Play basketball with your brother. Offer to make a healthy side for your holiday dinner. Simple techniques like these will keep you in fighting shape for the new year!

Hang Out with Your Family

It's true—they aren't just cash machines! You will always be your parents' child, but as you become an adult your relationship with them will change. While at college, you will still rely heavily on your parents for financial and emotional support. You've been gone for several months, and they've missed you. You may want to go out all the time and visit your local friends, but carve out a good chunk of time to spend with your folks. Don't act aloof or moan about how you wish you were back at school; that's unkind and hurtful.

Watch football with your dad, cook dinner with your mom—any kind of small activity means a lot. Share with them some of the things you are experiencing at college, and be open to hearing their thoughts and answering their questions. You may find that you really like your parents, even if you wouldn't choose to go back and live at home again.

Thank Your High School Teachers—and Mean It

High school may seem like a distant memory to you now, but it was four years of hard work, determination, and support from your teachers that got you into college. College breaks often start earlier and end later than high school ones, so if you have time before the holidays, round up some of your high school buddies and pay a visit to your favorite high school teachers while you're home. Tell them about college and all you're experiencing, and thank them for all the help they provided you as a high school student. Similarly, make a point to thank everyone who helped you get where you are: coaches, mentors, guidance counselors, and family members. Seeing you as a happy, active, and thankful college student will make their day!

Lend a Helping Hand

If you do not need or cannot find a job while you are home for winter break, you still need to do something to fill your time. You might consider shadowing a professional in your desired career field. You could also volunteer at a community service organization such as an animal shelter or soup kitchen. These experiences can help you in many ways. If you shadow a professional, you will gain good experience and a valuable reference for future jobs or internships. And if you contribute to your community through volunteer work, you will be doing something fulfilling and worthwhile—as opposed to sleeping in every day and watching a lot of television.

Reflect on Everything

Granted, you've only been a college student for four months, but your life has certainly changed since you graduated from high school. Lie on your bed at home and think about how everything is different now, and reflect on the new person you've become. Is there anything you would like to have done differently? What are you most looking forward to in the spring? Do you have any advice for your old self? Hang out with a local friend and reminisce about your memories and old habits. Thinking about the past can keep you grounded in the future.

Read a Book

Many experts say that to be a good writer and a good learner, you should be a good reader. Make a point over your break this week to visit your local library or borrow a book from a friend. Find one that interests you—whether it be mystery, young adult, nonfiction, essays, poetry collections, or the dictionary—and make time to sit and read it.

Reading for pleasure is one of the great hallmarks of successful students. Even if reading is right up there with cleaning the toilet for activities you don't enjoy, keeping up a pattern of reading comprehension over break will make it easier for you to transition back into scholar mode when the semester begins again. Check out the *New York Times*' bestseller list in your favorite category and see what's hot out there, or ask a friend what they are reading.

Review Your Financial Patterns

Today, sit back and think about your fall semester. No, not the parties and the friends you made; think about your spending patterns over the few months you were an active student. Look at your old bank statements to see ATM withdrawals and electronic purchases and try to pinpoint the major purchases you made—or the amount of minor purchases you made that equaled big bucks.

Small-item purchases may seem like no big deal at the time, but they certainly add up throughout a few months. If you noticed frequent ATM withdrawals on the weekends, try and remember what you spent the cash on. If your bank statements reveal you're spending $20 a week at Starbucks, note that is about *$300* you've spend on grande mocha latte beverages.

If you notice and understand your spending habits, you'll be in a better position to correct them as they are happening. (Oh, and ask someone for a travel coffee mug for your next birthday.)

Run for It!

If the idea of running makes you tremble in your sneakers, or if you've tried running before and didn't enjoy it, odds are it was because you were trying to do too much too quickly. It's very easy to hear "running a few miles" and think you're perfectly capable of doing it, but unless your body is prepared you'll end up winded or injured. If you're all clear medically to try a jogging program, consider going for it—the only equipment you need is a good pair of sneakers, so the cost-effectiveness is right there.

Try walking for a half-hour a day—no running just yet. Once you feel comfortable walking a fairly long distance, alternate walking and jogging a few minutes apiece. Make sure you alternate, even if you feel you can jog more than a few minutes. You're building up your stamina. Slowly increase the time you're jogging so it outpaces the time you are walking. Several popular walk-to-run programs say that it will probably take you a few months to get to a comfortable jogging pace, but even then, use common sense. Stop when you're tired or winded and make sure you hydrate yourself before and after your run.

Bring a friend with you. It's good company and a good rule of thumb—if you are too out of breath to keep a conversation going, you're overdoing it. And if it's too chilly or snowy to run outside, find a gym with treadmills or investigate local indoor tracks.

Understand That Change Is Good

It's only been a few months, but when you reunite with your old high school gang you may be shocked at how much your dear old friends have changed since the summer. Some of them will have made new, close friends at school, or even have boyfriends or girlfriends now. It can be a shock and you can feel saddened, threatened, and insecure about your status as their friend, resulting in a nasty attitude.

Don't be unkind or jealous. You have your own new pals as well, so don't begrudge your friends for having theirs. Ask questions about your friends' experiences, listen to their stories, and offer advice if they ask for it. Your friends are still your friends, and change is a part of life. Promise to visit, and invite them to visit you. You'll always have this time together, no matter what happens, so don't waste it by scowling and being rude.

Note: Winter break is also a good time to take a look at any romantic relationships you're involved in, particularly if your hometown significant other is still in high school or at another college. Are you both happy with the arrangement? Do you want to keep the relationship going? Have a serious talk if you're having doubts.

See What's Happening While You're Away

Most colleges lock up for break, but it's possible that your school has a few events going on. It may be too much trouble or cause problems for you to go back for one of these events, but if you're close by and are looking for something to do or want to help out, check out your college's website and see what's going on over winter break.

Winter break is often the time colleges host transfer orientation sessions, where students enrolling in the school from other colleges for spring semester come and learn more about the university. Shoot an e-mail to the coordinator and ask if there is anything you can do to help, from handing out brochures to breaking down tables and chairs—this not only gives you something to do, but it also puts your name in a few people's ears. When it comes to jobs on campus or internships, this is a great connection to have!

Reach Out to an Old Friend

If there is a friend or classmate you haven't seen since graduation and are curious about, track them down and give them a call asking how they are. Use Facebook if you don't have their telephone number; either ask them for it via a private message or send a private message to say hello.

Ask how their first semester of college went, or how they are doing. If your friendship was rocky when you last saw each other, consider this an olive branch. Wish them well, and ask if they would like to hang out before break ends. Be considerate of their relationship status, if that applies here, and make sure to keep your correspondence on the level.

College can make you see how silly high school fights or fading friendships can be, so try to keep your friends in your life. It's as easy as texting or messaging on social media to keep in touch. If you don't get a response, then chalk it up to experience and move on.

Map Out Your First Day

You remember your first day of fall semester, right? Even though you knew where your classes were and what time you needed to be there, you still felt nervous and unsure. Shake those feelings of doubt and anxiety for spring by mapping out your first day!

Look at your schedule and ask the following, writing down your answers and making a "day map":

- When is my first class? When are my other classes?
- What time should I wake up?
- How much time should I give myself for getting ready?
- How much time will I need for breakfast?
- Do I have any assignments or readings I should complete before the first day?
- Do I have any breaks in between classes?
- If so, do I have enough time to eat/nap/work out? If not, where should I go?
- When should I have lunch?
- Should I bring any snacks to tide me over?
- What time does my day officially end?

Having a clear route of your day can help you manage your time and keep you from running around like a maniac trying to make it to class on time while shoving a doughnut in your mouth and brushing your bed head!

SPRING SEMESTER

Welcome back! Let's hope your winter break was restful, because spring semester is already underway. You know how this goes; after all, you've done this before, right? Not exactly. Spring semester is a little different and can be more fast-paced than fall, but it's nothing you can't handle!

Be a Good Loser

As you return and get geared up for a new semester, you might view your grades from the fall for the first time. If your grade is lower than you anticipated, feel free to e-mail your professor and ask why. Don't be combative; simply state that you are surprised by your grade and would like to discuss it further. Track your performance in the class throughout the semester and calculate your grades on other assignments without your final, then gauge what your score must have been to result in that final grade. It's possible, although very rare, that there was a grading error. It's also possible that your professor will not be able to return your message right away (and may be buried in similar e-mails and voice-mails from other students), so be patient.

There is nothing wrong with advocating for yourself, but consider your performance. If you studied hard for the final but did the bare minimum for the rest of the semester, or vice versa, your grade may be spot-on. Don't burn a bridge with a professor that you may meet again in another class! Not getting a good grade can be upsetting, but consider your own role in it before you fire off an angry e-mail, and learn your lesson for the new slew of classes you're taking this semester.

Insure Your Stuff

If you had an unfortunate experience of being robbed last semester, or simply want to have some extra security when it comes to your things, consider insuring your belongings. You should do this if you have many high-level, expensive items that you absolutely need to have with you on campus and cannot afford to replace or repair yourself.

Colleges usually do not carry insurance that covers theft or damage to student property. Unless the school is negligent, which rarely happens, you'll be responsible for repair and replacement costs of damaged or stolen items. If your family's homeowners insurance does not cover your belongings while you're at college, you should consider signing up for renters insurance, either through a school-sponsored program or an insurance agency.

Adapt to a New Schedule

Your fall schedule may have been ideal for your fitness routine, but odds are you made some adjustments yourself and accommodated your habits to fit. Your spring schedule may have afternoon classes instead of morning, gaps where you didn't have gaps before, or classes in buildings on the other side of campus. If you're a routine-minded person, this can throw everything you built last semester into a tailspin.

Work with your schedule as best you can. If a course you absolutely need is only offered in the middle of Ultimate Frisbee practice, propose that your team practice an hour later. If you typically go to the gym in the morning before class but now your schedule has you up and ready at 8 A.M., consider moving your gym session to the afternoon. If you have a class way across campus and far from the gym, use this distance to work up a sweat—avoid taking public transportation unless you're concerned for your safety.

In college, your schedule changes every semester, so it's best to learn flexibility rather than just giving up on your fitness and health.

Say No to All Drugs

Marijuana has been a popular drug among college students for decades. It clearly affects memory, and college students in particular can't risk this damage while taking classes. Also, marijuana is easily detectable, so students who use it run a great risk of being caught by college authorities or law enforcement officials.

Ecstasy is another drug—used in many clubs—that you may run into. Repeated used of ecstasy has been shown to do irreparable damage to the human brain. Cocaine, heroin, and LSD are also found on many college campuses. The dangers of these drugs aren't limited to their physical effects; taking drugs can also cause you to suffer academically, socially, and economically. In addition to being dangerous, these substances are very expensive.

Steroids remain a popular drug choice among a small group of college students. Athletes or students who enjoy working out a lot may take steroids to help their performance. However, steroids can do serious and sometimes irreparable damage to the body, and athletes who are caught using steroids can be excluded from competition, lose scholarships, and harm their team's reputation.

Drug offenses can follow you for the rest of your life. Don't think it's a big deal? Well, if you get caught with any illegal drugs, the offense can come up in a background check years from now when you're applying for jobs, and a drug conviction can automatically disqualify you for financial aid, scholarships, study abroad opportunities, and work study, which for many students means the end of college. So think twice before taking them!

Schedule Your "Wants" and "Needs" for the Semester

Once you have placed the big items in your schedule (like classes and study time), it's time to figure out when you are going to do everything else. The key to managing this tension and effectively managing your time is to create a balanced schedule. If you do this successfully, you will be able to tend to all of the "needed" items and most of the "wanted" items, creating a happy lifestyle.

Several important parts of your college life should always take precedence over leisure activities in your schedule. These needs include your education, your health, and, possibly, your job. These items deserve extra time in your schedule and extra attention in your life. If you don't do well in your classes, take care of your health (both mental and physical), and maintain a job (if this income pays your tuition), then your college career could end as quickly as it began.

Once you have allowed enough time for your needs, be sure to allocate some time to your wants. These activities include extra-curricular interests such as sports and clubs, entertainment such as movies, concerts, and plays, and general relaxation and social time. Though you will not have time to participate in every club or sport that interests you, and you probably won't have enough time (or money) for a weekly trip to the movies, you should be able to find a balance between your needs and wants.

Having a set schedule makes living your daily life much easier, because many decisions have already been made on your behalf—by you!

Ask Someone on a Date

If that cute guy from your psychology class last semester is in another class of yours this semester, or if that nice girl from the coffee shop is working the morning shift again, consider plucking up the courage to ask for a date. The worst thing they can do is say no, so be brave and give it a try!

Fortunately, your college campus is full of fun and easy dating opportunities. When you have found one person whom you want to get to know better, consider these activities:

- See a movie on campus or at a local theater
- Go to a sporting event
- Watch TV in your room or the residence hall lounge
- Eat dinner off campus
- Take a walk through a residential neighborhood
- Visit a local tourist attraction
- Study together
- Go to a local club
- Visit an art show or campus museum

While you're dating, keep two important things in mind. First, be a good listener. This will impress the person you're dating and will allow you to get to know her better. Second, and perhaps most importantly, be yourself. You want to know who she really is and she wants to know the same thing about you. Telling lies or exaggerating stories will only mislead and confuse your date.

Take a Yoga Class

It's not just sitting, stretching, and breathing, you know! There is more to yoga than stretching your body into contorted positions in order to attain peace of mind. Yoga is an integrated system; a philosophy of life with a rich body of wisdom. It provides guidelines for thinking, action, diet, healing, and relationships, plus it can strengthen your arms, legs, and core. Your school may offer a yoga class in its fitness center, but if not, ask about any local studios or gyms that may offer it.

There are several simple techniques you can use to adopt yoga in your daily life. For example, as you prepare to start your day, deliberately slow your breathing by taking deeper breaths. Slow down your physical actions and train your eyes on only what you are doing. Choose one daily routine. For example, if you are combing your hair, move deliberately, watching your hand movements and posture. You do not need a mirror because it can be distracting. Think only of what you are doing and nothing else. The next time you perform this action, be as deliberate as before, but change your movements and posture to accomplish the same thing.

Recite an affirmation that reminds you of your essential goal for the present. Phrase it as though you have already accomplished that goal. For example, use positive affirmations such as "I am strong for others" or "I am healthy." As you say the words, picture those sounds as being as pure and colorless as the air that enters your body.

Start Treating School Like Your Job

College is a full-time job. You should start treating it like one if you aren't already.

Most adults wake up each morning, get dressed, grab breakfast or coffee, and race out the door to work so they can provide for their families. Well, guess what? Your job is to be the best student you can be. And it isn't always easy. So how can you do your job really well? Just like a "regular" employee: showing up on time, working hard to impress the boss, being nice and pleasant at work, being a team player, demonstrating leadership, and through community involvement or volunteer work. How do people get promoted and attain positive job recognition from bosses? They work hard by committing to doing the best job possible. You can be successful at school with the same method! Treat your professor's assignments and classes like a boss giving you a work assignment.

For example, let's say your boss for Introduction to Art History stresses that he values the importance of remembering the names and dates of important pieces of art. Now you know what he wants: memorization. Make a stack of flash cards for yourself with a picture of the piece of art and its name and artist, or highlight your class notes or textbook and memorize away. Or, perhaps your philosophy teacher tells you his class will be in a lecture format and that you will be quizzed exclusively on what he tells you in lectures. Now you know to pay extra-close attention to the lectures.

Remember, if you don't show up to work or slack off, you get fired. Same is true in college!

Bottle It Up!

Instead of purchasing bottled water and drinks from vending machines or from the local café, invest in a reusable water bottle to fill up in the morning and bring with you to class, the gym, and to meetings. Like purchasing coffee, bottled beverages can slowly take a toll on your finances, even if you only have one per day. So why not purchase a nice water bottle that you can fill with *free* water from your dining hall or from a water fountain?

There are numerous studies and debates about chemical leakage from certain types of plastic water bottles, so go for a metal one or one that is clearly marked "BPA-free." Your school bookstore will have some that will keep you hydrated and show your school spirit at the same time. Bottoms up!

Take Care of Your Skin

You are a relatively clean college student, right? You shower every day and change your clothes, and you try to keep up your appearance for social and health reasons, but are you taking good care of your skin while you're at school? You may be having problems with acne, which is completely normal. You've spent time at home and are back at school, adjusting to the water in the showers and your new schedule. Acne is a disorder of the sebaceous glands that causes clogged pores and pimples on the face (and occasionally the neck, chest, and upper back). Acne occurs when the sebaceous glands produce too much sebum, which can combine with dead skin cells and block the pores. The pores can become infected (most often with bacteria), creating more inflammation. If your face wash isn't cutting it, here are a few herbal remedies you can try:

- Calendula (Calendula officinalis): An infusion of calendula can replace commercial toners made with alcohol and other potentially drying ingredients.
- Guggul (Commiphora wightii, C. mukul): Modern research shows oral doses can be as effective against severe (nodulocystic) acne as the drug tetracycline.
- Juniper (Juniperus communis): Native Americans made an infusion from the branches of this evergreen shrub to use as an oil-balancing hair and skin wash.
- Tea tree (Melaleuca alternifolia): Research shows that a topical tea tree preparation works as well as benzoyl peroxide in clearing pimples, with far fewer side effects.

Also, even in the dead of winter, remember to apply sunscreen to your face and other exposed body parts!

Be a Smart Dater

You may have scored a date with a person you like a lot, but remember to date sensibly and smartly. Successful dating does not mean that you and he will be together forever. Dating is a process through which you get to know someone better, and you will likely date many people before you find one special person whom you want to be with for a long time. It is rare that a person marries the first person she dates. To fully appreciate this, ask your parents and relatives how many people they dated before finding their spouses. Their answers may surprise you. If you go on a few dates and things aren't clicking, don't think of the dates as failures. Every time you date someone, you always learn a little more about yourself.

Be wary of someone who:

- Pushes for a quick and serious commitment
- Pressures you to drink when you don't want to
- Pressures you to engage in sexual acts when you don't want to
- Threatens violence or makes you feel unsafe
- Uses physical or verbal abuse to get you to do things
- Is jealous and possessive of you and your time
- Threatens self-harm if you leave

This also goes for your friends. If you or a friend is dating someone who behaves this way, don't be afraid to seek help from the campus police. This behavior is not okay, and it's certainly not how people treat people they love, so be smart and take care of yourself.

Visit Your Student Activities Office

On any given day a variety of activities are happening across your campus, and this is especially true at the beginning of a new semester. A handful of these activities are organized and sponsored solely by faculty or staff, but most events occur because students have made them happen. You can become involved in this exciting experience by joining one of the many programming boards on campus.

Your student activities office is probably the hub of event planning on campus. The administrators in this office work with students to help sponsor fun and meaningful activities for the campus community. They will have opportunities for students to join programming boards for big concerts, fall and spring festivals, homecoming events, comedians and other specialized entertainment, and cocurricular events like lectures and exhibitions. The student activities office is also likely to have a sizable budget and needs student help to determine how best to spend that money.

Simply approaching your student activities office is the easiest way to get involved on a campus programming board. In most cases, you will not have to be elected, but you will need to regularly attend all meetings and help set up and clean up after events. While you can certainly volunteer for a committee that especially interests you, be sure to inquire about committees with only a few members. If you join a small committee, you will have the opportunity to have a larger voice right from the start.

Learn about a Friend's Culture or Religion

Even if you have no religious background, you can still attend the services, meetings, and events of most campus religious groups. If you are interested in a particular group, consider attending a meeting or mass with a friend who is already a member. She can give you a little background about the organization, as well as introduce you to her friends in the group. As with anything, be respectful of your friend's organization and their ceremonies.

Religious organizations offer students the chance to continue practicing a lifelong faith, begin practicing a new religion, or just become a part of a new community. These commitments can be very simple—you could plan to attend meetings once in a while—or you can take on more responsibility by becoming an event coordinator or the treasurer of the group's funds. If you are interested in learning more about the religious organizations offered at your college, ask your activities office staff for information.

Culture and religion are closely intertwined for many students, and religious organizations often help students connect to their cultural heritage while they're away from home. In other cases the two are slightly or completely different, and for these students, involvement with a cultural organization helps bridge the gap between a home community and a new college life. Most colleges have organizations to accommodate almost any cultural group.

Fight Stress Before It Even Arrives

Your semester is just starting, so you might not have had a moment of stress yet. But you remember well from last semester how not-fun being stressed out can be. Stress is a natural part of life. Quite often, it's psychological stress that gets you out of bed in the morning or to the gym in the evening. It's what makes you perform well at the office or in the classroom and do basically everything that you need to survive. Unfortunately, too much stress—problems that go on too long or demand too many of your resources—can wreak havoc on your health. Chronic, unresolved stress has been linked to a host of diseases, including cardiovascular disease and cancer. It's also been tied to many mental disorders, such as depression.

- Studies have linked lemon balm, an extract from the mint family, to relieving stress. Today, pick up some lemon herbal tea or lemon lotion to keep in your room for when those stressful moments strike. Brew a cup of tea or rub the lotion on your hands and inhale the scent.
- Prepare a stress battle plan for when those feelings come up. If you think you'll stress about a certain class, think of some ways to fight back, such as asking your professor about difficult assignments in advance.
- A lot of school-related stress is also grounded in guilt, especially when the problems are a result of a lack of effort on the student's part. Avoid this by staying up-to-date in your classes and attending every day.

Look Into Online Classes

If your schedule is becoming too much to handle and you don't want to quit any clubs, check out your school's catalog for any online classes you can take in the future. Many schools are adopting the online class format to reach a wider student base (such as older students with families, students who live far away, or professional students who work during the times classes are typically held). Your workload will not be lighter for these classes—you'll still be responsible for the same amount of homework and assignments—but the relief of not having one more place to be during your busy day may be enough to make it worth it.

Some classes are conducted via Skype or iChat, and all students have virtual face-to-face dialogue with their professors weekly regardless of their time zone or location. This is called a synchronous format of learning. Other courses take place through chat rooms, online bulletin board postings, and text dialogues, which is known as asynchronous learning. For some classes, professors introduce themselves to students through a YouTube clip and then conduct a text- and e-mail–based course for the remainder of the term. In others, students never see a professor, but just "listen" through messages or postings.

It may not be advisable to take an online course in your first year, but it's a great option for summer classes when you move back home!

Explore Job Opportunities Around Town

You've probably noticed already that this semester is a little easier in terms of scheduling. You typically know now how much time classes require, how many hours a day you have free, etc. Now would be a good time to explore the possibility of a part-time job in your college community. Don't be too proud; money is money and if a local place is willing to work with your schedule, there is no reason why you shouldn't explore the opportunity. Here are some possible jobs for you to consider:

- Ice cream scooper
- Coffee shop worker
- Grocery clerk or bagger
- Fast-food worker
- Landscaper or lawn mower
- Car wash attendant
- Babysitter
- Dog walker
- Retail stocker
- Shopping mall kiosk attendant
- Restaurant host or waiter

Your brush with the working world will put things into clearer perspective for you. And you'll never look at a $5 bill the same way again once you realize what it takes to earn it!

Get to Know the Superfoods!

College diets are never the easiest things to work with—with your schedule, the dining hall menu, and your appetite, you really need to make each meal count! Try to work in a few "superfoods" when you go for your meals.

Superfoods are particular types of food that contain high amounts of phytonutrients, which are necessary for the proper functioning of the body. They provide important health benefits, but taken as a whole they become a major defense against the ravages of free radicals, environmental toxins, and heavy-metal contamination. Twenty foods are almost unanimously found on all the superfood lists. Here are some common ones you can probably find in your dining hall, whole or as part of a meal. Stock up on these:

1. Apples (fight free radicals)
2. Blueberries (most antioxidants ever)
3. Broccoli (helps prevent cancer)
4. Garlic (nature's antibiotic)
5. Avocados (full of good fat)
6. Beans (lower cholesterol)
7. Kale (powerhouse of nutrients)
8. Green tea (liquid antioxidants)
9. Oats (the wonder grain)
10. Sweet potatoes (rich in vitamin A)
11. Yogurt (builds strong bones)

Know the Ins and Outs of Apartment Living

You may be tiring of the residence hall life, and think you would prefer renting an apartment next year. Start looking and studying up now, because you're not the only student at your school interested in renting one of the finite apartments around town. Some things to know:

- You have many more responsibilities at an apartment. You clean your own bathroom, you pay for rent and utilities, and you are responsible for your apartment's upkeep and maintenance. There is no RA to keep you on track.
- If you don't live on campus, you are technically a "commuter" student at your school. That means no meal plan, so budget for groceries.
- You may think you're saving money by living off campus, but really crunch those numbers and make sure—between rent, groceries, utilities, and other expenses, you're spending a lot more than you think.
- Being off campus isolates you from campus activities, and you may miss out on interesting events and opportunities. Is that okay with you?
- If you move in with roommates, there is no RA or housing office to help you with disputes.
- Safety is an issue in an apartment. Don't let strangers know that you live alone if you do not have roommates. For example, on your answering machine message say, "We are not home now" to give the impression that several people live in your apartment. Similarly, only put your last name on your mailbox.

Find an Intramural

Intramurals are a great opportunity for you to have a lot of fun with new friends and get some good exercise in the process. You will see advertisements for intramural sports programs in your school newspaper, posted online, or at the sports center. When you see one that interests you, gather people from your residence hall and register a team. If you are feeling competitive, recruit those people who you know are good athletes. If you just want to have fun, pick people whom you enjoy spending time with and who will not take the competition too seriously. Also, you will get the opportunity to name your team. This may seem silly, but take a little extra time to brainstorm about fun team names as a group. You may come up with a name that is intimidating or funny, or one that incorporates the first letters of all your teammates' names. You and your teammates may even decide to make your own T-shirts or jerseys to wear in competition.

If you don't want to start your own team or can't find anybody who is interested in a particular sport, check with the intramural office, which is probably located somewhere in the athletics department. Often this office will have a sign-up sheet for people who are interested in playing but don't have a team. Another group needing one or two more players may contact you and invite you to join them. You will still get the opportunity to play and have fun, as well as meet new people.

Intramurals are a year-round occurrence, though the sports will vary by season. Regular participation in intramurals will help you learn new skills and keep your body healthy, and you'll be able to interact with other students that you might not otherwise meet.

Make Plans to Invite a Professor to Lunch

You may feel incredibly awkward doing this, but try to get over that. You will need your professors when you try to find a job, work with a community service coordinator, plan classes, and much, much more. Professors are also great receptors for you to try to work out your academic (and sometimes even social) concerns. They will make useful suggestions to help you improve, and they appreciate students who come to them to seek help. Don't be afraid or intimidated, no matter what your classmates may say about a teacher. Professors select this profession because they genuinely want to educate and connect with students.

If you have a favorite professor now, ask a few classmates to come with you and invite your professor out for coffee or to grab lunch at the dining hall. Discuss the class and the subject matter, and share personal stories and interests. If you feel strange about meeting with a professor you currently have in a class, ask a professor you had last semester whose class you enjoyed.

It also won't hurt to stop by during your professor's office hours to have a conversation. These connections last a lifetime and are important to cultivate now.

Be Zen Today

When you hear the word "Zen," you probably think of a blissed-out-looking person sitting, completely at peace. But being "Zen" isn't the absence of thought; it's actually letting your mind wander and go naturally where it wants to go. Zen teachings speak considerably about the mind: its tendency to wander, run a habitual course, and become absorbed. It is referred to as the monkey mind, because like a monkey it jumps from branch to branch.

The activity of the mind is, paradoxically, "mindless." There is, however, more to the dimension of mind than this activity. And that's what Zen meditation is meant to enter. Sit on your bed or on a yoga mat on the floor and give it a try.

- Attention: Becoming aware of the mind's activity. It is possible to detach from thoughts by viewing them as each passes by. Pay attention to the mind.
- Visualization: There are some "countering" techniques that can be used to slow the mind's moving from thought to thought. Visual scenes, seed thoughts, everyday objects, and actions may be in the immediate environment or mentally evoked.
- Focus: Each time the mind wanders from a visualization, it is brought back. Naturally, this goes back to developing attention and visualization, but one must be gentle in the process, and not force or concentrate the mind.
- Quieting: The senses are quieted to achieve and maintain focus. This may entail entering a serene environment in which all stimulation is minimal and reflects a theme of serenity.

Put the Highlighter Down and Step Away from the Book!

Some students are "highlighter happy," tackling a required reading assignment by using a bright yellow highlighter as a machete. As they read, they highlight anything that looks remotely important, could be worth remembering, might be on a test, or is confusing. When a highlighter-happy student's mind starts to wander, she doesn't really worry: as long as something is highlighted, she believes she has "covered" it. When highlighter-happy people are done reading, more of the page is bright yellow rather than white. They are satisfied with their work, certain that they have read the chapter thoroughly.

Unfortunately, these students are often surprised when they do poorly on the final exam. Don't be this student. Highlighting can be a useful way to call out important points, but when you overdo it, all you get is a yellow page that you haven't really read and a headache from all the fumes. Try copying important points into your notebook instead and referencing the page number where the information came from.

Another point to consider: when you try to sell back your $50 textbook at the end of the semester (with the pages yellow and crispy from ink), the bookstore may offer you a substantially lower amount than you expected, or not accept it at all. All that the clerk asks is, "Who wants to buy a neon yellow textbook?"

Look Into Becoming a Resident Assistant Next Year

Being an RA is rewarding in many ways: you get to help new students acclimate to college life, you're involved in several campus activities, and it is technically a job so you receive money for it. If you're interested in student activities and campus life, it may be a perfect job for you.

RAs are usually students with at least one semester of college under their belts. The job requires patience, a passion for working with people, and the fortitude to remain confident in the face of criticism. The benefits include a stipend or a discount on tuition or room and board for their services, and they often get residence hall rooms to themselves. The skills that they learn in this job are extremely transferable to most careers that they will embrace in the future.

Talk to your RA about the channels he or she went through to get the position. You'll probably have to interview with your student life office and undergo an orientation period, and that process typically starts in the spring. Get on it!

Watch Out for Germs

Since you're in the height of the typical flu season, you may notice that you're getting colds and sore throats more often than usual. Living in close quarters (as one does in a college residence hall) means living with lots of germs. You might get sick more frequently than you did in high school. Colds, coughs, and sore throats are the most common complaints on campus, followed by stomach distress. If your college has health services, they can usually provide you with some over-the-counter medication that will make you feel better.

To avoid these germs altogether, make sure you consistently wash your hands with warm soap and water, use tissues when you sneeze (or sneeze into the crook of your elbow if a tissue can't be found), and rub hand sanitizer on your hands, all the way up to your wrists and in between your fingers. Drink plenty of fluids, especially orange juice and tea.

If you are spiking a fever, or have unusual pain or distress, make sure you access health services immediately. After hours, you should call public safety. They can determine if a trip to the emergency room is necessary or if you can wait until the following day to be seen by someone on campus.

An important plea from your professor and your classmates: Try not to attend classes when you are sick. While you want to try to have a perfect attendance record, your teachers and classmates do not want to be sneezed or coughed on. E-mail your professor in advance and explain your situation, being sure to attach any assignments due that day to the e-mail or having a friend turn them in for you.

Be on Alert for Eating Disorders

Eating disorders affect between 1 and 3 percent of the population, and various problems with eating, exercise, and weight affect many more. These illnesses are especially prevalent on college campuses, where physical appearance and popularity are common topics of conversation. Eating disorders can have serious psychological and physical consequences; therefore, you must be able to recognize signs of an eating problem in yourself and your friends, as well as know where to get help. Some signs to watch out for include:

- Visible and/or rapid weight loss or gain
- Frequent complaints of fatigue or feeling cold when others do not
- Appearance of illness: pale complexion, circles under eyes, thinning or dull hair
- Eating very little or not at all, or more than would be expected at one sitting
- Disappearing after meals or being observed vomiting after meals
- Exercising excessively
- Seeming depressed or anxious
- Making negative and distorted comments about own body or weight

If you are concerned that a friend may have an eating problem, it is important to discuss it with the person. For example, you could say, "I've noticed that you rarely eat meals with us anymore. I'm worried about you." Suggest that the student consider talking to a professional at the campus counseling or health center. Consider offering to accompany the person to her first appointment.

Ask a Professor for a Letter of Recommendation

Whether you're applying for a summer program, a job, or an internship, you'll need a letter of recommendation (probably at least two) from a professor. These recommendations are testimonies that educators provide your colleges, graduate schools, or future employers about your performance and contributions in their classes. These recommendations are taken very seriously and serve as an important piece of selection criteria. Sometimes they are the only way an evaluator can get a real sense of who you are as a classmate or team player, which offers them an indication of your potential.

- Make sure your professor is familiar with you and your work. Don't show up to your lecture professor's office for the first time and ask—you're one of the hundreds he teaches, and one of the hundreds that ask him for personalized letters.
- When you ask your professor to write you a recommendation, provide him with a copy of your student resume, which lists your extracurricular activities, community service, awards, honors, jobs, hobbies, and interests.
- Ask your professor to write a letter well in advance of the deadline. Your professor is very busy, and to expect him to drop everything to write your letter, which is due tomorrow, is not wise.
- Provide your professor with a sample of graded work from her class with comments if applicable.
- Write a thank-you note and let the professor know whether you were admitted into the program, etc., or when you expect to find out.

Plan a Spring Break Trip

Your spring break is approaching! With extensive planning and a big enough budget, you can transform your break into an exotic vacation.

The first decision you must make is what kind of vacation you want for spring break. Beach packages have long been the most popular among undergraduates, but this is not the only option. In recent years, many companies have begun offering ski vacation packages. The next decision to make about your trip is who to take with you. How many people can split one package? Which friends are fun travel partners? Which friends will get everyone in trouble? Everyone involved must have the same goals for the trip. You're going on a spring break trip to get away from the pressures and hassles of college life and to truly enjoy yourself. Therefore, you need to choose your group carefully.

One detail that you need to seriously consider is lodging. What does "hotel accommodations" mean? Ask the company to elaborate on the size, style, and location of the rooms. Read their website carefully and be very skeptical if there is no telephone number listed.

Another important element is travel. You can assume that getting to and from your spring break vacation location will be your responsibility, but what about after you are there? If your hotel is three miles from the beach, will a shuttle be provided? Will you have to walk through a rough neighborhood to get to the nightlife? Is there at least a shuttle to get you to and from the airport? If such services are not included in your package and you plan to take taxis, be sure to build that into your spring break budget.

Take a Quick Trip

You may not have the budget to take an elaborate break trip, or simply have no desire for the traditional trips, service opportunities, or visits home. There are still a variety of options for you, and they don't necessarily involve studying for hours on end. One-, two-, or three-day trips can provide the perfect getaway for those who want to conserve money and still have some fun.

Break periods give students a wonderful opportunity to take quick trips. For example, if you are "stuck" on campus during a break, consider taking day trips to local attractions. If your campus is close to a national park, a historical monument, or a museum, you have a wonderful opportunity to see something new. Get together with other students who have remained on campus for the break and go visit.

Another option for a quick trip is visiting old or new friends. You might go see a high school friend who is attending another college. Even if your break does not coincide with his, he may still enjoy having a visitor, showing you around his campus, and introducing you to his friends. Another option would be to visit the home of one of your college friends. Someone who lives only a few hours from your college may enjoy having you come over for a day or two.

Quick trips may also include going to see a show or a concert. If your campus is in or near a large city, it is worth seeing what shows or other cultural events are taking place in that city during your break period. And even if you won't have a tan when classes resume, you will have enjoyed several fun experiences.

Pack Your Books Along with Your Bathing Suit

Why in the world would someone want to study during spring break? If you are going to do schoolwork, then doesn't it just make sense to stay on campus and set up camp in the library? Absolutely not. Spring break is an optimal time to get away from campus and recharge your batteries as you prepare for the last part of the semester. However, a little studying during this week of rest will serve you very well. Your classes may not meet during spring break, but that does not mean that there are not impending assignments, papers, and projects that need to be done.

As much as you don't believe it, you will not spend every second partying on break. You'll need rest and relaxation, and might find yourself stretched out on your bed before dinner with a few hours to kill. Why not brush up on your class notes from psychology while you unwind?

The danger of taking study materials with you on break is that they may become damaged or lost. For this reason, you should back up your items—put copies on flash drives or on external hard drives and make photocopies of notes. Leave your original items at school so you will not fall behind if something happens to your materials on break.

Learn to Love Your Spring Break Budget

You booked the hotel, the flight, and the airport shuttle, but one of the most overlooked details of spring break packages is food. You are going on this vacation for the fun, the location, and the friends, but you still have to eat. It is unlikely that your package will include all meals, but some packages include items such as a continental breakfast or some sort of buffet unless you are going to an all-inclusive resort. Find out what is included and what meals you will have to provide for yourself. And remember to build meals into your spring break budget. Also include items that relate to eating and drinking, such as cover charges for clubs. These are the seemingly small expenses that can exhaust your budget before the week is half over.

Be wary of companies that offer spring break packages. The glossy photos and well-designed fliers will make promises before you even read the first word of their advertisements—and they love to throw around the phrase "all-inclusive," which means your initial payment covers your entire trip—but might not apply to food and drink. In fact, the first few words of the ad probably won't mean a whole lot for your spring break experience, but the last paragraph is critical. Before you sign up for any spring break package, read through every bit of fine print. Be sure you understand all the details before you hand over your money.

Know What and How Much You Drink

On spring break, you may run into situations where the alcohol is flowing and everyone is having a good time, particularly if you are in a country with a lower drinking age. Bear in mind that your weight and body fat affect how your body processes alcohol. Heavier people can usually drink more without feeling the effects of alcohol. However, a person with high body fat content will feel the effects of alcohol more quickly than a person of similar body type who has less body fat. For example, a 200-pound couch potato will feel the effects of alcohol sooner than a 200-pound linebacker.

A frightening danger of alcohol use is the amount of time it takes the body to process alcohol. In general, one beer, a glass of wine, and a one-ounce shot of liquor each contain the same amount of alcohol. It will take your body approximately one hour to process one ounce of alcohol. So it is a good idea to limit yourself to one drink per hour, as long as you don't drink for hours on end. However, it's important to keep in mind that different drinks are usually consumed at different paces. While a beer is sipped over time, a shot is usually consumed all at once. Four shots in one hour will be more difficult for your body to manage than four beers in four hours.

If you insist on drinking over spring break, try alternating a glass of water between drinks and having a robust meal before going out partying. This can help absorb the alcohol and help your body process it faster. Of course, your best and safest bet is to opt for alcohol-free beverages.

Be Safe on Your Trip

Just like at school, basic safety rules should be followed when you're on your trip. Safety begins before you even leave, when you're still in the planning stages of your trip. Choose to include friends who share common values with you. For instance, other countries have very stiff penalties for transporting illegal drugs, and if one member of a party traveling together is found with such contraband, the entire group may be held responsible. If you have a friend who is an irresponsible party animal, you may spend the majority of your trip babysitting her and avoiding dangerous situations instead of having your own fun, which is not fair.

When traveling away from your home, especially in other countries, try to always stay in groups or pairs, never flash large sums of money in public, and always carry your passport safely. Ask your trip coordinator or hotel receptionist what the protocol is for emergencies, and share this information with your friends.

Call your parents when you arrive and let them know how things are going. The more people who are aware of where you are and what you are doing, the better.

Volunteer for Spring Break

A completely different type of spring break experience, one that has been gaining popularity on college campuses in recent years, is a break spent working on community service projects. Many times this sort of spring break is set up by an office or organization on campus. Your campus office of community service or religious life will have some information. The experience can involve staying at the college or within the local community, traveling to a different part of the country, or sometimes even traveling out of the country. While you probably won't be staying in hotels, you will be with other college students, and your basic needs will be met.

An alternate spring break trip can be hard work, but the work you will do is completely different from your day-to-day life at college and will ultimately leave you feeling refreshed and enthused. After spring break, when you're explaining how you spent your time to friends at college or family at home, the energy in your voice will convey to them that you were part of something special. Alternate spring break trips may include working with widely established organizations such as Habitat for Humanity, or with local entities such as domestic violence shelters. Some trips involve living and working at a Native American reservation or nature reserve. There are as many possibilities as there are people in need of your services. Only a week of your time could change the lives of dozens, or even hundreds, of people.

Investigate Internships

You might not be able to secure an internship your first year, but sooner is better when it comes to finding opportunities. Many of these internships carry through breaks, so your spring break could be booked up before you know it.

Your campus career center is an obvious place to go when searching for internships. Jump on their website today and see about making an appointment to speak with a career counselor. Some career centers even have counselors who specialize in internships. Most career centers will maintain a book of the most popular internships for students at that school. The same information may be available on the career center's website. If you don't find the type of internship that you are looking for using these resources, ask a career counselor about other lists or ways of searching for internships. There are a variety of guides for specific fields, such as human rights, environmental work, and sports.

The career center can do more than just help you find an internship. The counselors can help you figure out the best way to approach the internship sponsor. You may need to go through a formal process or contact a particular person at the host agency. There may also be a particular etiquette for making the initial contact, and the host agency is bound to have specific questions for you that go beyond your motivation for the internship. Your career center will help you prepare for all of these situations.

Learn Calming Travel Techniques

You are leaving for spring break soon, and you're nervous about the traveling you will be doing. Whether you have a problem with flying or just being in a car or on a train for long periods of time, or you're just nervous about the trip itself, know that you're not alone in this anxiety.

Today, take some deep breaths and relax, then think about all the fun memories you're about to make. Assure yourself that air travel is safe and that you'll pay careful attention to the flight staff. You'll also take every safety precaution you can once at your destination, and will do your best to make sure your friends do the same.

A group meeting before the trip begins just may be the key to reducing the stress before it even starts. Meetings are organized discussions where every group member contributes her opinion on a topic. Invite each member to share any concerns about the upcoming vacation as well as one or two activities she would like to do on vacation. Try to compromise with one another.

A quick tip: Leave a little room in your suitcase for souvenirs you'll pick up on your trip. Shipping costs can be a nightmare from some places.

SPRING BREAK

You may be on your way to a tropical island, venturing to a building site for Habitat for Humanity, or heading home for a week with the family. No matter what you're planning, make sure you devote time to keeping up with the lifestyle you live at college. These simple tips will help you.

Check Your Syllabus for the Week

You may be on spring break, but any projects or assignments assigned by your professor are still due the week that classes resume. Unlike winter or summer break, spring break happens in the middle of a semester, so you're still enrolled in the same classes when you leave and when you return. Make sure you allot some time to work on your assignments over break, even if it's only a short time every day. And don't leave it until the last minute or until you return from your trip! There is nothing worse—or more counterproductive—than having a panic-filled Sunday night in which you try to do all your homework, unpack, and put aloe on your sunburn.

Write It Down, Make It Real

Especially if you use a credit or debit card over your break (when you don't physically see the money leaving your hand), you can easily overspend or rack up some serious debt on trivial, small things like meals, rounds of drinks, and souvenirs. To help with this, bring a small notepad with you or find a note-taking app for your phone. Every time you make a purchase, note it. What did you buy? How much did you spend? What is your day's spending total? How about the whole week's total? The number may shock you, but seeing it in black and white can dissuade you from whipping out the plastic every time you see a cute T-shirt or want a drink.

Take a Half-Hour a Day to Move

You will be eating and drinking a lot of unhealthy things on your break, so you should make time to move and exercise every day.

Many times on vacation you'll take walking tours, see the sights, travel to local attractions, swim in the ocean, ski on a mountain, or dance until the wee hours in a nightclub, which is great—do it all, as long as you're moving! Even for as little as a half-hour a day, try to do some moderate exercise. Run on the beach in the morning. Take a refreshing walk with a friend. You'd be surprised what you can fit into your schedule.

Know That Crime Doesn't Take a Vacation

If you're going to a notably popular spring break spot, you'll most likely be among a crowd of college students who, like you, are looking forward to a fun week with their friends. But these vacation hot spots don't only attract other coeds: they also attract people who target these students for robberies, assaults, and fraud. Make new friends and be social, but be on your guard, and take simple precautions:

- Never accept a drink from a stranger, or let your friends accept one. If someone wants to buy you a drink, let the bartender or wait staff make and serve it.
- Never walk anywhere alone at night, particularly if you have been drinking. Don't let your friends do it, either.
- Keep an eye on your purse or wallet when you go out. Don't flash money or credit cards in public.
- Know the number for your credit card's member services line. If your card is lost or stolen, immediately call that number to cancel it, and any charges accrued since.
- Never go back to a hotel room or private area with someone you just met.
- Report any suspicious behavior to police. If you're wrong, that's okay. But if you're right, you're helping keep everyone around you safe.
- Stick with your friends. You arrive together, you leave together.

Don't Just Party

If you're in a new place on vacation, it can be tempting to just party and do the same activities every day for your whole trip. Don't deprive yourself of the sights and sounds of the locale you're in: visit some local beaches, see some museums, research any attractions or festivals and take time to check them out. You'll party enough, but you'll regret not doing more once your vacation's over.

Participate in Student Culture

If you're in a college break hot spot, there will definitely be some student-centered activities going on, like carnivals, television specials, and other break-themed events. Don't be afraid to get involved. Dance like a crazy person, laugh with your friends, and make memories. Be cautious and avoid any exploitative activities or people that make you uncomfortable, try not to let strangers take your picture, and above all, remember this and repeat it when you're feeling invincible: **The Internet is forever. The Internet is forever. The Internet is forever.**

Know When to Walk Away

The week is already over? It may seem like it flew by, but your time in paradise has ended. To avoid the panicked packing and getting everyone ready to go, start packing everything you don't need the night before you go. Leave out your clothes for the next day, your necessary toiletries, and travel supplies. Everything else can go into your suitcase. Place your dirty clothes on the bottom. Try rolling your clothes into tube shapes to save room.

When everyone else is running around like a chickens with their heads cut off the next day trying to pack, you'll be calm, serene, and ready to go.

Proofread Everything (And Then Have Someone Else Proof It, Too)

Always proofread your assignments before turning them in. When you proofread, you are looking for errors specifically in grammar, spelling, and punctuation. It can often be difficult to catch them because you're so accustomed to the essay that you simply do not see them. In order to proofread effectively, you need to read in a much more focused manner. Read through it once, twice, and then aloud so you can actually hear your words.

If you feel comfortable, give your assignment to a close friend, mentor, or teacher other than the one who assigned the paper to you. Sometimes fresh eyes can make you see things you missed or may not have considered. Conversely, beware that too many reviewers can take your voice out of the work you created. So pick and choose the feedback you receive and do not second-guess yourself or your instincts.

If you truly have concerns about a certain paper or assignment, bring it to your school's writing center. A trained tutor will help you work through your paper's issues and shape it. A writing center tutor will not correct your mistakes for you; she will only help you see them yourself. So don't expect to drop off your paper and pick it up later, like dry cleaning.

Get the App for That

If you have a smartphone, look for a budgeting app. Most apps usually cost a few dollars, but it could be money well spent once you start using it effectively. Most budgeting apps, like Mint, iReconcile, and Expenditure, require your banking information so they can alert to you low balances in your accounts, and help you set a budget by giving you a specific amount you can spend on a certain activity.

Mint.com also has a web version that you can use if you don't have a smartphone. You receive weekly updates and e-mails regarding your accounts and your spending.

If you are uncomfortable sharing your banking information with an app or a website, don't underestimate creating an old-fashioned manual budget in Microsoft Excel or in your notebook. Whatever works for you!

Crack the Nutrition Code

First of all, it's very important to try to avoid eating processed foods whenever you can. College is perhaps the most difficult environment in which to do this, but it is possible—and the benefits are many. Try to always choose the whole foods that are complete as nature intended them. Processed foods such as grains, sugars, and flours are often stripped of their natural nutrients. Even when vitamins and minerals are added back in later—through a process called "enriching," where nutrients lost during refining are added back in to enrich the product—the total effect is never the same.

Another confusing term for consumers is *fortifying*, and many of today's foods are *fortified* with added vitamins and minerals. *Fortifying* milk with vitamin D is one example; adding folic acid to specific foods is another. *Enriching*, then, means putting back into a refined food nutrients lost during processing; *fortifying* means perhaps adding back lost nutrients, but also adding in others that may not occur naturally in a particular food.

Take the example of rice: White rice may cook faster and have a more adaptable taste, but when the outer bran layer is stripped away, the rice grains lose much of their beneficial fiber and minerals. As proof, one cup of brown rice contains 3.5 grams of fiber. One cup of white rice contains less than 1 gram. Even enriching white rice doesn't make up the difference in the loss of fiber and minerals.

Don't be fooled by labels and tricky words—be an educated eater!

Don't Ignore Yourself

If you are feeling sad for a good part of the day, sleeping a lot or not at all, crying frequently, spending too much time alone, eating too much or not at all, or missing classes, you may be depressed. Depression is different from sadness because it lasts longer, runs a bit deeper, and often requires outside help to be resolved. You should immediately make an appointment at counseling services. Depression is not uncommon among college students, so don't think you are alone in feeling the way you do. In fact, most people experience depression at several points in their lives and are able to manage the experience successfully, often without medication. Counseling services can help you find ways to alleviate your distress. Depression is usually not something you can "get over" on your own. It usually requires professional intervention, so don't wait to see if you will simply feel better in a few days. Also try to remember that with help, you will begin to feel and function better, which in turn will help you get back on track.

If you are vigilant about taking care of yourself, which includes reaching out for help, your depression will probably not cause a major disruption in your life; but initially you may find you have to force yourself to leave your room, go to your classes, and stay connected with friends. Depression often causes people to want to stay in bed under the covers, but that's the worst thing you can do. You need to maintain as much normalcy in your life as you can, as it will help you begin to feel like yourself again. Working through one episode of depression will also prepare you to deal with similar problems you or a loved one may have in the future.

Make Your Room Attractive

Your room is also a place of opportunity by virtue of the people you attract to it. There are certainly people in your residence hall whom you don't know, so why not extend the olive branch and be more inviting as they pass by?

When you are hanging out or studying in your room, keep the door propped open. The music you are playing or the way you have decorated your room may attract people with similar tastes. One or two people walking down the hall may see your open door and take a moment to check out how you have set up your room. If you say hello and invite them in, you can begin to get to know each other. This will give you the chance to talk about the things in your room that are special to you, such as family photos, posters or paintings, or a favorite book or movie. Of course, there will be times to keep your room door closed, such as when you are sleeping or changing clothes. Otherwise, keeping your door ajar is an easy way to potentially meet new people—but make sure your roommate is okay with being as social as you.

Unfortunately, this is also an opportunity for some less-than-kind people to see what you have in your room in the way of electronics and other items, so always keep your room locked and secure when you are not there.

Plan a Game Night

Today, plan a game night for people on your floor and some of your own friends. Get some board games (local thrift stores are a great option if you don't have any games) and decks of cards, and invite people to come play. Besides individual rooms, there are a couple of other places in your residence hall where you can meet. Your residence hall will likely have a lounge—a room or open space with several couches, a TV, or other entertainment equipment. These areas would be great spots. Check with your RA to make sure the space isn't being used.

Look for really interactive games that many people can play together like Twister, Trivial Pursuit, and others—if you can and you have one, try hooking up a Wii or Xbox Kinect in the lounge and have dance parties.

The best part about having game night in the lounge is that you'll attract the attention of people passing through to go to their rooms, and may gain some extra players!

Practice Some Visualization

Oh, boy, it's happening again. That time when the schoolwork speeds up, your time slips away, and you're buried under a pile of homework, activities, and obligations. Stress is back! Today, learn visualization exercises you can use to bust it when it rears its ugly head.

Here is one basic technique that you can start doing right away. You should try to do this exercise a few times first so that it will work more effectively during an actual stress emergency.

As you practice this exercise, you'll be able to experience that feeling of safety and happiness more and more quickly—in as little as thirty seconds—just by closing your eyes and breathing deeply. Even during an exam, you can take thirty seconds to close your eyes, breathe deeply, and relax.

Sit in a chair with a firm back and place your palms, face up, on your thighs. Close your eyes and take deep breaths. Concentrate for a few moments only on your breathing, on the feeling of air going into and out of your lungs. Next, picture yourself someplace you've been where you felt safe and happy. See yourself there. Use all your senses. Remember the sights, smells, and sounds of being there. Think about this scene for several moments, continuing to breathe deeply. Enjoy the feeling of safety and serenity you know while you are there. At the same time, know that you can always return there, where you feel safe and happy, when you need to. Sit for as long as you like in this place. When you are ready to leave, count to ten, and then open your eyes.

Do the Extra Credit, Even If You Don't Need To

Who says nothing in life is free? The best-kept secret in school is extra credit. When it comes to extra credit, do it! Find out how the extra credit or homework points contribute to your final grade so you can remind yourself of how important it is. Any time a teacher offers extra credit, they are seeking answers to a few of these questions:

- Who can figure out this extra-tough problem?
- Who is willing to do a bit more work on top of what is assigned?
- Who is planning ahead and wants to maximize his chances of having a great grade in my class by securing a safety net of sorts, just in case he doesn't do as well as he wants on a paper or final exam? Or who wants to put a few extra points accumulated in the GPA bank?

What's wrong with being the student who is the answer to any of those questions or assumptions? Nothing.

Think of extra credit as free money. It's out there for you to take and keep. And here's the greatest secret of all. If you do the extra credit and get it wrong—even if you miss every part of the assignment either once or every time—you are no worse off than before you attempted it.

Note: It's wonderful to try for extra credit to get a few extra bonus points, but you should *never* rely on it to pull up a failing grade, nor should you ask the professor to assign you extra credit projects because you've slacked off on the other class assignments.

WEEK EIGHT

Manage Your Credit

So you somehow got yourself a credit card (or three) and have rung up a few charges. Your parents are fuming, and you are not too pleased with yourself either. Here are some simple tricks you can use to get control of your credit.

Step one is always to cut up the cards or lock them away. Period.

Second, to really get a handle on your debt, develop a written plan. Each month, pay the minimum balance on all credit cards except the one with the highest interest rate. Pay as much as you possibly can on this card each month until it's paid off. Use all available money for this payment including overtime pay, tax refunds, bonuses, money generated by reducing expenses, and your bottle deposit money.

When you've paid off the first debt, pause briefly to pat yourself on the back and then start in on the next debt with the highest interest rate. Pay as much as you possibly can each month, including the amount you were previously applying to debt number one. Continue to pay the minimum balance on the others. Keep moving down the list of debts until they're all paid off. This is the only time you should ever pay the minimum balance on any credit card.

And seriously, give the cards to your parents for safekeeping. You cannot be trusted!

Look Into Birth Control Options

If you are currently sexually active on campus or considering becoming so, it is important that you investigate ways to protect yourself and your partner. Safe sex is the responsibility of both of you. If you are unable to have an open conversation about this, you and your partner need to wait before having sexual contact. If you talk about this issue early on in your relationship, you'll be prepared for planned or spontaneous sexual encounters.

A variety of birth control methods are available over the counter. The type of birth control you want to use is a very personal decision. Talk to your health center staff or primary physician about birth control. Your conversation will be confidential and you can learn about what is available, the risks involved with each method, and other important facts. Your health and safety must be your primary concern, and it will be largely your responsibility.

Know that no matter which birth control option you go with, there is a chance it will fail. The absolute safest choice you can make is to abstain from sex. This will protect you from an unwanted pregnancy, sexually transmitted diseases, and other emotional or physical repercussions. Some students who choose abstinence have reported that they have just as much fun as everyone else at college, have fewer emotional crises, and are still accepted by their friends. Abstinence is a choice, and one that you should consider along with your other birth control options.

Lose the Negative Nancys and Energy Vampires

You may find, as you begin to form real friendships in college, that some people resist when you try to withdraw from them, time- and energy-wise. They may need you as an audience and source of attention. These people, who take more than they can give, are a major source of relationship stress. Relationship expert Dr. Judith Orloff calls these people "energy vampires" because they literally drain the blood of a healthy relationship—your precious time and energy—right out of you.

Whether it's a roommate who only wants to talk to you to complain about her boyfriend, or your friend from high school who drains your positive moods with her whining about wanting to go home, energy vampires are everywhere on campus. Today, make a point to change your relationship or lose them forever— you have your own stresses and worries; you don't need theirs, too!

- When your roommate starts to complain about her boy-friend, chime in with your own experience or your latest relationship problem. If she responds and engages in what you're saying, great! If she brings the conversation back to her, then tune her out.
- Your friend from home thinks she is entitled to you as a friend because you went to high school together. This isn't so. When she starts complaining, advise her to find things she enjoys on campus, or to look into commuting to school.
- Don't become an energy vampire yourself; always act engaged with other people and think outside of yourself.

Look Into a Summer Program in Another Country

If you cannot leave campus for an academic year or even a full semester, ask your campus study-abroad coordinator about summer opportunities. There are a variety of programs lasting from five to eight weeks in the summer that can give you a solid experience in another country. Many times these programs occur through a course offered on your campus and may involve traveling to several countries. Summer programs still offer you the chance to learn about another country, its culture, and its people. Shorter programs may allow you to have the best of both worlds—study abroad for academic credit and a summer job to pay for the experience.

An increasing number of schools are also developing study-abroad programs for intersession or break periods. January is often an opportunity for faculty to take a group of students to another country for a few weeks. This trip is typically done in the context of a particular class, but is usually available to students regardless of their declared major. Sometimes these classes will be interdisciplinary, giving a few professors the opportunity to collaborate on a course in which the students may think broadly about the location and the subject matter. A significant advantage for many students is that January trips abroad often involve heading to a warmer place. Spending three weeks of January in Mexico, for example, may be a more attractive option than staying on campus in New England.

Make Connections with Your School's Alumni

Alumni offices sometimes work in conjunction with career services or other campus offices to set up internships for students. This is an excellent opportunity for an undergraduate to work in her desired field and be mentored by an alumnus. The alumnus is likely to look out for you during the internship, give you advice, and help ensure that you have a good experience. He will be proud that a student from his college is working hard for his company, and the work you do will reflect well on him, too.

At some point, you'll probably see signs around campus advertising the alumni office's annual phone-a-thon. This is the period where volunteers, usually students, call alumni to solicit donations. This actually represents a good opportunity for you and your friends. If you volunteer to be a caller during this program, you could earn some money and make connections with professionals in your field. Some colleges give a prize to the student who is able to raise the most money over the course of the phone-a-thon. In addition, you will get to answer alumni questions about what is going on around campus and what activities you enjoy most. At best, you will be able to connect with a few alumni and perhaps begin a relationship that will help you after college.

One reason that alumni work with undergraduates is their passion for the college. They valued their experience at the college and want to help other students. After you work with an alumnus, send him a postcard depicting a scene from the campus. If the experience was particularly helpful, consider sending a souvenir from the bookstore along with a thank-you note.

Take Screen Breaks

Sometimes you'll be working on a paper that you think you'll never finish or researching journal articles in the library when you realize you've been staring at a screen for the past hour. This isn't good for your eyes or your mental health.

The Mayo Clinic recommends the 20/20/20 rule for computer eyestrain, but it will work to relieve all computer stress. Stop using the computer every twenty minutes and look at something twenty feet away for twenty seconds. Better yet, every twenty minutes take notes by hand, clean your workspace, or return a phone call without looking at the computer screen to give your body and mind a much-needed break.

Give your head a quick massage. Close your eyes. Place your hands, palms up, in front of you. Sink your head into your hands, and gently massage your temples and forehead with your fingers. Then massage your eye sockets with your palms. End the massage by breathing deeply three times. All that relaxation really can come from the discomfort of your desk.

Become an Effective Listener

Hearing is passive; it means some sound has reverberated in your ear, whether or not you wanted it to, and there's been a noise. Listening, on the other hand, is an active process. It implies that you must do something to accomplish it. It takes action and, often, work to listen well.

The same principle applies to classroom lectures. There may not be the same amount of noise in a lecture room as on a crowded train but you still have to work hard to listen to the professor's words. The first step to effective listening is to realize that listening takes effort. It won't happen on its own and it's not something that is going to take place automatically just by your being there. Go into situations where it's important for you to listen, and listen carefully. Concentrate. It may be difficult at first, but in time you'll get better.

It is difficult to listen to someone if you are not giving all your attention to that person. Ideally, you should look at the speaker's face the entire time she is talking. In a lecture, though, this is not always possible because you also need to look up and down at your notes from time to time. If you can't write and look at the professor at the same time, make certain to look up from your notes frequently.

Listening, like any skill, improves as you work at it. As you try to concentrate in different situations, you'll find you get better and better at it. Practice always helps.

WEEK NINE

Think about Ditching Your Car Next Year

If your school has allowed you to keep your car on campus this year (a rarity, considering that many schools ban freshmen from keeping cars on campus to preserve space), consider leaving it home next year. Sure, it's nice to have a car on campus so that you can easily get to the store or get home for a weekend. But how much have you used your car this year? Has it sat in the parking lot between visits home?

Not only does your college charge you for the privilege of having your car, but your insurance rates may go up. In the big, busy campus parking lots, it's not uncommon for a car to acquire dents or worse damage, and vandalism does occur. Parking tickets can also be very costly, and some colleges institute a strike rule; in other words, after you acquire a certain number of tickets, your car will be banned from campus.

Have other students been pushy about asking for rides or if they can borrow your car? If it's been a problem, this is another plus to leaving it home.

Rethink Your Diet Plan

So you hit the gym every morning and play club sports three times a week, but the number on the scale isn't going down—in fact, sometimes it's going up! You're doing everything to stop the Freshman 15 from striking, but nothing is working! The problem may be that your diet still isn't perfect, and you think regular exercise gives you a free pass to snack on Doritos, cheese fries, and ice cream.

If you need to lose weight, there is only one way to do it. You must burn more calories than you consume. There are dozens of diet plans, programs, pills, and shakes vying for your dollar. But the only healthy way to lose those excess pounds is by controlling portion sizes, understanding which foods your body needs, and incorporating exercise into your daily routine.

Cutting calories takes attention, and burning them takes effort. There's no getting around it.

You can lose about a pound a week if you eliminate or burn 500 calories a day. To help you gauge this, an 8-ounce container of low-fat, plain yogurt has about 150 calories. People who run regularly burn about 100 calories per mile. Eat less, exercise more. Sounds simple enough, right?

Make a Plan for Your Roommate Situation Next Year

Maybe you and your roommate hit it off and are planning to room together next year, too. If so, that's great! Your school should be sending you information on room selection for the next year as the spring semester draws to a close, so keep an eye out.

However, perhaps you had a few conflicts throughout the year, or just don't feel you are a good match for living together next year. This is okay, and a natural occurrence when it comes to roommates—sometimes it works, sometimes it doesn't. But if you don't wish to continue living with your roommate, inform him immediately that you will be seeking alternate arrangements so he can do the same. Be kind and don't use this opportunity to unload a laundry list of things he does that you hate or reasons why you're moving on; simply state that you would prefer trying a new roommate next year.

If you and your roommate somewhat get along, make an effort to keep in touch with each other. If you decide not to live together after your first semester or year, remain friends on campus and try to meet once in a while for lunch. If you work to build and maintain the friendship, it should not fade away.

Join a Special Interest Group

Special interest groups cover a wide range of formal and informal topics. Each academic department usually has an affiliated club advised by a professor or group of professors. Language departments are a good example of this; they often have clubs that sponsor film series, meals, discussions using only the particular language, and even trips to observe cultural events or displays. Sometimes language programs will sponsor a house or residence hall floor where only that language is spoken. These are generally open to both native and non-native speakers.

Departments such as biology and economics will also often have active clubs on campus. The biology club may visit a state park to examine plants and animals in the area. An economics club may visit the city's financial center and give members a chance to network with influential business leaders.

Your campus may have a student organization dedicated to environmental sustainability. Similarly, your college may have a group of students who are interested in artistic expression. These art expression groups tend to be very active on campus and may sponsor shows, take members to events in the local area, and encourage students to express their individuality.

Most campuses have a group for gay, lesbian, bisexual, transgender, questioning, intersex, and pansexual students, as well as their friends. These organizations vary greatly; some focus on member support and others on campus activism. They may have office space in the student union or housing on campus.

Start Your Own Special Interest Group

Consider starting a group focused on your particular interest. If you gather a group of students who share your interest, you can lobby your school for the resources necessary to begin a new special interest group. You will also gain valuable leadership experience by enduring the start-up process.

Though there are many formal special interest groups on campus, the informal special interest groups are more numerous and often more important to students. Such a group might consist of the friends you always eat dinner with, or the people you decide to live with in a suite or off-campus apartment. Such affiliations will not feel like special interest groups to you, but that is precisely what they are. You will choose to affiliate yourself with a group of people because of common interests and values. These are the people whom you are comfortable with, whom you can spend a lot of time with, and who are there for you when you need support.

Practice Mindfulness Today

Mindfulness refers to bringing your awareness to the present moment. It means paying attention to what you're doing, how you're doing it, and what's going on around you in each moment. When you're in the present moment, you can enjoy the peace of being "right here, right now," where regrets about past events or concerns about future possibilities won't cause you stress.

There are many ways to practice mindfulness. The more you practice being mindful, the more often you will start to live that way, sometimes without consciously thinking about doing it. Here's an exercise you can do as often as you like.

Daily Mindfulness Exercise

1. When you can remember, at any point in your day, stop what you are doing for a moment.
2. With your eyes closed deepen your breath, and send your awareness to the various parts of your body starting with the top of your head and moving downward to the feet.
3. As you send awareness to each body part, inhale and imagine sending energy to that body part. Exhale, and imagine releasing stress.
4. After you've brought your awareness down to the feet, notice if anywhere in the body you feel discomfort. Make small movements of the body to release tension and stiffness.
5. Finally, take a few very deep inhalations and exhalations.
6. Open your eyes and take another moment to appreciate that small break.

WEEK TEN

Move to the Front of the Room

If you don't sit close to the front of the classroom already, try and grab a seat there today. Why is sitting up front so important? Proximity to your professor is crucial. The boss is up front, looking out and teaching to a classroom full of faces. The faces often blur together from class to class, especially if your professor teaches multiple courses to multiple students. So how can you be certain to be recognized and appreciated as an individual employee—er, student? By sitting close to the boss. While it may seem to you as though your professors know you very well, remember that you are one of at least 100 or several hundred students they teach throughout the course of the day. Be sure they really do know you. Sitting up close just makes that easier for them.

If you select a seat in the first three rows, you will also be less tempted to doze off, chat with classmates, check your text messages, or goof around. Physical closeness to your teachers is a key to them "knowing" you better as a student. You will probably be called on more, and that will force you to be better prepared and will serve as an incentive for you to perform well in that class. Sit up straight. Be focused and serious about your job. What is your job again? Absorbing, assimilating, and learning the material that is being presented to you. Take notes, listen well, and maintain eye contact as much as possible.

Go Easy on the ATM Withdrawals

Your first time at college means that you probably have your first debit or ATM card. It can seem like a magical piece of plastic that makes money come out of nowhere, but you need to know that money comes from somewhere, and there is only a finite amount of it. Keep an up-to-date list of what you've spent and how much you have to avoid overdraft fees.

Keep a few warnings in mind when using ATMs. First, if your bank or network does not own the ATM you are using, there might be an extra charge for using that machine. Charges usually range from 50 cents to $2 per transaction. Keep in mind that frequent use of such ATMs will quickly deplete your bank account. Find an ATM that's in your network instead of regularly using machines that charge the extra fee. If you do use a machine that charges a transaction fee, be certain that you include that fee when you balance your checkbook.

A second caution for ATM use is security. While most ATMs are in well-lit areas and monitored by videotape, you still need to exercise caution at these machines. Shield the keypad when you enter your PIN code so that nobody can read it over your shoulder. Also, take care to shield your PIN from security cameras as well, since crooks have recently been caught installing their own tiny cameras at ATMs to record users entering their PINs and then robbing the cardholder. Be aware of who is around you while you are at the ATM, and don't count your money out in the open.

Snack on Something Before You Go to an Event

As you have surely discovered during your time at school, food is everywhere.

Trays of cookies, sugary sodas, cupcakes, muffins, and other delicious delights are the usual fare at college events, and even if you're not hungry you can find yourself snacking on them for something to do.

Whether you are sitting in your room, hanging out in the lounge, or having fun at a party, you will find that there will always be food nearby. Even receptions and special events on campus often include food. Though free food excites most college students, you will have to learn to resist the temptation to eat whatever is put in front of you. Eating too much junk food will cause you to gain weight and suffer from any number of digestive problems, including cramps, diarrhea, and constipation. While these greasy, gummy, crumby foods may be tempting, you'll have to exert some self-control to keep your body healthy.

Try eating something filling before you go to events. Carrot sticks are great, but will they fill you up enough to keep you from going for the chocolate chip cookies? Maybe not. Go for a hard-boiled egg, some pita chips, or some hummus instead. And bring a water bottle with you so you have something to hold instead of nervously reaching out for snacks.

Use Caution on Public Transportation

If your college is in or near an urban area or city, you will probably have access to public transportation. This kind of transportation includes buses, taxis, and trains. There are various times when these modes of transportation can be of use to you, but they require planning. Always make sure you keep yourself safe. When you want to use a bus or train, look for paper schedules in your student center or look for schedules online. Be sure to plan to get to the station or bus stop well in advance of the scheduled departure time, because buses—and especially trains—stay on schedule and do not wait for delinquent passengers.

Check with your student center or college website to find out if your school has a special relationship with any cab companies regarding discounts or special pickup areas. For safety, always try to travel in groups or pairs, never flash large sums of cash in public, and always keep $10 hidden in your wallet or purse for cab fare in case of emergency.

Keep a Journal of Your Experiences

Aside from being a great way to keep a record of your day-to-day activities (and something you can look back on with great fondness), keeping a journal can help you score a perfect job or internship. Start one today! You can use a paper journal or a free online version like Blogger or WordPress.

In grade school, many students spend the first day of school talking about what they did during vacation. Some students have to write short essays about their experiences. In college, the experience is similar but the reasons are different. When you are putting together your next resume, the career counselor is going to ask what you have been up to and what you learned from the experiences. Your academic advisor may ask you the same thing.

If you have a cool internship, job, or are working with a volunteer organization or school group, it is worthwhile to keep a daily or weekly journal. Writing down a few sentences on a regular basis can help you recall important events and demonstrate to yourself how much you learned from the experiences. If you worked a job primarily for the money, keep a copy of the job description and make notes of additional responsibilities you had. No matter what type of experience you had, take some time to write down what you learned and how you think it benefited you.

Find a Mentor

Your friends, family, and upperclassmen can offer you advice on many things, but a professor is perhaps best qualified to offer specific advice about your education. For that reason, finding a faculty member who can serve as your mentor is extremely important. In addition to offering you advice, a mentor can help you negotiate the school's bureaucracy, discuss your future career or educational plans, write letters of recommendation, and much more.

Finding a mentor takes time and effort. There's no sign-up sheet for mentors, and no professor is going to knock on your door to volunteer. You need to find a professor whom you like and respect, and then work to establish a relationship. At some point, you will take a course with a professor you really like. You can initially see this person during office hours or after class. On the first couple of visits, simply discuss the course. If the professor seems receptive, you can eventually ask for advice on other aspects of your education and volunteer more information about your own interests and goals.

Seek out a mentor who might be able to guide you further into an internship under their advisement or who can assist you in networking with colleagues or partners they know in the working world. Mentors do not have to be teachers. They can also be coaches, employers, school administrators, graduate students, or residential advisors.

Learn to Avoid Repressing Your Feelings

In college, you are constantly surrounded by people: professors, roommates, friends, classmates—the list goes on. Things can happen and you can get angry, but you repress that emotion to either be polite or not make a fuss, or because you're afraid to upset someone. This is not healthy. There are many ways you can express your emotions fairly. Here are some of the common ways repressed anger works:

- Projection—seeing your problems in someone else's life. Jennifer Aniston must be single because relationships are impossible, which you've been saying for years.
- Displacement—redirecting anger at a safer target. You snap at your roommate because you got a bad grade on a test you didn't study for.
- Passive aggression—lashing out at another in indirect ways. You deliberately refuse to let your friend borrow a shirt because she teased you last week.
- Isolation—separating emotionally from a stressful or traumatic event. You describe your roommate's laptop getting stolen with no emotion whatsoever.
- Somatization—expressing feelings of anger at another as physical pain or anxiety. You suffer from a headache after a snippy conversation with your classmate.

All of these are unhealthy ways of dealing with anger. Today, make a promise to be honest about your feelings; you'll find it is much more relaxing to say, "I'm frustrated because you have been eating my snacks," or "Professor, I feel confused by my grade because I thought I followed your directions," instead of bottling it up inside.

Borrow Your Friend's Notes

Have you ever heard that anecdote about the three blind men walking down the street? They encountered an elephant, and when each man touched it, they reported three completely different objects. That's how some lectures can be: what you take away from it may be completely different than what a classmate does.

No two people take exactly the same notes. There's a good chance that someone else caught something you missed during a lecture. If you have gaps in your notes or don't understand a section you've written, look at a friend's notes. There's absolutely nothing wrong with sharing notes with a friend. Just make certain the friend is a reliable note-taker. You don't want to borrow from someone who doesn't take decent notes; you might wind up copying down incorrect information. If you know someone who seems to you like a smart student and efficient note-taker, however, you can begin to exchange notes on a regular basis if she is willing.

Do not borrow someone else's notes just so you can skip class or snooze during the lecture. Pretty soon they'll catch on and stop lending them to you.

Learn about Your Credit Report

Any time you borrow money or use credit, your credit rating is affected. If you rent an apartment, your utility bill payments show up on your credit report. Any time you take out a bank loan, such as for a car, or use a credit card, your credit rating could be affected. When you try to get new credit, such as securing a new credit card or getting a loan to purchase a car or house, the lender you are working with will check your credit rating. If you have consistently paid your bills on time, you will probably get the credit you are seeking and get good rates. However, the more problems you have on your report, such as missed payments or high balances, the more difficulty you will have getting credit.

This all serves as a caution to you. You want to get through college with as little debt as possible. When you do incur debt, you want to treat it carefully. It's not only your college education that could affect you for years to come. If you start to be concerned about your credit rating, you should seek assistance quickly. There are nonprofit agencies that can help you understand your credit report and give you a crash course in personal finances (financial management) at no cost. Your local bank or college bursar's office may have resources that you can use, and your parents are a good source of counsel as well. These are better options than those that charge fees for the same services.

The big three credit report agencies are Equifax (*www.equifax .com*), Experian (*www.experian.com*), and TransUnion (*www.trans union.com*). Check them out and see where your credit report stands.

Find Out Your Basal Metabolic Rate (Or How Many Calories You Need)

Basal metabolic rate (BMR) is the rate at which your body burns calories while at rest. It is the level of energy your body needs to keep your normal body processes going, such as your heartbeat, breathing, body temperature, and transmitting messages to your brain. Your BMR uses 60 percent of your body's total energy needs.

There are different methods for estimating caloric needs for individuals. Though just an estimate, the BMR can give you a general idea of how many calories your body needs. Whether you are overweight, at your healthy weight, or underweight, it is important to know how many calories you should be consuming for good health and to reach or maintain a healthy weight. The following simple equation can help you easily estimate your caloric needs:

1. Figure your BMR by multiplying your healthy weight (in pounds) by 10 for women and 11 for men.
2. Figure your calorie needs for physical activity. Multiply your BMR, from step 1, by the percentage that matches your activity level: sedentary, 20 percent; light activity, 30 percent; moderate activity, 40 percent; very active, 50 percent.
3. Add calories needed for digestion and absorption of nutrients in your body. Add your calories for BMR, from step 1, and your calories for physical activity, from step 2, then multiply the total by 10 percent.
4. Total your caloric needs by adding the calories from each step.

Be a Good Friend

In college, you'll have some built-in friends and some new friends you'll make on campus. You like them, they like you, and you have a grand old time together. But part of being a good friend is knowing when to step in—especially when your friend is engaging in dangerous or inappropriate behavior.

If you have a friend who is exhibiting forms of mental health issues like depression, be there for him as best you can. Trying to cheer up a depressed friend may help initially, but if the depression persists encourage him to seek professional help. You alone cannot be responsible for how a friend is feeling. Be supportive as he works through his depression, but don't let it become the focus of your friendship.

If a friend is partying constantly, coming back to her room dead drunk and passing out, throwing up, and missing classes, step in. Let her know you're worried about her health and concerned her behavior will get her removed from school.

One of the most important parts of being a good friend is telling the truth, even if it makes you seem like a wet blanket.

Think about Transferring

Perhaps you got to college and realized that the school isn't right for you. The classes may be interesting, but the majors may not fit your career plans. Perhaps the school's sports are fun, but the social scene isn't. Or maybe a college will turn out to be too far from your family home. College is probably still the answer for you in this case; the challenge now lies in finding and transferring to the right college.

There are both good and bad reasons to transfer schools. Unfortunately, it's hard to distinguish between good and bad reasons in the midst of a difficult time. The decision to transfer can be emotionally stressful for you and your family, and it can also be expensive. However, if your reasons for transferring are sound, in the long run this decision will be worth every difficult moment and every expense incurred.

Bad reasons to transfer out of a college include poor roommate relations, homesickness, and missing a boyfriend or girlfriend back home. These are all temporary issues that can be fixed relatively quickly. In fact, transferring usually doesn't fix these issues; it just moves the problem from one college to another. Students with these types of difficulties should seek assistance from an RA, a college counselor, and family members.

Remember the adage: "The grass is always greener on the other side of the fence." Take the time to really examine your reasons for wanting to transfer. Because transferring can be a lot of work and can cost you in "time to graduation," stay put if the problems you are having at your current location would be problems for you at any other location as well.

Look Into Transfer Schools

The first step to transfer is to make a list of what you are looking for in a new school. You should focus on why you to want to transfer—for example, because of specific majors offered by a college or because your preferences have changed. For example, some students will start at a large college and decide that they really want a small campus. Other search criteria will remain the same for students who are transferring, such as a school's location or cost.

Next, you need to contact potential new schools and find out what specifically is required of transfer applicants. Most schools have a separate application process for potential transfer students. A transcript of college work completed at the former school will be required and sometimes a statement from a dean or discipline system administrator indicating that you are in good standing with the current college will also be requested. Poor grades or some disciplinary infractions will not necessarily keep you from transferring, but admissions counselors want to have a good idea of what kind of student they are considering. If you have poor grades or disciplinary records, you should submit an additional essay detailing the difficulties you had and explain why these problems won't occur at the new school.

When you have narrowed down the list of new schools to two or three, it's time to speak with an admissions counselor, preferably during a campus visit.

Establish and Keep Your Roots

College is an intense experience for students, and even after one semester most students have built very meaningful friendships. Transferring is often difficult in part because it means leaving the friends you have come to value so much. The longer you are at a school, the more friends you will have, and the deeper the friendships will be. Most of the time, these friends will mean more to you than many of the friends you had in high school. However, you should not let these friendships stop you from pursuing your goals at another institution. There are ways to maintain these friendships, even from another campus. Finding ways to keep your friends will nourish your heart and keep a small part of you at your current school.

Students don't become friends because they attend the same college. Certainly the campus serves as a common meeting place, but people choose to become friends because of shared interests, values, and memories. After you have graduated from college, these friendships will endure. Things are no different for a transferring student. You'll be leaving the college before your friends, but your friendships should remain.

You should leave your first college with an address book full of contact information from your friends. And as soon as you know your contact information at your new school, you should send out that information. E-mail, social networking sites, and instant messaging will make it easy for you to stay in touch, even if your school is far away from your friends.

Make Friends with Your Librarian

Researching for an essay or paper can be a painstaking and tedious process. It can also be very rewarding if you think of yourself as an investigator trying to find clues to help sort out your assignment. Being a researcher means you seek the ideas of others to confirm or deny your thesis statement or assigned topic. You become part of a much bigger world of academia once you research a project or paper.

Unless you are researching in a very antiquated library that uses old-fashioned card catalogs only, most libraries nowadays list their sources on computer. The entries are usually organized four ways: by author, title, subject, or keyword. If you have a specific source in mind, you can consult either the author or title entries to find out if the library has the source and where it is located. If you are merely looking for general sources, though, you can search according to the subject.

Most libraries organize their subject catalogs according to the standard list of subjects set by the Library of Congress, although some libraries have their own classifications. The library should have a subject list available for you to consult. Sometimes a subject will be divided into subcategories. Try to find whatever subject or subcategory most closely relates to your topic.

Ask a librarian to help you with your research. They are more than happy to assist and teach you the skills you need to know to be a great researcher.

Keep a Stash of Laundry Money Ready

Remember that some college washers and dryers require money to operate. (You may have already found this out the hard way!) However, some schools build the cost for laundry into your college fees and set their machines to run without direct payment. Others actually deduct the money from your college debit card. In these cases you can usually get your money's worth by doing sixteen to twenty loads of laundry each semester. Other schools use a card system in which the machine debits your charge from a central account.

Because some colleges and most laundromats still require quarters for each load you wash, save your quarters every time you get change back from a purchase. A load of wash will probably cost between $1.50 and $2, and you'll be charged a similar amount for a cycle in the dryer. Always have extra quarters on hand in case a machine takes your money but doesn't work, or the dryer doesn't dry your entire load in the first cycle. Keep a small container for quarters in a safe place somewhere in your room. Aside from laundry machines, quarters can also be used in vending machines around campus.

Find Out What Your Blood Pressure Is

Go to health services today and ask them to take your blood pressure. High blood pressure occurs when the pressure of blood flowing through the blood vessels increases and remains elevated. This increase in pressure means that the blood flow is pushing against the arterial walls with a stronger-than-normal force. Blood pressure is measured in millimeters of mercury (mmHg) and consists of two numbers usually written one over the other. The top number reflects the systolic blood pressure reading—this is a measure of the pressure when your heart contracts, pumping the blood out. The bottom number reflects diastolic blood pressure. This reading measures the pressure when your heart rests, refilling with blood in between contractions.

High blood pressure is dangerous because it usually gives no warning signs or symptoms, like diabetes and high cholesterol. The only way to know whether your blood pressure is high is to get it checked, and not just once. Ideally, your blood pressure should be lower than 140 mmHg over 90 mmHg (usually spoken as "140 over 90" and written as 140/90).

To keep a healthy blood pressure, avoid processed meats, cheeses, canned foods like soups and vegetables, salty crackers and snack foods, salad dressings and condiments like soy sauce or barbecue sauce, and any other foods prepared with salty seasonings. Caffeine and alcoholic beverages can elevate blood pressure in some people. Foods that can reduce blood pressure levels include fruits and vegetables that are rich in potassium, such as dried fruit, bananas, and melons.

Use Social Media Wisely

You know that Facebook and Twitter are natural enemies to pro-ductivity: you can spend hours tooling around on them rather than studying or doing your homework. But they can also be great ways to connect with other people.

When you're using social media, really think about what you're putting out there and who is reading it. It may be tempting to fire off an angry status update about your roommate snoring all night or tweet about how much you hate your literature professor, but consider what you're saying. The Internet is forever, as you know, so your status won't disappear on its own—even if you delete it later it could have already been read and shared. What if your roommate saw your post about her snoring or a friend filled her in? She'd be hurt and you would have an awkward situation on your hands. Or if your professor happened upon your Twitter feed or was directed to it by another student or a standard Google search? It might not affect your grade but it will certainly affect your relationship with that professor.

A good rule to follow is: "If you wouldn't say it out loud to the person, don't say it about them on the Internet." Vent to a trusted friend or write it down and tear it up instead.

Start Looking for a Summer Job

You may have coasted by winter and spring breaks with the excuse of not getting a job because your time off was so short, but that won't fly for summer.

As a college student, your summer experience must include two things. First, it must be meaningful. You must do something more than you have done in past summers, something that will further your academic or career interests. At the end of the summer, your resume should be stronger and you should be a more attractive candidate to a future employer. Second, you need to make money. College expenses extend far beyond tuition, meals, and books. After a year of college, you'll have an idea of how much money you need to earn during the summer. Ideally, you'll also be building a savings account to help you get established after graduation.

Combining these two goals may be difficult. For example, you may find the perfect internship, one that gives you good experience and connections in your future career field. However, the internship may be unpaid, and you'll essentially be a volunteer. In such cases, you'll need to earn money with a second job outside of your internship, and finding a job that has the right hours might be difficult. In such situations, students often find the summer busier than the school year. However, these experiences will pay off in the end.

Check with your professors, your school's career center, and places around your home for some leads.

Apply to Be a College Tour Guide

You know this place pretty well by now, wouldn't you say? Visit your student life office or admissions office and offer your services as a campus tour guide. If any positions are available, you would have to undergo some training and learn new information about your campus, but if you're enthusiastic enough and willing to do the work, it could be very rewarding.

You probably remember your tour guide from over a year ago, and how seasoned and smart she was about the campus? You would take crowds of interested high school seniors and their parents around campus, answering their questions and offering information about the school. If you love college and love your school, it could be a perfect match for you, not to mention a gateway into similar jobs on campus.

Consider Commuting Next Year

If you are having difficulty adjusting to living on campus or simply wonder if you can save more money by living at home and commuting to school, consider this possibility for next year if you live close enough to make the drive a few times a week. Commuter students don't have to pay room and board so their fees are considerably less, but they can still have access to mostly everything that resident students have, with the exception of meal plans and dorm access. You should still be able to retain school insurance through your full-time status.

Deciding to commute can relieve a lot of stress, particularly if you are finding yourself traveling home nearly every weekend for work, to take care of family matters, or to maintain a romantic relationship. But make sure to consider what you'll be giving up. Commuter students have a tougher time staying involved on campus because they typically travel for their classes alone and have little flexibility; study groups that meet at night or impromptu events are usually out of the question. It's not impossible to be an involved and active commuter student, but it's much more work.

Really think about your reasons for wanting to commute. If you're doing it to save money, or because you are needed at home for family matters, those are strong reasons. If you are doing it to be closer to a boyfriend or girlfriend at home, it could be something you regret someday, especially if the relationship ends. Giving up a spot in your school's residence halls is easy, but getting it back as an upperclassman is close to impossible, so make sure it's really what you want before you let the housing office know.

Keep That Old Paper!

You might receive a paper back with an awesome grade, or a test filled with such glowing praise from your professor that your mom would put it on the fridge in a second—either way, hold on to your graded assignments.

It's very useful to consider saving some of your old graded papers, writing, tests, research papers, or projects. Why? Here's one reason: Some graduate programs, scholarships, or awards committees will ask for writing samples or examples of good work you have done in college. If you have saved some of your best work, complete with positive teacher comments, this request will be easy for you. Many students dump work at the end of the school year only to realize later they may have been better off keeping some of it. Even a graded math test that shows your work and thought process can be insightful. A paper you reprint off your computer is of less value than a graded one with teacher comments. So save those papers with grades and teacher comments in case you are asked to provide photocopied samples later.

Get Thrifty

If you find that you're spending money as quickly as you get it on clothes and home wares and simply cannot imagine cutting down your shopping trips, think about finding a local thrift store to do your shopping.

Your school may be near a Salvation Army or other thrift store that carries used clothing, furniture, books, and other items—at a fraction of the cost of a traditional department store. Plus, what you find at these places is usually unique and interesting, like a T-shirt from a long-ago event or a dress from the 1960s. And since the place is located near your school, odds are that departing upperclassmen may have dropped off their own used clothes, so you may just find clothes that are your style.

These places generally put out merchandise that has been washed or cleaned, but to be extra careful, throw your new shirt in the next load of laundry before wearing it or get your new dress dry cleaned before donning it for a date.

Get Up for Breakfast

Even though sleeping in an extra half-hour and munching on Pop-Tarts is much easier, try and wake up in time to have a balanced breakfast. It really is the most important meal of the day, and without it, you're dragging through the morning on a caffeine high, only to crash in the afternoon. So set your alarm earlier and march over to the dining hall to grab some eggs, toast, and cereal.

The easy breakfast options that you can keep in your room are usually chock-full of sugar, carbs, and calories, with no real nutrients. They give you a sugar high that doesn't last—plus they make you hungrier for more junk when the sugar high wears off. Get up, get a real breakfast, and get on with your day.

Smooth Out Any Conflicts

The semester is almost over, so now is the time to fix any problems you may have encountered with your roommate, a friend, or a classmate. Don't sweep these problems under the rug! Part of being an accountable and responsible college student (and future adult) is taking responsibility for your part in a dispute.

Sit down with your roommate and make any necessary apologies about violating the roommate agreement or bringing alcohol into the room or whatever the wrong, and ask what you can do to make it right. If you're planning on living together again next year, you want this resolved, and if you're not, you don't want to end your relationship on a sour note.

Likewise, call your friend or e-mail your classmate and talk through your problems. Make it clear that you want to know what you can do to fix the situation. If your friend or classmate is unresponsive or cold, just repeat that you want to fix the problem, make your point, and end the conversation. No sense in talking to a brick wall.

Know that these conversations should not be an invitation to drudge up any previous arguments or assign blame, call each other names, or determine who is right. This is good training for your professional life, when you will have to solve problems as diplomatically as possible.

Submit to Your School's Newspaper

Do you have any thoughts or opinions about what's going on at your school? Talk to your college newspaper to see about submitting your work for publication. Perhaps the editor is looking for someone to write a piece on a certain topic or college event, and you're just the person.

Read through some past editions of your school's paper to see its style and tone before writing your article. When you're done, have a friend proofread it or bring it to your school's writing center to make sure it's ready to go.

If your piece isn't selected, don't let that stop you. Keep writing and submitting, and sooner or later, you'll be a published author. Keep these clippings, because graduate programs and future employers will be interested in your portfolio.

Go to an Open Mic Night

Your school might host a weekly or monthly open mic night, or a local coffee shop may host one. An open mic event is an event in which amateur musicians, poets, writers, singers, and more share their craft with a crowd.

Today, look into an open mic night to attend. It's a great chance to hear local music and art, especially if it's on campus. And if you're a singer or musician or poet, pluck up the courage to sign up yourself and sing a song or read something you wrote. These events are composed of amateurs trying to learn their craft so don't worry about not being pitch-perfect or hitting a few sour notes here or there. The environment for these events is generally very supportive, and you may walk out with a few new friends who share your interests.

Use Food to Battle Your Mood

This may sound like permission to indulge in comfort food every time you feel bummed out, but it's not. Food remedies have been around for thousands of years; many people treat basic mood conditions with food rather than medicine. If you're feeling bummed out today, these foods may help you feel better.

A variety of chemicals in the brain (for example, serotonin, dopamine, and norepinephrine) influence your mood. Some amino acids consumed through protein in foods are precursors for the brain chemicals, meaning that they are converted to the chemicals once digested or absorbed. Tryptophan and tyrosine are two such amino acids. Meat, fish, poultry, eggs, and milk are complete proteins, meaning that they supply all nine essential amino acids, some of which are important for mental health and improved mood. If you are a vegetarian, currently there are two plant sources considered to be complete proteins: soybeans and quinoa.

Carbohydrates come from a variety of sources, but simple carbohydrates such as sugars and sweet snacks lead to a spike in insulin. This can be followed by a crash that depresses the mood. Stick with whole grains, beans, vegetables, and other complex carbohydrates. They take longer to digest, resulting in longer-lasting energy and less of a crash in mood.

Don't Try to Outsmart Your Professors

Some students think they can easily outsmart the professor. Keep in mind, though, that your professor was once a student, too. Any tricks you think of your professor has probably thought of, too. Consider this popular story passed on from one student to another about an incident that supposedly took place at a college in the United States. As the story goes, four college buddies decided to take a weekend ski trip, even though they had a major exam coming up that Monday afternoon.

They had a great weekend partying, but on their way home Monday morning, they realized none of them had studied. They decided to skip the exam and make up an excuse. When they went to class the following Wednesday, they told the professor they had been driving to class Monday morning from their off-campus apartment, when they'd gotten a flat tire several miles away from school. They tried to fix it as fast as they could, they said, but the flat detained them for several hours and forced them to miss the exam. The professor expressed sympathy for their plight and told them they could make up the exam that Friday. The four friends were thrilled that they got all this extra time to study.

They showed up at the classroom Friday completely prepared for the exam. The professor passed out the test and when the four friends turned over the exam, they were horrified to find this one question, "Which tire on your car had the flat?"

The moral of this story: Don't lie to your professor. Respect the time he or she puts into preparing for the class, and be accountable for your behavior.

Sell Your Junk

As you're slowly packing up the objects in your room you don't need anymore so you're not frantically packing as your parents pull up to your residence hall (you're doing this, right?), you may notice a few things that you bought or brought with you that you genuinely think you have no use for. It might be the tennis racquet you bought before you realized you hated tennis, or a phone charger that doesn't fit your new phone.

Whatever it is, consider selling it either to a person you know or via an online site like eBay or Craigslist. It's a great way to make some extra cash and free up some space in your living quarters. Of course, when dealing with online interactions, be smart and safe. Never meet with a buyer; always include the cost of shipping the item in your offered price. Your school or residence hall may have a bulletin board. Advertise the item there!

Set a reasonable price or no one will come knocking, and make sure you're honest about the condition of the item. And definitely make sure the item you're selling belongs to you (don't laugh, people have sold borrowed items before!).

I Scream, You Scream

We all scream for ice cream! As the weather gets warmer, out come those delicious frozen treats in the dining halls, and a heaping ice cream cone sounds like just the ticket on a warm spring evening. And it is a great treat—once in a while. But as you know, there is a difference between driving to the ice cream parlor and having tubs and tubs of the stuff at your fingertips in the dining hall. Self-control!

Try to restrict it to once a week. If that's too difficult, invest in some smaller pints of frozen yogurt or sherbet from your local grocery store. They fit in your dorm's freezer and satisfy that need for a cold treat—but without all the calories and fat.

Don't Get Scammed

Throughout your time in college, you'll become an expert at dodging all kinds of salespeople trying to get your cash: credit card companies, long distance carriers, cell phone providers—the list goes on. These people know that you're a young adult on your own and don't have your parents running interception for you anymore. And if you're technically an adult (eighteen years old or older), you are legally allowed to commit to all kinds of things like cell phone contracts, some credit card agreements, and the like. Know first and foremost that it doesn't matter that you were a kid only last year: if you sign these agreements, you are legally obligated to make any payments they require in their contracts.

There is a reason these companies call college students, particularly new freshmen: you are of age to commit but don't have the experience to know when you're getting a raw deal. And a shiny credit card that can purchase all kinds of stuff sounds pretty darn tempting to a college freshman.

Odds are you probably have a cell phone already, probably under your family's plan. You either work part-time, have money saved up from a summer job, or can rely on your parents to send you money as needed, so you probably don't need a credit card. Anytime you are approached or called by a telemarketer trying to sell you something, kindly thank them and decline. If it's something you think you'd want, ask them to send you more information. Share it and discuss with your parents before committing. And remember the cardinal rule: If something sounds too good to be true, it probably is!

Build a Brag Sheet

A brag sheet is a place for you to list everything you have done outside of your classroom—after school, on the weekends, and during summers. It is basically an extracurricular resume. List all honors, awards, accomplishments, extracurricular activities, summer experiences, internships, employment, community service, and athletics in which you have participated or achieved, as well as hobbies and interests that you have. Include a column listing the hours per week and weeks per year dedicated to each activity. Keep this growing log in a document on your computer and track your involvement. Don't forget about any awards or honors you have won in these activities!

Brag sheets are great to have on hand when you're applying for internships, graduate programs, and awards—plus it helps a very active student see it all on paper.

Think about the Big Picture

Around the close of freshman year, many students feel lost in their studies. Their friends have already chosen majors and are excelling, while they have no identified path yet. Today, dive into your dreams and figure out your goals.

To determine a big-picture goal, consider your purpose in attending college in the first place. If the only reason is because your parents said you must, you are not going to be very happy. There must be *something* you hope to gain in your studies, and it doesn't necessarily have to be the same thing your parents or professors want or expect. You may, for example, want to develop specific skills to help you in a certain career. Or you might want to receive high grades so you can get into the graduate school of your choice. There might be more personal factors involved as well, such as the desire to better yourself, to become a more educated person, and to experience new ways of thinking and seeing.

Your "big picture" is a personal one, and it can be different from everyone else's. Keep this big picture in mind as you study and navigate school. Without a sense of this big picture you can easily feel unfocused; however, if you maintain a clear sense of what you are doing and why, you are more likely to remain on track.

Try to see how each task you go about in your to-do lists and schedule fits into your big-picture goal. If you see how each agenda item contributes something to your goal, you'll remain much more focused on your work and you'll also find your studies more fulfilling.

Color Yourself Relaxed

One of the leading alternative therapies out there is art-based—did you know that? There is something relaxing about creating a beautiful piece of art with paints, pencils, or even crayons. If you're feeling stressed today, break out the colored pencils or crayons (seriously!) and color. You don't have to be a great artist, just use simple strokes to make nondescript designs and color them in. Color outside the lines if you want to!

If you don't want to color, then search the Internet for some easy crafts you can make in your dorm. There are several sites devoted to repurposing old products into new pieces of decorative art, such as turning books into hanging mirrors, old pages into paper flowers, and tons more. Invite a friend over to make her own craft.

You'll feel more relaxed and have a beautiful new project to decorate your room!

Don't Toss Your Notes

Many students are so relieved when the semester is over they throw away all their notes. You've worked hard taking those notes! And more importantly, you never know when you might need to refer back to them. Be assured that many of the courses you take will interconnect, particularly those within your major or concentration. As you move on to more advanced levels of coursework, you'll find you need to refer to notes from earlier courses to refresh your memory about certain key points or fundamentals.

You also may take courses that seem completely unrelated to one another, only to find that some point or issue will come up that you have previously addressed elsewhere. For example, you may be reading a novel in an English class that refers to specific events from your history class. If you've taken a history class about that period, you can read your notes and get more information about those events, which in turn can help you understand the novel and allow you to contribute more to class discussions. Imagine how impressed your teacher will be if, in class discussion, you can provide some of that background information. So save your notes!

At the end of the semester, label and put each set of notes someplace safe and accessible. Consider purchasing a file cabinet to store them in or large clear plastic containers you can easily buy at an office supply store. If you've been using a loose-leaf notebook, you can take the pages out of the binder and put them in a folder. That way you can reuse the binder next semester. Just make certain you label the folder with the course title and year.

WEEK FIFTEEN

Consider the Cost of Classes

Even after you've been attending a school, you should continue to think of yourself as an educated consumer. Your school may have a tremendous range of offerings: there are many different courses as well as many different teachers. Both teachers and courses, though, can range in quality. It would really be a shame to spend money for college credits and end up in courses that do not excite or appeal to you. Sometimes a course won't be good because its content isn't something that interests you. More often than not, though, the deciding factor is the professor. A dynamic teacher can make the most mundane of subjects seem interesting. A poor teacher, however, can make the most fascinating subject matter a total bore. Before you select classes, do some research to be sure you'll get what you want.

Bottom line: if you didn't learn this lesson your freshman year, learn it now. *You are paying for this experience and are a guest at your college's pleasure.* When you are making class selections for the fall, don't waste your money or time on courses that you don't need, want, or have an interest in.

Quit—or Don't Start—Smoking

You may be a smoker, may have started when you got to school, or don't smoke. If so, you should have quit a while ago, should quit right now, or never start. Besides being a drain on your wallet (a pack of cigarettes can cost you upwards of $7), your health and the health of others is affected, and that smell never really comes out of your clothes.

Smoking is the largest cause of preventable death worldwide today. A smoker will live an average of ten to twelve years less than a nonsmoker, and a smoker has a 70 percent higher risk of heart attack and a ten times greater risk of developing lung cancer than a nonsmoker. Visit your health services office to learn about options for quitting.

Don't Start Any Fires

Seems like that would be pretty easy, right? Wrong!

Between banned appliances in your room like hot plates and hot pots, and unattended laundry, it can be easier than you think to start a fire in your residence hall. Be an aware and attentive resident; don't be that person everyone stares at outside when the fire alarm goes off.

- If you're not sure, check with your housing office to see if you're allowed to have certain appliances in your room. Typically, colleges only allow microwaves. Don't sneak in any illegal appliances (hot plates, hot pots, and electric kettles are the usual big no-no items). Your college has banned them for a reason—they are not safe.
- Make it a rule to always empty the lint filter before and after you use the dryer. A clean lint filter allows the dryer to be more efficient, drying your clothes more quickly and completely. A clogged filter is also a safety hazard, particularly when a dryer is being used with high heat settings or very large loads. Every year there are small fires in laundry rooms that could have been prevented if students emptied the lint filters.
- When using your dorm's kitchenette, don't walk away when something is in the oven, even if it's only for a few minutes.
- Never smoke or light candles or incense in your room. Even if you are very careful and watch the flame, the smoke can still set the alarm off.

Practice a Random Act of Kindness

Doing something nice for someone really does make you feel good. Something very small you do around campus can make someone's day. Today, try to find something you can do to bring joy to someone else.

- Pick up trash on the ground near your dorm.
- Give someone directions.
- Tell a friend that you like his outfit or hairstyle.
- Lend an ear to your roommate if she needs someone to talk to.
- Smile at people as they walk by.
- Thank your professor for a great class.
- Thank your dining hall staff for the meal and for serving you.
- Call your parents to say hello.
- If you can afford to, buy a coffee for the person in line behind you.
- Offer to help someone with a task she is struggling with.

If you're at a loss when thinking about what good deed you can do, think about what someone could do for you at that moment to brighten your day—and do that!

Start a Blog

Blogging is a great way to document your life at college. You can post entries, pictures, and memories all in one spot. Visit Blogger .com or Wordpress.com to start your blog; you can start one with a friend and share posting duties, devote your blog to one topic (e.g., your clubs or activities), or just have a private area where you can post your thoughts.

Starting a blog is also a great way to keep in touch with everyone at home. Share the link with your parents, grandparents, family, and friends so they can see what you're up to (if you do this, make sure the content is suitable for your family to see!) without constant catch-up phone calls and e-mails.

Either way, a blog is a fantastic way to record your time at school. You'll be able to look back on your posts with great fondness someday!

Forgive Yourself

You slacked off and got a bad grade on an assignment. You said something really mean to your roommate. You were short with your parents on the phone. You skipped the gym and ate ice cream instead. You lied about yourself to a stranger to impress him. There are plenty of reasons you can get angry, frustrated, or even disgusted with yourself throughout your time in college. But know that you are not the first person to get a bad grade, fight with her roommate or parents, or go straight for the mint chocolate chip instead of the treadmill—and you definitely won't be the last.

Today, examine what you feel guilty about and work on forgiving yourself. Ask:

- Can I do anything to fix this problem?
- Once I've done that, what else can I do?
- Will feeling guilty improve the situation?
- Is there anything else at play here? Insecurity, anger, depression?
- How can I move on?

Once you have answered all these questions, it's time for you to forgive yourself for being a human and move on. Yes, you messed up and you are facing the consequences (a bad grade, a mad roommate, etc.). If you've done everything you can to make a situation right, you can't beat yourself up forever.

WEEK SIXTEEN

Present Yourself Well

Some professors might assign a presentation in place of a final exam. A few tips will help you no matter what the subject matter. For example, always dress nicely for your presentation. This will make a difference, even if your professor doesn't grade on it. Get a good night's sleep before your presentation. If you start yawning halfway through your remarks, you'll lose your audience. And as always, there is no substitute for thoroughly knowing the subject of your presentation. You need to be prepared to explain or demonstrate what you are talking about and answer questions on the spot.

The biggest mistake students make with presentations is failing to rehearse prior to the presentation. Whether you rehearse in front of friends or just in front of a mirror, make sure to go through your entire presentation at least once. Also, practice standing and talking naturally, using helpful (but not distracting) hand gestures and referencing (but not reading) your note cards. It is also imperative that you practice using any visual aids included in your presentation. Be certain that you have a backup plan in case the technology fails at a critical moment. Time yourself or have your roommate time you—sometimes you'll find that your presentation is over or under a set time limit.

The final tip for making presentations is to be confident. Even if you are uncertain about your material, you need to speak as though you have no doubts. Your confident appearance will help ease your nerves and convince your audience, your professor, and yourself that you are thoroughly prepared for the presentation.

Consider Selling Your Textbooks Back

Be warned: if you sell your textbooks back to your college book-store, be prepared for the possibility that you'll receive *much less* than what you paid for them. The sticker shock may stun you for a minute, but understand that the bookstore has to acquire books they can resell. Even if you bought the book brand new, it is now used. You removed the shrink-wrap, folded the pages, highlighted sections, and doodled in the margins. Perhaps the class your books are for is not being offered next semester, or the professor is ordering another text for the class. Either way, don't expect to walk out making a profit or breaking even on what you spent on your books last semester, but selling your books back after finals is a great way to make some extra cash.

Before you lug every textbook you used this year down to the bookstore to sell it back, consider what you're doing. If there is any chance you will refer to a book—particularly if it was used in a course that is part of your major—it is probably worthwhile to hold on to it. You can always try to sell it back later, but you never want to be in a position where you have to buy the same book twice!

Get Exam Ready

Get enough sleep TWO nights before your exam. Sometimes a lack of sleep from a previous night doesn't hit you the next morning but lags a day. So get your rest leading up to your test and eat healthy! On the day of the test, eat a well-balanced meal with some protein to give your body an energy boost. Don't eat too large a meal, though—that will make you sleepy.

Try this healthy parfait for those busy exam days. A small Tupperware container filled with it makes a portable, delicious, and energy-boosting breakfast!

CRUNCHY CREAMY YOGURT PARFAIT

[Low-fat, Gluten-free, Vegetarian, High-fiber]

Yogurt parfaits are traditionally a healthy choice, and they're easy to make at home in no time at all. Mix and match different cereals, yogurt flavors, and fruits for more delicious combinations.

Serves 1

2 tablespoons bran flakes cereal

4 ounces sugar-free vanilla yogurt

¼ cup sliced strawberries

Layer the ingredients in a tall travel cup, starting with the bran flakes, then the yogurt, and finally the strawberries.

Be Honest but Proactive

You could be fretting a great deal about an upcoming final exam. If it helps, talk to students who have taken classes with your professor to find out what the exam might be like. A professor's style is usually consistent regardless of the class she is teaching. However, a student who has had your class with a different professor may not give you accurate advice. Solicit advice primarily from people who know your professor well. It may be tempting to ask about previous tests and what questions appeared if your professor is known to reuse exams. Some tips to keep your conversation on the level:

- Do not ask for or accept information from previous students on what content will be on the final. This is dishonest. Simply ask about the professor's testing style and that student's experience with the final exam.
- If you have questions about the format of the exam (essay, short-answer, etc.), ask your professor first. Often they will share this information. If not, expect all possibilities.
- Never take a graded test or paper from another student to review and possibly use in your own exam. This is not only cheating—it's also plagiarism.
- Do not look at anyone else's paper during an exam or even give the impression that you might be looking. Keep your eyes on your own paper.
- If anyone asks you to provide answers or assist them in cheating, say no.

Most colleges have a very strict academic code in place when it comes to cheating and plagiarism. If you are caught, you can fail the exam or even the class, or even find yourself before the school judicial board to face possible punishments like expulsion from school.

Volunteer Locally

The secret is this: Volunteer work does not have to be a drag. Take something you already like to do and extend it into the area of community service. If you enjoy drama, volunteer at an after-school Boys and Girls Club or community center program to teach kids drama games and improvisation. Often it is as simple as completing an application and showing up during open hours.

Volunteer Dos and Don'ts

- **Do** volunteer to do something you enjoy and find meaningful.
- **Do** strive to make deep connections and commit yourself to the volunteer activity.
- **Do** seek out connections with the people you work with at your volunteer site, not only the recipients of your time but your co-volunteers and volunteer coordinator too.
- **Do** keep a personal log of hours you have committed to each organization.
- **Do** work hard as a volunteer since it can sometimes turn into a paid gig.
- **Do** work beyond the hours that are the minimum requirement of your school (if there is one) to demonstrate your longevity and sincere commitment to the organization.
- **Do** show up on time, ready to work, with respect and commitment.
- **Don't** volunteer because you think it "looks good" for college or graduate school.
- **Don't** disparage or speak down about your co-volunteers, the organization, or people you serve.
- **Don't** treat a volunteer job as unimportant just because you are not being paid for your time.

Look for a Summer Job on or Around Campus

If you love your college town and don't want to leave, or you rent an apartment there all year, consider finding a job around town for the summer.

The career center is a frequently overlooked place to go when looking for a summer job. If this office can help students find a job after graduation, why can't the staff also assist with jobs for the summer? While this is not one of its primary missions, your career center is already set up with many of the resources necessary to find a good summer job. For example, companies may post summer job openings at your career center. The career center can help you put together a resume targeting your desired job and will likely help you prepare for the interview. Your career counselor will also be able to help you revise your resume after the summer job ends so that you can highlight your experiences and make yourself more attractive to future employers.

Prepare for the End (of the Year!)

You're in your last week of school today, and your dorm is starting to get packed up and looks almost as bare as it was when
you moved in last fall—seems so long ago, huh? You're about to
enter another transition period of your life: moving back home for
the summer as a college sophomore. You'll need to get a summer
job, re-establish a relationship with your parents and siblings, and
say goodbye to your new friends, new routines, and new surroundings. It can be very stressful. Today, make a list of things
you can do to make the transition smoother.

- Friend your new pals on Facebook, follow them on Twitter,
  and get their e-mail addresses and cell phone numbers.
  Make sure they have your contact info, too.
- Make one steady plan to meet, if you can, in the summer.
  If a meeting is impossible (distance, money, work commitments, etc.), make a plan to Skype or all meet in a chatroom.
- Have a conversation with Mom and Dad about coming
  home. See what ground rules they would like to abide by,
  and which ones they are willing to bend. This way you don't
  come home and run into conflict right away.
- If time permits, when your parents come to pick you up
  organize a lunch with your roommate or new friend. Your
  parents can see whom you spend your time with, and seeing your two worlds meet can make the transition home
  easier.
- Remind yourself that you'll be back in the fall!

Look Forward to Next Year

Most colleges don't require that you choose a major before your junior year, but you may have made your decision this year about the direction you want your education to take. Think about the fall semester and how you want to arrange your schedule to meet your goals.

It's important to choose a major that interests you, but it should also lead you to a career or graduate program once you graduate. If you only have a general idea of a career that you might enjoy, declare a less-specific major, such as business or communications. This will prepare you for a wide array of jobs and still allow you to further shape your education in graduate school.

When you know what your major will be—or at least your first major, since you will be able to change your mind—sit down with your academic advisor and discuss your plans. Do it today or tomorrow because the school year is rapidly winding to a close and you want this done before you break! Your registrar will have the official major declaration form for you to complete, and you can investigate possible classes in your major for the fall semester.

Save Your Supplies

With the semester over, or very nearly so, you may be prepared to burn, throw, toss, or destroy your school supplies in celebration: pens, pencils, notebooks, and sometimes rulers, calculators, or other equipment. But before you do, take a look at what you can salvage for next semester.

Did you fill up your entire five-subject notebook? If not, clip the written pages together or remove them to store elsewhere, and leave the blank ones. Remove the contents of your folders and binders so you can reuse them. Your pens still work, right? The stapler hasn't stopped stapling? The highlighters may be a little crispy on the end but still do the job. Save yourself some money (and don't throw out perfectly usable supplies) in the fall and store these away in your backpack—they'll be ready and waiting when you begin classes again.

You remember how much you spent on these supplies at the beginning of the year or semester. There is no rule that you must start every semester with new supplies, so don't be wasteful. Keep the ones that work!

Go for the Green!

Smoothies are a great way to get a lot of nutrients in one bottle. It can be easy to fall into the creamy, sugary, fatty kinds of smoothies, so this summer try and go for a green smoothie, or a smoothie that is jam-packed with fruits, veggies, yogurt, and all kinds of good stuff.

Here's a good recipe to start with, but experiment with your own favorite veggies and fruits to get your perfect combination.

GREEN TEA GREEN SMOOTHIE

Add powerful antioxidant-rich green tea to the vitamins and minerals provided by the rich greens and citrus!

Recipe Yields: 3–4 cups

1 cup spinach

2 lemons, peeled

½" piece of ginger, peeled

1 tablespoon raw honey

2 cups green tea

1. Combine spinach, lemons, ginger, honey, and 1 cup of tea in a blender and blend until thoroughly combined.
2. Add remaining 1 cup of tea as needed while blending until desired consistency is achieved.

Use Caution at End of the Year Parties

Parties are an important part of the college experience. A balanced lifestyle includes having fun as well as studying, working, and exercising. Parties give students a chance to escape the rigors of classes, meet and form friendships with others, play games, listen to music, or dance.

Many colleges will host events at the end of the school year, like large concerts where a national band or musician comes to play, a carnival, or a festival to celebrate another year accomplished. Many students can get swept up in this fervor—along with the fact that the year is ending—and have a little too much fun partying. Use your better judgment and have fun responsibly, and encourage your friends to do the same.

Pack It Up!

You may be realizing that despite your best efforts to clean your room when you left for winter break, you forgot a few items and acquired a few more as the spring went on. The basic truth is that you will leave your college residence hall with more than you came with, so account for this when you move back home. Today, look around your room and determine what you can bring home with you, what you want to keep, and what you don't mind parting with forever. Get a big garbage bag and sort through your clothes. Anything you don't wear that has no sentimental value, throw it in the garbage bag! When the bag is full, bring it to your local Salvation Army or used clothes drop-box.

Throw out or eat any perishable food (bring home or donate packaged stuff) in the fridge and give it a good scrub. Remove your posters and wall hangings (make sure they left no residue), roll them up for next year or toss, recycle, or give them away. Sweep and mop the floor and wash the windows. Double-check your closets and drawers for any stray items—when your RA does his final sweep of your room, all things left behind will be tossed.

When you moved in, your RA made meticulous notes about your room, including any existing damage (chipped mirror, stain on curtain, etc.). When you leave, the RA does another sweep, compares that list to the room's state now, and marks any new damage that has occurred since. As such, you could be fined for any new stains, holes in the walls, and scuff marks that happened throughout your tenure. So if you were careless, this summer you can watch out for that bill for the cost of replacing, repairing, or retouching an item.

Go Around Your Campus in One Day

Today is one of your last days on campus, so make sure you do everything you enjoy one last time (while wrapping up some loose ends)!

- Visit the gym and use your favorite machine or take your favorite fitness class.
- Eat your favorite meal at the dining hall.
- Walk around the campus with a friend.
- Say goodbye or send notes or e-mails to your favorite professors.
- Thank the dining hall and residence hall staff members for all their work.
- Return any library books (you don't want those fines piling up over a whole summer!) and thank the librarians who helped you with your research this year.
- Get a coffee from your favorite local café.
- Visit your friends in other residence halls. Help them pack if they need it.
- Make sure your own packing is as close to done as possible.
- Stop by the bookstore and purchase a small souvenir for yourself.
- Take pictures of yourself, your friends, and your campus.

You'll be back in a few months, but that doesn't mean you shouldn't take a farewell tour of your school before you take off.

Organize a Farewell Meal

Before the moving chaos begins, try to organize one last meal with your roommate and friends. You can splurge for brunch at a local eatery or just go to the dining hall together for the last time this year. Laugh at the funnier moments of the year and reminisce about the times and memories you shared.

Don't stress about the summer, or the move home, or even what next year will bring. Just have fun together while you eat. Tell each other about your summer plans. Make arrangements to visit if you can. Keep it positive and upbeat!

SUMMER VACATION

It's summer! You're back in the swing of things with your high school friends, your family, and your local job. And you're officially a college sophomore! To start the new school year off right, here are some things you can do this summer to keep your momentum pumping.

Brush Up on What You Learned

Don't automatically assume that since you passed your classes in your freshman year you no longer need that information. Those classes and lessons are the building blocks of any future knowledge that you'll acquire in school. Look at your schedule for the fall. If you have a science course that is a step up from the one you took freshman year, review your notes. If you have a Writing II class, then peruse your graded papers from Writing I to see what you need to work on. Learning is a journey, not a destination.

Save Your Earnings

You saw firsthand this year how expensive college can be and how easy it was to blow through your budget. Save as much as you can from your summer job to avoid being broke your sophomore year. A good rule of thumb is to split your paycheck into three parts: 50 percent of it should go to your needs (any bills or debt), 30 percent to your wants (movies, concerts, dinners out with friends, etc.), and 20 percent to your savings account. Mess with the numbers if you want more in your savings or less in your wants. You'll be grateful for all this planning in September.

Don't Slack Off

Keep up your exercise routines over the summer. Since the weather is warmer, you should be able to run, walk, swim, or play a sport outside. If you can, work out at the same time you did while you were at school—it will be easier for you to maintain your routine.

Since you're not surrounded by all that dining hall food, it should be easier for you to monitor your diet. Watch out for those barbecue foods, though!

Play Nice

To be frank, it can really suck to be away from your friends and your college, especially if you had a wonderful freshman year. But that's no excuse to be a gloomy, irritable brat at home. Your family has missed you, and it can be hurtful when you act aloof and make it clear you wish you were somewhere else. Be kind and engaged with your family and friends. After a few weeks, you'll fall back into your home groove.

BE ACTIVE | FRIDAY

Keep in Touch

Keeping in touch with particular professors can also be specifically beneficial to you. Professors from a college can serve as references for jobs or graduate schools. They can also serve as mentors and advisors, and are often happy to do so even when you are at another institution. They can help direct a job search, provide networking opportunities, and perhaps even collaborate on research projects. These relationships are well worth maintaining. Send an e-mail to a professor and inquire how her summer is going to get the ball rolling.

Introduce Yourself to a New Roommate

If you're getting a new roommate this coming year, reach out and introduce yourself on Facebook or e-mail.

- What do you like to do for fun?
- How would you like to decorate the dorm room?
- Which appliances or decorations can you bring on move-in day?
- Are you in a relationship? If so, will your significant other be visiting the room often?
- What kind of social life are you hoping to find at college?
- What is your favorite movie, book, or song, and why?
- What will you miss most about your family?
- What are you most looking forward to about this year?

Deal with Family Stress

Welcome to three months (maybe more, depending on your school's schedule) of being back home! Even though you lived with them for eighteen years, you may find readjusting to home life after a year at school is pretty hard. You've spent nine months living your own life with every bit of freedom possible, so being a son or daughter, brother or sister again can be a transition.

If your family instantly stresses you out, you react to them out of habit. Remember the two ways to deal with stress: responding to stress, where you make a conscious decision to act, and reacting to stress, where stress takes over and you instantly lose your mind to it? You have a mind. You're aware. Take a moment to reflect on a recent family situation that proved very stressful to you. Write down what happened, and pinpoint the exact place where you reacted rather than responded to stress. Practice using "I" statements with this family member the next time she begins to stress you out, and when the opportunity arises—which it undoubtedly will—be bold but kind. Communicate your needs, resist the family drama, and be kind yet firm. You can care without being stressed out of your mind. Sample phrases include:

- "I get irritated when you set curfews for me. Can we work something out?"
- "I feel violated when you touch my stuff. If you want to borrow something, ask."
- "I'm sorry I yelled, but I felt very angry when you made plans without asking me."

APPENDIX A: COLLEGE 101

Laundry Basics

It turns out that doing laundry is just a little more complicated than throwing clothes in the washer, adding some detergent, and coming back later to put everything in the dryer.

The first thing you should do is figure out how often you need to do laundry. Don't wait until you're wearing your last pair of clean underwear to drag a heaping basket to your residence hall laundry room. A good rule of thumb is to do laundry once a week. And remember to bring:

- A laundry basket and laundry duffle bag for trips home
- Laundry detergent (a big bottle should get you through the semester)
- Fabric softener if you use it
- Dryer sheets

Sorting

Next, you need to sort your clothing into groups by color and material. Read the tags on your clothing to see if any items warrant special care; if so, place those items in a separate pile. At the very least, you should sort light and dark colors. Whenever possible, you also want to separate delicates from heavier items. While you are sorting your clothes, be sure to go through all your pockets, remove pins or stickers you placed on your clothing, and tie drawstring ends together. Tying up drawstring ends (on a hooded sweatshirt, for example) will keep the string in place throughout the washing and drying process. Also, be sure that each pile of laundry is the right size. Too few items will waste water in the washing cycle, and too many items can overload the washer and keep the dryer from being effective.

Detergent and Setting Options

Next, you must choose a detergent. There are many detergents to choose from, and you can select one based on brand, fragrance, and price. While this can get complicated because of the array of detergent, bleach, and pretreating products that exist, a simple general-purpose detergent is sufficient for most college students. You also have a choice between powder and liquid laundry detergents. One advantage of powders is that they take up less space in your residence hall room. However, some people find that powders clump, which can sometimes lead to poor laundry results. Liquid detergents come in large plastic jugs that take up more space, but they won't clump. The best thing to do is try both options and see which one you like better. In any case, thoroughly read the directions for your chosen laundry detergent before using it.

Once you're standing in front of the washing machine, you will have a few more decisions to make. When do you add the detergent and what temperature should the water be? If you're using powder detergent, you generally want to add the detergent after the washing machine has started to fill with water. This will give the detergent some time to dissolve in the water before you add your clothes. Liquid detergent does not require much time to dissolve, so you can choose to add it before or after you put in your clothes. The correct water temperature depends on what type of clothing you are washing. Many clothing labels will list what temperature the water should be, and college laundry rooms often have temperature guides posted on the walls to assist you. A good rule of thumb is to use cold water for dark colors and new clothes, hot water for whites or particularly dirty clothes, and warm water for everything in between.

Stains and Other Crises

Whether you're a sloppy eater or just a victim of circumstance, you are likely to find a stain on your clothing, a button missing from your shirt, or a rip in your pants at some point in your college career.

- When you find a stain on your clothing, first try removing the stain with a small amount of laundry detergent or dish soap. Use cold water and be gentle as you work with the stained area.
- If the stain is more persistent or has set in, you need to pretreat the stained area when you are about to do a load of laundry. You can use a small amount of liquid detergent or a pretreating product to do this. Follow the directions on your stain remover and read cautions carefully in case the remover will not work well with a particular kind of stain or fabric.
- You may need to soak your stained clothing before washing it in order to loosen the soil and give the stain remover or detergent a chance to activate. This can be done using a small bucket of warm water or a presoak feature, if available, on your washing machine.
- Before you place your clothing in the dryer, check to see if the stain came out in the wash. If not, do not put the item in the dryer; doing this will only cause the stain to set and likely become permanent.

Repairing Buttons

At some point during your college career it is likely that you will lose a button from a shirt. You can purchase a small sewing kit, complete with several colors of thread and a few needles, at most drug stores, and perhaps even in your college bookstore. If you manage to save the button or find it in the washing machine at the end of a cycle, you can simply sew the button back on to your shirt. If the button is lost, you can often find a replacement at a craft store, and some shirts have spare buttons sewn on the underside of the bottom hem.

For many new students, sewing a button on a shirt is a completely foreign activity. If you are not confident about this or other clothing-related matters, inquire with your friends to see if one of them can teach you how to reattach the button or do whatever you need to do. You can also ask an RA for assistance, or visit a local sewing shop or tailor in town.

Repairing Rips

Rips and tears are often harder to deal with and may require waiting until your next trip home to repair. You can easily get an iron-on patch and apply it yourself, but that will only work for some types of clothing. You may also find a tailor at a local dry cleaner who can repair rips and tears easily for a minimal charge. Do not necessarily abandon clothing that has been damaged in this way; just be patient while you figure out the best solution.

APPENDIX B: WHAT TO BRING

You probably already have everything packed and ready, but just in case, here's a refresher for next year:

TOILETRIES
- ☐ Soap
- ☐ Soap dish, preferably covered
- ☐ Toothbrush
- ☐ Toothbrush case
- ☐ Toothpaste, dental floss, and mouthwash
- ☐ Hairbrush or comb
- ☐ Hair dryer, if you use one
- ☐ Shampoo and conditioner
- ☐ Cotton swabs
- ☐ Nail clippers and file
- ☐ Shaving cream and razors
- ☐ Deodorant
- ☐ Contact lens care equipment, if needed
- ☐ Over-the-counter medication for headaches, joint pain, stomach distress

Clothes
In addition to your basic shirts, pants, shorts, skirts, underwear, and socks, don't forget these items:

- ☐ Bathing suit
- ☐ Bathrobe
- ☐ Exercise clothing
- ☐ Nice dress

- ☐ Pajamas
- ☐ Rain jacket and umbrella
- ☐ Sport coat
- ☐ Sweaters
- ☐ Sweatshirts and sweatpants
- ☐ Ties
- ☐ Shoes: dress shoes, casual shoes, and sneakers for working out

APPENDIX C: INTERNET RESOURCES FOR COLLEGE STUDENTS

There are numerous fun and useful websites for college students. From buying textbooks to keeping in touch with family at home, there are resources on the Internet to help you with virtually any task or problem. Though you will certainly discover others during your college career, here are some Internet resources to give you a head start.

Academics

SparkNotes
A collection of study guides, including literary and nonliterary topics
www.sparknotes.com

Rate My Professor
Student ratings of professors at colleges around the country
www.ratemyprofessor.com

Cramster
Online homework help for many majors 24/7
www.cramster.com

Alternative Spring Break

Alternative Breaks
Many alternative spring break opportunities
www.alternativebreaks.org

Live United

Alternative spring break opportunities offered through the United Way charities

http://liveunited.org/take-action/alternative-spring-break

Jewish National Fund

Alternative spring break trips for Jewish students

www.jnf.org/asb

Humor and Games

The Onion

A critically humorous news source

www.theonion.com

Fark.com

Obscure and unbelievable news stories

www.fark.com

Sporkle

Games, entertainment, and trivia

www.sporkle.com

StumbleUpon

A personalized browsing tool to help you find interesting websites

www.stumbleupon.com

Miniclip

Online games site

www.miniclip.com

College Humor
Amusing pictures, movies, and games
www.collegehumor.com

MadBlast
Movies, music, television and games that parody popular figures
www.madblast.com

JibJab
Political parodies and cartoons
www.jibjab.com

eBaum's World
"Media for the masses"—jokes, games, videos, and cartoons
www.ebaumsworld.com

HomestarRunner
Popular online cartoon
www.homestarrunner.com

Bored.com
Dedicated to procrastination and entertainment, with games, media, and links
www.bored.com

Milk and Cookies
Games and humorous news stories
www.milkandcookies.com

Darwin Awards
Honors those who improve the gene pool by removing themselves from it
www.darwinawards.com

Personal Space on the Web

Xanga.com
"The Blogging Community"
www.xanga.com

LiveJournal
A site for online journals
www.livejournal.com

Angelfire
Provides free web space
www.angelfire.com

Webs.com
"The next generation of free web hosting"
www.webs.com

Movies and Music

IMDb
The Internet movie database
www.imdb.com

Netflix
Movies for rent online
www.netflix.com

Sidereel
TV and movies online
www.sidereel.com

OVGuide
Online video guide
www.ovguide.com

TV Duck
Free movies and TV online
www.tvduck.com

Hulu
Free movies and TV online
www.hulu.com

CMJ
"New music first"; music reviews, reports, and news
www.cmj.com

Pollstar
Popular music resource
www.pollstar.com

AllMusic
A place to explore new bands or genres
www.allmusic.com

AllMovie
Film and actor reviews and movie sales
www.allmovie.com

Textbooks

Amazon.com
Books, including new and used textbooks, and other products
www.amazon.com

Barnes & Noble
Books, including new and used textbooks, and other products
www.barnesandnoble.com

Half.com

An eBay partner site with new and used textbooks, as well as other products

www.half.ebay.com

efollett

Online location of a popular college bookstore

www.efollett.com

Bigwords.com

Helps students find the best deals on textbooks

www.bigwords.com

Chegg

Low-cost textbook rental site

www.chegg.com

Travel

StudentUniverse

A place to find cheap domestic and international flights, as well as resources for traveling in Europe

www.studentuniverse.com

Lastminute.com

A resource for last-minute travel

www.lastminute.com

easyJet.com

Cheap travel within Europe and helpful to students studying abroad

www.easyjet.com

Expedia Travel

Flights, cruises, hotels, and travel packages

www.expedia.com

Orbitz Travel

Flights, cruises, hotels, and travel packages; Expedia competitor

www.orbitz.com

Southwest Airlines

Great prices if they travel to the vicinity of your destination

www.southwest.com

Hostelworld.com

Search over 25,000 hostels in more than 180 countries

www.hostelworld.com

Cheapo Air

The name says it all

www.cheapoair.com

E-Cards

All 4 Free

An Internet greeting card index

www.rats2u.com

Hallmark.com

The online site of the popular card and gift store

www.hallmark.com

Blue Mountain

Popular cards available to send online

www.bluemountain.com

Other Interesting Sites

Webshots
A place to post photos for friends and family
www.webshots.com

Facebook
An online directory connecting people through social networks at colleges and beyond
www.facebook.com

Campusfood.com
Online source for local restaurants that deliver
www.campusfood.com

Classmates.com
An online database of high school graduates
www.classmates.com

Doodle
Helps groups of people find shared availability for meetings, parties, etc.
www.doodle.com

Consumer Reports
A nonprofit organization and print magazine with product reviews and other information
www.consumerreports.org

Huffington Post
Breaking news and opinions
www.huffingtonpost.com

INDEX